THE ISAAC QUESTION

TEMPLARS AND THE SECRET OF THE OLD TESTAMENT

A Novel by
David S. Brody

Eyes That See Publishing
Westford, Massachusetts

The Isaac Question
Templars and the Secret of the Old Testament

Eyes That See Publishing
Westford, Massachusetts

ISBN 978-0-9907413-1-2
1st edition

This is a work of fiction. Names, characters and incidents are either a product of the author's imagination or are used fictitiously. Except as otherwise noted in the Author's Note, any resemblance to actual events or people, living or dead, is entirely coincidental.

Cover Art by Kimberly Scott
Printed in USA

THE ISAAC QUESTION

TEMPLARS AND THE SECRET OF THE OLD TESTAMENT

David S. Brody

Praise for David S. Brody's Books

"Brody does a terrific job of wrapping his research in a fast-paced thrill ride that will feel far more like an action film than an academic paper."
—PUBLISHERS WEEKLY (*Cabal of the Westford Knight*)

"Strongly recommended for all collections."
—LIBRARY JOURNAL (*The Wrong Abraham*)

"Will keep you up even after you've put it down."
—Hallie Ephron, BOSTON GLOBE (*Blood of the Tribe*)

"A riveting, fascinating read."
—MIDWEST BOOK REVIEW (*The Wrong Abraham*)

"Best of the Coming Season."
—BOSTON MAGAZINE (*Unlawful Deeds*)

"A compelling suspense story and a searing murder mystery."
—THE BOSTON PHOENIX (*Blood of the Tribe*)

"A comparison to *The Da Vinci Code* and *National Treasure* is inevitable....The story rips the reader into a fast-paced adventure."
—FRESH FICTION (*Cabal of the Westford Knight*)

"An excellent historical conspiracy thriller. It builds on its most famous predecessor, *The Da Vinci Code*, and takes it one step farther—and across the Atlantic."
—MYSTERY BOOK NEWS (*Cabal of the Westford Knight*)

"The action and danger are non-stop, leaving you breathless. It is one hell of a read."
—ABOUT.COM Book Reviews (*Unlawful Deeds*)

"The year is early, but this book will be hard to beat; it's already on my 'Best of 2009' list."
—BARYON REVIEW (*Cabal of the Westford Knight*)

"An enormously fun read, exceedingly hard to put down."
—The BOOKBROWSER (*Unlawful Deeds*)

"Fantastic book. I can't wait until the next book is released."

iv

—GOODREADS (*Thief on the Cross*)

"A feast."
—ARTS AROUND BOSTON (*Unlawful Deeds*)

About the Author

David S. Brody is a *Boston Globe* bestselling fiction writer named Boston's "Best Local Author" by the *Boston Phoenix* newspaper. A graduate of Tufts University and Georgetown Law School, he is a former Director of the New England Antiquities Research Association (NEARA) and is a dedicated researcher in the field of pre-Columbian exploration of America.

He has appeared as a guest expert on documentaries airing on History Channel, Travel Channel, PBS, and Discovery Channel.

The four previous novels in his "Templars in America Series" have all been Amazon Kindle Top 10 Bestsellers.

The Isaac Question is his eighth novel.

For more information, please visit
DavidBrodyBooks.com

Also by the Author

Unlawful Deeds

Blood of the Tribe

The Wrong Abraham

The "Templars in America" Series:

Cabal of the Westford Knight:
Templars at the Newport Tower (Book 1)

Thief on the Cross:
Templar Secrets in America (Book 2)

Powdered Gold:
Templars and the American Ark of the Covenant (Book 3)

The Oath of Nimrod:
Giants, MK-Ultra and the Smithsonian Coverup (Book 4)

Preface

In this novel I return to the Templar-based themes I first explored in *Cabal of the Westford Knight.* Specifically, I focus on the Knights Templar as one link in a chain of secret societies that stretches back to include first the ancient Egyptians and later the mysterious Druids, and then moves forward to include the Freemasons as the modern-day successors to the Templars. Anyone who doubts these connections should simply wander into a Masonic lodge and observe for themselves the abundance of Egyptian and Templar-related symbolism in the lodge architecture and décor. More subtle are the connections to the Druids—but these are there as well, for those who look carefully.

As I tracked my way to the intersection point of these four groups—Egyptian, Druid, Templar, and Masonic—I found myself again standing in the shadow of Scotland's iconic Rosslyn Chapel. The Chapel's architecture and decorations featured not only Druidic, Templar, and Masonic symbolism as befitting Scotland's long history with each of these groups, but Egyptian motif as well. What, I wondered, was the historical tie between Scotland and ancient Egypt?

The answer, I soon learned, lay hidden in the mystery of Princess Scota.

Scota, in turn, led me back to ancient Egypt and caused me to take a fresh look at the Book of Exodus. What I found, frankly, shocked me. I will not reveal those findings here, but suffice it to say the findings led me to a clearer understanding of many of the events recounted in the Old Testament, events that frankly had never made much sense to me.

As in my previous novels, I use artifacts and historical sites as evidence for the "secret" history my story tells. In this book, I focus on the dozens of mysterious stone chambers that dot the landscape of New England and eastern New York. Who built these chambers, and why? And do these chambers have anything to do with the mysterious Baphomet skull worshiped by the Templars? More importantly, do these chambers help us better understand the truth behind the Book of Exodus stories?

Readers of the first four books in the series will recognize the protagonists, Cameron and Amanda, and also young Astarte. However, this novel is not a sequel to the prior four and readers who have not read the earlier novels should feel free to jump right in.

As in the previous stories in the series, if an artifact or object of art is pictured in the book, it exists in the real world. (See the Author's Note at the end of this book for a more detailed discussion covering the issue of artifact authenticity.) To me, in the end, it is the artifacts that are the true stars of these novels.

I remain fascinated by the hidden history of North America and the very real possibility that waves of European explorers visited our shores long before Columbus. I also, in researching this novel, have become fascinated by the hidden truths within the Old Testament stories. It is my hope that readers share these fascinations.

David S. Brody, August, 2015
Westford, Massachusetts

Note to New Readers

Though this is the fifth book in the series, it is a stand-alone story. Readers who have not read the first four should feel free to jump right in. The below provides some basic background for new readers.

Cameron Thorne is a forty-year-old attorney whose passion is researching sites and artifacts that indicate the presence in America of European explorers prior to Columbus. His fiancée, Amanda Spencer-Gunn, is a British museum curator who moved to the U.S. from London while in her mid-twenties and shares his research passion; she has a particular expertise in the history of the medieval Knights Templar. They reside in Westford, Massachusetts, a suburb northwest of Boston. They are in the process of adopting a ten-year-old orphan, Astarte, whom they met while investigating artifacts in New York's Catskill Mountains with her uncle, who later died. Cam and Amanda are part of a growing community of researchers investigating early exploration of North America.

To my daughters, Allie and Renee

Anyone who has ever loved a child as I have loved both of you understands the absurdity of God's demand upon Abraham

The Book of Genesis, Chapter 12

Verses 11-19 describe how the patriarch Abraham allowed the Pharaoh to take Abraham's wife Sarah into his harem, and how the Pharaoh paid Abraham a bride price for the privilege:

11 *As he was approaching the border of Egypt, Abraham said to his wife, Sarah, "Look, you are a very beautiful woman.*

12 *When the Egyptians see you, they will say, 'This is his wife. Let's kill him; then we can have her!'*

13 *So please tell them you are my sister. Then they will spare my life and treat me well because of their interest in you."*

14 *And sure enough, when Abraham arrived in Egypt, everyone noticed Sarah's beauty.*

15 *When the palace officials saw her, they sang her praises to Pharaoh, their king, and Sarah was taken into his palace.*

16 *Then Pharaoh gave Abraham many gifts because of her—sheep, goats, cattle, male and female donkeys, male and female servants, and camels.*

17 *But the Lord sent terrible plagues upon Pharaoh and his household because of Sarah, Abraham's wife.*

18 *So Pharaoh summoned Abraham and accused him sharply. "What have you done to me?" he demanded. "Why didn't you tell me she was your wife?*

19 *Why did you say, 'She is my sister,' and allow me to take her as my wife? Now then, here is your wife. Take her and get out of here!"*

[New Living Translation version]

Traditional Depiction of Abraham's Family Tree

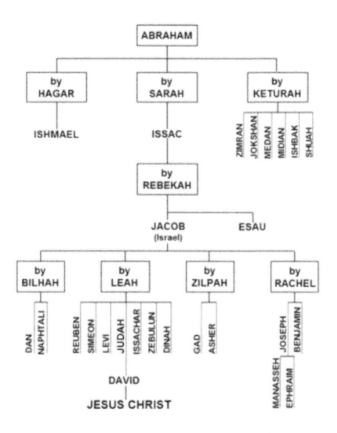

Warning

If you believe that the Old Testament is the literal word of God, you are likely to be offended by some of the themes and revelations contained in this novel.

Prologue

May, AD 515
World's End, Southwest Coast of Ireland

Brendan stumbled, startled. A tall, gnarled Druid stood in his path, as if one of the majestic oaks had magically transformed itself into a human and lumbered out of the grove to block his way. That human's name, Brendan knew, was Omarlin. His apparition was not magic, but merely another of the old man's countless tricks. But it was unwelcome nonetheless.

Omarlin raised his knobby walking stick at Brendan and smiled, the old man's white teeth radiating from within the dirt-covered, wrinkled leather of his face. "Greetings, young Brendan." He stood erect on bare feet, the gold thread of his long green robe sparkling in the morning sun. The smell of earth wafted off the Druid.

Brendan stepped back, preferring the briny scent of the ocean wafting up from the cliffs beneath them. He had thought himself alone, here at the westernmost tip of the known world, a place others called World's End. It had been three years since the old Druid, who was known to wander as far as Gaul, had been to these lands. And there was no reason for him to be here now.

"We agreed you would stay away. You are not welcome here."

Omarlin's smile widened into a menace. He pointed his walking stick at Brendan like a wand. "Careful lest I turn you into a sheep and let the farm boys have a go with you."

"You know I put no stock in your magic, Omarlin." Even so, he shifted so the old man's wand aimed not at his chest. "Only Jesus can work his magic here."

Omarlin's green eyes narrowed. "Ah, yes, that new god of yours." He waved his hand dismissively. "You and the other

1

simpletons may worship whatever gods you please." He leaned forward. "But must you steal our holidays? There are hundreds of days in the year; why must your Christian holy days always coincide with our festivals?"

The old man had a point. It was easier to get the villagers to come to church on the days they already considered to be sacred. Brendan merely shrugged. "I don't suppose you came all this way to discuss the calendar."

But the wizard would not let it go. "A few days ago, on Beltane no less, I entered a village only to have my ears battered by the sounds of Christian prayer. Are you claiming this is mere happenstance?"

Brendan held the old man's gaze. "Forty days following Easter we celebrate the blessed Ascension. That is the day our Lord Jesus finally ascended to heaven, after comforting his followers." He shrugged again. "It just so happens to coincide with Beltane."

Omarlin laughed and grabbed his crotch. "The *Ascension*. Yes, that is a proper name for it. On Beltane every cock in the village ascends like a maypole and finds a bit of heaven inside some young maiden." He cackled again. "*Ascension*."

Brendan crossed himself. But the Druid was correct: After the villagers attended church this past Sunday to celebrate the Ascension, the sounds of singing and dancing and grunting continued deep into the night, making sleep—and even prayer—impossible.

Omarlin continued. "Speaking of which, how is your mother?" He paused and raised an eyebrow. "She was a beauty, she was, and an enthusiastic celebrant of Beltane." He spread his arms and leered. "It is possible, in fact, that your father I be."

Brendan took a deep breath; he would not let the wizard bait him. "She is well, thank you. And I was born midsummer so you cannot be my father, thanks to God."

"Well, perhaps then you were a product of immaculate conception, like that Christ of yours." He winked. "Not a bad consolation prize, if you cannot be of *my* seed."

Brendan balled his fist. "Enough, Omarlin. Enough of your blasphemy."

2

The Druid raised his chin and laughed. "Calm yourself, young Brendan. I reckon even this Jesus of yours must have a sense of humor." He furrowed his brow as he studied his one-time protégé. "He must have one, in fact—why else would he insist you shave the top of your head like that? You look like a monkey some Saxon I once knew kept as a pet."

Brendan's face reddened. "We monks wear our hair in this style because Christ was forced to wear a crown of thorns."

"So you've been ordained then, have you?"

Brendan straightened himself. "I have."

"And does that mean you have taken a vow of celibacy?" Omarlin practically spit out this last word.

"It does. I have."

The Druid sighed. "Well, at least you won't be populating Ireland with more of your kind. There's something for that."

Brendan folded his arms across his chest. Last he heard, Omarlin had been in Glastonbury, across the eastern sea, no doubt causing trouble. Now the trouble had come to Brendan. "What is your business here, Omarlin? I have work to do."

"Yes. Saving souls, no doubt. Spreading your precious gospel."

"Aye. As you no doubt already know, we sail tomorrow."

"Tomorrow already?" Omarlin looked deep into the woods, as if seeing the future and weighing whether to alter it. His voice dropped. "Brendan the Navigator, they will call you." Then he nodded, as if what he saw had decided things. "That be why I am here."

"To undermine me while I am at sea? I warn you, the villagers will not return to the old ways in my absence." Brendan had worked tirelessly to Christianize the area; he would not allow the pagan ways to return.

The Druid waved the comment away. "I care nothing for your fishermen and farmers. But your voyage—that intrigues me. I have long fancied sailing to the ends of the ocean. There are tales of lands far to the west." He smiled. "I will join you. And two of my novices as well."

So that's what this was about. "That you'll not. I have a loyal crew of fourteen. All Christians."

3

"Yes. And one with a gambling problem." Omarlin flicked his wrist and a diamond-shaped clear stone filled his bony hand. "Recognize this?"

Brendan reached for it without thinking, only to have Omarlin snatch it away. "The sunstone," Brendan stammered. "*My* sunstone."

"No longer, I fear. The dice be not kind to your first mate."

Brendan's jaw tightened. It would be suicide to sail without a good sunstone—the stone made the sun visible through clouds and even fog. And without knowing where the sun was, it was impossible to navigate. Brendan forced a smile. "God will be my sunstone then. I will trust him to guide me." He turned to leave.

Omarlin laughed. "That may be well and good for you, Brendan. But I wonder how many of your crew will agree."

Brendan exhaled. Omarlin had a point. Their belief in God was not as strong as Brendan's. And perhaps God was sending a message through the dice. Brendan turned back. "Away for many years we will be." At least if the old Druid were with him, he could not stir up trouble here at home. And fourteen monks should be able to control three heathens. "There is no surety we will even survive the voyage."

Omarlin smiled again and shrugged. "Such is life. Never have I begun a journey certain that I would return from it."

Brendan eyed him. There was something the sneaky Druid was not telling him. "Truly, why do you want to come?"

Omarlin held his eyes. "I am an old man, and I have seen all there is to see between here and Rome. I wish now to cross the great ocean." He removed an ornately carved limestone box, half a cubit square, from within the folds of his robe. He held the box reverently and lowered his voice. "And like many old men, I have a final task I must complete before my death."

Chapter 1

1,500 Years Later
Boston, Massachusetts

The real estate closing had taken longer than it should have, which meant Cameron Thorne's parking meter was set to expire. Wearing a suit and carrying a briefcase, he pushed through the door of the Registry of Deeds building and jogged, angling toward North Station. The subway usually didn't run on time, and the streets sometimes didn't get plowed, but Boston never missed a chance to issue a parking ticket.

It took him a few seconds to adjust to the bright sunlight of the spring afternoon, so it wasn't until the man running toward him was only a few yards away that Cam saw the fear and panic on his face. A few times a year someone approached Cam to ask for an autograph, thinking he was the Boston-born actor Matt Damon. This was clearly different.

"Hey, you a lawyer?" he gasped, eyeing Cam's dark suit and briefcase.

"Yeah, I am."

"Buddy, you gotta help me!" The man shoved a green and yellow lottery ticket into Cam's chest and turned, scanning the urban streetscape behind him.

"I'm sorry, what?' Cam said. The guy was about average height, like Cam. Fit, maybe thirty. His blue eyes bore into Cam's.

"This ticket's a winner," he blurted, pronouncing winner as if it ended in 'ah' rather than 'er.' "But the guys from the neighborhood heard about it and they want half." He angled the ticket into Cam's chest a second time and backed away, leaving the glossy cardboard strip caught between Cam's suit coat and shirt. "Well, fuck 'em." He licked his lips. "I'm trusting you to do the right thing, you know? I'll be back in an hour, after I lose these guys." He gestured with his chin down the street. "Meet me in the Dunkin Donuts bathroom, the one on Causeway Street, okay?"

Cam blinked, his hand involuntarily catching the ticket as it slid. "I don't know." He tried to hand the ticket back.

"Please, man," he replied, refusing the ticket. His eyes bore into Cam's, pleading. "Just an hour. What's that saying, do a random act of kindness? I really need that now. I'll give you a thousand bucks."

Something about the man's desperate urgency touched Cam. And he couldn't really think of a reason to say no. "Well, okay. But I don't want your money. You can just buy me an iced coffee."

The man smiled and patted Cam on the shoulder. "Thanks, man. You got it. An extra large." He turned. "Really, thanks," he yelled over his shoulder as he sprinted toward the parking garage across the street.

The entire encounter took less than thirty seconds.

Shaking his head, Cam resumed the walk to his car. What had he got himself into? It had happened so quickly that he didn't really have a chance to think it through. He glanced at the ticket, wondering what would possess someone to hand a winning lottery ticket to a total stranger. And also wondering what he would do if the guys from the neighborhood showed up. Actually, he knew what he'd do—he'd hand them the damn ticket.

He fed the meter and, with an hour to kill, bought a newspaper and found a bench near the TD Garden sports arena. He examined the glossy rectangle of cardboard—as the man claimed, the scratch ticket was an instant winner, for $500,000. Half a million bucks, just like that. He looked back toward the parking garage, shook his head and, tucking the ticket into his breast pocket, phoned his fiancée Amanda. "You won't believe what just happened," he said, chuckling.

As the hour passed, Cam grew alternately curious and resentful about the lottery ticket incident. Curious that someone would give a winning ticket to a complete stranger rather than settle for half, and resentful that he had been inconvenienced—and perhaps put into danger.

He walked the half block to Dunkin' Donuts, replaying the encounter in his mind. Skilled at reading facial expressions, a talent honed over years of reading juries, Cam sensed there was more to the story than the man had let on. He considered simply turning the ticket over to the police, but the hour was almost up and his curiosity won out. And, arguably, the man had entrusted the ticket to Cam in Cam's capacity as an attorney, which imposed upon him a duty to act as a fiduciary in the man's best interests. Arguably. He would turn the ticket in and be done with this if the owner didn't show up soon.

By 2:30 the Dunkin Donuts was mostly empty. Cam scanned the dining area, did not see the man and followed a hallway toward the restrooms in the rear of the building. He pushed the door open and entered. Empty. Sighing, he unfolded his newspaper, leaned against the wall and waited.

Ten minutes passed. Nothing. He couldn't wait much longer. Though he was a lawyer by trade, he had developed an expertise in the history of European exploration of America before Columbus; tonight he was scheduled to give a lecture at a Masonic lodge as the guest of a local veterinarian who had taken an interest in his research.

Cam checked his watch again before finally deciding to do the obvious: He urinated. As he was zipping up the door swung open. He tensed at the sound of heavy feet approaching quickly. He began to turn, but someone dropped a black hood over his head and pressed a sharp blade against his neck in what seemed like a nanosecond.

What the—?

"Don't move, or I'll cut your throat."

Cam's first impulse was to resist, but the strong hands of his assailant, plus the cold metal of the blade, froze him in place.

A cloth covered Cam's nose and mouth, and he smelled a sickly-sweet odor like melting candy. A wave of dread washed over him. *Chloroform.* He began to struggle.

"Just relax, skipper. Everything will be okay."

Cam felt his body sag. His last thought was that the man pronounced skipper as if the word ended in 'ah.'

Cam awoke, his heart pounding but his brain unable to ascertain why. Smoke filled his nostrils and a loud beeping assaulted his ears. A few seconds passed as his cogency returned. His body jolted. *Fire.*

Adrenaline surging, he sat up and looked around. A dimly lit room, a couch underneath him. Gray smoke billowed from some source against the far wall, sunlight causing the dark particles to dance. *Sunlight.* He turned. Light poured in from a window next to him. Cam yanked; the window opened easily, leading to a black metal fire escape. Exhaling, he began to climb through.

"Waaah."

He froze.

The sound came again, audible between the wails of the fire alarm. "Waaah." There. From behind a door opposite the couch. *A baby.* Cam did not hesitate.

Using the lapel of his suit coat to cover his mouth and nose, he strode across the room and shouldered open the door. The space was dark, the crying sound louder. "Waaah." Fumbling, he found a light, his eyes burning. The room was small, no bigger than a glorified closet. A pantry perhaps. No crib, no bed, no furniture. And no baby. "Waaah." He focused in on the sound over his own coughing. *There.* Sitting on a shelf next to a box of spaghetti. An MP3 player with a pair of small speakers next to it. *What the –?* Cam punched the stop button. The crying ceased.

Swatting the MP3 off the shelf, Cam spun and fought his way back toward the open window. The smoke had thickened, so he dropped to his hands and knees and crawled, the taste of ash filling his mouth and the lack of oxygen dizzying his head. The light from the window beckoned like a beacon, but the ten-foot span of the room felt like a football field. Finally he reached the couch, pulled himself onto it, and rolled out the window onto the fire escape.

Panting, his eyes still burning, he allowed himself a few seconds to breath. But fire or not, he needed to get out of here.

Presumably whoever had abducted him would be back. He pulled himself to his feet, ready to descend the metal stairs. On his first step the rusted metal of the landing dissolved beneath him. He grabbed for the frame of the stairway, clawing for something to keep him from falling, but his fingers found only air. He barely had time to look down to see himself crash, feet first, into a large container of some kind. Cardboard boxes cushioned his fall, but a stab of pain shot up his left leg.

Panting, Cam slowly shifted his body atop the boxes. Other than his leg, he seemed to be okay. Looking up at the fire escape, he saw he had only fallen one flight. Smoke billowed from the open window, and the fire alarm continued to caw. He tried to stand, using his right leg; a box gave way beneath him and he lurched to the side, falling against the side of what he guessed—based on the familiar smell—was a plastic garbage dumpster.

As he began to stand again, the top of the dumpster swung down and slammed shut over him, plunging him into darkness. "Hey," he yelled, pushing upward at the lid. A loud click froze Cam—the sound of a padlock snapping into place. Desperate, he shoved upward again, smashing at the secure plastic cover with his shoulder and arms.

As he pounded futilely, the dumpster began to roll.

The everyday sounds of the city echoed within the dumpster, taunting the entrapped Cam as he rolled along, bumping occasionally over curbs and potholes. He exhaled slowly, trying to control his racing heart. His afternoon had transitioned quickly from baffling to stupefying to mind-numbingly dangerous. His leg throbbed, he couldn't stop coughing and the dank smell of rotting food caused his stomach to heave. He had no way to escape the rolling dumpster, and no idea of why he was in it in the first place.

Sweating both from the heat of his confinement and from fear, Cam felt around in the darkened dumpster for some way to escape. Shoving the boxes aside in the approximate six foot by four foot space, he groped and found a drain hole, plugged with a plastic stopper, in the bottom of the container at one end. He reached into his breast pocket, relieved to find his Swiss army knife nestled inside his handkerchief—his captors had taken his cell phone but must have missed the knife. After removing the drain plug and discarding his jacket, he stretched on his stomach, wedged the blade into the hole and sawed into the hard plastic, fighting to enlarge the opening as the dumpster bounced along. It was slow going, the plastic thick and the blade increasingly dull. Cam figured he needed an opening at least a foot-and-a-half in diameter to slither through. But he had no idea how much time he had.

The sweat now pouring off his face, his nose and mouth only inches from the stench at the bottom of the dumpster and the scurrying of rat paws audible from the far corner, Cam carved and sawed. As he panted and coughed, his stomach turned and he vomited, the turkey sandwich from what seemed like a lifetime ago mixing with bile and acid and blackened saliva; he was able to turn his head in time to direct the spew onto a box, which he pushed aside. A couple of times he dug the blade too far down and the knife kicked back off the pavement, dulling the edge and once gashing his palm. Blood now mixed with sweat and vomit and stench as he worked the knife fiendishly, stabbing at the thick plastic like a slasher in a teenage horror film.

The dumpster stopped, jolting Cam from his task. He sat up, his senses alert. Seagulls cawed and, even through the stench of the dumpster, he smelled the salty air of the harbor. His chest tightened, fearing what might be next. A few seconds passed and the dumpster began rolling again, accelerating as it descended down a slope. For some reason an old golf adage popped into his head: *Everything rolls toward the water*. The wheels hit a bump and the container went airborne and tumbled. He braced himself. He knew he did not have much time.

The splash both confirmed his fears and drove home the point that he had no time for fear. If he didn't think quickly and rationally, he would soon drown.

Water poured through the hole. Though the dumpster for now bobbed atop the waves. the opening—his intended salvation—had become a gaping liability. Realizing he had little time, Cam threw his weight against the side of the dumpster. It tipped partially before righting itself. As it did so, he threw himself against the opposite side. Again, the dumpster swayed before settling back to its original position. Cam was like a weighted keel in a sailboat, keeping the vessel from overturning. But Cam *wanted* to overturn. *Needed* to overturn before the water swamped the container and turned the dumpster into a coffin. Continuing to throw his body alternately against each side—rhythmically, like rocking a car out of a snow bank—Cam finally toppled the dumpster onto its side. He exhaled and peered out the opening. The hole sat a couple feet above the water line.

But his relief was short-lived. With the dumpster now on its side, the ocean seeped in through the lid joints. Not as fast as through the hole, but already almost a foot of cold, dark water sloshed at his feet. The dumpster wouldn't remain buoyant much longer. Cam took a deep breath. He had bought himself both a few minutes and hopefully the chance for a cold swim. Grabbing the knife, and working with even more desperation than before, he sawed and jabbed at the opening. Using his hands to rip back the jagged plastic, he finally succeeded in folding back a section of his prison wall.

Light and air poured in as Cam glanced out. The bottom of the hole rested less than half a foot above the water line. Taking a deep breath, he squirmed through the opening, the sharp edges of the plastic cutting through his shirt and piercing his chest. Gritting his teeth against the pain, he thrust forward with his legs, the plastic clawing his skin. With a final push he tumbled out, splashing into the cold spring waters of Boston Harbor.

The cold numbed him, and the salt water stung his cuts, but the sunlight and air on his face felt glorious. Treading water, and on the lookout for yet another attack, he saw he was less than fifty feet from a stone retaining wall protecting the city from the ocean tides. A small crowd had gathered. With so many eyes on him, he sensed he was, finally, safe.

Floating on his back, exhausted, he kicked toward the retaining wall. A policeman yelled to him, and a few seconds later a firefighter dropped a rope ladder down the side of the wall.

"You okay?" the cop yelled.

11

The firefighter looked ready to jump in. "Yup," Cam waved weakly, his teeth chattering. He turned on his stomach and swam the final few yards, his hands no longer feeling the cold sting of the water. He grabbed for the ladder and blinked the salt water from his eyes. "But you're never going to believe my story."

Cam knifed across the wake, his water ski sending up a rooster tail made orange by the setting sun. He angled toward the beach, released the rope, and sank in waist-deep water, thankful that the lake was fifteen degrees warmer than the ocean had been three days earlier.

Amanda waded out in her shorts and kissed him. She didn't compete anymore, but she maintained the grace and toned figure of a world class gymnast. "Not bad for an old man. Happy fortieth birthday." She handed him a red plastic cup. "Cheers."

"Captain Morgan?" he asked.

She grinned. "No, Metamucil on the rocks. You're at that age now, Cameron."

He tilted his head and tried to knock the water from his ear. "Very funny. Sure you still want to get married?"

Amanda shrugged. "It would be bad form if I walked away now." She clinked her cup to his. She was a decade younger than him, and her long blond hair and princess-in-a-fairy-tale features often turned heads. "Perhaps I'll just take a young lover."

"Speaking of which, Happy Beltane." Today was May 5, the date of the old pagan fertility celebration.

She arched an eyebrow. "Hmm. So it is. As a Brit, I should have known that. Beltane and your birthday on the same day. Even you could get lucky tonight."

He held her green eyes for a few seconds like a smitten sixteen-year-old. As she smiled back at him, he rotated his shoulder, which ripped at the scabs on his chest and completely ruined the moment for him. The whole abduction earlier in the week still made no sense to him, from the lottery ticket to the fake baby to the dumpster being rolled into the harbor.

Cam sipped his rum and stepped out of the ski, his left ankle still tender from the fall from the fire escape. The advantage of an early May birthday was that he could spend the morning on the ski slopes in Vermont and still have time to water-ski in the evening at their Massachusetts lakefront home in Westford, thirty miles north of Boston. The disadvantage was that his forty-year-old body ached. But in a good way. He exhaled. "I'm starving."

Amanda tossed him a towel. "The grill is fired up. A burger and corn on the cob, just like you requested. Astarte should be home from soccer practice any minute."

"And ice cream for dessert?"

She rolled her eyes. "Yes, and a pony ride also." She handed him a thick white envelope as he stepped ashore. "This came in the mail today; I thought it might be important. And the detective called from Boston."

"Did he have any news?"

"They have security camera footage showing some bloke carrying you out the back door of Dunkin Donuts and tossing you into a plastic dumpster in an alley. Then further down the block another camera shows him pushing the dumpster along. Then nothing."

"Can they see the guy's face?"

"Not really. He wore a cap and kept his face turned away from the cameras. Same build as the chap you described."

"It makes no sense. If the guy thought I wasn't going to give the ticket back, I guess I can understand him knocking me out with the chloroform. But why the rest of it?" Cam shook his head. He didn't expect they would catch the guy if they hadn't done so by now—because Cam wasn't seriously hurt, it would not be a high priority case.

He focused instead on the letter. The return address indicated it was from the Middlesex County Registry of Deeds. Someone had handwritten his name and Westford home address across the front. "I wonder why it came here instead of my office." As a real estate attorney he often received documents from the various county registries. He dried his hands, opened the envelope, and unfolded a two-page document entitled 'DEED' across the top.

"What is it?"

Cam scanned the document, flipped to the second page, then rescanned the first page. It made no sense. "It's … a property deed." He shook his head. "To some land in Groton."

"You seem confused."

"I am." He shook the papers. "The deed is to *me*, in my name. Cameron Thorne."

Amanda's green eyes widened. "As in, the property is now in your name?"

"Some company in England just deeded me six acres."

"It's Groton, Massachusetts, not Groton in England, right?"

He flipped again to the second page. "Yes." The idyllic town of Groton, Massachusetts, known for its prep schools and early Colonial history, abutted Westford.

"Wow," she said playfully. "That's a better gift than I got you."

He barely heard her. "It must be some kind of mistake. Somebody probably cut and pasted my name off some other real estate transaction I was involved with."

"Well, then, why do they have your home address?"

He exhaled. "Good question."

"Are you working on anything in Groton?"

"No, actually. And nothing involving this English company, One Wing Industries, either."

"Perhaps they have the wrong Cameron Thorne?"

"Maybe. But six acres of property in this area is worth … I don't know, at least a half million bucks."

"Just like the lottery ticket," Amanda said.

Cam looked up at her. "That is a weird coincidence. But it still makes no sense. The guy in Boston wasn't British—he had a townie accent. And why would he give me property in Groton?" He looked at the signature line. "And this deed was signed back in March."

"So, like you said, maybe it's a mistake."

Cam made a face. "I've been doing this a long time. That's quite a mistake." He studied the first page again. "It says here the purchase price was one dollar."

"That seems odd."

14

"It's actually fairly common when you want to gift a property to someone."

"But why would some company want to gift six acres of land to you?"

He rubbed the towel over his face. "I have absolutely no idea."

Despite staying up late celebrating his birthday, Cam awoke at six the next morning. He wanted to be at the Registry of Deeds as soon as it opened, so he threw on sweats and running shoes, wrapped his left ankle, put Venus out, and hit the pavement just as the sun rose above the trees on the eastern end of the lake.

There had to be some explanation for the Groton property transfer, but despite an hour-and-a-half of Amanda and he bouncing ideas around they hadn't come up with anything that made any sense. They had done an Internet search for One Wing Industries but found no connection between the London company and the property in Groton, and definitely nothing that connected the firm to Cam.

Cam ran hard, sweating the rum out of his system. A diabetic since childhood, he was usually more careful about his alcohol intake. As he ran, he wrestled with the twin mysteries of his abduction and the property conveyance. Three-and-a-half miles later, both mysteries still unsolved, he sprinted into the driveway, did some quick stretches, and entered to find Amanda and Astarte seated at the breakfast table of their modest two-bedroom Cape.

"Figure anything out?" Amanda asked.

"Yes. Running faster does not make me smarter. I still have no idea what any of this is about." He kissed Astarte on the top of her head. "Also, that eating the entire quart of ice cream was a bad idea. Sorry, Astarte, you can have raisins for dessert tonight."

She grinned up at him. She had been living with them for almost two years, since her uncle died. Without family, the girl had latched first onto Amanda as a mother figure and then grown close to Cam as well; they were thrilled to be formally adopting the

15

bright-eyed ten-year-old immediately after the wedding. "I know you didn't eat it. I hid it in the freezer in the basement."

Cam chuckled. "Great. Outsmarted by a fifth-grader."

He showered, then walked Astarte to the bus stop. She surprised him with a question on the way. "Why do you think Abraham agreed to sacrifice Isaac?"

She must have been learning about this at Sunday school. He sensed an orphan's vulnerability beneath the inquiry. Stopping, he crouched down to look her directly in the eye. "Honestly, I've never understood that story." And he understood it even less as his love for Astarte had taken root and grown. "No parent would dream of injuring their child. I know both Amanda and I would do anything to protect you."

She nodded, but he saw doubt in her wide cobalt eyes. "Even if God commanded it?"

"Yes, even if God commanded it. I think the Bible contains lots of stories that are exaggerated or get garbled over time. This is one of them. God would never ask a parent to hurt their own child, and no parent would ever do so even if commanded." He stood. "But now I think I hear the bus coming. Race you!"

Twenty minutes later Cam was in his SUV on the way to Lowell to visit the county Registry of Deeds, the mystery of why Abraham had obeyed God's odious command pushed to the back of his mind. An old mill town, Lowell sat on the banks of the Merrimack River; the river flowed due south from the mountains of New Hampshire before fish-hooking near Lowell back to the northeast and dumping into the Atlantic. Cam's route through Chelmsford and into Lowell tracked the river and he let his mind wander, trying to imagine the waterway as it existed in its pre-industrial state. If European explorers had traveled to New England before Columbus, as Cam and Amanda believed and as Cam had written about in his recently-published *Across the Pond* book, chances were they had used the Merrimack as their highway.

He parked on the street and entered between the massive pillars of a grand, but tired, gray sandstone building. Cam hoped to find the history of the Groton property—how and when had One Wing Industries acquired it?

Working backwards, pulling books from the shelves of the cavernous, dust-filled hall, he learned that One Wing Industries, Inc. had acquired the property less than a year earlier, in October, purportedly for $1.2 million, from an entity known as Middlesex Semiconductor. Middlesex Semiconductor, in turn, had acquired the property in 1989 from a man named Fletcher, whose family had owned the property for generations. He examined the deed from Middlesex Semiconductor to One Wing Industries and compared it to the deed transferring the property to him—it was an identical conveyance, entailing the same six acres off of Main Street. So what had happened in the past year to change the parcel's value from over a million to a single dollar? Or was this just some kind of mistake?

He tried another tack and searched the records for any mortgage that might have been placed on the property. If the property had a value of $1.2 million, but also had an outstanding mortgage of, say, $1.1 million, and the mortgage was in default, then that might explain why an owner would walk away. Or, in this case, give the property away. But, again, he found nothing. One Wing owned the property free and clear. Or, to be more precise, he owned the property free and clear.

Running out of ideas, Cam did a search for other properties One Wing might own in the county. Nothing. Squinting, he examined the name of the notary public who notarized the signature of the One Wing corporate officer who signed the deed—nobody he knew. Exhaling, he sat back and eyed the stacks of plastic-covered land records lining the shelves of the high-ceilinged room. Sunlight filtered through the high windows, illuminating the dust particles floating above him. It was as if One Wing Industries were as illusory as the dancing dust.

He phoned Amanda.

"Any luck?" she asked.

"Yes. But none of it good," he said, summarizing his work. "I'm going to drive out and check out the property. Want me to swing by and pick you up?"

"Sure."

Twenty minutes later Cam turned off of Main Street and onto a narrow paved driveway just west of Groton's downtown area.

Fifty feet up the drive a chained gate blocked their path; in fact, the entire parcel appeared to be enclosed by a high chain-link fence.

Cam rattled the gate. "Locked."

Amanda eyed the fence, the ex-gymnast in her sizing it up. "I could climb it, but I don't fancy the barbed wire on top."

"You know what, there was a hardware store a half-mile back. And we own the property, so we can do whatever we want."

"Good point. I'll wait here. I want to walk around and investigate."

Fifteen minutes later Cam returned with a pair of bolt-cutters. Amanda had been joined by a Groton policeman.

"Cam, can you show Officer Greely a copy of the deed, please?"

The officer squinted and examined the document. "And you are Cameron Thorne?"

"Yes."

"You wrote that book, *Across the Pond*, right?"

Cam smiled. "It depends on whether you liked it or not."

Officer Greely chuckled. "Loved it. I'm big into history, especially the Templars." The book had documented how many of the early American explorers had ties to the outlawed Knights Templar. The policeman jotted a few notes in a small pad.

Cam asked, "Any idea why the property is fenced off?"

"Been that way for years. When I was a kid we used to play back in the woods. There's a brook that runs through that had some good trout. Also there's some kind of stone structure up there." He smiled. "Some of the kids—not me, of course—used to go drinking there. Then they built some kind of factory or something." He gestured. "And the fence."

The officer looked to be about Cam's age, which meant he had been a young teenager just before the property was sold to Middlesex Semiconductors in 1989. "What kind of stone structure?" Cam asked.

"A chamber built into the side of the hill. You know, like a farmer's root cellar."

Amanda and Cam exchanged glances. They had been studying stone chambers as possible evidence of pre-Columbian exploration, and Cam had written a short chapter on them in his book as something that invited further study. It was the first hint at some kind of connection between the land and Cam, though admittedly a flimsy one. Maybe someone who read *Across the Pond* wanted them to study, and even own, the chamber. But then why not just call him up and ask him to take a look?

Cam turned back to the policeman and held up the bolt-cutters. "Unless you have a problem with it, we're going in."

The officer shrugged and turned to walk to his car. "Knock yourself out. It's your land." He stopped at his car door. "But you might want to lock it back up. There must have been some reason the owner didn't want people rummaging around back there."

As the policeman drove away, Cam snapped the padlock and Amanda pushed open the hinged chain-link gate. Cam drove forward toward a frost-heaved parking lot set back from the street. Beyond the lot lay a cement slab the size of three or four tennis courts, the foundation for what once had been some kind of building. "Looks like a decent-sized operation," Cam said. "Maybe 25,000 square feet of space, assuming only one story." He turned and studied the parking lot. "And the lot is big enough for fifty, maybe sixty cars."

"And they made semiconductors?" Amanda asked.

"They did, until for some reason they stopped." He looked around. "And then they apparently knocked the building down."

The land sloped up from the street and, as the cop said, a stream ran down the side of the parcel. "Let's head up the hill and see what's in the woods back there," Cam said. "I'd like to see that chamber."

The rear of the property, beyond the parking lot and building slab, was overgrown; Cam pushed aside the branches and thorns as mosquitoes buzzed around them. They crested the hill and continued down the back, northern side, slipping on last fall's wet leaves. At the bottom of the slope a chain link fence delineated the rear boundary of the parcel.

"Here's the chamber," Amanda called. He turned; she was facing back up the incline toward the crest, pointing. "You can see the opening in the side of the hill, next to that oak tree. We walked right by it; it's only visible from below."

19

Cam scrambled up toward the squat opening. "Look at the roof lintel," he said as he approached. "That's a big stone. Whoever built this meant business."

"And whoever built it was either really short or they didn't intend to use it for storage of any kind." The roof was only a few feet tall and the opening perhaps two feet wide. "I don't think you could get a wheelbarrow through. And if you were going to carry something, you'd have to do so bent completely over."

They stopped just outside the opening.

Stone Chamber Opening

"I'm guessing the tree grew up around this," Cam said. "So the chamber's got to be at least fifty or sixty years old."

"I would imagine much older." She took a step forward and directed her cell phone light toward the opening. "Let's go inside."

Cam touched her elbow. "Wait. Some animal might be holed up in there." He found a small stone and side-armed it into the chamber; it echoed as it hit the back wall. They waited a few seconds but nothing scurried out. Amanda ducked in, her phone illuminating a narrow stone passageway strewn with debris on the dirt floor.

Cam again focused on the roof slabs. "More huge stones across the roof," he said. "They must weigh tons." He followed Amanda; the passageway ran deep into the hillside, perhaps fifteen feet. "And you're right, no way could you get a wheelbarrow through here."

Stone Chamber Passageway

At the end of the passageway Amanda gasped.

Cam froze. "You okay?"

"Yes, fine. I just wasn't expecting *this*." She illuminated a domed inner chamber with a massive slab capping the roof. "We have these beehive chambers all over the British Isles," she breathed.

Stone Chamber Domed Ceiling

"The Druids built them, right?" he asked, knowing that would make them over a thousand years old.

21

She nodded, entranced.

Cam, too, stared at the intricate stonework of the circular inner chamber, measuring approximately ten feet in every direction. He exhaled and smiled. "A beehive is a good description." Or an igloo.

While Cam removed debris from the chamber floor, Amanda paced off the chamber's dimensions, took some pictures and began to sketch the structure. Twenty minutes later she handed him her schematics. "Overhead and side views," she said. "When I was a young lass, I wanted to be an architect."

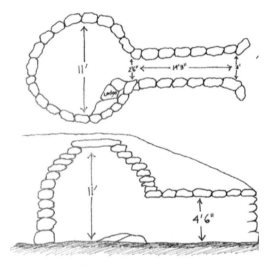

Chamber Drawings

"Nice, thanks," Cam said. He stared at the drawings, then at the chamber walls and ceiling. "Do you think this was ceremonial?"

"Yes. Often these beehive chambers were oriented so that the summer solstice sunrise or sunset ran down the chamber's passageway and illuminated the inner sanctum. It would only happen once a year. It was done to mark the longest day of the year, as part of their ceremony venerating the sun."

Cam oriented himself. "So the opening would need to face due east or due west."

"Actually, a bit north of east-west since we are north of the equator. On the summer solstice the sun rises on the northeast horizon and sets in the northwest."

Cam nodded. "Of course." Crouching, they walked through the passageway and exited the chamber. Cam pictured a map of Groton in his head as he looked toward the horizon. "Main Street runs northwest so that means...." He grinned. "This chamber opens to the northwest."

"About thirty-three degrees north of due west," Amanda said, examining the compass on her phone. She took his arm. "And remember that quartz stone on the back wall? I bet the sunlight on the solstice hits that quartz and makes it glow."

He exhaled slowly. Was it really possible this had been built by explorers from the British Isles back in the Dark Ages? Perhaps ancient, sun-worshiping Druids?

Together they stared at the chamber. She leaned her head against his shoulder. "Well, I know where I plan to be on the summer solstice."

Chapter 2

Friday, finally. Bartol let his mind wander. It was the only way to keep from going crazy from the monotony—eight hours every day, week after week, sanding and rolling and edging, the sharp smell of paint filling his nostrils so bad that even his dinner tasted like frigging latex. But if he wanted to live off the grid, getting paid in cash was his only choice.

And, to be fair, he had played hooky on Monday.

Today he stood on a ladder atop a modest saltbox colonial—of course, 'modest' in Weston still meant over a million bucks, prices crazy from all the foreigners moving to Boston. He didn't know who owned this house and he didn't care. He was content to be high on the ladder, alone with his thoughts.

The Charles River glimmered in the distance over the tree tops. On the far side of the river stood an incongruously-placed stone tower. Bartol had researched the tower: Built in the late 1800s by a wealthy industrialist, the tower marked what the industrialist imagined to be the medieval settlement of Norumbega, as described in Norse legend. Nobody took the tower seriously anymore. Nobody, that is, except Bartol.

David S. Brody

Norumbega Tower, Weston, MA

Bartol studied the tower as he painted, wondering if the site did indeed mark a thousand-year-old settlement established by his Viking forbearers. The exact location might be off, but Bartol didn't doubt that the Norse settled in North America. Not that it mattered to most people—today's politically-correct, liberal elite purposefully downplayed the amazing achievements of Europeans over the past centuries. Well, people would care when the barbaric Arabs overran Europe, wiped out Judeo-Christian culture and set their eyes on America. Then they would be glad for soldiers like Bartol, trained and ready to defend his country.

A co-worker, Sully, interrupted his thoughts. "Hey, Bartol, you want a sandwich?"

"No thanks. I brought my lunch." He always made his own meals, avoiding the processed foods that poisoned the body. He was a soldier, his body his most important weapon.

Sully continued to look up at him. For some reason it bothered him that Bartol chose not to eat with him and the rest of the crew. "So is Bartol your first name or your last name?"

"It's my only name."

Sully was a bear, the alpha man of the crew, outweighing Bartol by fifty pounds. He couldn't let Bartol have the last word. "Well, it rhymes with asshole."

25

Bartol turned slowly, looked down and fixed his gray-blue eyes on Sully. "Yeah, I suppose it does." He was willing to come down the ladder if Sully pushed it, but he was past the point in his life where he needed to prove anything to anybody.

Sully shrugged and began to walk away. As he passed Bartol's ladder, he side-kicked it with a heavy work boot. The ladder skidded and tilted, sending Bartol in a slow arcing descent. Reacting instantly, Bartol grabbed at the roof gutter and jumped from the falling aluminum. He caught the gutter, hanging one–armed, seething at his co-worker's idiocy. As if to add an exclamation point to his thought, the ladder crashed to the ground, paint splattering. Finding a foothold on some window trim, Bartol grabbed the gutter with his second hand and began to hoist himself onto to the roof.

Suddenly the gutter moaned and pulled away from the fascia. *Shit*. Again reacting without thinking, Bartol swung himself sideways toward an oak tree, grabbing a branch with a free hand like a monkey just as the gutter fully gave way. As he swung, his weight caused the branch to bend, leaving his boots only four feet above the ground. He dropped. And landed next to a leering Sully.

"Sorry that you tripped over my ladder," Bartol said. He didn't wait for the larger man to respond. Feigning a punch with his right hand, Bartol instead fell back and swung his right leg out to sweep Sully's feet aside, knocking him to the ground. Bartol leapt atop him, grabbing him in a choke hold and straddling his back. Sully roared, the sound muffled by the choke, and pushed himself to his feet, Bartol still riding his back. The larger man stumbled backward toward the house, apparently with the intent of squishing his adversary against the wall. Bartol held on, baiting Sully. "Come on, big boy. Everyone's watching."

Another roar, and Sully threw himself backward against the house. But Bartol was quicker, somersaulting himself over Sully's head and landing on his feet like a Saturday morning wrestler just as the big man crashed back-first into the clapboards. With a grunt, he crumbled to the ground, moaning.

Bartol took a dollar from his wallet and dropped it on his co-worker's cheek. "You know what, I changed my mind. I'll take a water. I seem to have worked up a bit of a thirst."

26

A few of Sully's buddies had circled the pair but, seeing what Bartol had done to Sully and intuitively fearing his cold ferocity, they shrugged and carried their friend away, leaving Bartol alone.

Which was all he really wanted in life—to be left alone. By his alcoholic mother; by a Big Brother government obsessed with monitoring and tracking its citizens; even by his old army buddies who couldn't seem to see that the country they fought for had already sold out. The war was over, America and its experiment with democracy had lost. All without the enemy firing a shot. The Democrats had opened the borders, legalized the millions of immigrants overrunning American cities, and bought their loyalty with welfare and food stamps. The political balance of power in America had changed permanently, with those leeching off society outnumbering those contributing to it. At some point—unless the Arabs had already destroyed the country—the true Americans might rise up, and when they did Bartol would be ready to join them. But until then he refused to pay a penny in taxes and refused to allow the government to intrude into his life. He had cut up his driver's license, closed his bank account and credit cards, bought a bicycle, and changed his name. He lived about as far under the radar as anyone could. Other than his coworkers and the old woman who rented him a small apartment on the second floor of her row house in Boston, nobody even knew he existed. He rode public transportation when not using his bike, went to the library when he wanted to read or surf the Internet, rigged up some rabbit ears to an old Zenith television set, and kept a stash of weapons and other survival gear locked in a storage unit under a fake name a short walk from his apartment. At twenty bucks an hour he easily earned enough to buy food and supplies, pay rent, and keep his survival stash fresh. In short, he was having no trouble surviving. But surviving was not really *living*.

Bartol righted his ladder, making sure to place it near a window ledge this time just in case Sully came back for revenge. He re-ascended, turned back to the tower and exhaled, clearing his head. How had America gotten here, to this dead end? There was a time when the promise of America had captured the imagination of the world. Though the designs were dissimilar, the stone tower reminded Bartol of Rhode Island's Newport Tower, a structure built by America's earliest explorers. He had recently read *Across the Pond,* a book by a local author documenting the many sites and artifacts that evidenced a history of Europeans—northern Europeans, to be precise—crossing the Atlantic to explore and settle in America. It was amazing research, giving his ancestors the credit they deserved. Bartol did not support Hitler and his lunatic policies, but he did agree that the cultural achievements of the white race were far superior to any other group in the world over the past five hundred years. Advances in critical thought, human rights, technology, medicine, culture, and (as *Across the Pond* compellingly explained) exploration all originated with Caucasians. Not that all Caucasians were exemplary; Sully was proof of that. But, on average, there existed a quantifiable level of superior accomplishment. Unfortunately, the world now equated the notion of white supremacy with Nazi homicidal insanity. Just because Bartol believed the white race had created a society superior to any other in the world did not mean he wanted to kill off the others. It just meant he didn't want them infesting his country unless they were going to work hard and contribute to it.

As if to prove his point, a couple of Hispanic workers moved their ladder near his, rap music polluting the air as they bobbed their empty heads. These were among the best of their race, actually holding down a job. But had they ever read a book for pleasure? Watched an evening newscast? Had so much as a single original thought? Bartol did not love the Jews, but at least they accomplished things—their contributions to world culture far exceeded their population numbers. Hitler had been an idiot to try to exterminate them. But the Arabs and the Africans and the Hispanics—what had they contributed in the past five hundred years other than terrorism, bad music and crack cocaine?

He shook his head. No, that wasn't fair. That was hyperbole. There were plenty of Arabs and Africans and Hispanics whom he respected and admired—he had fought side-by-side with some of them in Iraq. Just not enough to make up for all the others.

Alone in the house with Astarte at school and Cam at his law office catching up on work he had missed while researching and inspecting the Groton property all morning, Amanda took advantage of the warm spring afternoon and brought her laptop out onto the deck overlooking the lake.

Venus curled up at her feet, her fawn-colored face positioned to capture the sun angling between the deck balusters. Amanda, too, turned to the sun, closed her eyes, and let out a long sigh. She didn't normally stress over such things, but the wedding plans had occupied most of her time the past couple of months. Her mother lived in England—and was in many ways even more distant emotionally than physically—so Amanda had done much of the planning herself. Cam helped, as did his mom, but it still felt like every time she made a decision two more popped up in its place. Now, with the Labor Day weekend date only four months away, Amanda finally felt like she had things under control.

Which meant she could get back to her research. She had long been fascinated with, and had recently focused on, Baphomet, the mysterious head the Knights Templar were accused of—and admitted to—worshipping. Many historians believed the head represented some religious secret the Templars had discovered, a secret so threatening to the Church that it outlawed the entire order, torturing and executing its leaders. Amanda was content to let Cam write the books and give the lectures. What she loved was spending hours rummaging around in the dusty corners of history ruminating over questions like this: Why would a Christian monastic group worship a head which was so seemingly at odds with Christian religious practices? In fact, in its most famous representation, the Baphomet figure bore a strong resemblance to the devil. Amanda found the image, first drawn by the French occultist Eliphas Levi in the 1850s, and pulled it up on her screen. Amanda had always focused mainly on Baphomet's head; this illustration included his entire body.

Baphomet

She studied the figure, wondering at his horns and his wings and the star and moon figures—the image was full of esoteric imagery. But she would return to these sensationalized, devil-like aspects of Baphomet later. For now she focused on the question of why the Templars would worship a head of any kind, devilish or not. The Third Commandment expressly prohibited the worship of any graven images or idols, and the Templars had to know that the medieval Church had a zero-tolerance policy toward any kind of unorthodox worship practices. So why would the Army of the Church risk everything by worshiping some mysterious skull? Did the skull embody some religious secret the Templars had discovered during their time in the Holy Land?

As if in response, a black crow flew overhead, cawing, waking Venus from her nap. The Labrador Retriever growled and arched her ears, then returned to her slumber as the crow banked away, its call echoing across the lake. Amanda watched the bird fade into the distance. If there had been a message in its caw, it had been lost on Amanda.

She returned to her notes. There were more than a dozen differing theories trying to explain Baphomet, but Amanda had yet to uncover one that made sense to her. She herself theorized that Baphomet represented a fusion between the medieval practice of relic veneration—in which bones and personal effects of saints were collected and displayed by churches and monasteries under the belief that the saints, so-honored, would intercede with God on the parishioners' behalf—and the pagan practice of worshiping the head as some kind of representation of the divine. This head worship, known as the Cult of the Head, was practiced by numerous non-Judeo-Christian cultures as well as by the Druids of the British Islands. Somehow, Amanda was beginning to believe, the Templars had taken relic worship to the next level and combined it with the ancient Cult of the Head beliefs.

Her theory, of course, begged the question: Who exactly was Baphomet, and why had the Templars worshipped his skull?

Zuberi Youssef drove one-armed, the stump of his right arm resting on the armrest of the rented Cadillac SRX crossover as he navigated the streets of Waltham, a few miles west of Boston. He raced through a yellow light, the vehicle jumping at his touch. It felt good to drive—usually he was being chauffeured around Europe or the Middle East by one of his bodyguards. But today was just father and son. Eighteen-year-old Amon sat in the passenger seat, his posture erect and his face expressionless.

Zuberi lowered his voice. "I understand, my son, that you not are happy with this decision."

Amon began to respond in Arabic but Zuberi quickly cut him off. "In America, only English." The boy had the advantage of learning English as a youth and spoke it almost fluently. Zuberi had begun speaking it only as an adult and still struggled.

"Very well. I am not happy with the decision. No. But I accept it. I understand your reasoning, Father."

He said it matter-of-factly, without bitterness. Amon, unlike his brash older brother and his spoiled younger sister, had always been level-headed and practical. When he was young Zuberi called him the Little Banker because he was always saving his candy and hoarding his money. Zuberi smiled ruefully. "In some ways you be punished for being agreeable, for being obedient, for doing what is best for family. Even if it not make you happy."

"I do not look at it as a punishment. Brandeis is a fine university."

"Yes, but Brandeis is not Tufts or Columbia. I know you prefer to attend these instead." Zuberi sniffed; not that any of the options constituted a hardship. When Zuberi was Amon's age he was fighting alongside the Americans with other Egyptians in the Gulf War. He had made many useful friendships during that year. And he had lost an arm to an Iraqi mortar strike. Not a fair trade, but not as one-sided as it first appeared.

Amon bit his lower lip. He was tall and olive-skinned like his mother, though much more handsome. From his father he inherited a pair of large, dark brown eyes and a curious intellect. "If I had studied harder, perhaps I could have gained entrance to Harvard."

"And I would insist still you go to Brandeis, my son."

Amon simply nodded and turned to stare out the window.

"We are Muslims in Judeo-Christian world, Amon. A world that becomes more fractured and also more anti-Muslim. But as businessmen we need to do business across all borders. This is why I moved our family to Scotland—a European company can do business that Egyptian company can not." Amon had been twelve at the time of the move—then, like now, he had accepted the decision stoically while his older brother cursed and made threats. But there were still doors closed to Zuberi. "The Jews in America and Europe are very powerful and very rich. We need to build bridges; we need friends in the Jewish world; we need to win their trust."

Amon nodded again. "I will do my best."

Not that Zuberi had planned things that far in advance, but the boy's name meant 'the hidden one'—Zuberi's plan was to hide the boy in plain sight amongst their would-be enemies. If war broke out with the Jews again, Zuberi intended to profit. Zuberi *always* profited. He sold weaponry in times of war and heavy machinery in times of peace to rebuild that which had been destroyed. The key was to foresee which was coming next.

Zuberi spoke again. "You know the American proverb: 'Keep friends close and enemies closer.' Four years you spend at

Brandeis. I care not about your grades or what classes you choose or if you smoke or gamble or bring women to your bed—"

Amon interrupted. "I do not do those things, Father."

Zuberi smiled as he turned onto a side street a block away from the Brandeis campus. "Not yet, perhaps. But, again, fine it is that you experiment. I care only that you build these bridges. Find Jewish friends. Support Jewish causes. Condemn Islamic acts of terror. Show to the Jews that Muslim can be their friend." He lowered his voice. "And *be* a true friend, Amon. Do not only pretend. All men have good in them—find the good even in the Jews and embrace it. Only then they will trust you." Zuberi swallowed. *But please, Allah, do not let him fall in love with a Jewish girl.*

They pulled up to a bright yellow two-family Colonial home on a street full of similar structures. Zuberi continued. "In September you move into dormitory with other freshmen. But in summer you live here."

"This is the house you purchased?"

"Yes. It is for you. Maybe offer good rent to Jewish students you want as friends. This summer you learn the campus, learn Boston, learn Waltham, make plans how you are going to build these bridges." Zuberi put the car into park. "I help you carry suitcases."

Amon opened his door. "That is not necessary, Father. I know you have a meeting to attend." He grabbed his bags from the back seat, leaned back through the door and offered his hand, turning his wrist so Zuberi could shake with his left hand. He held his father's gaze. "I will not disappoint you."

Zuberi nodded, surprised at the moisture pooling in his eyes. He rubbed his bald head with his hand. What a softy he had become, living amongst the Europeans. He turned his head before Amon noticed. "Go with Allah, my son."

Cam spent a few hours in his office Friday afternoon returning phone calls and getting ready for a Monday closing—this one preferably less eventful than last week's. But his mind remained focused on the stone chamber and the strange way it had appeared in his life. He didn't believe in coincidence, so the fact that he had just written a book on pre-Columbian history and the fact there was an apparently ancient chamber on the property must somehow be related. And from that it followed that, for some reason, someone wanted Cam to own—and investigate—the stone structure. He shook his head. "They could have just asked," he muttered not for the first time.

He phoned Amanda. "Hey, I'm done here. I was going to shoot back to Groton and snoop around Town Hall, see if anyone knows anything about this property."

"Fine," she said. "Astarte just got home. We're going to take a walk around the lake with Venus."

"Hey, before you go, check out this email I just got. I just forwarded it to you."

He gave her a few seconds to read it. "Who is Bartol?" she asked, seeing the name of the sender.

"Never heard of him."

The message was a rambling one, but essentially the sender—an ex-Army Ranger—claimed to be a fan of Cam's book and believed the politically correct would target Cam, perhaps violently, to suppress his research. Bartol was offering to serve as Cam's bodyguard if Cam ever felt in danger.

"Well, looks like you've made a new friend."

"I'm not sure I need friends like this. He sounds like a kook."

Amanda had studied psychology in London. "Guardian angels are generally well-meaning. But some of them are so compulsive they end up developing something called Guardian Angel Complex."

"There's a specific complex for guardian angels?"

"You actually see it a lot. They get so concerned with fighting their enemies that they forget to protect their charges. The animal rights groups are a good example. In the name of liberating' animals they break open cages, only to have the critters die in the wild. They become obsessed with taking action, even if it ends up being counterproductive."

"So I shouldn't invite this guy over to dinner?"

"It depends—do you want to be let out of your cage?"

Cam typed a quick, non-committal response to the email and, twenty minutes later, parked in front of Groton's brick, Italianate-style Town Hall. He wandered in, found the tax assessor's office on the second floor, and asked for the file on the property. Two years ago, before the building had been demolished, the property was valued at $1.15 million, $850,000 attributable to the structure and $300,000 to the land. Middlesex Semiconductor had sold to One Wing Industries for just over that amount, but for some strange reason One Wing had then conveyed to Cam for nothing. There were some notes describing the structure before it had been demolished, but nothing that shed any light on the mystery.

Cam handed the file back to the clerk. "Can you tell me if the taxes are current?" One possibility was that the owner was so far in arrears on the taxes that the property was essentially worthless. The clerk, an elderly man wearing a blue blazer with a Freemason's pin, nodded and stabbed at his computer keyboard. Often the elderly were allowed to offset their tax bills by doing volunteer work. "They are paid up through last quarter. The next payment is due June 1, just over a thousand dollars."

Over the next few weeks Cam would need to decide whether to pay them or not. "Can you print out a copy of the bill?"

"Sorry, the printer is on the fritz. If you give me your name I can mail you a copy Monday."

"Great. I'm the new owner." Cam showed him the deed and gave him his name and address. "Thanks."

Cam descended the stairs and found the Town Clerk's office. "I was wondering about the old Middlesex Semiconductor property. I noticed it's fenced off and the building is torn down."

A tall, straight-backed woman wearing a light blue cardigan nodded. Pushing sixty, she had a no-nonsense way about her that reminded Cam of a high school vice-principal. Behind her the three desks in the office were free of clutter and the room otherwise immaculate. "Presumably it is fenced off to keep people out," she sniffed.

He tried a different tact. Sometimes immaculate people liked lawyers, perhaps because of the presumed orderly nature of their work. He wished he was not wearing jeans and a tennis shirt. "I am an attorney and I have a client, a developer, who asked me to check into this property for him."

She softened a bit. "The man who owned the company died a few years ago. His widow sold out to a British company last fall, but they fired all the workers, shut the place down and demolished the building after only a couple of weeks."

"Any idea why?"

"The explanation I heard was that they only bought it to get rid of their competition; apparently Middlesex had developed some expertise in a certain kind of semiconductor. By shutting them down, they removed their main competitor."

Cam nodded. That made some sense, at least. But it did nothing to explain how the property ended up in his lap. "Has the new owner tried to sell the property?"

She shrugged. A wall clock ticked loudly high on the wall behind her. "I have not seen a For Sale sign posted."

"But why knock down the buildings?" he asked, more to himself than to the clerk.

"I heard they stripped the buildings before they demolished them, took all the high-tech machinery out. I do know they did not bother to apply for a demolition permit. The town fined them five thousand dollars."

"Okay, thanks for your time." Maybe once stripped the buildings had little value. Or maybe the owner planned to redevelop the property. But then why give it away? He began to walk away but turned back with a final question. "Is there anything else at all you can tell me about the property? Anything you might have heard, rumors or such?" His years practicing law had taught him that sometimes the 'catch-all' question actually caught something.

The clerk crossed her arms in front of her chest and blinked three times in rapid succession as her cheeks reddened. "I beg your pardon, but I am not one to spread rumors." She spun away. "Good day to you."

Cam watched her back; his own back tingled, a familiar sensation that often portended danger. She may not be one to spread rumors, but as the town clerk she was in an ideal position to hear them.

After dropping off his son Zuberi drove to the Brandeis campus and found a quiet, shaded spot at the edge of the parking lot to unroll his prayer rug. He had an hour before his meeting. Turning the prayer rug so it faced just south of east, toward Mecca, he supplicated himself.

The wooly, dusty smell of the rug comforted him. Every rug's design uniquely reflected its owner's village—Zuberi's rug featured a royal blue image of his local mosque set on a silver background. The rug carried the aromas of home with it as well. When Bennu was small, she used to climb on the rug to pray with him—she told him the rug smelled like a wet camel. He smiled at the memory and wondered how his little bird (Bennu being the Arabic word for heron) had turned into such a spoiled brat of a teenager. Actually, he knew the answer: Her mother had died in a car accident when she was seven and her father had dragged the family from Cairo to Scotland, and then remarried. He sighed. He did not miss his first wife. Theirs had been a loveless marriage, arranged by their parents; she was a hairy, malodorous bear of a woman who knew nothing about business and cared even less. But the children, especially Bennu, missed their mother. He sighed again. Perhaps his bird might still soar someday.

He rubbed his smooth head, trying to clear his mind and focus on his prayers. He was not a religious man—the idea of some omnipotent god sitting in heaven micromanaging life on earth seemed ludicrous to him. Yet the spark of life must have come from somewhere, and the scientific theory that life began in some primordial soup when a couple of molecules bounced into each other seemed equally ludicrous. In the end, he prayed not because he believed anyone was listening but because it settled him, focused him. His prayer was a simple one: *Give me strength to be the best I can be.*

Five minutes later he opened his eyes, brushed the dust from the knees of his gray suit, rolled up the rug with his one good arm and retrieved his briefcase from the Cadillac. He was fortunate to have a son who would inherit his business—in today's world, he knew, it was not always so. Nasser, in fact, wanted only to race fast cars and chase fast women. And there had been a time he was not so certain about Amon—the boy did not necessarily have the ruthlessness or cunning needed to be a successful businessman.

"Must I work in the family business, Father?" the young Amon had asked, his large brown eyes wide with innocence.

Zuberi had smiled even as his heart clenched. "No, my son. If a man's future was governed by his origins, no bird that came from an egg would ever fly."

"But can I work with you if I choose to?"

"Yes, of course." He had smiled. "But if you choose to fly with me,"—and, looking back, he now realized he had been mixing his metaphors—"you must promise to fly as high and far as possible."

Now, in one of life's strange twists, they had flown together to suburban Boston, to the largest Jewish university in the Western world. In a few minutes Zuberi would be meeting with the chair of the History Department and some dean with a fancy title. He had a proposal for them, and he was prepared to put some dollar signs behind it.

In truth, it was his wife's proposal. He had remarried a few years ago, three years after moving to Edinburgh, the marriage more of a business arrangement than a love affair. Many generations had passed since Carrington McLeod Sinclair's family could count themselves among the landed gentry of eastern Scotland. She was, in fact, the daughter of a chemist and a taxi driver—the family's modern-day claim to fame was that Carrington's mother had been part of the team that cloned Dolly the sheep at the Roslin Institute in 1996. But the Sinclair name still carried cache in Scotland, and Zuberi understood that certain doors were open to a Sinclair that would not open for an Egyptian named Zuberi Youssef. She, in turn, longed to take her place atop Scottish society, which was why she had kept her mother's Sinclair surname while dropping McLeod after the marriage, becoming Carrington Sinclair-Youssef. Their union was not one of physical affection, but a certain level of fondness between the two had developed—a pleasant surprise to Zuberi after his first marriage.

And a bonus. It was never a bad thing to get more than one bargained for.

There were some in the Sinclair family, Zuberi knew, who compared his marriage to Carrington to that of Mohamed al-Fayed's efforts to marry his son Dodi to Princess Diana back in the 1990s. There were some similarities, of course, but al-Fayed had made the mistake of allowing his pride and his emotions to blind his judgment—marrying his son to the princess had become an obsession with Mohamed, one that eventually took Dodi from him. Zuberi had not aimed as high. Nor had he paid such a high price. As a business associate and countryman of al-Fayed, Zuberi had attended Dodi's funeral, hugged the grieving father, even shed tears with him. Dodi's death was a loss not just to his family but to all Egyptians, a missed opportunity to enter the inner circle of European society and power. Zuberi's marriage to Carrington did not allow him access to that inner circle, but it brought him a few steps closer. And he and Carrington had plans to shoulder their way even nearer.

He phoned her in Edinburgh as he walked. "Hello husband," she answered. "Have you settled Amon?"

"Yes. My son is agreeable, as always. How is Bennu today?" He knew better than to ask about Nasser—the boy was on some yacht in the Greek Isles.

Carrington exhaled a short laugh. "Another crisis. A boy invited her to the school dance, but then his parents forbade it."

Zuberi gritted his teeth, the back of his neck burning. "Why?"

"You know why, Zuberi. And Bennu knows why also. She has locked herself in her bedroom."

He chortled. When he was a child, his entire family lived in a two-room, mud-brick home. There was no bedroom to lock oneself in. The house Carrington had insisted on purchasing—a renovated castle overlooking the city, once owned by the family that produced Drambuie liqueur—had more rooms than he could count, plus another entire building for the servants.

His wife continued. "She claims she won't come out unless you agree to move back to Cairo. She has already missed her dinner."

He stopped and leaned against a tree, the sun on his face. Scotland was a liberal, open-minded country, but remnants of the old-time landed gentry still continued to socialize only with each other. "These noble families forget Scotland was settled first by Egyptians." Scota, after whom Scotland was named, was in fact the daughter of a Pharaoh. "It is Bennu who should be … what is your expression … looking down her nose to them."

"Yes, well, someday that might be the case. But for now her nose is buried in a pillow."

He kicked the tree. Zuberi spent almost as much time worrying about his daughter as he did his business. Carrington knew better than to try to play the mother role with the girl—reaching out to her would only push the girl further away, like a child swimming after a beach ball in the ocean. She allowed Zuberi, and the governess he had hired, to raise the girl. She played the role of a concerned, but properly distant, aunt. "I am at Brandeis now, heading into the meeting," he said.

In this matter, unlike in the parenting of Bennu, Carrington took an active role. "Any word yet from Cameron Thorne?"

"No. I call him when I hang up with you."

"We need him, I believe. I watched a video of him giving a lecture at a conference—he is very compelling. And he is becoming well-known based on his book. Be persistent, Zuberi."

He chuckled softly; his wife had no idea how persuasive he could be. "I plan honey and vinegar both to catch this bee."

"But Mr. Thorne is of no use to us if Brandeis turns us down."

He laughed again. "Before I phone you I go to Brandeis website to look at course catalog for next fall. They have class called 'European History of America Prior to Columbus' listed."

Her laugh met his. "Already? Before we've even come to an agreement?"

"They need to put in catalog in April when students choose classes." But it gave Zuberi a free look at Brandeis' hand.

"Have you settled on a figure?" Carrington asked.

"I will begin with million dollars. From what I read, Brandeis has financial problems. A few years ago they try to sell their art collection—the students and faculty object, but the money problems continue."

"Is a million enough?"

"Perhaps no. But we know now they are already committed. I will hint at more money in future. And I can negotiate always higher."

"The benefits to our family, and to your business, could be many times that."

He smiled. "This I know. And to you I give thanks, my wife. I will phone you after meeting."

The certified mail notice had arrived at their house on Tuesday. Cam had been carrying it around in his wallet for three days—as a lawyer, he understood that certified mail was often used for mundane matters as well as important ones. Only today, after leaving Groton Town Hall, did he have time to swing by the post office to sign for the letter.

As he pulled into the parking lot his phone chimed. While driving through a dead zone he had missed a call from Zuberi Youssef. Cam smiled at the memory of the strong-willed Egyptian. He and Amanda had met Zuberi and his wife Carrington last October; they were visiting from Scotland and arranged through friends for Cam to show them the Westford Knight carving. Cam had shown the carving to hundreds of visitors over the years. But he would never forget that blustery, Columbus Day weekend.

Nor the ironic significance attached to the timing of their discovery.

He smiled as he replayed the scene in his mind:

Cam squatted and splashed a few ounces of water on the battle sword carved into the bedrock. A cold fall wind blew across the hill as the sun dropped to the horizon in the western sky, numbing Cam's moistened fingers. The visitors from Scotland—a husband and wife—bent low over him.

"How old do you think the carving is?" the man asked. In his mid-forties, Zuberi Youssef spoke with a Middle-Eastern accent.

The Issac Question

He had only a stump for one arm; he dragged on a cigarette using the other, his dark eyes locked onto Cam.

Cam waited for a truck to pass; the carving was located atop a hill along an ancient Native American trail which in modern times had grown into a main thoroughfare in town. "The legend is that Prince Henry Sinclair came to North America in 1398." Cam smiled. "I know that's not very old in European terms, but for us it sets the clock back a hundred years."

Using an old rag, Cam spread the water over the entire face of the carving and dabbed the excess away. Stone carvings were best viewed at night, using low angle light after moistening the rock. He held his flashlight low to the bedrock and maneuvered his body to block the streetlight. The outline of a battle sword jumped off the rock.

"Now I see it clearly," the woman exclaimed. She looked to be a decade younger than her husband, though she was one of those people who seemed to have morphed from teenager directly to middle-age; at one point she pulled a tissue out of the sleeve of her cardigan sweater, the way Cam's grandmother used to do. A Sinclair herself, Carrington outlined the sword with her finger as Cam snapped a picture with his new camera, focusing on the pommel, hilt and cross guard of the weapon.

Sword from Westford Knight Carving

42

"It's a two-handed battle sword," Cam explained. "Like a claymore."

The woman smiled. She was not pretty, but her face—pink-cheeked from the cold—was friendly and her eyes intelligent. "Like in that horrible movie, Braveheart,*" she said. "The film was a load of bollocks, but at least the history was spot on: The Sinclairs fought alongside William Wallace and later with Robert the Bruce at the Battle of Bannockburn in 1314."*

Cam nodded. Legend held that the outlawed Knights Templar also fought on the side of the Scots against the English that day, ensuring victory and eventually leading to Scottish independence.

Carrington added, "Prince Henry possessed a fleet of ships in the Orkney Islands, where he ruled. And his mum was a Norsewoman, so he certainly knew the tales of the old Viking journeys across the North Atlantic. He probably even had some old maps."

Zuberi rubbed his bald head. "I see sword, but I do not see knight."

Cam nodded again. "Much of the carving has faded over time." He pulled a photo from his pack. "This is a rubbing that was done about twenty years ago. It shows the knight as he once looked." The knight was purportedly one of Sinclair's men, Sir James Gunn, who died during the exploration.

Rubbing of Westford Knight Carving

43

Zuberi grunted. Cam wondered how much he was just indulging his wife by visiting the site, though he didn't seem the type to defer to her much. "How can you be certain carving is old?"

"It was written about in the 1870s in a town history," Cam replied. "Even then it was considered a historical mystery of unknown origin, attributed to the Indians. But the Native Americans did not have iron tools needed to peck into the hard bedrock."

Cam splashed more water on a scratched area above and to the right of the sword's pommel and held his flashlight low, his free hand in his pocket to keep warm. "This gives us a good comparison. It was carved in the 1870s by some local boys—they thought it would be fun to give our dead knight a pipe to smoke."
He smiled. "So they scratched one into the rock with a knife."

"Peace Pipe" on Westford Knight Carving

"It looks more like toothbrush than pipe," Zuberi said, pointing at the series of parallel vertical scratch marks.

Cam nodded. "It does, yes. But it also helps with the dating question. Since we know the pipe was added about 140 years ago, we can analyze the weathering patterns within the carved surfaces of the pipe and compare them to the sword. The weathering on the sword is significantly older, again pointing to a much earlier date."

Zuberi again grunted noncommittally while Cam and Carrington studied the head area. After a few seconds, the Middle-Easterner said, "What is this?"

Cam looked up. Zuberi was pointing to an area near the tip of the sword where Cam had inadvertently spilled some water. "What?" Cam had never seen anything carved in that area.

Zuberi's face was inches above the stone. "I see five-pointed star."

Cam crab-walked over, flashlight in hand. He peered in and gasped. His first reaction was that his guest was playing some kind of trick on him.

"What is wrong?" the man asked.

Cam closed his eyes and took a deep breath. He leaned over and peered in again. This time he could not wrench his eyes away. He swallowed and fumbled for his camera, afraid the image would somehow disappear if he did not record it immediately. He snapped a shot and stared at the display screen, as if seeing it on the camera somehow made it more real than on the stone itself. There was no doubt.

"What is it?" Carrington asked.

"It's too good to be true, is what it is," he answered as he snapped another shot. "It's a Hooked X."

Hooked X Mark on Westford Knight Carving

45

The Issac Question

"A what?" Zuberi asked.

Cam shivered, his body reacting either to the cold or, more likely, to the discovery. "An X, with an extra fork on the upper right stem. It's a runic character that has been found on rune stones in North America, but never in Europe or Scandinavia. If this is real..."

He lifted his head to study his guests. Was there any way they could have somehow planted this? He bent over again and peered at the carving, using a jeweler's loupe to examine the carving closer. The carved areas were smooth and uniform, the result of decades if not centuries of weathering. This was not a modern hoax. And it was clearly an intentional, deliberate mark—the carving, located just where an artist would sign a portrait, was oriented in the same direction as the sword and knight, and the mark itself was offset by a deep dot on either side of the X, a kind of punctuation often found in runic inscriptions.

After what must have been several minutes, Cam lifted his head again. Carrington and Zuberi were staring at him, waiting. He realized he was being rude. Rude to the people who may have just rewritten the history books. He took a deep breath. "Like I said, we've seen this character on other carvings. And we've always theorized these other carvings were related to Prince Henry Sinclair. But we never had any proof." He smiled at Carrington. "It's possible your husband just found conclusive proof your ancestors were here a hundred years before Columbus."

Seven months had passed, but Cam still smiled at the memory. The discovery had occurred on Columbus Day, of all things.

He and Amanda had returned the next day, and for many days thereafter, using three dimensional imaging and other technologies and experts to evaluate the carving. In the end, it came down to the science: The weathering of the Hooked X matched the weathering of the sword, and the tool used to carve each was the same. Whoever had carved the Westford Knight had also carved the Hooked X.

The finding had been a tipping point, finally swaying many of the skeptics who had rejected evidence of European exploration of

America before Columbus. The mark tied the Westford Knight carving to Minnesota's Kensington Rune Stone, Maine's Spirit Pond Rune Stones and Rhode Island's Narragansett Rune Stone—carvings separated by thousands of miles and hundreds of years. No longer could skeptics claim that each of these was its own, freestanding hoax. Instead, the skeptics were left to argue that the four carvings were part of some unknown, convoluted, centuries-old conspiracy. But the argument fell flat. In a classic application of Occam's Razor—the principle that among competing hypotheses, the one with the fewest assumptions should be selected—the public sensed the truth: The carvings were authentic.

Cam had quickly incorporated the Hooked X discovery into what was scheduled to be a December release of *Across the Pond.* He then spent several months following the book's release lecturing and doing radio and television interviews. Now, finally, the launch of the book behind him, he had settled into a routine that allowed him to continue his research.

He dialed Zuberi's number.

"Cameron, hello!"

"Hello Zuberi. How are you?"

Zuberi spoke loudly and slowly, aware that his thick accent might be difficult to understand. "I wonder if you have chance more to think about our offer?"

After the discovery of the Hooked X, Zuberi and Carrington had insisted on taking Cam and Amanda out to a late dinner to celebrate. As the evening wore on, Carrington—dressed in a pantsuit from the 1990s and frequently looking to her husband for permission before venturing an opinion—became increasingly enthusiastic about the idea of teaching the Prince Henry Sinclair story in American schools. Why should it be so readily dismissed as legend, she argued, when the evidence was so compelling? Cam and Amanda had dismissed the proposal as one of those fleeting dinner-table ideas sparked by good food and a few glasses of wine. Cam had been shocked when an email arrived a week later outlining their idea of endowing a chair at a Boston-area university to focus on the study of pre-Columbian history—and proposing that Cam's rear end sit in that chair.

But Cam thought this had been resolved. "As I wrote back to you, I was very flattered to be considered for this job but I am not a professor. I am not even technically a historian." He majored in history in college but did not hold a master's degree. "Plus I don't really like the idea of being part of academia." It was the academic types, in fact, who were the biggest naysayers when it came to the idea of explorers arriving before Columbus. He wanted to research, not spend his days debating and arguing. "I don't really think I'm the right person for the job."

"This is what makes you perfect man for job!" Zuberi bellowed. "If we want professor egghead we hire professor egghead. But we want someone who is outsider. Someone with passion and energy and mind open." The egghead comment caused Cam to recall Zuberi rubbing his bald head during dinner with his one good hand. Amanda had commented that she thought he looked like Yul Brynner in *The King and I* with his piercing brown eyes and dark, angry eyebrows. The Egyptian lowered his voice and continued. "The job pays very well, Cameron."

The money was tempting. Amanda worked part-time as a museum curator, but once they got married the plan was to have a baby or two. Cam's law practice generated enough income to support a single guy, but not a growing family. Book royalties were climbing, but Cam had earmarked that money for Astarte's college fund. "Honestly, I'm tempted. But I want to spend more time researching, not less."

"This job is to allow you to do research!"

Cam laughed. "No, it will allow me to sit in faculty meetings and grade papers and defend myself from attacks from the mainstream historians. Maybe twenty years from now, but this is not the right time." He glanced at his watch; speaking of time, the certified letter would have to wait as the post office had just closed.

"The world, it changes quickly," Zuberi said. The Egyptian was probably only a few years older than Cam, but he had a worldly air about him that made him seem much older. And his wealth gave him a self-assuredness that bordered on arrogance. "So you think more and I phone you next week. Say hello to Amanda."

Cam laughed again. He did not want to be rude. "Okay, Zuberi. Our best to Carrington. Bye."

"Professor Thorne," he whispered as he restarted the engine. He shook his head—it didn't sound right. And it didn't feel right, either.

Zuberi's Friday afternoon meeting with the Brandeis officials was not going well. Which meant it was going precisely as Zuberi expected. Zuberi and two others sat around a conference room table that overlooked a pond on the edge of the campus; Zuberi scowled at the modern art adorning the room's walls while a waiter served coffee, tea, and bottles of flavored water.

The History department chair—a bookish, older man wearing an oversized beige blazer and a pair of thick glasses that sat crooked on his nose—complained that the field of pre-Columbian history was a fringe area of study that would taint the reputation of the entire university. Zuberi tried not to roll his eyes: The Americans, like most cultures, spun their history to support their idealized view of themselves. For example, he had recently read that the Spaniards built a thriving community in Santa Fe, New Mexico a decade before the Pilgrims arrived on the Mayflower. But nobody ate gazpacho on Thanksgiving.

Meanwhile, the associate dean—a toothy, sharp-featured, wavy-haired woman in a navy blue suit—was trying to pay lip service to the concerns of the department head while at the same time working to ensure the fat fish on her line did not swim off to nibble at another university's bait. It was the classic good cop, bad cop routine, but the fact they were meeting at all, and the inclusion of the course listing in the fall catalog, meant that Zuberi had already won. They would eventually agree to his proposal; it was just a matter of him making an offer too good to refuse. As the department head rambled on about the absence of any solid evidence proving exploration before Columbus, Zuberi contorted his face into a look of pensive concern and recalled the old

Winston Churchill joke one of his new Scottish friends had told him:

"Madame," Churchill said in a bar to a well-dressed, middle-aged woman. "Would you be willing to sleep with me tonight for a million pounds?"

"Well," the woman stammered, fixing her hair and blushing, "I am very flattered, sir. Yes, yes I suppose I would."

Churchill smiled and bowed. "Excellent. Now, would you be willing to do so instead for five pounds?"

The woman's eyes widened. Exhaling, she slapped Churchill's face. "I never! Five pounds? What kind of woman do you think I am?"

He bowed again. "I believe we have already established that, my dear. Now we are merely haggling over price."

That's what was happening here. The department head was simply haggling over price. Zuberi replied to the academic, smiling sideways at the dean as he did so. "My wife and I believe absence of evidence of early explorers is because American universities ignore this corner of history. If universities have resources," here he paused and sipped his water, "and if universities have financial commitment, we believe evidence can be found." He raised an eyebrow. "And as I say, my wife and I stand behind our belief with generous endowment." He shrugged, continuing to focus on the department head. "Of course, we know nothing about how it works inside university history department. Our hope is to write check, help select professor—we think the author Cameron Thorne is good choice—and then go away." He flicked his fingers to the sky. "We trust university such as Brandeis knows how best to use the money." It wasn't a bribe, but it was pretty damn close. No doubt the department head had some pet projects he would love to fund or perhaps a nephew or even a mistress he needed to put on the payroll.

Zuberi played his final card. "As I say, Brandeis is our first choice, as our son Amon is freshman here in September. But we understand if you are not interested. Then we will have meetings with other universities."

He sipped his water. Normally he didn't like flavorings in his water, but he had to admit this tasted pretty good.

Tamara Maxson watched the door close behind Zuberi Youssef, waited a few seconds to be sure he was out of earshot, and spoke into the American flag pin she wore on the lapel of her blazer. "He's gone. Come on in."

A back door opened and a paunchy, forty-something man marched in. Tamara turned to the elderly professor. "Thank you for your time, professor. You played your part expertly."

He shrugged and smiled. "I treated a fool with impatient disdain. It was an easy part to play."

"Shabbat Shalom," she said, shaking his hand.

"And to you, Dean Maxson." He checked his watch. "I am always happy to help the Mossad. But not even you can protect me from my wife if I don't make it home with the Shabbat groceries before sunset. Goodbye."

The paunchy man dropped into the professor's vacated seat and exhaled, the smell of tuna fish wafting across the desk. Tamara waved the air away with a legal pad. Moshe was a brilliant and lethal field agent, but he had the social graces of a warthog. He spoke. "He's up to something, no doubt."

"But what?"

Moshe scratched at his skull with his fingernails, propelling small flakes of dry skin to settle on his brown sweater vest. "Could it be as simple as it appears on the surface? Is he trying to pump up the Sinclair name with this Prince Henry bullshit to elevate his social status?"

Tamara shook her head. "It's never that simple with Youssef. He plays chess while the rest of us play checkers; there's always a game behind the game." One of the leading arms dealers in the world and by far the largest in the Middle-East, Youssef thrived during times of even-sided war, where both sides inflicted heavy damage but neither succeeded completely. He had, in fact, occasionally aided Israel when it appeared the Arabs might gain the upper hand. "And don't forget, it's not just the Sinclair name he is trying to glorify. He's also pushing this Princess Scota stuff."

51

"Which will enhance the standing of Egyptians in Scotland," Moshe added. "But, again, why? You can't convince me he cares two shits about what country club he belongs to or whether some Scottish tightwad invites him over for dinner."

Tamara cocked her head. "I disagree. I think he does care about this stuff, if for no other reason that he has aspirations for his children. Why else would he marry the Sinclair woman? But you are right, there is more to this than just social standing."

"Well, we'll just have to play it out."

"Brandeis is not going to be happy about having this Thorne character teach here." Brandeis had agreed to give Tamara a fancy title and an office as a cover, but they got a bit prickly when the Mossad's mission crossed over into academia.

Moshe waved the comment away. "Like it really matters if anyone came over before Columbus; the Native Americans were already here." He wiped his nose with the back of his hand. "Besides, Brandeis gets to keep Youssef's money."

"So what next?" she asked. Technically Moshe was senior to her, though he rarely pulled rank.

"I say we dig into this Thorne guy a little deeper. For some reason Youssef has a hard-on for him. Why? What makes Thorne so special?"

☥ ☩ ⬥

"New plan," Cam announced as he opened the front door. Amanda stood in the kitchen, stir-frying chicken and vegetables, while Astarte set the table. "After dinner, let's get our camping stuff and do a sleep-over in the stone chamber."

"Yeah!" Astarte replied, running to meet him with a hug in the foyer. "Can we make s'mores?"

"Of course." Cam kissed Amanda and grabbed a mushroom from the pan. "We can't light a fire inside the chamber but we can definitely have one outside the entrance." He turned to Amanda. "You up for it?"

"What about your trip to Washington?"

Cam had accepted an offer to visit the Masonic House of the Temple in Washington, D.C., the headquarters for Scottish Rite Freemasonry for most of the country. "My flight leaves at ten. We'll just get up early."

She paused and chewed her lower lip. "Fine with me; you don't have to ask twice to get me to go camping."

"What? I know that look."

She stabbed at the vegetables. "I just don't fancy you going to Washington. I don't trust Randall Sid." Randall Sid was a high-ranking Freemason from Boston whose twin brother, Morgan, had lured Cam and Amanda into a plot to assassinate a U.S. Senator, a scheme that was foiled only after a young CIA operative had been killed and Cam and Amanda's lives endangered. Randall had not been part of the stratagem, but he did feel responsibility for his twin's crimes. Whether out of a sense of guilt, or because Randall believed Cam's research and glorification of Masonic history was helping spur membership, Randall had over the past many months offered Cam rare and increasingly revealing access to Masonic secrets and lore. "He's using you, Cameron. His brother was a murdering scoundrel, and I fancy Randall even less."

"I don't trust him either. And I agree he's a cold fish. But you can't put a price on the information he has been sharing with me."

"Yes," she sighed. "And that's what's bothering me. To those whom much is given, much is expected." She fixed her eyes on his. "What do they expect from you?"

Cam tried to keep things light. "At least with him I know my enemy. Unless you think he's the one who dropped me into Boston Harbor."

"I just don't trust them."

"You've been reading too many conspiracy theories. The Masons are harmless. Heck, even Venus' veterinarian is an active member. And you like him fine."

She smiled. "That's because he gives Venus treats."

Astarte bounced into the room, ending the conversation. After dinner Cam loaded the SUV with their sleeping bags and air mattresses, filled a backpack with supplies and snacks and retrieved a book from his library on stone structures of New England. He was fairly certain the chamber was ancient, but there

53

were certain construction techniques that would help date it and also help determine whether the structure was Native American or European.

An hour later, in the twilight, Cam pulled the SUV to a stop in front of the locked gate of the Groton property. Amanda unlocked the new lock Cam had installed and Cam drove to the old parking lot area.

"Should I lock it again?" she called as he and Astarte began to unload the SUV.

"Good question." On the one hand he didn't want a bunch of teenagers crashing into their chamber with a case of beer. But it seemed odd to lock themselves into their own property like some reclusive millionaire. "You know what, close it but don't lock it. If anyone trespasses, Venus will hear them."

"What's that smell?" Astarte asked as a warm nighttime breeze washed over them.

Cam sniffed "What smell?"

"It smells like ... Starbursts."

"The candy?" Cam asked.

"I get a hint of it also," Amanda said, approaching. "Sweet, like Astarte said."

Cam shrugged. "Who knows? Let's get away from the busy street." He smiled. "Time to find some nature."

By the time they approached the chamber on the back side of the rise in the rear of the parcel, almost a quarter mile from the road, the sounds and smells of civilization had faded away. Cam removed more debris from the chamber while Amanda made a fire and Astarte tried to catch fireflies in a paper cup.

"We call them glowworms in England," Amanda said.

"But they don't crawl like worms, they fly," Astarte responded.

Cam emerged with a full black trash bag from the chamber. "We called them lightning bugs when I was a kid. They make light to attract mates in the spring; it's actually a bit early for them, probably because it's been so warm."

"My teacher says it's global warming," Astarte said.

"Might be," Cam responded. "But it might also be just a natural cycle of temperature changes. The earth has had lots of mini Ice Ages." Cam had been investigating the effects of a cold period during the late 1300s in Europe that wiped out the Greenland settlements—most scholars believed the cold discouraged ships from traveling the north Atlantic, but Cam believed instead that the reduction in crop yield had pushed European explorers to brave the icy Atlantic in search of more fertile land. "Amanda, do you know what the climate was like in the middle of the 6th century?" He tossed the trash bag to the side and turned to Astarte. "That's when historians think the Irish monks might have come to America and built this chamber."

Amanda answered his question with one of her own. "Why do you think Irish? These chambers are all over the British Isles."

Cam squatted next to her and watched the fire. "I was reading a bit about Brendan the Navigator, the Irish explorer. The legends say he left Ireland around the year 515 and explored the western sea. He sailed in a boat made of ox skins called a *curragh*—an Irishman named Tim Severin in the 1970s built the same kind of boat and sailed across the Atlantic in it."

She nodded. "I've heard the stories. But Brendan was a Christian monk, and the chambers in Europe are believed to be built by Druids."

"Actually, the legends say that Brendan had fourteen monks with him plus three pagans. Maybe the three pagans were Druids. Even if not, Christianity in Ireland in the early 6th century was just taking hold—it was a long way from Rome and many of the old pagan ways were still followed." He tapped at his smart phone and found an image he had bookmarked. "Here's a mosaic showing medieval Irish monks worshiping the sun. They were really just Christianized pagans." He turned the screen toward Amanda and Astarte as he took a seat on the cooler.

Early Medieval Irish Monks Worshiping Sun

She nodded. "Christianized pagans, like you said."

"And these are the guys who would have traveled with Brendan."

"The legends of the Brendan voyage always resonated with me," Amanda said. "Ireland is at the far west of the British Isles, a good kicking-off spot for crossing the Atlantic." She blew lightly on the fire. "But to answer your question, the first half of the 6th century was one of the coldest in history."

"How do they know?" Astarte asked. She had found three sticks and was pulling the s'mores supplies from the pack.

"By looking at tree rings," Amanda replied. "Scientists believe there may have been a massive asteroid hit or volcanic eruption that polluted the atmosphere around that time, blocking the sun's rays."

Cam nodded. Amanda and he had been so focused on the mystery of the land conveyance that they hadn't spent much time theorizing about the origins of the chamber. They both loved this kind of mystery, as did Astarte, so the evening promised to be an interesting one. "So, again, a good time to go exploring, looking for food and good land and maybe warmer temperatures," Cam said.

"Okay," Amanda replied, "so let's run a bit with your Saint Brendan theory. I wrote a report about the Brendan journey back in secondary school—as I recall, he encountered a mountain spouting fire, floating crystal palaces, a smoking hill, a sea monster with horns growing from its mouth, little furry men … I may have missed something. But would a sailor heading west from Ireland encounter these things?"

Cam shifted forward on the cooler. "I bet Astarte can figure all these places out. Let's start with a mountain spouting fire—what does that sound like to you?"

She replied, "A volcano."

He nodded. "And we have active volcanoes in Iceland even today, due west of Ireland. What about a floating crystal palace?"

Astarte bit her lip, then brightened. "I know, an iceberg!"

"Excellent," Amanda said. "Next thing was a smoking hill. We showed you pictures of this once, Astarte, from when we went to Iceland."

She smiled and nodded. "The steam comes up from underground like fog," she said, describing the geothermal springs beneath Iceland's surface.

"What about the sea monster with horns growing from its mouth?" Cam asked.

"A walrus?" Astarte replied.

"Probably," Amanda answered. "And little furry men?"

"Were Eskimos little?" the girl asked. "I know they wore animal furs so they probably looked furry."

"Generally, they were smaller than Europeans," Amanda replied.

"So, based on this," Cam said as he scratched Venus under the chin, "Brendan and his crew would have come across the northern part of the Atlantic—all these encounters occur in cold-weather locations."

"Just like the Vikings did later," Amanda said. "And don't forget, the last stop on Brendan's voyage was a land of plenty, a veritable paradise."

Astarte raised her hand. "I know—America!"

Astarte handed out the sticks and they each impaled a marshmallow.

"So let's get back to specifics," Amanda said. "Brendan sails over, trades with the Native Americans, maybe tries to convert a few of them, builds a chamber to mark the summer solstice as they did in Ireland, and then moves on. Is that it?"

Cam blew the flames down on a marshmallow. "It's never that simple," he smiled. "The legend says he was away for seven years. I think they stayed for a while here in America and built a whole complex down in Connecticut. Parts of it are still standing. It's called Gungywamp."

Astarte giggled. "That's a funny name."

"It's a Gaelic name—that's the language they speak in Ireland," Cam said. "Gungywamp means 'Church of the People.' Some historians believe that Gungywamp was Brendan's headquarters; from there he sent his monks out to try to convert the Native Americans. There are chambers all over New England just like this one—Vermont, out near Worcester, on the Connecticut-New York border—probably built by Brendan's monks."

Amanda pulled a marshmallow off her stick and squished it along with a wedge of chocolate between a couple of graham crackers. "Let me guess: Road trip in our future."

Cam grinned. "Of course." He licked the dessert from his fingers and stood. "But for now I want to compare the construction of this chamber to the techniques in this book."

Amanda and Astarte looked at each other and crinkled their noses. "We'll stay here and guard the s'mores," Amanda said.

"Yeah," Astarte added as Venus licked the marshmallow from her fingers. "Chocolate's not good for dogs." She slid another wedge onto a graham cracker. "So we better finish it all to be safe."

Dressed in black, Bartol slipped through the unlocked gate, hid his bicycle in the brush and moved silently toward the sound of laughter and the smell of campfire. Careful to stay downwind lest the dog catch his scent, he moved stealth-like, keeping to the shadows with a soft foot and sharp eye. He didn't need his night-vision goggles—the light of the fire illuminated Cameron Thorne and his family like actors on a stage.

For tonight at least, Bartol planned to be an audience of one.

But going forward, Bartol had a plan, a vision. The world needed more thinkers like Cameron Thorne, advocates willing to pull aside the curtain and not censure the truth. Better yet, it needed people like Thorne to evolve into leaders—revolutionaries like Benjamin Franklin, Thomas Paine, Vaclav Havel and even Julius Caesar had been prolific authors before becoming statesmen. Thorne had taken a few small steps, appearing on television documentaries and radio talk shows, but did he have what it took to become a true leader?

Up until this week, Bartol would have shrugged his shoulders at the question. Not now.

Bartol had learned in his Army Ranger training that a true leader exhibited five essential characteristics: intelligence, commitment, integrity, courage, and resourcefulness. Nobody graduated law school or authored a breakthrough research book without both intelligence and commitment. It was the other three qualities Bartol was unsure of.

Which was what this past Monday's ordeal had been all about.

Integrity: Would Thorne pocket the scratch ticket? Nothing had been stopping him; as far as Thorne knew, the guy who handed him the ticket didn't know Thorne's name and didn't have any way to track him. Bartol had planned it all out—learning when Thorne had reserved a closing room at the Registry of Deeds, buying a fake scratch ticket online, and finally shoving the ticket into Thorne's hand—but of course Thorne had no way of knowing that. Many people would have taken the half million bucks and bolted.

Courage: Thorne went back into a smoke-filled apartment— Bartol's North End studio still reeked of smoke—to rescue a baby. Thorne had no way of knowing, again, that Bartol staged the whole thing and that there never was any baby or real danger.

Resourcefulness: This had been tougher to orchestrate, but in the end Thorne had earned high grades. Cutting his way through the dumpster and then rolling the dumpster onto its side before it sank was an impressive escape for someone not trained in survival skills.

"Good job, Thorne," Bartol whispered, still crouching behind a tree. "I appreciated not having to jump in and drag your ass out of the harbor."

When the idea had first hit Bartol one day at work, so quickly and violently that it almost knocked him off his ladder, he dismissed it as a fantasy. But the muse had been an inspired one, perhaps even divinely so. The more Bartol considered it, the more it made sense. Perfect sense. People like Thorne needed soldiers to help him fight against the liberal elite and the politically correct and the other enemies of true Americans. And Bartol was a soldier without a battlefield, a believer in the true greatness of America but with no banner to march behind.

It was the cause he had been looking for, a way to give some meaning to his otherwise empty existence.

Fishes swim. Birds fly. Lions hunt. And soldiers fight.

Bartol scampered up a slight ridge that offered clear sightlines and unshouldered his pack. He removed a portable steel stick ladder, fit the pieces together, and leaned it against a thick oak tree. He then unclipped a hunter's treestand—it looked like a folding beach chair—from his pack. Scurrying to the top of the twenty-foot ladder, he tied the treestand to the trunk, tugged on it to make sure it was secure, descended the ladder to retrieve his pack, and finally nestled into his perch.

His plan was simple: Watch the author, get to know his routines and his habits. In that way he would be able to detect any interruptions in his routine that might put Thorne in danger. The key was to anticipate danger before it arrived. In Thorne's case, his vulnerabilities were obvious: First, his fiancée. And second, the girl. Anyone who wanted to get to Thorne could easily target either of them.

Bartol leaned back, considering the possibilities, as the girl's laughter wafted through the trees. Thorne's work was important, perhaps crucial. He was the one, it seemed, destined to rewrite the history books and help reestablish the supremacy of the Northern European bloodlines. It was Thorne's gift, but also his burden.

The girl and the fiancée might be luxuries Thorne could not afford.

After an hour Cam reemerged from the stone chamber. He waved his reference book in the air. "I think we have ourselves a very old chamber."

Amanda smiled up at him; his enthusiasm for life was one of his most endearing qualities. That and his boy-next-door wholesomeness. "How old?"

He grinned. "I just told you: *Very* old."

"*Very* is not a number, Campadre" Astarte announced, using her new pet name for him. She called Amanda 'Mum.' Both names hinted at the parental relationship which had not been formalized yet.

Cam lifted Astarte, plopped onto the ground in her spot next to Amanda and dropped the girl onto his lap. "Ah, the wisdom of a ten-year-old. Before I get to the age of the chamber, I want to tell you about the Druids. Do you remember Merlin in the King Arthur stories?"

Astarte nodded.

"Well, he was a Druid."

"I thought he was a wizard."

Cam smiled. "In many ways they're the same thing. Druids knew a lot about science and nature, and they used that knowledge to convince the common folk that they had magical powers. So, for example, they often built their shrines in areas where strange lights appeared at night. Sometimes these lights came from swamps, from the methane gas; sometimes they appeared along geological fault lines where tectonic plates containing quartz deposits rubbed together and caused strange blue lights to shoot from the ground."

Amanda nodded. "I've heard of that; the lights are called earthquake lights."

Astarte said, "So the people thought the Druids were doing magic. But it was really just nature."

"Exactly." He handed Astarte his cell phone. "So, remembering all that, I want to do a little experiment. Which way is north?"

Astarte looked into the sky, found the North Star and pointed toward it.

"Correct," Cam said. "Now, open the compass on my phone and go stand in the entrance to the chamber."

Astarte did as instructed, Amanda wondering what Cam was up to. "Hey," she said, "the compass is pointing the wrong way, toward the street."

Cam nodded. "It's an old trick, a hint that the Druids built this chamber. They often buried magnetic stones at the entrance to their chambers. It was another way to convince people that they had magical powers."

"I don't get it," the girl replied.

"Well, those people didn't know about magnets. So if the Druid priest floated a piece of metal in a bowl of oil, he could make the metal spin around like magic because of the magnet buried beneath the bowl. Anyone seeing a metal bar spinning around for no reason would think the Druid had strange, special powers."

"Well played," Amanda chuckled, amazed at the random collection of knowledge Cam had somehow acquired over his life. "What else did you find inside the chamber?"

"The big thing is there's no evidence of any modern quarrying work in any of the stones. That means the chamber definitely dates back before 1800."

Amanda smiled. "Does that qualify as *very* old?"

"No. It still could have been built by Colonial farmers as a root cellar."

Amanda made a face. "This chamber feels too … *elaborate* … to be a root cellar. It's too carefully constructed. It feels ceremonial to me." Plus it looked like the Druid-built chambers all over Europe.

"I agree," Cam said. "From what my reference book says, the corbelling construction technique—the way they used the stones to support the dome—is the same as they used in the British Isles to build chambers a thousand years ago, and even before that."

She nodded.

"Plus," he continued, "look at the land around our chamber here. We're on a pretty steep slope, so this was not exactly prime farming land. And from what I saw from the land records, the nearest farm was almost a quarter-mile away. So why build a root cellar here?"

"You wouldn't. And if you did, you'd make the entrance wide enough for a wheelbarrow," she said, repeating her earlier argument. "Plus the floor in there is damp—you'd want something drier to keep your vegetables from rotting."

Astarte jumped in. "What about the Native Americans?" She was half Native American herself. "Could they have built it?"

"Good question," Cam said. "The Native Americans did build sweat lodges, sometimes with stone." They used these for purification ceremonies. "But why would they have buried magnetic rocks? And I don't think they built with this corbelling technique."

"And what about ventilation?" Amanda asked. "There's a small vent hole in the chamber, but wouldn't you need a full chimney in a sweat lodge?" She was trying to be objective about this, but she had seen so many similar chambers in the British Isles that she couldn't believe this chamber was built by either Colonists or Native Americans. It was not that she thought the Native Americans were incapable of building such a structure, merely that in the case of this chamber they had not.

They sat for a few moments in silence, staring at the flames. Cam winked at Amanda and shifted. "I think I'm going to have a snack." He was up to something, probably sensing Astarte was getting bored. Amanda just didn't know what.

He pulled a small jar of mayonnaise from a freezer bag in the backpack and opened the lid. "Amanda, can you hand me a spoon?"

Astarte watched, her head angled to the side. Keeping a straight face, Cam dipped the spoon deep into the jar and extracted a large white glob. Amanda snickered; the vanilla pudding box she had spotted in the garbage bag at home suddenly made sense. Eyeing Astarte, Cam slowly slid the spoon into his mouth and sucked it clean.

"Gross!" she shouted, her face contorting. "Yuck. Disgusting."

Cam dipped the spoon in again, sucked it clean and licked his lips. "What? It's just egg yolks, oil and vinegar." He held out the spoon. "Here, try some."

"No way."

He pushed the spoon closer. "Just one bite. Come on."

Astarte rolled away and leapt to her feet, Cam scrambling after her and waving the spoon as Astarte shrieked and scurried toward the woods. Venus, tail wagging, followed.

As their laughing voices faded, Amanda sighed. How strange life was, how odd its twists and turns. A few years ago she had moved from London to Westford hoping for a fresh start. Initially, she had been miserable here—alone and friendless. Then Cam appeared, then Venus, and then Astarte, and now she couldn't imagine a life without them. It was almost too good to be true.

She sighed again. Too good to be true was also an apt description for this land deed. She had a funny feeling about it: Things that seemed too good to be true usually were.

Chapter 3

Rachel Levitad was not having a good day. Final exams had ended and she wanted to go home. But her flight to Chicago had been cancelled, which meant she was stuck on campus another two days. It felt like finishing a marathon and then being told you had to stick around the finish line for the rest of the weekend. She crumpled her coffee cup, tossed it into the recycle bin, and headed for the exit door of the campus student center.

She had always considered herself hardworking and pretty resilient. But freshman year had beaten her down. Partly it was the culture at Brandeis—the students delighted in overachieving, as if spending Friday night in the library were something to be proud of. But mostly it was just that she was done. Done with competing, done with cramming, done with dining hall food. She had finished the marathon. Now it was time to go home and let her parents treat her like a kid again.

Most students had finished finals earlier in the week and the campus was largely abandoned. She had come to the student center to grab a cup of coffee and take a break from packing.

"Excuse me." A tall, olive-skinned boy stepped in front of her from next to the ATM machine. "Can you assist me with this?"

Rachel sighed. "Sure." She stepped toward the screen. "You've been here all year and haven't figured out how to use this yet?"

"I just arrived yesterday," he said quietly. His accent was foreign, probably Middle-Eastern. "I will be beginning classes in September."

"And you're here already?"

He shrugged, his large brown eyes sad but confident. "My father wants me to learn my way around and get comfortable here."

"Well, I suggest the first thing you do is get familiar with the shuttle bus system." She smiled. "It's pretty intense here: You'll want to get into Boston once in a while to get away." She took his card and helped him navigate the touch screen.

He bowed to her. "Thank you very much. If you are ever in Scotland, I will teach you how to use the bank machine there."

"Scotland?" She stopped herself, not wanting to be rude. She had assumed, based on his accent and skin tone, that he was Arabic.

"Originally from Egypt." He bowed again. "My name is Amon Youssef." He held her eyes with his and offered his hand.

"Hi," she stammered as she ran her hand through her hair. "Rachel Levitad. Originally from Chicago. That's in the central part of the country." She hoped she wasn't being patronizing.

"Famous for its slaughterhouses, deep-dish pizza, and Oprah," he grinned. "I have been studying American geography."

"I see that." He fell in beside her as she made her way to the door. The words tumbled from her mouth before her brain had a chance to check them. "I was just about to grab lunch in the dining hall. Want to join me?"

He smiled, a gesture that seemed to come easy to him. "I am told the food here is only tolerable. Perhaps it would be wise for me to get used to it before classes start."

"Yeah, sort of like shrinking your stomach before a hunger strike."

He laughed at that, his eyes twinkling like a pair of bright stars. A strange tingling feeling coursed through her chest, and an even stranger giggle bubbled from her mouth. She exhaled— perhaps the next forty-eight hours would not be so bad after all.

Cam's flight landed at Reagan National Airport without incident. He grabbed his backpack, crossed the parking lot to the Metro station and rode into the capital, emerging from the McPherson Square subway station not far from the White House just after noon.

He had an hour to kill. Dry air and a deep blue sky made the warm spring day ideal for walking. Cam checked his blood sugar, grabbed a slice of pizza and a Diet Coke and began strolling up 16th Street. The last time he had been in the Washington area, almost a year-and-a-half ago, he had also been on 16th Street, meeting clandestinely with senior CIA operatives a dozen blocks north of here at Meridian Park. The park had been so-named because Thomas Jefferson hoped the world would accept 16th Street as the new prime meridian; notable landmarks located along the north-south line included the White House, the Washington Monument, the Jefferson Memorial, the aforementioned Meridian Park and, curiously, the Freemason's majestic House of the Temple.

Cam shook his head—the Freemasons always seemed to have their hands in things, always seemed to be in close proximity to the seats of power. Many, in fact, believed the Masons had been behind the design of the city, and that its layout reflected Masonic imagery, symbolism and belief. The Masonic Brothers Cam knew claimed that they were not part of a secret society, merely a society with secrets. But the more Cam researched, the more he found the hidden hand of the Freemasons—along with their precursors, the Knights Templar—pulling the puppet strings of history. Which is why he had quickly accepted the offer of a private tour of the Temple from Randall Sid.

Of course, Amanda was correct: Randall and his Masonic cohorts weren't giving Cam access to their secrets for nothing. It was likely the master puppeteers planned to use him as one of their puppets. For now Cam was willing to risk having his strings pulled. But only because—to mix the metaphor—he was fascinated by the secret look behind the curtain.

The beige limestone building dwarfed its surroundings, occupying half a block on the east side of 16th Street. The building was numbered 1733, and Cam had read that the hulking structure featured 33 columns, each 33 feet high—all a nod to the importance of the 33rd degree in Freemasonry. The ornate Neo-Classical architecture, in the same style as the Jefferson Memorial, evoked a sense of ancient culture—a pair of massive marble sphinxes flanked the front staircase as if expecting an ancient

Pharaoh to stroll down 16th Street. Cam angled his head: He would need to ask Randall about the sphinxes.

Cam climbed the stone stairs two at a time. A bronze lion door knocker dominated the dark oak door; Cam was about to lift the knocker when the door opened silently in front of him. A tuxedoed man wearing a Masonic apron smiled and greeted him. "Welcome. May I help you?"

Cam's eyes looked past him, surveying the massive marble-floored atrium area. More colossal columns lined the walls and another pair of Egyptian-style statues, these complete with cartouches, guarded the staircase at the far end of the hall. "I'm here to see Randall Sid."

The tuxedoed receptionist gestured to a wood-paneled seating area in the corner of the atrium. "Please wait here."

Cam nodded and wandered slowly toward the seating area, his eyes scanning the ceiling. More Egyptian motif, along with the expected Masonic symbolism. But, again, why the Egyptian décor? What did the Egyptians have to do with Masonry?

A hidden door opened across the room and a short, elderly, brown-skinned man wearing a tuxedo and bright red fez stepped through. Cam knew a bit about Masonic custom—only the Masters were allowed to wear hats within the lodge, as a sign of their status, so it was apparent that Randall stood at or near the highest rung on the Masonic ladder. Somehow, here in the ornate Temple, the hat—which would have looked ridiculous out on the street—added to the solemnity of their meeting.

The man offered a perfunctory hand-shake and a curt, "Hello, Cameron."

So unlike his brother, who had been loquacious and charming … and also a snake in the grass. "I'm excited to be here."

Randall nodded. "As you should be. Few people are welcomed into our inner sanctum."

He turned and led Cam past the Egyptian statues and onto the central staircase. Massive bronze lamps, again with Egyptian motif, illuminated the round, marble stairway. "I have to ask," Cam said, figuring he might not get a straight answer the first time he inquired, "why all the Egyptian symbolism?"

Randall pursed his lips. "As with many of your questions, Cameron, I will need to be careful with my answers." Unlike his twin, who spoke with a patrician accent, Randall sounded like a Boston cabbie; he was, in fact, the owner of a driver's education school. It was one of the fascinating things about the Masons—a driving teacher or a plumber or an insurance salesman could rise to the pinnacle of the organization.

Cam smiled. "Well, if I asked you the obvious stuff, you'd get bored with me."

Randall showed a set of gray, even teeth. When Cam had first met Randall's twin, he thought the man resembled an older, shorter Barrack Obama. "True enough." He took a deep breath. "Many people know of the ties between Freemasonry and the Knights Templar." Scores of books had been written on the subject, and in Cam's mind there was no doubt the outlawed Templars had morphed into Freemasons during the late medieval period. Randall continued, "But very few know about the connections between Masonry and the ancient Druids."

Cam turned. Again with the Druids.

"There are some fascinating similarities," Randall said. Cam tried to stay a stair behind the shorter man, to even up their height. "For example, the Druids had elaborate initiations in which ancient secrets were passed from a high priest to a new candidate. The candidate then went through a ritual death before being arisen into enlightenment during the third degree of his initiation."

Cam nodded; his host may as well have been describing the Masonic initiation ceremony rather than the Druidic one.

Randall continued as they slowly ascended. "Thomas Paine, the famous American patriot, wrote the following in an essay in 1805." He cleared his throat. "*Masonry is the remains of the religion of the ancient Druids, who, like the priests of Heliopolis in Egypt and the Magi of Persia, were priests of the sun.*"

Cam mulled over the words. The Masons. The Druids. The Egyptians. The Magi—also known as the Wise Men who greeted the baby Jesus. Quite a group.

It was an amazing statement. But Cam knew better than to question his host's memory; his knowledge of all things Masonic was encyclopedic, and showing off this knowledge Cam had learned over the past few months seemed to be his life's joy. Cam pressed on. "So you're saying both Masons and Druids are sun worshipers, along with the Egyptians?" He'd leave the Magi out of this for now.

"I'm not saying that, Thomas Paine is."

"Well, is it true?"

"I believe, yes, the Druids worshiped the sun. As did the Egyptians."

A half-answer, or perhaps two-thirds. But not full. Apparently Randall was not going to comment directly on Masonic sun worship, something Cam had always suspected was an important part of Masonic ritual. The Masonic calendar year began on June 24, the date historically marking (due to inaccuracies in ancient calendars) the summer solstice—the longest and therefore sunniest day of the year. And the Masons named their initiation oath—called the Oath of Nimrod—after a pagan king, Nimrod, who was closely associated with the sun god, Baal. Cam began to press the point when he noticed Randall staring at a point high on the far wall. Something about the man's facial expression caused Cam to turn and follow his line of sight: A radiating bronze star symbol stared back at Cam.

Star Symbol Decoration, The Masonic House of the Temple

Cam smiled and turned back toward the high-ranking Freemason, who had his index finger in the air, ready to make a point. "You are familiar, no doubt, with the singular importance the Temple of Solomon plays in Masonic ritual?" Randall asked.

"Of course." The construction of the Temple gave birth to Freemasonry.

"You may find it interesting that the word Solomon is comprised of three smaller words—the Latin 'sol,' the Hindu 'om,' and the Egyptian 'on'—all of which mean sun in their respective language."

Cam found it more than interesting. Randall had essentially confirmed the sun-worshipping roots of Freemasonry. Without, of course, directly answering Cam's question.

Cam decided to push further. "I noticed something earlier in our conversation: I asked about the Egyptians, and you told me about the Druids."

Randall looked up at Cam and again showed his gray teeth. "And why do you think that might be?"

He reminded Cam of one of his law school professors, who prided himself on his ability to tease insights from his students. "I'm guessing there must be some close connection between the Egyptians and the Druids."

They reached the top of the staircase and Randall motioned for Cam to take a seat on a padded bench outside the main Temple chamber. Apparently they would finish their conversation here. "As you know, there are Masonic secrets I am forbidden to tell you. But I can talk freely about the Druids. And I can also point out that the Druids were heavily influenced by the priests of ancient Egypt."

And, as he had previously said, many believed the Druids and Masons possessed similar roots. It was easy to connect the dots: Randall was explaining to Cam—without actually voicing the words—that the Masons traced much of their knowledge and ritual back to ancient Egypt. Which, of course, explained the décor not only here in the Temple but in all the lodges Cam had been in: They all, for example, contained obelisks, as did many Masonic burial markers. Not to mention, of course, the most famous obelisk in the world—the Washington Monument, supposedly part of the Masonic design of Washington.

Point made, Randall stood in front of the enormous leather-covered doors to the Temple room, the building's main ceremonial space. "Each door weighs three hundred pounds, but they are perfectly balanced on their hinges." He smiled and with a single finger pushed them open. "Just as a Mason hopes to be."

They entered a massive, square room with a domed skylight soaring eight stories above them. The opulence of the room reminded Cam of a European palace, or perhaps one of the gilded Newport mansions. But his thoughts were elsewhere. As Randall described some of the more mundane architectural details, Cam focused on the Egyptian motif and connections between the Masons, the Druids and the ancient Egyptians.

Cam tried to redirect the conversation as they made their way back down the circular staircase to the library in the basement of the building. "Can we talk more about sun worship?"

"Why?"

"Because, as Thomas Paine pointed out, it seems to be a common thread running through history."

"Of course it is. Without the sun there would be no life."

"Yes, but the same can be said of food and water, but nobody worships those."

Randall raised an eyebrow. "Have you ever observed Catholics receiving Holy Communion, or Jews blessing the wine and bread before a meal?"

"They are receiving and giving thanks, not worshipping. There's a difference."

"Fair enough. And you think this sun worship is important?"

Cam pondered the question. "I think it is important to understanding Freemasonry. Assuming, of course, that Thomas Paine was correct and you really do worship the sun." He stopped on the landing and spread his hands. "Do you?"

Randall checked his watch. "What time is your flight home?"

"Eight o'clock, last flight."

"Could you leave tomorrow morning instead?"

Cam sensed it would be worth the fifty dollar airline change fee. "Sure."

"Good. After dinner there is something I want you to see."

It was not a direct answer to his question about Masons worshipping the sun, but Cam had spent enough time with Randall to understand that a partial response was preferable to a full lie.

Amon leaned forward across the dining room table. What a strange and delightful young woman this Rachel was. Humorous, irreverent, opinionated. So unlike the girls he knew in Scotland, all of them intent on fitting in rather than standing out. Perhaps it was just the difference between secondary school and university.

"So here's the thing," she said, lightly touching Amon's hand, "you're going to get a *great* education here. As good as it gets. But the dynamic is really weird. You have all these Jewish kids from the northeast who know each other from summer camp and trips to Israel. But Brandeis prides itself on being open and diverse, so it also attracts a bunch of students from the Middle East."

He raised his hand. "Like myself."

She smiled, showing a set of straight, white, wet teeth. She was not pretty in the conventional sense, but her face was pleasing to look at, especially when she smiled and her hazel green eyes grew wide with joy. "Well, the reality is that if we were in the Middle East rather than Boston, you and I would probably be trying to kill each other."

The idea pained him. He held her eyes. "I would do no such thing."

She waited a second before responding, then burst out in laughter, the sound echoing in the near-empty dining hall. "You are so serious, Amon! Perhaps *you* wouldn't try to kill me, but the point is that others would. But here, we go to class together, eat together, even live together. And everyone acts like it's no big deal. But beneath the surface there's all this … tension. I think that's why the social life here is so bad. Nobody wants to let down their guard."

"Is religion really such a big deal? I thought in America it is not so much."

She leaned back and exhaled. "Let me give you an example. I took a really neat class on the Old Testament this semester. We spent a lot of time on the story of Abraham." She paused. "I'm sorry, I shouldn't assume you know the Old Testament."

"Abraham is an important figure in Islam also. He is the father of Ishmael." Amon glanced at the clock on the wall, surprised that almost two hours had passed since they first sat down. "Please continue."

"Yes, of course he is. Anyway, Professor Siegel was one of those hippies left over from the sixties who loved to question authority. One night he invited a bunch of us to his house for dinner and he started sharing some of his research with us. I don't think the administration was very happy about what he was working on; he said they didn't want him to share this stuff with his students." She took a sip of her tea. "Anyway, from what he told us, there are a lot of things that are … odd … about Abraham's story."

"Please continue."

She held up one finger and took a deep breath. "First, when Abraham and Sarah came to Egypt, he was worried the Egyptians would see Sarah, who was very pretty, and want to steal her from him. So instead of fighting to keep her, wimpy Abraham came up with a plan to tell everyone Sarah was his sister, not his wife." Amon made a face to make sure she knew he did not approve of this. "Well, sure enough, the Pharaoh came along, saw Sarah and wanted her for his harem. So what did Abraham do? He negotiated a bride price and sold her off. Later, after the Pharaoh had, as the Bible would say, 'known' her, he learned she was already married to Abraham, which apparently was bad form even for a Pharaoh. So he summoned Abraham and accused him of cheating him and making him look a fool, which Abraham did. Now here I would think the Pharaoh would kill Abraham, but he showed mercy and instead just exiled Abraham and Sarah from Egypt." She paused again and smiled. "But he gave Sarah a handmaiden to take with her! What possible reason could there be to give Sarah—who also had lied to him and duped him—a handmaiden? My professor suggested it was because Sarah was far into her pregnancy with the Pharaoh's child. He says a handmaiden is really just another word

74

for midwife." She paused to let her words sink in. "If so, what ever happened to this child?"

Amon had never heard this story, but he had no reason to doubt Rachel's version of it. "This is hardly the behavior one would expect from a patriarch." If Amon had a beautiful wife like Abraham, he would fight to keep her.

"You think? But wait, it gets better. Later, after their son Isaac was born, God told Abraham to take Isaac and bind him to an altar for sacrifice. Well, I'm sorry, no father would obey this command. It goes against every human instinct and emotion."

Amon considered his own father. Amon's mother, before she died, used to joke he would sell his family into slavery if the price was right. But it had been just that, a joke. Rachel was correct— the story went against the basic human instinct to protect one's offspring. As distant as Amon's father sometimes was, he would never intentionally do anything to harm his children, no matter what deity commanded it. "So do you think this story is somehow wrong?" he asked.

"The story's not wrong, but the premise is. All we have to do is look more carefully at the ancient texts—the clues are all there." She leaned forward. "Do you know the Talmud—that's the book of Jewish law—says that when Isaac was born Abraham invited all his neighbors to a feast to celebrate, but only a few of them came? They didn't believe the child was his."

"Why is that?"

She continued without answering, though she did smile at him as she held his eyes. "And did you know that after they left Egypt, basically after the Pharaoh divorced Sarah, God made her change her name from Sarai to Sarah, meaning 'queen.' And," she paused here for effect, "he promised that Sarah 'shall be a mother of nations; kings of people shall be of *her.*' Not of Abraham, but of her. *Her* children shall be the kings of nations."

Amon was still not sure where this was going, but Rachel's passion swept him along in her wake.

"Look at the clues, Amon: Sarah sleeps with the Pharaoh, who gives her a handmaiden. Then God tells her to change her name to queen and promises that her children shall be kings. Then many years later Isaac is born—Sarah is supposedly *ninety* freaking years old by then—and God promises him a kingdom if he gets circumcised. And, by the way, as I'm sure you know, circumcision is an Egyptian custom. Oh, and when Abraham tries to throw a party celebrating the birth of his new son Isaac, everyone mocks him."

Now Amon understood. "Aha! You think Isaac is the son of the Pharaoh, not Abraham."

"It's not what I *think*. It's what the Old Testament pretty much says, if you have half a brain. Why else would Abraham agree to sacrifice him?" She shrugged. "Isaac wasn't *his* kid."

Amon had trouble believing they would teach such damning material at a Jewish institution. "This is the official Jewish position?"

"No." She laughed. "God, no. Like I said, the administration forbade the professor from teaching it. They threatened to fire him if he did."

There was something to this, something important that Amon could not put his finger on. It related somehow to the story of Scota leaving Egypt and eventually settling in Scotland, a story his father and step-mother were intent on promoting. He would phone his father later. But for now he was focused on Rachel and her wet teeth and dancing hazel eyes. He smiled. "At this dinner, I imagine it made many of the Jewish students uncomfortable?"

"It sure did. I don't give a shit because I don't believe in the Bible anyway in the literal sense, but lots of religious Jews do. Let's just say the room got really quiet." She grinned. "So I raised my hand and ask, as innocently as I can, 'Does this mean the Pharaoh is the father of the Jewish people?'"

Amon laughed and leaned forward again. "So we are cousins, then, the Jews and Egyptians, all descending from this pharaoh?"

She nodded. "I suppose so."

"This is good." He grinned. "It means there is no need for you to try to kill me."

Cam spent the rest of Saturday afternoon in the House of the Temple, examining Masonic ritual items and poring through ancient Masonic writings in the high-ceilinged library reading room. Plaster busts of famous Freemasons kept watch over him just in case he had the urge to slip one of the priceless tombs into his briefcase. He had made some headway in understanding the Masonic connections to Egypt and the ancient Druids, but he had the strong sense that there were deeper, more fundamental secrets that the Masons kept hidden.

Rubbing his eyes, Cam set aside an illustrated text recounting the construction of the Temple of Solomon by the earliest Masons and stood to stretch. He remembered as a child reading a story about a boy who lived on a primitive island in the South Pacific and believed the island to be the entirety of the universe. Later, of course, the boy learned that the world was many times more complex and many times more mysterious than what he had originally believed. Cam felt that way now as he explored the House of the Temple and wondered how much more complex and mysterious the true history of the world was, a history hidden and preserved over the millennia by secret societies like the Freemasons.

From the shadows, Randall appeared. As if reading Cam's thoughts, he asked, "Have you ever read an account of World War II from the Japanese perspective? Or the Civil War—known as the War of Northern Aggression in some southern states—from the point of view of a Southerner?"

Cam shook his head.

"Well, you should. It might make you question history as you know it."

"What history?"

"All history. The Old Testament, specifically. Unless you believe it is the divine word of God—which I doubt you do—then it must have been written by man. As such, it is as flawed and skewed and propagandized as any other recounting of history."

Cam had never heard the Old Testament described as propaganda before, and he wasn't sure what the Masonic elder was getting at. "What does that have to do with the Egyptian connection to the Freemasons?" That was, after all, the focus of his research.

The elderly man showed his gray teeth. "Think about the Book of Exodus. Written by one of the parties—the Israelites—involved in the conflict in Egypt thirty-five hundred years ago. We call it the Holy Bible, but why should we believe it to be any more accurate than the Japanese version of World War II?"

Cam wasn't sure how to respond. Randall held his eyes for a moment before abruptly glancing at his watch. "Six o'clock. Time for dinner."

He led Cam to an ornate banquet hall featuring portraits of George Washington and introduced him to a handful of other senior Brothers from the D.C. area. They dined around a large table in one corner of the massive room. Try as he might, Cam was unable to guide the conversation back toward Egypt or the Druids or sun worship or even the accuracy of the Old Testament. Apparently the group had decided that Randall, and only he, would spoon secret information to Cam.

Instead they discussed Cam's research, questioning him about the ancient artifacts scattered around the continent, many of which seemed to point to exploration by their forbearers, the Knights Templar. This was an aspect of history not taught in the Lodges, and the Brothers seemed captivated by the information.

"What makes you so sure the Newport Tower is not Colonial?" one asked. Many historians argued the structure was built as a windmill circa 1675.

Cam smiled. "Just look at it. It's a round stone tower with Romanesque arches. Does it look like Colonial architecture to you? And more to the point, what self-respecting engineer would build a windmill on eight shaky pillars?"

He pulled up an image of the structure on his phone.

Newport Tower, Winter Solstice

He continued, summarizing many of the points he made in *Across the Pond*. "Not to mention all the astronomical alignments. The Tower marks the winter solstice, and also the 35 possible days of Easter. Whoever built it used it as a calendar as well as some kind of ceremonial site."

"Then why didn't the archeologists find medieval debris when they dug?" another challenged. "All they found was Colonial stuff."

"I'll answer your question with a question: When you go to church, do you throw your trash out under your pew?" Cam smiled. "Of course not. Well it's the same with all these ancient religious sites—ask any European archeologist. The sites are pristine because people treated them with reverence. And that includes not dumping their trash."

"So who built it?"

Cam leaned forward in his chair. "I don't know for certain, other than it predates the Colonists. But the Easter alignments tell me it's a Christian group. There is some carbon-dating of the mortar which dates the construction to the early 1400s. And the architecture is very similar to Temple Church in London, built by the Knights Templar." He sat back. "So I think the best guess is it was built by Prince Henry Sinclair and his group. Prince Henry was in New England in 1399 and his family had long and close ties to the Templars. When I asked a Native American tribal chief who he thought built it, he also answered Prince Henry."

Randall ended the conversation by ceremoniously checking his watch. "We will have to continue this discussion at a later time, though I will say that I concur with Mr. Thorne's reasoning—as some of you may know, Masonic records show that Rhode Island's earliest Freemasons took an active interest in preserving the Tower." He stood. "Sunset is at 8:05 tonight. That gives us an hour to get across town and go through security." He turned to Cam. "I have a car waiting."

"Security?" Cam asked.

Randall smiled sardonically. "You don't think you can just waltz into the Capitol building without passing through security, do you?"

Cam updated Amanda on his plans with a text from the car and twenty minutes later they pulled up to the guard house outside the front entrance to the Capitol. A young man in a dark suit greeted them as they stepped out of the car and led them to a private entrance on the ground floor of the Capitol, where they passed through a metal detector and a pat-down. The staffer escorted them along a back hallway to an elevator, which lurched up a few stories and let them out on a balcony overlooking the famous Capitol rotunda.

"We are actually halfway up the dome," Randall said. He smiled and removed his hat. "And we are going higher."

The staffer led them to a steep, narrow metal staircase. "You'll want to use the handrail," he said. "There are actually two domes here, an inner and an outer. These stairs run between them." Cam looked up—the stairs wound their way through a web frame of interlocking steel girders that reminded him of the Eiffel Tower. They would be ascending between the two domes, the senior Freemason being given secret access to the inner sanctums of government just as the conspiracy theorists proclaimed.

Fascinated, Cam climbed, gladly enduring the pain in his ankle from his fall into the dumpster. He knew better than to ask what Randall wanted him to see, though obviously it had something to do with sunset. They emerged on a landing; the staffer pushed opened an arched wooden door and a burst of wind buffeted them. Cam stepped onto the balcony and surveyed the city below, then turned to look up at the colossal bronze Statue of Freedom looming over him like a mythical goddess. For a statue carved in the early 1800s, the figure was surprisingly progressive. No knitting needles for this lady—she carried a sword and wore a battle helmet. And, in another surprisingly inclusive gesture, a Native American blanket adorned her shoulder.

But it was not the statue Randall wanted Cam to see. They gazed out over the city, the warm wind swirling around the dome and the lights of the capital flickering on as the sun began to set. The Washington Monument, by law the tallest structure in the city, rose above them to the west along the Mall—the famous obelisk would, being due west of the Capitol, mark the equinox sunsets. Randall pointed to the northwest, toward the White House. "Pennsylvania Avenue runs from here to the White House; it is laid out at a very specific angle. That is why there is a jog at both ends—it was the only way to keep the angle precise while also allowing the road to not pass directly through the White House."

Cam knew the Freemasons played a prominent role in the design of the city, including sacred geometry and Masonic symbolism in its layout. But he was unsure to what extent the layout was reflective of sun worship. He had the sense he was about to become enlightened.

Randall continued. "As you know, in some ancient cultures the cross-quarter days—the days halfway between the solstices and equinoxes—were the most important days of the year. Even more so than the solstices and equinoxes."

Cam nodded. When Randall spoke of the ancient cultures, it was code for the Druids and the Egyptians before them.

"In some ways the cross-quarter days most truly mark the seasons," Randall explained. "Climatically, August 5 is the height of summer, and February 5 the height of winter."

Cam had read about this. "And May 5, Beltane, marked the beginning of summer, especially in agricultural communities."

"Correct. Which is why in many societies Beltane was the single most important day of the year." Randall pointed to the setting sun, still a couple of inches above the horizon. "As I'm sure you've already deduced, on Beltane the sun sets directly over the

White House. We are two days past, technically, but the alignment remains almost exact."

Cam had witnessed many alignments at both the Newport Tower and New Hampshire's America's Stonehenge site, and they never failed to fill him with awe. There was something noble and admirable and even wistful about man's age-old attempts to synchronize his world with the sun, moon and stars.

Randall redirected Cam's attention to the southwest. "And on Imbolc, at the peak of winter, the sun sets atop the Jefferson Memorial."

Cam nodded. Another cross-quarter day. And another tie between the Masons and the Druids. "The chambers in New England that we think the Druids built mark the solstices and equinoxes, not the cross-quarter days. So why the difference here?"

Randall pursed his lips. "First of all, I think you'll find the New England chambers mark both. As for Washington, the designers of the city needed to be careful. They could not make things too obvious—even in their day, the Masons had enemies. Aligning the city to the cross-quarter days was more subtle than using the solstices and equinoxes."

Made sense. "Why did they mark the sunsets and not the sunrises?" Cam asked, thinking about their stone chamber in Groton.

"For the Druids, the day begins at sunset. Just like the Jews."

Again with the Druids. Cam had been studying the Freemasons for years, but the strong Druidic influence on them was completely new to him.

Randall continued. "Are you familiar with Royal Arch Masonry?"

"Not really." More revelations coming.

"Without getting too deep into the subject, suffice it to say that Royal Arch is the primary degree in Freemasonry." He paused. "Typically it is symbolized by a crest or banner featuring four creatures." He raised an eyebrow. "I suggest you use that phone of yours to find a picture of the banner."

Cam quickly found many versions of the banner, all containing the four creatures. He showed one to Randall.

Masonic Royal Arch Banner

"That will do. Can you identify the four creatures?"

Cam peered at the phone. "Going clockwise, looks like an eagle, a lion, a bull, and a man."

"And how are you with your zodiacal signs?"

"Let's see: The bull is Taurus, the lion is Leo ..." He shrugged. "I don't know what the eagle and man symbolize."

"The eagle, along with the scorpion, is a symbol for Scorpio. And man is a symbol for Aquarius, the water-carrier." He paused, as he liked to do before making a point. "So we have Taurus, Leo, Scorpio and Aquarius."

It hit Cam. "Those four signs match up with the cross-quarter days." May 5, and also early August, November, and February.

"Exactly. In fact, the cross-quarter days fall at the precise midpoint of these zodiacal cycles."

Cam blinked. "So the Masons ... this Royal Arch degree ... they are marking the cross-quarter days."

"Not just marking, Cameron. Venerating." He lowered his voice, as if somehow someone could be eavesdropping on their conversation atop the Capitol dome. "Freemasonry venerates the cross-quarter days. Just as the ancient Druids did."

Cam felt like a man who had just been taught to read. He knew that Masonry was full of ancient symbolism and allegory, but he had no idea it tied back so closely to the Druids. It struck him again that there was so much he didn't know, hadn't seen.

Randall directed their attention back to the White House. The sun, as it always seemed to do, dove to the horizon in the final few minutes before dusk. The yellow orb rested precariously and momentarily atop the center of the White House roof, as if impaled on the soaring flag pole, while the dying embers of sunlight blazed a fiery trail up Pennsylvania Avenue.

Cam exhaled and turned to Randall, who stared back at him, ready to speak. "So, Cameron, the question is this: Do you think is it a coincidence that the Founding Fathers felt the need to align the two most important structures in Washington to the Druidic festival of Beltane?"

The back of Cam's neck tingled. He straightened. "As a general rule, I don't believe in coincidences."

Tamara's cell phone buzzed, interrupting the Saturday evening Havdalah service marking the end of Shabbat. Her eleven-year-old daughter elbowed her. "Mom, turn that off."

Tamara bit her lip. A text from Moshe; he wouldn't bother her unless it was important. "Sorry, I have to take this," she whispered. "Be right back."

"But Mom, it's Shabbat. You're not supposed to work."

"If God didn't want me to work, he would have made sure I didn't have cell coverage."

She edged out of the aisle and into the lobby. "Call me ASAP. Urgent," the text read.

Tamara jabbed at her speed dial.

"It is done," he said.

"The professor?" She knew they were on a secure line.

"Yes. A speeding car hit him in a crosswalk in Newton Center as he got off the train. Hit-and-run. He is not dead, but he will not be returning to the classroom anytime soon. The car has been disposed of and our agent on his way back to Tel Aviv."

She sighed. It was too bad, really. But Professor Siegel had been warned not to disclose certain things. And the Isaac Question, as they called it, was at the top of the list.

Moshe continued. "But I fear we are too late. We have been tracking Youssef's son. Earlier today he spent a few hours with a freshman named Rachel Levitad. She was a student in Siegel's class. Our agent is a lip-reader. She is certain this Rachel recounted to Youssef's son the details of the professor's theory about Isaac's parentage."

She closed her eyes. "Well that sure sucks." An Arab arms dealer was the last person they wanted to possess this kind of information. For years the Israelis had been waiting for some sharp Islamic scholar to take a careful look at the Old Testament and point out the many flaws in the assertion that the Jewish people had some God-given right to the land of Israel. But the Muslims were so busy poring over the Koran—and so repulsed by the thought of diving into the ancient Jewish texts—that they had left the assertion largely unchallenged.

"We need, as the Americans say, to somehow put the toothpaste back in the tube," Moshe said. "We can't have the Isaac Question spreading into Muslim academia."

"What do you suggest? A second 'accident' would be too convenient, would raise suspicion—the Americans are not idiots. And in any event I don't think it wise to make a blood enemy of Zuberi Youssef."

Moshe cursed. "You are correct, unfortunately. I think for the moment our hands our tied. All we can do is watch and learn."

"Youssef is back in Scotland. In the meantime the best way to learn about his plans is by watching Thorne."

"Agreed."

She ended the call and returned to the sanctuary. "Mi Chamocha," the congregation sang. This prayer was not usually sung during Havdalah, which made it even more ironic. This was the song the Israelites sang as they crossed the Red Sea on their way out of Egypt. Thanks to Professor Siegel's indiscretions, the world might soon learn that the Exodus story was a bit more complicated than was taught in Sunday school.

Cam purchased a Diet Coke, settled into a leather chair in the hotel lounge and waited for the clerk to notify him his room was ready. He closed his eyes, the imprint of the setting sun resting atop the White House still burned into his retinas. What a fascinating day. He had flown to Washington hoping to peek behind the Masonic curtain, to catch a glimpse or two of the secret society's secrets. Instead he had been nearly blinded by them.

He phoned Amanda to update her on his day and say goodnight to Astarte. "It was definitely worth missing my flight. Just to be up in the dome was amazing." He shook his head. "And then the alignment. I need to bring you back here."

She laughed. "You sound almost giddy."

"Yeah, I'll never get to sleep. Maybe I'll grab a beer at the bar." He paused, trying to put his thoughts into words. "I've learned so much, but I sense there's something deeper, something even more important still hidden from me. I feel like a guy who knows there's something amazing around the corner, but I can't see it, no matter how far I crane my neck."

Amanda replied, "I know it's a cliché, but with the Freemasons, it seems there's always another layer of the onion to peel away."

They said goodbye and Cam checked his email. Randall Sid had dropped him off only fifteen minutes earlier, but already he had sent Cam a message. "Read this," the email stated, "if you want to learn more about the Druids."

Cam opened the attached file and began reading. He had always thought of the Druids as being Irish or Celtic, but apparently they lived all over Europe in the centuries before Christ. Eventually the invading Romans pushed them westward to the British Isles. Nobody seemed to know where the Druids came from, but the author of this article theorized that they were the remnants of Egyptian priests loyal to the sun-worshiping Pharaoh Akhenaton, forced from power after trying to push sun worship on an Egyptian society unwilling to give up its pantheon of gods. Akhenaton, his priests, and his entourage fled Egypt and made their way to the European continent, the author concluded. This paralleled Zuberi Youssef's story of Princess Scota fleeing Egypt and her descendants eventually settling in Ireland and Scotland. And it was consistent with so much of what Cam had learned today, tying the Druids and Egyptians and Freemasons together in some kind of mismatched group of sun worshipers.

The unanswered question, of course, was this: Was the story of Scota and the story of the Druids the same story? Freemasonry had long been closely associated with Scotland, with many historians believing the society originated there. And, of course, there was the Sinclair family connection to consider—for centuries the clan patriarch was the hereditary grand master of Scottish Rite Freemasonry. Did this close association between the Masons and Scotland stem from the Druidic ties to ancient Egypt?

Cam allowed his mind to race: Freemasons, Druids, Egyptians, Sinclairs…

Of course. He grinned, almost laughing out loud. Tapping at his phone, he pulled up an image of Rosslyn Chapel, built by the Sinclair family. In seconds he found what he was looking for: By one count there were hundreds of representations of Green Men carved onto the Chapel walls and ceilings. A gargoyle-like Druidic symbol of fertility who was sometimes painted green, the Green Men consisted of human heads springing from the vines and roots and branches of Mother Nature, a clear nod to the ancient pagan beliefs.

Rosslyn Chapel Green Man

But why, Cam had often wondered, were the Green Men so prominently displayed alongside dozens of examples of both Masonic and Egyptian imagery in a Christian chapel?

The answer came to him, a simple and neat one: The Chapel, he realized, was built as more than a chapel. It was built as a mural, a storybook in stone. Through its hundreds of carvings, the Chapel told the history of Scotland, of its roots in Egypt, of its centuries of rule by the pagan Druids, of its close ties to Masonry, and of its eventual conversion to Christianity. The story was all in plain sight, a story of sun worship and paganism alongside the more traditional Christian symbols.

But the Druidic Green Man was most visible of all. And he screamed a truth that told Cam he was on the right track with his research. Even if he still couldn't see what was around the corner.

Randall Sid took the opportunity to close his eyes and perhaps nap for ten minutes as the sedan raced from the hotel near the airport toward the House of the Temple. Since arriving in Washington he had been in meetings upward of twelve hours every day; no doubt tonight the other Sovereign Commanders would want to rehash the Cameron Thorne situation. Randall yawned; he was seventy-eight and had never worked harder in his life.

Trying to save Western society was exhausting.

He focused on clearing his mind, but trying to save Western society was also one of those tasks that gnawed at you and made it hard to sleep. Instead he considered the meetings yet to come. Last year fifty Sovereign Commanders from all over the world had convened in London with an unprecedented agenda: Develop a strategy to control and eventually end radical Islam's attempts at undermining Western society. Collectively the group had influence over almost every head of state, major corporation, and international institution in America and Europe: When conspiracy theorists claimed the Freemasons ran the world, they were not all that far off. Governments came and went, but the connections made through Freemasonry spanned generations, crossed borders, and bridged religious differences. Now, after a year of work, the Sovereign Commanders were reconvening in Washington to implement some of the dozens of stratagems they had considered.

Randall pulled a document from the briefcase at his feet and examined the list of countries represented at the conference. The list included most of the Western democracies, but other than Turkey the group lacked Middle-Eastern representation. Which is where Cameron Thorne entered the picture. Thorne had, somehow, forged a relationship with one of the most powerful men in the Middle East—arms dealer Zuberi Youssef. It was gaining access to men like Youssef that would be crucial to the group's success.

The driver dropped Randall at the rear entrance to the House of the Temple just before nine-thirty. Randall climbed the grand staircase and found the Sovereign Commanders meeting in the Temple room. He expected to slip in unnoticed, but apparently they had been waiting for him.

The men were seated at mahogany desks rimming the room. A jowly Spaniard, who had been elected the group's leader, addressed him. "Most Worshipful Randall Sid, we await your update. The more we discuss this, the more we are in agreement that Zuberi Youssef is key to our plans. If we can somehow exert influence over who he sells arms to, this would go a long way toward emasculating the extremists." All the Sovereign

Commanders in the room were equal in status under the rules of Freemasonry, so the Spaniard sat at one of the mahogany desks rather than in the raised, throne-like chairs at either end of the ornate hall.

Randall walked to the center of the room, the acoustics making a microphone unnecessary. "As you know, I spent the day with Thorne. He's very curious about the Masonic connection to the Druids and ancient Egyptians. I did what I could to solidify this connection in his mind."

The Spaniard replied. "And you think he is curious about this connection because of his relationship with Zuberi Youssef?"

Randall shrugged. "I'm not certain. But it seems reasonable. Youssef has been promoting the Scota legend, which ties the Scots to the ancient Egyptians and also to the Druids." He paused to explain. "Those who believe in the Scota legend believe Princess Scota and her followers spent many generations in Europe after fleeing Egypt, working their way east to west, before finally ending up in Ireland and then Scotland. The Egyptian-trained priests in her group continued their training and teaching in Europe, eventually spawning the Druids."

Heads nodded. Randall turned the conversation back to Thorne. "And Youssef, knowing Thorne is an expert on the Templars, is trying to recruit Thorne to work for him."

"To what end?" a voice called out.

"I believe because Youssef's wife is a Sinclair and Youssef wants Thorne to validate the Prince Henry legend and thereby add to the Sinclair cache." Randall shrugged again. "Of course, the way one becomes an expert on the Templars is by studying the Freemasons."

A tall, elderly Brother at a desk near the entrance stood and cleared his throat. He sported a red tartan kilt under this tuxedo jacket. "Pardon my interruption," he said in a Scottish accent, smiling and nodding.

"Most Worshipful Duncan Sinclair," the Spaniard said. "The floor is yours."

He bowed. "To belabor your point, if the way one learns about the Templars is by studying the Freemasons, then the way one learns about the Freemasons is by studying the Sinclair family."

Only a few wisps of white hair crisscrossed his liver-spot-covered head, but his blue eyes danced with life. "As my Brothers know, it was the Sinclair family that conceived of—and later implemented—the strategy of folding the outlawed Knights Templar into the Scottish stonemason guilds during the fourteenth and fifteenth centuries. That is why, for centuries, the head of the Sinclair clan served as hereditary Grand Master of Scottish Rite Freemasonry." He straightened himself. "I am a continuation of the close ties between the Sinclairs and this Brotherhood." He bowed again. "But I must say, I have never met this Zuberi Youssef fellow or his wife, Carrington." He shrugged. "Ours is a large clan."

The Scotsman sat and Randall summed up. "I agree with our strategy that building some kind of relationship with Youssef is crucial. And I believe one way we can do so is through Thorne, especially if Thorne agrees to take this professorship at Brandeis University. But Thorne's not an idiot: He knows Youssef will want him to research the Scota legend. If the legend is bunk, Thorne will refuse. I think the only way Thorne will even consider working with the Egyptian is if he believes the legend is real."

"So you showed him the Druidic sunset illumination?" the Spaniard asked.

"Yes. And other things."

"Excellent." The Spaniard nodded. "This is one of those occasions when sharing our secrets serves a greater good." He paused. "Now, is there anything else … anything at all … we can do to ensure Thorne accepts this university position?"

Randall smiled. "I'm one step ahead of you."

Chapter 4

After returning from Washington early Sunday morning Cam had spent the rest of the day doing yard work and coaching Astarte's soccer team. At dinner Astarte slipped a blob of mayo under a scoop of his ice cream. Lucky for him she couldn't stop giggling and he avoided a ruinous dessert.

Sitting under the stars on their deck Sunday evening, Cam had shared with Amanda the fascinating connections between the Freemasons, the Druids and the ancient Egyptians.

"You know," she said, "I keep running into the Druids in my research on Baphomet and the Cult of the Head."

"I'm not surprised," Cam replied. "The Masons, the Druids, the Templars—from what I can see, they're all branches of the same tree that has its roots back in ancient Egypt. It's all about sun worship."

Back in the office on Monday, he slipped out during lunch to retrieve the certified letter he had been unable to retrieve last week due to Zuberi's phone call. The pleasant weekend weather had devolved into a rainy, gusty mess; he drove with his wipers on full and kept both hands on the steering wheel to keep the SUV in its lane.

Rain jacket dripping, he pulled back his hood and entered the post office. He slid the green slip across the counter and the clerk handed him a thick white business-sized envelope with a return address reading 'Environmental Protection Agency' and a downtown Boston address. Cam cocked his head. Like the property deed, if this were some kind of business-related correspondence it would have been sent to his office address.

Cam opened the envelope and unfolded four sheets of heavy stock paper. The bold words across the top staggered him like a kick to the gut:

Urgent Legal Matter: Superfund Notice of Liability

Barely able to breathe, his eyes raced across the legalese and settled on the sentence that promised to change, and potentially ruin, his life: *"EPA has determined that you, as the current owner of the Site, are a responsible party under the federal Superfund Law for cleanup of the Site."*

It all suddenly made sense: The sweet smell wafting from the parking lot; the buildings being torn down; the fence surrounding the property; and of course the property being deeded to him in the first place. Who gives away six acres of prime real estate for nothing? Nobody, of course.

He knew he needed to call Amanda, though it was the last thing he wanted to do. He walked to the car, oblivious to the rain, climbed into the SUV and rubbed his face with his hands. Exhaling, he pushed the speed dial button. Without preface, he blurted, "I'm in big trouble."

"What, Cameron?"

"The property is contaminated." He summarized the letter. "This chemical, TCE, is apparently seeping into the groundwater." He choked out the words. "It causes cancer. That's what you and Astarte smelled the other night."

"Oh my God, is she in any danger?"

"I don't think so; she only sniffed it for a second, and she didn't drink any water from the brook."

Amanda exhaled. "But why are you in trouble. You didn't *do* anything. Why should you be liable for the cleanup costs?"

"That's the way the goddamn Superfund law works." He fought to control his breathing. "It's called strict liability. Anyone who contributed to polluting the property, and anyone who ever owned the property after it was polluted, is liable for one hundred percent of the cleanup costs."

"That's bloody ludicrous."

Ironically, he had written a paper in law school defending the policy. "The idea is that the government shouldn't have to pay for it. The EPA probably already squeezed everything they could from Middlesex Semiconductor and the owner's widow." He swallowed. "Now they want to squeeze me."

"What about the British company?"

"I'm guessing they didn't leave any money here in the U.S. Looks like they bought the property, discovered it was contaminated, fenced it in, and got the hell out of here."

"How much are we talking?"

He closed his eyes. "Everything I've got. Everything." What an idiot he had been. "All my assets. The house, my savings, my retirement account, future book royalties. These sites cost millions to clean up, and I'm on the hook for it all."

She was silent. He sensed her fighting to maintain control, though he wouldn't have blamed her if she blew up. Her voice raised an octave. "What about the fact that you didn't even *want* the blooming property. Someone just handed it to you out of the blue."

He sighed. "I was thinking about that. But we have the cop who saw me cut the lock and enter the property, and he knows who I am. In the law, that's called exercising dominion and control. Once I did that, the transaction was complete." He continued. "And just to top off my stupidity, I told the tax assessor's office to send me the property tax bill when I was at Town Hall last week."

She asked the obvious question. "What if you had gotten the Superfund letter before we went over there?"

He rubbed his eyes with his hand. "Then I would have rejected the tender and gone to court to rescind the transaction." Just five lousy days.

"Well, damn it all. Who would do this to you, Cameron? What kind of sick bastard would pull the pin and drop a grenade in your lap?"

Cam slumped against the steering wheel. "The same guy who handed me a lottery ticket and then pushed me off the pier?"

Amanda considered it. "That makes no sense. No sense at all. The deed was dated *before* the lottery ticket shenanigans, after which you were supposed to drown in the harbor." She continued her metaphor. "Why drop a grenade in the lap of a dead man?"

"I agree." He felt weak, almost sick. "But other than that, I have no idea."

Numbed by the EPA letter, Cam mindlessly navigated his way home. He had been involved with a Superfund case once before—a gas station owner who disposed of used car engine oil at a licensed disposal site was held liable for cleanup costs at the site even though he had behaved perfectly legally the whole time. And the government had been ruthless, squeezing the poor guy for almost a quarter of a million dollars. Cam did some math in his head—the lake house was worth maybe a hundred grand more than the mortgage, he had about twenty thousand in savings and another forty in his retirement account, and he owned some shares of Google worth maybe another ten. Plus he was due a quarterly royalty check of about fifteen thousand. Altogether, less than $200,000—not nearly enough to pay for even the smallest Superfund cleanup. Even if the EPA took it and let him walk, where would they live? How would he pay for the wedding? Would the EPA attempt to garnish future earnings and book royalties as well? What about Amanda taking time off to have a baby? And Astarte's college?

He banged the steering wheel, cursing. Who had done this to him, and why?

He took a deep breath and exhaled, forcing his mind to focus on the mystery rather than fixate on the misfortune. If he could figure out who had orchestrated this, he might still wriggle out of it. The obvious question was, did the stone chamber have anything to do with the conveyance? Almost assuredly. Whoever did this must have suspected Cam would be more likely to exercise dominion and control of the property once he saw the chamber. Another owner, uninterested in the chamber, might not have been such a cowboy and charged onto the property like Cam did. So it was likely the culprit targeted Cam at least partially because he or she knew of Cam's interest in ancient stone structures.

Which basically narrowed the possible culprits down to Cam's friends, family, associates, and anyone who had attended one of his lectures or seen him on a television documentary or read his book. Not exactly an intimate group.

There was, also, one additional clue: Whoever did this had a good knowledge of the law, or at least access to a lawyer who did. But that still left thousands of possibilities. Without an apparent motive, there was no way to identify the culprit.

He cursed again. *What a fucking nightmare.* And the worst part about it was that Amanda and Astarte were going to have to live through it with him.

Amon collapsed back into the plastic seat of the subway car and closed his eyes. The taste of Rachel's lip gloss lingered in his mouth just as the smell of her perfume wafted from his clothes. He sighed, exhausted and exhilarated by the past forty-eight hours. They might have stayed in bed for another week had she not had to catch her Monday flight to Chicago. As it was, Rachel left half her belongings in her dorm, she and Amon barely having the time to stuff a few suitcases and rush her to the airport.

She had blown him a final kiss, grinning from the front of the security line. And then she was gone, swallowed by the airport body scanner tunnel.

Cocooned in rapture, Amon almost missed the subway transfer to North Station where he would catch the commuter rail back to Brandeis. He had willingly spent sixty dollars on a taxi to get them to the airport, figuring the extra hour it gave them in his bed to be worth ten times the cost. But there was no urgency in his return trip. There was nothing for him in a Waltham without Rachel. When he got on the train he would phone his father. But for now he stretched out and wallowed like a cat in the winter sun....

His father answered on the fourth ring. "Yes, Amon, is everything okay?" He must have been sleeping because he spoke in Arabic.

"Everything is fine, father."

Zuberi switched to English. "But it is past midnight."

Amon looked at his watch. He had completely lost track of time. "I'm sorry," he mumbled, "it is still evening here. I can phone you tomorrow."

"No, no, I am awake. How are you, my son?"

They made small talk, Amon omitting any mention of Rachel. There would be time enough to discuss this if the romance continued. "I had an interesting conversation with a Brandeis student that I wanted to share with you." He related Rachel's recounting of the Abraham story, his father interrupting often with a comments and questions.

"She said," Amon concluded, "that it could mean the Pharaoh, not Abraham, is the real father of the Jewish people."

"Very interesting," his own father replied. "I believe the Pharaoh at this time was Tuthmosis III." He paused, filling the silence with a clicking of his tongue. "This could be very important."

"Why is that, father?"

"First thing I think is, this helps explain the story of Joseph. Do you remember?"

Amon related the story as he recalled it: Joseph was the son of Jacob, who was the son of Isaac. Jacob had many sons but Joseph was his favorite. His brothers were jealous of him so they sold Joseph into slavery in Egypt. While in Egypt Joseph ended up in jail but then correctly interpreted one of the Pharaoh's dreams, thereby winning his freedom and also winning the confidence of the Pharaoh, who eventually made Joseph his vizier, or prime minister.

"So, my son, what part of this story gives you questions?"

Amon considered the inquiry. "The vizier was usually part of the royal family, not a foreigner and definitely not a slave."

"Very good. But if what you say about Abraham is true, then Joseph—who is Isaac's grandson—is cousin to this Pharaoh, yes?"

"Aha," Amon exhaled. "Now the story makes more sense. Somehow Joseph proved his lineage. So now, when his dream interpretations prove correct, he is given a position befitting his royal blood."

His father exhaled. "You do good work, Amon. This is important information, and it is only one week in America. We will discuss more later—I think we find more in this story. Remember, many scholars believe Moses was also part of Egyptian royal family. Maybe all pieces are part of one big puzzle."

Amon thought about remarking how the name Moses was similar to the name of the Pharaoh Tuthmosis III, but he assumed his father had already made the connection. "Good night, father."

"You do good work," he repeated. "I am proud of you."

Cam spent the next twenty-four hours alternately moping, apologizing to Amanda and lashing out in anger at his unseen enemy. He had nothing pressing at the office—and little ability to focus in any event—so he paced around the living room most of the morning Tuesday ignoring both Venus' whines for him to play with her and Amanda's attempts at normal conversation.

Desperate to do something productive, he dropped onto the couch and used his laptop to research the chemical, TCE. For decades, trichloroethene, a colorless solvent used to clean metal parts in industrial use, had been seeping into the groundwater beneath factories all across America, slowly making its way into drinking water supply sources downstream. The technology existed to remove the cancer-causing chemical from groundwater, but it took time and money—lots of both.

After lunch on Tuesday, during which Cam did little more than pick at his sandwich, Amanda came up behind him while he sat and draped her arms over his shoulders. "Hey, honey, maybe you should go to the office for a few hours? Astarte will be home soon and she's sensing something is wrong."

He nodded and sighed. "You're right. I'm about as much fun as ants at a picnic. Give me a few hours to try to rally."

She kissed him on the head. "That assessment's a bit harsh, don't you think?"

"Not really. I'm definitely a downer."

She cuffed him playfully on the side of the head. "I meant it was harsh on the ants."

As he drove he tried to force himself to depersonalize the situation and analyze it coldly, rationally. If he had hired himself as a lawyer, what would Attorney Thorne advise? "Find a lawyer who's not such a fucking idiot," he murmured.

But he pushed himself to go through the exercise. The primary objective should be, obviously, to get Cam-the-client out from underneath the liability spotlight. But the strict liability of the Superfund law provided very little wiggle room. Failing that, a second objective would be somehow to shield or shelter Cam-the-client's assets from the long, sticky paws of the federal government. *Cover your assets*, it was called.

He had advised clients on how to hide assets during the last real estate downturn and he knew some pretty creative and effective tricks. But most of these tricks required a decent lead time—a client would approach him early on, with trouble far off on the horizon, and Cam would craft a plan to convey assets to a spouse or to a trust or to a retirement account or to some offshore bank. One client even converted two hundred thousand dollars into gambling chips, hid them, and cashed them in once the litigation was over. But, again, this only worked with a long lead time. And it only worked against banks or other creditors who did not have the power of the federal government.

He went through a mental checklist of other strategies. He had, in the past, worked with clients to hide funds by prepaying their federal income taxes. One client under duress from a bank had declared $420,000 in income on his tax return rather than the actual $120,000 and paid an extra $100,000 in taxes; later, after the litigation, he claimed a clerical error, filed an amended return with the IRS, and received the $100,000 back as a refund. But even that wouldn't work here—the EPA, as a sister agency to the IRS, had access to Cam's filings and would more than likely see through the ruse. Another client slowly emptied his bank account by purchasing scores of $1,000 American Express gift cards, which he then used for living expenses; Cam could purchase a few of those now, but there was no way he could empty his account without the EPA getting suspicious.

The reality was that his current assets—savings, home, retirement, stocks, royalties—were probably lost, either forfeited to the government or squandered on legal fees. At best he could come up with a plan to limit the loss. That meant protecting Amanda's assets, and protecting his future earnings. But it sucked to be sucked dry.

Amanda had never seen Cam so dejected. He hadn't even wanted to kick the soccer ball around with Astarte yesterday after school.

She power-walked through the neighborhood, headphones playing U2, Venus trotting along beside her in the early afternoon sun. The idea of losing a couple of hundred thousand dollars along with their house obviously didn't thrill her, but it hadn't debilitated her like it had Cam. She had grown up in a wealthy but dysfunctional family—given the choice for Astarte and any future children they might have, she much preferred a loving husband and father over a wealthy one. And it's not like they were going to starve; she and Cam were both professionals who could increase their work hours if necessary. Sure it might mean cutting back on their research, but such was life...

And then it hit her. *Of course.* She pulled her phone from her pocket and jabbed at the speed dial. "Cam, listen. What if whoever did this is trying to stop you from doing further research?"

"How would this stop me?"

She resisted reminding him how mopey he had been the past couple of days. "Well, first of all, this litigation is going to totally distract you for the next however many months. And, more to the point, it's going to force you to work more hours and focus on income generation rather than research." She took a breath. "I think someone did this to knock you out of the game."

"Then why give me land with a stone chamber?"

"That was just the bait, to get you to swallow the hook. My guess is you haven't thought about that chamber since you received the EPA letter."

Silence for a few seconds. "True, I haven't. Maybe you're onto something. But who? Who cares enough about this stuff to put together such an elaborate ruse?"

She hadn't gotten that far. In the past both the Catholic Church and U.S. government had tried to block their research, but in those cases there had been an obvious connection between the research and some secret those entities were trying to hide. But not this time. "All right, let's brainstorm. What about the Freemasons?" They had not been thrilled last year when Cam connected some of their rituals to the pagan god, Baal. "I told you before I don't trust Randall Sid."

Cam shook his head. "I don't think so. They've been pretty supportive of my research."

He had a point. In the past year Cam had been invited to lecture at a dozen Masonic lodges, and based on the emails he received they were buying his book by the truckload. Not to mention Randall had been spoon-feeding Cam Masonic secrets.

"Maybe we're thinking too broadly," Cam said. "Are we researching anything specifically right now that might be threatening to anyone?"

"I'm looking at Baphomet. I don't see how that threatens anyone, and I don't think anyone even knows what I'm doing. What about you?"

He sighed. "I started looking into the Scota legends a few weeks ago. Zuberi has been sending me stuff to read." Cam had shared some of his research with Amanda—Zuberi claimed that thirty-five hundred years ago a daughter of an Egyptian pharaoh married a prince of Scythia, a land known today as Iran. When her father the pharaoh was deposed and exiled, this daughter, known as Princess of Scota (the name Scota being a derivative of Scythia), fled to her husband's homeland with a group of followers before later sailing west. They settled first in Spain and eventually continued across Europe to Ireland and Scotland, where their descendants lived today.

Cam continued. "It turns out, Zuberi may be right about Scota. Ever hear of the Declaration of Arbroath?"

"The Scottish Declaration of Independence. We learned about it in school."

"Right." In the year 1320 the Scots sent a declaration to the Pope, requesting that he force England to respect Scottish sovereignty. Many historians compared the petition to the

American Declaration of Independence in term of importance. Cam continued. "The Declaration of Arbroath began by reciting the history of the Scottish people. I have it right here; I'll read the relevant parts: '*Most Holy Father and Lord, we know from the chronicles and books of the ancients that the Scots journeyed from Greater Scythia and dwelt for a long course of time in Spain. Thence they came to their home in the west where they still live today.*'"

"That's pretty matter-of-fact," Amanda said. "From Scythia, across to Spain, west to Scotland."

"And it matches Zuberi's version of the story, though to be fair it doesn't say anything about Princess Scota being the daughter of a pharaoh."

"How could it?" Amanda asked. "Think about it. The Scots couldn't very well claim to be descended from the pharaoh who ruled during the Exodus and then expect the Pope to do them any favors. The pharaoh of the Exodus was probably the biggest villain of the Old Testament."

"Good point. And Zuberi sent me other sources that fill in the blanks and document the Scota stuff, including some strong DNA evidence linking the Scots and the Egyptians. I have to admit, Zuberi makes a strong case. So I'm willing to buy that the Scots descend from the Egyptians. But getting back to your original question, why would anyone care? And like you said, I don't think many people even know what I'm working on."

She considered his question. "Well, if the Scots really do descend from Egyptians, I could see where that might have some interesting repercussions in the Middle East. Perhaps the Israelis would rather not have Scotland tied historically and ethnically to Egypt?" It was a reach, she sensed.

"Maybe."

"Look, just because we don't know exactly who it is doesn't mean we can't deduce why it was done. Someone wants to stop your research, Cameron. No, I don't know who it is. But that has to be the reason. Like I said, they want to knock you out of the game."

"I guess you could be right."

He still seemed down, listless. She tried another tack. "I know you're bummed out about this. Someone outsmarted you, and I know how you hate that."

"They ran circles around me, Amanda." He exhaled. "They kicked my ass."

"And that's usually my job, so I'm pissed also."

He forced a chuckle.

She continued. "So, yes, they kicked your ass. But why? Like I said, because they want you to stop your research." She paused. "So are you going to let them get their way? Are you going to curl up in the corner and feel sorry for yourself?"

He exhaled again. She knew he knew she was right. But she also knew how fragile the male ego could be.

She nudged him further. "The man I fell in love with wouldn't let whoever did this get what they want, Cameron."

For the next few hours Cam thought about what Amanda had said. She was right—someone was trying to stop his research. But knowing that didn't change his predicament. He wrestled with his decision all afternoon, pacing around his office. But it really wasn't a decision at all. He had no choice. Not that Amanda would see it that way.

They had dinner as a family, Cam trying to be upbeat—Astarte had sensed the turmoil over the past two days. She had been through enough, raised by an uncle after her mother died and then, after his death, taken in by Cam and Amanda. She deserved some stability and normalcy. Not that she was going to get it.

After dinner Cam and Astarte went outside and played catch with a Frisbee, Venus racing back and forth between them and intercepting more than a few of their throws. As dusk set in and the mosquitoes came out, he snatched a throw out of the air and turned toward the house. "Okay, shower time for you," he said as they pushed through the front door. "You done your homework?"

"I have a little math to do."

"Need any help?"

"Nope. I like math."

"Good. After your shower and homework, we can watch the rest of that movie."

Amanda watched Astarte leave the room and turned to Cam. "I'm glad she fancies mathematics. And I'm glad her school doesn't have any of that gender bias one sometimes hears about."

"I never understood that," Cam said. "In ancient times only women could do math; men were thought too stupid. That's why the root for the word math is the same as for mother—they both come from the name of the Egyptian goddess, Maat. Mathematics literally means 'mother wisdom.'"

"You are just filled with fascinating little pieces of trivia."

"You know that beer ad with the most interesting man in the world? I'm the most interesting man in the house."

"Only because Venus is female."

Two hours later they took turns kissing Astarte goodnight. "There's something I need to talk to you about," he said to Amanda as they moved into the living room.

"Is it a wine talk or a tea talk?" Amanda asked.

He smiled sadly. "More like whiskey. But I'll settle for wine."

"Okay," she said, pouring a large glass of Pinot Grigio which they would share, as was their custom. They sat together on the oversized chair looking out over the lake, Venus at their feet. As always, Amanda smelled flowery fresh with just a bit of muskiness mixed in. On most days he would have nuzzled her neck.

"Okay, a couple of things," he said. "First, I'm going to have another conversation with Zuberi about taking that teaching job. He called last week to offer it again."

"What did you say?"

"I turned him down. But that was before the Superfund shit hit. I think we're going to need the money."

"But you hated the idea about being stuck in a university setting. I believe the expression you used was, 'Why would I want to collaborate with a bunch of people who have their heads up their asses?'"

"Yeah, well, I also hate the idea of insolvency. And I'm going to talk to him about some ways to structure the deal so the government can't grab my salary."

"Nothing illegal, I hope."

"No. But, for example, take some of my salary and use it to hire you as my assistant." He took a deep breath and forced himself to look her in the eye, to let her see the hurt inside him. "Which leads to me next item: We need to postpone the wedding."

Amanda coughed, a bit of wine escaping and dribbling down her chin. "Why on earth do we need to do that?"

"The obvious reason is because we're not going to be able to pay for it—"

She cut him off. "Screw that. We can get married in our living room and eat take-out Chinese for all I care."

He knew she'd feel that way. "But more to the point is that, if we get married, the government will come after you."

"Why? I'm not on the bloody deed."

"No, so technically you have no liability. But I know the lawyers who work on these cases—they're the most competitive, Type A people in the world. If they think they can gain an edge by threatening you, they will." Many of the lawyers who did government litigation were considered hound dogs in the legal profession—they generally didn't graduate at the top of their law classes, but they were tenacious, and many of them chewed and slobbered their way up the ladder.

Cam continued as Amanda sat back, her eyes closed. "They have all the cards, all the power, and they know it. They won't let this die until they have every penny they think they can get." He took a deep breath. "If it weren't for Astarte, I'd even suggest you move out, just to keep you completely off their radar. They have no legal right to force you to contribute, but that doesn't mean they won't try. This is all just one big negotiation."

She slid off the chair and began to pace, the wine sloshing over the sides of the glass. "This is ludicrous, Cam. What about just signing everything you have over to them. Now. Tomorrow. Then by June it's all behind us."

Cam shook his head. "Whatever we offer won't be enough; they'll always think they can get more, maybe from my parents or maybe a payment plan going into the future. So we have to let this play out for at least a couple months, make them think they've gotten everything they can from me." He paused. "But getting married would put you right in the bullseye; they'll definitely want any assets my spouse has."

"Well it's not like I have a trust fund or anything."

"No, but you have some savings. And a car. And an income. It's bad enough I'll be insolvent. But we're going to need your money just to survive."

"Bloody hell, Cameron. Your government can be such a bunch of pricks." Tears pooled in her eyes as she stared out over the lake, the wind rippling the surface and bouncing the moonbeam as if in reflection of the turmoil in the house on the shore. "I want to get married in September, like we planned."

"I do too, honey. I do too."

"And what about Astarte?" she asked softly. "We can't officially adopt her until we are married. Think about her."

He exhaled. "I am thinking about her. About not having to move out of Westford, about being able to pay for her sports and dance classes and summer camp, about college."

"Damn it all." She kicked the couch. "This really fucking sucks."

Even in her anger, she didn't blame him. Or if she did, she was kind enough not to voice it. "I'm sorry I screwed this up, Amanda. I should've been more careful."

She flopped back into the chair, rested her hand on his thigh, and chugged some wine. She exhaled. "I don't blame you for this, obviously. Someone sucker-punched you, and all that you're guilty of is not seeing it coming. But I sure do wish you had not cut that padlock."

He closed his eyes. "Tell me about it."

Cam phoned Zuberi first thing the next morning, which was early Wednesday afternoon in Scotland. Actually, Cam had no idea if Zuberi was in Scotland—he could just as easily be in the Middle East or Asia. He really knew very little about Zuberi's business, other than it seemed to be worldwide and extraordinarily successful.

"Cameron," Zuberi bellowed, the emphasis hard on the first syllable. "Have you phoned to tell me your mind is changed?"

From his rear deck overlooking the lake Cam watched a mother duck lead her chicks ashore. Venus, too, watched; for some reason she did not bark at the ducks like she did at the squirrels. "Amanda and I discussed your offer, and I'd like to hear more about it."

"Excellent. Brandeis is very interested. I will endow a chair for study of history in America before Columbus." He laughed. "After this, anything is possible. As you Americans say, name your terms."

"First of all, I'd need to know I'm not going to be constrained in any way. I research what I want and how I want it. And my findings won't be censored."

"I agree! And Brandeis knows this also. This is why we choose you; we know you have strength in your beliefs. But we also know you are not fool. We have expression in Egypt: 'Wise man never takes step too long for his leg.' You will march toward truth, but not run into wall like fool, yes?" He paused to let his point sink in. "Now, what more terms have you?"

"I would be willing to teach a class in pre-Columbian history, but I don't want to teach anything else. I'm not a historian, so I'm really not qualified."

"Agree. We want you teach two classes, both in study of explorers to America before Columbus. One class is what I think they call survey class and other is more advanced—maybe teach about Prince Henry Sinclair."

Two was doable. But all this also entailed preparing syllabi and grading papers and holding office hours. "I would want an assistant. Twenty hours per week."

"Agree again."

"Nobody knows this material better than Amanda. Would you be okay with her taking the position?"

Zuberi chuckled. "Most men wish to keep wife away when they are with pretty college girls. But most men do not have wife so pretty as Amanda. But if you wish, why not?"

Cam laughed politely. "Sounds good so far. What are we talking for salary?"

"The salary we discuss is $100,000, plus, say, hourly twenty-five dollars for your assistant."

Cam was glad Zuberi could not see his face flush; the sum was significantly more than he expected for teaching just two courses. Of course, it was pocket change to Zuberi. Cam reminded himself of the Rule of Two Zeros—when dealing with someone as wealthy as the Egyptian, remove two zeros from the end of every dollar amount. So, for Zuberi, the expenditure of $100,000 compared to buying a new computer for a normal person. Not insignificant, but not life-changing either. "That is generous, thank you. I may ask that some of that be reclassified. For example, I would like to take some of it as a housing stipend, some as a car stipend, some as a life insurance stipend, et cetera, with the payments made directly to third-party vendors." The less money that ended up in his bank account, the less the government could attempt to garnish.

"I am businessman, Cameron. All of this is play for children. We structure things as you wish."

"Thanks." Cam appreciated him not pushing for an explanation.

"But there is one condition: What is saying you Americans have, publish or perish? Carrington and I would like research published. We want to see another book from you. And this will make Brandeis happy also. So salary is half for teaching and other half when book manuscript is complete."

Cam sensed a loophole. "When my manuscript is complete, or when it is published?"

"Complete. I know you have not control over publisher."

Cam exhaled. That was fair. It would be a busy year, both teaching and writing, not to mention fighting with the EPA and keeping his law practice afloat. But with Amanda's help it could be done. He took a deep breath. "I think, Zuberi, that we have a deal."

"Excellent," the Egyptian boomed. "And Cameron, I have one more idea."

"Yes?"

"Maybe you start teaching in summer. Why wait until September? We give you extra twenty-five thousand."

Cam considered it. The extra money would be welcome. And it might be nice to try out his lesson plan in the summer, when things would be more low-key. "When does summer semester begin?"

"First week June."

"Would Brandeis be ready for me yet?"

Zuberi chuckled. "They are ready as soon as I write check. I will talk with them."

The morning mist over the lake had begun to clear as the temperature rose. Cam had no more questions; Zuberi's terms were both reasonable and generous. "Thank you, Zuberi," he said. *You just saved my ass.*

The weeklong Masonic conference was finally winding up. The Spaniard had offered to ride with Randall from the hotel to the airport for his Wednesday morning flight.

The Spaniard's jowls shook as he slid into the back seat of the sedan next to Randall. He offered a tired smile. "I just received a phone call. Señor Thorne has accepted the position at Brandeis."

Randall knew better than to ask how they had intercepted the call; the Masons, like any secretive group, operated on a need-to-know basis. "Good. I will continue to cultivate my relationship with him."

"Yes. Until now you have been giving. Soon it will be time to take."

"Understood."

The Spaniard shifted in his seat so he was full face to Randall, large dark bags visible under his eyes. "Brother, there is something else you need to know." He exhaled, the smell of strong coffee wafting over Randall. "Things are worse even than we believed. ISIS is like a disease, crossing borders and poisoning the populace with its fanatical beliefs. And like most fanatics, it cannot be bargained with or reasoned with or in any way placated." He sighed again. "Due to ISIS aggression, many of our contacts in the Middle East have either fled or are dead. When we began this operation, Señor Thorne was one of many arrows in our quiver. Now he is one of very few." He put his hand on Randall's shoulder. "We need to somehow control Zuberi Youssef. And to do that we need you to somehow control Señor Thorne."

Cam had greeted Amanda with the good news about Zuberi's offer when she returned from her morning visit to the gym, then had gone off to the office with a bounce in his step for the first time this week. "My plan is to funnel a chunk of my salary to you as my research assistant," he said before leaving. "So instead of twenty-five bucks per hour, make it fifty. That, along with your museum job, should give you a high enough income to qualify for a mortgage to buy a new house for us. Maybe we can even figure out a way for you to buy back this one." The government wouldn't care, as long as it got its money.

She appreciated the good news, but the thought of delaying the wedding still felt like someone had reached down her throat and scalded her heart with a hot needle. She had tried to remain upbeat while Cam was glum, but the wedding postponement loomed on the horizon of her consciousness like a funnel cloud, threatening to suck her happiness away, break it into a million pieces and scatter it across the countryside. Her reaction, frankly, surprised her—she had never been one of those women who felt her life would be incomplete if she did not marry. But she had fallen in love not only with Cam, but with the idea of finally having a family. Her father had left when she was young, and her mother spent Amanda's childhood trying to find his replacement, often leaving Amanda home for long stretches with a sitter.

The story of her parents' marriage was an ugly one, the worst part of which her mother had only recently shared with Amanda. Amanda wasn't even sure she believed it—it could just as easily have been a tale fabricated by her mother to justify being such a neglectful parent. True or not, the story went that, early in their marriage, before Amanda was born, her parents went on vacation in Marrakech. Late one night they wandered the narrow, winding streets far from their hotel and became lost. They encountered a group of young Dutch tourists who invited them into a candle-lit room to smoke hashish with some Moroccan friends. The hashish mixed with whiskey, one thing led to another, and a few hours later her mother regained consciousness to find an Arab man atop her on the floor while her husband smoked in the far corner of the room. Unable to fight the man off, she succumbed until he finished, then angrily fled. Staggering back to their hotel, her husband at her heels, she turned on him, demanding how he could have allowed the man to rape her. Sheepishly, through bloodshot eyes, he had replied that he feared they were going to do what they wanted in any event, and because of his acquiescence they hadn't killed them and in fact the Moroccans had given him a week's supply of hashish and a leather wallet as payment for the use of his wife. Her mother hadn't divorced him immediately, she claimed, because she had just learned she was pregnant with Amanda. But the incident had poisoned their marriage. If it was true—a big if— Amanda couldn't really blame her mother.

In any event, Amanda now had little contact with her mother and none with her father. Marrying Cam would give her not only a husband, but allow them to adopt Astarte as well and then have babies of their own. A family, finally. Now it was all on hold.

And so, in a classic example of hope triumphing over both despair and common sense, she had so far this week procrastinated in notifying the function hall and caterer of the wedding postponement. Another few days should not matter—she had read once that where there is great love there are always miracles. Maybe something miraculous might still come along and save their wedding. She tossed the caterer's phone number aside.

Amanda showered, washing away both the sweat from her morning workout and the griminess she felt from reflecting on her mother's Marrakech ordeal. After dressing, she decided to dive back into her Baphomet research. She sat at the kitchen table, fingers on her left hand sliding across the track pad on her laptop while her right hand alternately grasped a cup of coffee and scrawled notes on a legal pad. She had been focusing on the Templar skull they called Baphomet being a continuation of the pagan Cult of the Head worship, and as she read further about the Cult of the Head she in turn found many connections to the Druids.

For example, at an ancient religious site called Roquepertuse in southern France dating to 500 BC, the skulls of the most learned of the Druids had been preserved and placed in niches within arched, Stonehenge-like stone pillars where they were venerated.

Roquepertuse, Provence, France, c. 500 BC

The Druids believed these preserved skulls possessed visionary powers, powers that would help guide and shepherd the living. Amanda smiled, remembering the Druidic trick involving the magnet and the needle: Had these skulls belonged to ancient charlatans who had wowed the villagers with similar parlor tricks?

The Druid belief in the visionary powers of preserved skulls was also reflected in a practice known as 'death's head at the feast,' in which the Druids placed a skull at the dinner table during important feasts. A lit candle was placed inside the skull, giving the skull the light needed to see into the future. These lit skulls, Amanda read, were the precursors to the lit jack-o-lanterns of Halloween.

The Druids seemed to be like Waldo in the *Where's Waldo* children's books, she mused, popping up in both her research and in Cam's. Sometimes that happened in research, she knew. And it was important not to suffer from something called apophenia, the proclivity to attach meanings to or see patterns in random events or occurrences—sometimes the decorations on a cookie were just that, decorations, and held no secret message. But her instincts told her the Druids were important to understanding Baphomet. Curious, she entered the words Druid and Baphomet in a Google search. Thirty minutes and a full sheet of legal paper later, she had a list of additional connections between the two.

First, the Druids worshiped the pentagram, or five-sided star, as a sign of the godhead; Baphomet, likewise, was usually portrayed with a pentagram on his forehead, or even as a pentagram himself.

Baphomet Depiction

Second, she learned that John the Baptist's executioner was a man named Mug Ruith, an Irish Druid who had somehow found his way to Jerusalem to study with the magician and New Testament figure, Simon Magus. Here she had paused, that quiet but insistent little voice inside her head calling to her: Hadn't she read once that some scholars believed the Baphomet skull to be the head of John the Baptist, the word Baphomet being a derivation of 'Baptism'? Had the Druid executioner Mug Ruith somehow absconded with John the Baptist's skull and brought it back to Europe, where the Templars eventually gained custody of it? It was an intriguing, and potentially explosive, possibility.

Third, she found further support for the conclusion Cam had reached, based on his trip to Washington, that Freemasonry and the ancient Druids were closely related. In a magazine entitled *PS*

Review of Freemasonry, she read, "There is a school of Masonic research holding that Freemasonry is descended from the Druids and other truly ancient Celtic priesthoods of the sun." This sun worship tied things back again to John the Baptist—and by extension to Baphomet: John the Baptist's birthday was celebrated on the summer solstice, the sunniest day of the year.

So what did it all mean? Nothing, yet. But the connections between the Druids and Baphomet reinforced her original theory that the skull the Templars worshiped was part of an ancient pagan Cult of the Head veneration.

As was so often the case with the Templars, it raised an intriguing and troubling question: Why had the so-called Army of the Church engaged in pagan head-worshiping rituals? That the head might have belonged to John the Baptist would explain some of it. But the veneration of Baphomet seemed to go beyond that.

Based on the number of Templars tortured and killed by the Church, their Baphomet worship clearly had hit a nerve at the Vatican. The Church would not move to wipe out an entire army simply because of some overzealous relic worship. Amanda sensed there was something else here, something more fundamental and more incendiary that the Church was trying to keep hidden.

After seven hundred years, the truth might never come to light.

Cam's phone rang as he navigated his SUV through late morning traffic on his way to a Wednesday real estate closing. He had asked an old law school classmate who now worked at the state Department of Environmental Management to snoop around the feds and see what he could learn about the Groton property. "Hey Mitchell," Cam said. "What did you learn?"

"As a kid I learned never to accept candy from strangers, and this week I learned the same applies to real estate. And I learned you're in deep shit."

Cam swallowed. Mitchell was his friend, but there was often a competitive tension between lawyers. Cam's predicament put

Mitchell above him in some judicial pecking order. "Yeah, I got that part already. Can you fill in some details for me?"

"This spill came in as an anonymous tip."

"When?"

"Last November. Some guy called in and said he noticed a blue liquid pooling up on the property."

"How bad is the contamination?"

"Actually, not terrible. It doesn't seem to have made it into the groundwater yet. And the nearby stream is clean."

"So can I get out of this cheap?"

Mitchell snorted. "If by cheap you mean millions rather than tens of millions, yeah. It's not the cleanup itself that's so expensive—though it can be, of course. It's the monitoring and testing and administrative work and legal fees that burn through the cash."

That was good news, at least. Nobody was getting cancer from this. Yet.

"I gotta say, Cam, someone must really be out to get you. This is brilliant, in an evil genius sort of way. But you should never have cut that lock. You know, offer and acceptance and all that first year contracts stuff."

"Yes, Mitchell, I get that." Cam took a deep breath. "Let me guess, One Wing Industries is judgment proof." It was a term that meant a defendant, even if found legally responsible, possessed no assets to pay any judgment against it.

"Pretty much. They're a wholly-owned sub of some larger corporation. Looks like it was created just to purchase Middlesex Semiconductor. Only asset is the land."

"What about the machinery?"

"They claim they scrapped it."

Of course they claimed that. And the EPA was not going to chase machinery across the Atlantic. "Does EPA think One Wing knew about this when they bought the business?" Normally a buyer would examine a property for contamination before the closing, to avoid potential liability.

"No. It doesn't look like they did much due diligence. They didn't care about the factory itself; they were planning to strip it and shut it down anyway. They just wanted to eliminate their competition."

"And the widow?" Cam asked.

"She netted almost a million for the property but the rest of the money, for the sale of the business, went to other stockholders. And most of her money's gone—she owed a chunk for taxes and the rest went to a nursing home."

"So I'm the only fish on the hook."

"Afraid so."

"Any chance they're going to reel me in, hold me up for some pictures and then throw me back?"

Mitchell snorted again. "Doubtful. I think they plan to skin and fry you—butter, garlic, and lemon. The EPA has been spending a ton of money the past few years and not recovering much. These guys know they might be out of a job if they don't start generating some income." He paused. "I don't need to tell you, Cam, don't bother trying to hide any assets. That'll just piss them off. And it opens you up to criminal prosecution for fraud. You don't want to go there."

"What about the fact that I'm sort of innocent in all this? You know, the whole idea of fairness?"

Mitchell guffawed. "Come on, Cam. We're talking about a bunch of lawyers here. Who gives a shit about innocence and fairness?"

Chapter 5

Amanda sang along to a classic rock-and-roll station while Cam drove south on Route 495, the rush hour traffic heavy but still flowing on a cool, bright Thursday morning. Through some connections Cam had tracked down a local woman to give them a tour of the Gungywamp property in Connecticut and, after grabbing sweatshirts and putting Astarte on the school bus, they jumped into the SUV for a day trip.

Amanda had bookmarked some sites on her phone. After an hour of rehashing their financial predicament, she changed the subject. "Enough of that. Time to talk about Gungywamp. As you said, the name is Gaelic for 'Church of the People.' It's a bit like America's Stonehenge, with mysterious stone chambers, rock walls, and other stone features that seem ancient."

"Do the chambers contain alignments?"

"One alignment marks the equinoxes."

Cam nodded. Some chambers marked the summer or winter solstice, others the equinoxes. "The issue, of course, is that the site could have been built by Native Americans, like Astarte said. Or the Colonists."

Amanda waved the comment away. "I think that possibility is a distant third. I found a letter dated 1654 from a fur trader describing stone walls and chambers there—that was before the area was colonized."

He raised an eyebrow. "I agree, 1654 is early."

She continued. "Plus, your Colonists had calendars; they didn't need chambers to mark astronomical events. And most of these chambers have no utilitarian use. I don't think life was so easy in Colonial times that farmers had free time to build play forts for their kids."

Based on what Amanda had seen, the chambers in New England resembled ones in the British Isles. But she understood that resemblance was not enough—in the end the question would be decided by hard evidence. She said, "Another reason some researchers believe ancient Europeans built the site is because a Chi-Rho symbol is carved on one of the stones."

Cam turned. "A Chi-Rho, as in the Christian symbol?"

"Yes." Amanda found a website and read aloud: "The Chi-Rho symbol combines the Greek letters Chi, which is written like an X, and Rho, which is written like a P. These letters make the first two sounds in the word *Christos*, or Christ." She turned her phone. "Here's what it looks like; this is on a church in Europe."

Chi-Rho Symbol

"Well," Cam said, "that would eliminate the Colonists and Native Americans. When was the Chi-Rho in use?"

After a few minutes of surfing, she smiled. "You're going to like this. One of the most famous examples of the Chi-Rho is in something called *The Book of Kells*, an illustrated Gospel book. It contains the most lavish and largest Chi-Rho symbol of the period." She paused for effect. "*The Book of Kells* dates back to sixth century Ireland. Same period as your man Brendan the Navigator."

Cam's head jerked. "You're kidding. That'd be amazing to tie this site back to the Brendan voyage."

She squeezed his thigh, happy to see him animated and excited. "From what I'm reading, the Chi-Rho at Gungywamp has faded, but you can still make it out." She pointed. "There's your exit."

Ten minutes later they pulled down a narrow paved drive not far from the New London Naval Base. A woman in her late twenties wearing sunglasses and a windbreaker marched over to greet them, shaking both their hands with a firm grip. "I'm Shannon Jilligan," she announced. "You'll need comfortable shoes. And tuck your pants into your socks to keep the ticks off of you. Then you can follow me."

Amanda guessed this Jilligan woman, based on her clipped speech, short hairstyle, and upright posture, was in the service, probably at the nearby naval base.

Shannon led them along a path through the woods at a brisk pace, explaining that this property was an old YMCA camp that had been donated to the state. "How did you get interested in this site?" Cam asked.

"I grew up in Putnam County, New York, just across the border from Connecticut about an hour north of the City." She spoke matter-of-factly, chin up and voice steady. She had one of those healthy, wholesome faces that didn't need makeup. "We had stone chambers in the woods that everyone said were built by the Colonists as root cellars. A few years ago I went to Ireland, where my family is from, and I saw dozens of similar chambers. I was stationed here at New London at the time, and when I heard about this site I came out here to take a look around."

"And?" Cam asked.

She looked sideways at him. "And nothing." She shrugged. "You asked how I got interested."

Cam tried again. "I meant, do you think these chambers around New England are related to the ones in Ireland?"

She walked in silence for a few seconds, swinging a walking stick she had picked up along the trail. "I don't think I'm qualified to make that determination. One of the reasons I agreed to show you around is I heard you—both of you—are good researchers. I'd like to hear what you think after showing you the site."

Amanda asked her about the Chi-Rho symbol.

"I can show you that," Shannon said. "In fact, it's just ahead."

119

She stopped alongside a boulder the size of a refrigerator. "This used to be part of a chamber." She gestured to the other rocks that had collapsed around it. "Researchers have identified as many as seven Chi-Rho symbols carved in these ruins."

Cam and Amanda peered closer. Amanda could barely make out a brown-colored P with a diagonal line slashing across from southeast to northwest.

Shannon handed them a piece of paper. "Here's a photo of a rubbing. I'm afraid the carving has faded."

Gungywamp Chi-Rho Rubbing

Amanda and Cam studied the rubbing. Amanda knew how difficult it was to work with centuries-old carvings. Over time, they faded—simple as that. "It looks like one of the X lines of the Chi is missing," Cam said. "The upper right stem."

"Not missing. They just incorporated it into the vertical line of the Rho, or the P," Amanda replied.

"Makes sense. You're carving into stone, which is never easy, so you might abbreviate a bit."

"That's one of the things that always bothered me," Shannon said. "Would they really modify a religious symbol like that?"

"Actually, it happened all the time," Amanda said. "I was looking at Chi-Rho symbols on our drive down today and I found seven or eight different versions. Different groups make minor modifications and, over the years, those modifications became magnified. I think it would be more surprising if a Chi-Rho symbol in Constantinople was identical to one in Ireland, over a thousand miles away." Amanda continued. "Think about all the different versions of the cross—in addition to the traditional Latin cross, there's a Celtic cross with a ring around it, the Templar's splayed cross, the Cross of Lorraine, the three-barred cross, the Sinclair scalloped cross, and probably a dozen others. But they all signify the same thing."

Shannon nodded, seemingly satisfied. She led them along, stopping to inspect a few structures that were clearly Colonial, before coming upon a stone chamber.

Cam grinned as Amanda snapped a shot. "A little sister to our girl in Groton," he said.

Gungywamp Chamber

They ducked into the chamber and Shannon pointed out a square hole high on the back wall. "On the equinoxes, the sun shines through that opening and illuminates a white quartz stone by the entryway."

Shannon continued. "There's also a winter solstice illumination." She stood in the doorway of the chamber, facing out, and pointed diagonally off to her right. "On December 21 the sun comes up in the southeastern sky and illuminates the same white quartz stone." She pointed with her left hand to a low spot just inside the chamber entryway.

Amanda and Cam exchanged a glance; the second alignment made it even more likely the chamber was built by some pagan, sun-worshiping culture. "We didn't know about the winter solstice alignment," Cam said.

Shannon nodded. "Most people don't. There's an excellent researcher from Yale who documents all this stuff, but most of the locals still insist Gungywamp is Colonial."

"Wait," Amanda said, "there's a professor from Yale researching this? I thought it was taboo in academia to study pre-Columbian contact."

"He got his masters degree from Yale in archeology, but he's not a professor there," Shannon replied. "Anyway, like I said, most of the people down here don't listen to him because they're convinced this is all Colonial."

Cam shook his head. "Yeah, can't be having smart people with master's degrees from Yale weighing in on this stuff."

They spent twenty minutes examining the chamber, Amanda again struck by the similarities between it and its British Isles counterparts, before Shannon led them up a slight rise to a flattened area marked by a circular formation of flat-lying stones. "We think this is an old mill of some type," Shannon said. "In Colonial times it was probably used to tan sheepskin to make vellum. There was probably a middle post sticking up from the ground, and some kind of farm animal would walk in a circle outside the ring to power the operation."

Gungywamp Stone Circle

As Cam and Amanda inspected the stones, Shannon said in a firm voice: "But it could be older than that."

Cam stood straight and eyed her, his lawyer's training tuned-in to the change in her tone. "What makes you say that?"

"A researcher named Whittall carbon-dated some charcoal from inside the mill back in the nineties." She paused. "The date came back around 550 AD. He thought the site was originally some kind of sacrificial alter."

A jolt of energy surged up Amanda's spine. She eyed Cam; he swallowed, his face pale and frozen.

"Are you sure of that date?" he breathed. The date was contemporaneous with Brendan the Navigator's voyage to America. And the Druids often sacrificed animals and sometimes even humans to their gods.

Shannon nodded, holding his glance. She sensed the importance of the find. "Yes, certain."

Researcher Jim Whittall had died in the late 1990s, but both Amanda and Cam knew of his work; he was as thorough and well-respected as any researcher of his era.

After a few seconds, Amanda filled the silence. "If it was charcoal, couldn't it have been Native American?"

Shannon shook her head. "That's the strange thing. The Pequot believe this land is haunted. I've spoken to a few of the tribal elders and they say there is no way their ancestors would come near this land, never mind stopp to make a fire." Shannon took a deep breath. "You may sense my hesitancy," she said. "Most of the people around here who study this site think it's either Colonial or Native American. The rest of us keep our mouths closed." She glanced back and forth between Cam and Amanda, holding their eyes. "But I can't get that 550 AD date out of my head. If it wasn't the Pequot, and obviously couldn't have been the Colonists, who else could it be?"

The question was rhetorical, and all three of them let it hang in the air. They made small talk as Shannon led them back to the parking area. Amanda thanked their guide, and Cam shook her hand. "Hey," Cam said, "by the way, why do the Pequot think this land is haunted?"

Shannon smiled, her first real smile of the day. "Apparently we are sitting on a geological fault line. When the tectonic pressure builds, strange blue lights come floating out of the ground like ghosts. It still happens sometimes if you come here at night."

Amanda's hand involuntarily went to her heart. "Oh my God, Cam. The Druids." She swallowed. As they had explained to Astarte, the Druids often built chambers around these earthquake lights. "The Druids really were here."

Bartol had picked an interesting second day to track Cameron Thorne. His landlady sometimes let him borrow her car to pick up groceries for both of them, not knowing of course that he didn't have a license. He had awoken early, called in sick, and driven to Westford to watch Thorne's home. He had not expected to be driving all the way to Connecticut.

Nor had he expected someone else also to be tracking Thorne.

Bartol crouched low behind the stone wall near the parking lot of the Gungywamp site and peered through his binoculars, careful to make sure the sun did not reflect off its lenses. Thorne, his fiancée, and a woman guiding them had wandered deep into the woods. Bartol had hung back on the off chance they had been followed and watched with surprise as a man in dark pants and windbreaker stalked them, darting behind trees and otherwise keeping himself out of sight. Now, an hour later, the man, fit and athletic, was jogging toward him back to the parking area, apparently far ahead of the returning Thorne and company.

Bartol smiled. The follower never expected to be followed.

Bartol burrowed himself deep into the nook of the stone wall, only a few car lengths from the dirt parking area, glad he had taken the precaution of hiding his landlady's car on a logging trail a few hundred yards away. The man pulled out a cell phone when he reached his car. Bartol, who had positioned himself downwind, cupped his ear, a clichéd gesture that actually did improve hearing.

"Raptor here, checking in. Thorne is looking at another stone chamber, like the one in Groton." Bartol detected a bit of an accent. "I have no idea what any of this has to do with Zuberi Youssef." A pause. "Okay, I'll stay on him. Shalom, Moshe."

Bartol's gut clenched. The guy was definitely following Thorne. And if he was checking in, he was part of a formalized chain of command. Moshe was a Jewish name, Raptor a field agent's code name, and Shalom a Hebrew greeting. And this Raptor had mentioned some guy with an Arab name. The pieces could fit: Was it possible Raptor worked for the Mossad? Bartol racked his brain: *Only reason for the Mossad to care about Thorne is because they want to silence him.* He felt the old, familiar surge of adrenaline heightening his senses and tightening his muscles. *Not on my watch.*

Crawling, keeping the car between himself and the agent, he maneuvered closer. The agent, Raptor, had completed his call and leaned against the rear trunk of his car smoking a cigarette. Still crawling, the smoke helping him ensure he stayed downwind of the agent, Bartol approached silently. Ten seconds later he pulled himself under the agent's sedan. He felt for the knife in the sheath on his calf, Raptor's all-terrain shoes and the bottom of his dark trousers silhouetted only a few feet away.

Knife between his teeth, Bartol inched closer to the rear of the car, knowing that even the slightest noise would alert the agent and probably result in death to Bartol. Sweat dripped into his eyes; he blinked it away, took a deep breath, and pulled himself to within a foot of the agent's legs. *Now.* Removing the knife from his mouth, he slashed upwards, across the back of the agent's right knee. The man screamed and toppled, spinning as he did so, his face falling to within inches of Bartol's.

The agent's eyes met Bartol's for a split second, surprise turning to fear turning to understanding. Bartol knew that after understanding would come some kind of defensive maneuver. He never let it get that far. Thrusting, he pierced the agent's jugular, twisting and slicing as he had been trained.

Bartol closed his eyes as the agent's blood sprayed from the wound and splattered his face. It had been a long time since he killed a man. It was never a thing to celebrate. But it sometimes was a thing to be proud of.

The Issac Question

Zuberi stopped to catch his breath and waited for his wife to catch up. The late afternoon sun had dipped low on the horizon, bathing Edinburgh in a soft golden glow. He had never viewed the city from up here, from the desolate crags of Holyrood Park. In the distance Edinburgh Castle stood, bastion-like, on a matching crag. The city rested in the middle, nestled between the twin volcanic protrusions. From this high angle Edinburgh resembled a medieval dragon, with the Castle the raised head, the city proper the notched backbone, and Holyrood Park the long, elevated, spiked tail.

"Wait while I take a picture, Zuberi," Carrington said, her plain, round face glistening with sweat. For six years she had tried to get him to hike these hills. She clicked a few shots. "It's a wonderful view. Do you want to climb all the way to the summit?"

He shook his head. This was a business trip, not a picnic. "Not today. I think we have not the time." The famous Arthur's Seat, the pinnacle of the stony hill, was a popular destination for tourists and residents alike. "I want to examine ruins."

She pointed. "We need to go off the trail a bit. St. Anthony's chapel is on the other side of that rock formation. I haven't seen it since I was a young lass." If she was disappointed with his response, she did a good job of hiding it. When he married her he had not expected her to be such a loyal and useful partner in his business ventures.

He had learned in business that the best way to cement loyalty was to make underlings feel important—even more than money and prestige, the feeling of being valued was the primary factor in determining an employee's job satisfaction. The same probably held true in his marriage. He asked a question to which he already knew the answer: "Tell me again history of ruins?"

Carrington took a deep breath. "No one is certain of the construction date, but local legend is that the chapel was built by the Templars, probably after they had been outlawed in 1307. Records show extensive repair work done in 1426, so the structure must have been many decades old already by then."

Zuberi nodded. After leaving Brandeis last week he had driven to Newport, Rhode Island to view the Newport Tower. If the Tower had indeed been constructed in the late 1300s by remnant

Templars associated with Prince Henry Sinclair, then it stood to reason the Tower's architecture would match contemporaneous structures in the Edinburgh area, near the Sinclair home of Roslin. "Here is picture of Newport Tower," he said, handing her his phone.

Newport Tower, Newport, RI

Carrington leaned in and furrowed her brow. She was somewhat of an expert on ancient castles and other stone structures. "Yes, I'm familiar with this. I can't believe the Americans think their Colonists built it. It is clearly Romanesque. Early Americans never built in that style."

"I agree. But if we wish to rewrite history, and have your Sinclair ancestors replace Columbus, we need strong evidence."

They rounded a rise and the chapel ruins rose up before them.

"What a spot," Carrington breathed. The chapel, or what was left of it, stood on the precipice of a cliff face. Below it, encircled by a ribbon of lush green vegetation, a sky-blue lake twinkled in the sunshine while, in the distance, beyond the city, the gray, angry waters of the North Sea estuary known as the River Forth swirled. Egypt possessed some picturesque landscapes, but nothing compared to the stunning, varied beauty of Scotland. Zuberi took it in for a few seconds, exhaled, and focused on the task at hand.

"Notice," he pointed. "The architecture of archway is same as Newport Tower." He gestured from the ruins to the close-up of the archway pictured on his phone.

Saint Anthony's Chapel   Newport Tower

"I see that," Carrington replied.

"And windows are similar also, with a single slab as a lintel and the other three sides rough," he added.

Saint Anthony's Chapel   Newport Tower

She again concurred. And she surprised him with additional information. "Did you know that there are ruins of a medieval church on the Orkney Islands that are similar to this architecture as well?"

"No, my wife, I did not." But he did know that in the late 1300s the Sinclair family ruled not only in Roslin, outside of

128

Edinburgh, but also a couple hundred miles north in the Orkney Islands off the northern tip of Scotland.

She searched through her phone. "I downloaded these. I thought you might wish to see them. In fact, this Eynhallow Church was built by Abbot Lawrence, himself a Sinclair."

Eynhallow Church, Orkney Islands, Scotland

The archway, especially, was a close match. "Excellent," he breathed. Another compelling piece of architectural evidence tying the Newport Tower to the Sinclair family. His wife was proving to be a valuable ally. He shared with her more information. "There is fireplace in Newport Tower. I think this means it could not be grist mill because of fire danger."

She nodded and surprised him yet again. "The fireplace flue is like devil horns; it goes up on two sides. That is a feature unique to Scottish architecture of the late 14th century."

He grinned. "Yes? Is that so?" More compelling evidence.

They spent another twenty minutes wandering among the ruins before Zuberi suggested they head down. It had been a productive visit, made even more so by Carrington's insights into the Orkney ruins and the Newport Tower fireplace flue. He made a spontaneous decision. "My wife," he said, "you have given great service to my business these months. In the morning I will instruct my banker to transfer half a million pounds to your account." They had an ironclad prenuptial agreement which gave her no claim to his fortune; she received only enough money to run the household, plus a small allowance. This gift would reward her for her service and loyalty.

She flushed. "Thank you, Zuberi." She took his good arm as they walked, obviously pleased by his generosity. "I assume you will send all this new information to Cameron?"

"Yes."

"We both agree he is the right man for the job. But how can we be assured he will reach the conclusions we want him to?" She gazed out over the city, toward Roslin to the south.

"First reason, because these conclusions are truth and Thorne is smart man." Zuberi paused.

"And the second reason?"

He exhaled. "The second reason is still a seed in ground. I will show to you when she blooms as beautiful flower."

Amanda had a twenty minute drive to work as a part-time museum curator in historic Concord, halfway between Westford and Boston. She had made the drive hundreds of times, her car almost knowing the way itself. As she navigated amid Friday morning suburban traffic she thought about the Groton chamber and the Gungywamp site and her research on the Cult of the Head—the thread that seemed to tie everything together was the ancient Druids. Who were they? Where did they come from originally? And what was their connection, if any, to the Templars and Freemasons?

Almost as if he were reading her mind, Cam called and exclaimed, "You need to meet me for lunch. There's a place in Lowell called Druid Hill. It has standing stones that line up to mark a bunch of astronomical alignments."

She was glad to hear the excitement in his voice after a tough week. "In Lowell?" The old mill city was only ten miles from Westford. "How come we haven't heard of this already?"

"I don't know. I just stumbled upon it by accident. I was looking at some of Whittall's old research—I figured if he studied

Gungywamp he might know of other Druid sites in New England. Listen to what he said about Druid Hill: 'There I saw a sight I had not seen since my travels in the British Isles. Situated on a mound were weathered megalithic stones. I was filled with disbelief—it just couldn't be—Western Europe, yes, but here in Massachusetts—no. The reality of the scene was astonishing.'"

"And it's still standing?"

"Yeah, apparently in a park next to a baseball field."

"What's the history of the land?"

"It first shows up on maps in the mid-1600s as an Indian reservation. After that it was used as farmland. As far as the old-timers remember, the standing stones have always been there." He paused. "Oh, and one more thing: It's a short walk from the Merrimack River."

Many of the ancient sites in New England were located along the Merrimack, which was presumably used as a main highway for explorers. "All right, you've convinced me. Lunch it is, one o'clock." She was only scheduled to work half a day anyway. "I'll expect something yummy."

"Deal. What do you want?"

"Surprise me. But don't dream of showing up without chocolate."

♀ ✠ ⬙

Tamara picked at her salad, watching a pair of blue jays chase each other around the branches of the maple tree outside her window as she lunched. Normally she loved the songs of spring—chirping birds, wind chimes, a baseball game on the radio, even a lawnmower in the distance. But today it all sounded tinny and hollow.

She forced herself to swallow a slice of cucumber. It had been twenty-four hours and Raptor had not returned from his assignment tracking Cameron Thorne in Connecticut. She didn't even know his real name. But she feared he would not be chirping this spring, or any other.

Moshe had been called to a morning meeting in Boston at the Israeli consulate in the Park Plaza hotel. They all assumed the worst.

She tossed her fork into the salad. None of it made any sense. Raptor followed Thorne and his fiancée and a local researcher into the woods, returned to the parking lot ahead of them, then … nothing. Even if Thorne had sensed he was being followed, there was little chance he would—or could—react by killing Raptor. Especially with witnesses around…

Moshe barged in without knocking, interrupting her thoughts. He bulled his way over, dropped into a chair and scratched at his scalp. "Let me know if my nose starts bleeding."

"Why?"

"That's how far up my ass the bureau chief put his foot."

She bit her lip. Moshe's crudeness was actually well down the list of his annoying habits. "No word from Raptor, I take it." He was someone's son, maybe someone's husband or boyfriend or even father. And he would not be home for Shabbat, or the High Holidays, or birthdays. It was worse for the survivors. She knew, because she was one. It had been more than eight years since her husband had gone out on patrol and not returned.

"Nothing. He called in around eleven. Routine surveillance." Moshe wiped his nose on his sleeve. "Then nothing."

Tamara felt bad for Moshe. He had trained Raptor, and apparently Raptor was one of the few friends Moshe had. "Could Thorne have done it?"

"I don't see how. Or why. The girl, Shannon Jilligan, says when she drove away they were getting in their car to leave. And nobody else was around."

"She's military?"

"Yup. Exemplary record." He shrugged. "I don't think it was Thorne."

"But it could have been. Raptor could have surprised them, maybe let his guard down, Thorne feels threatened…" She threw up her hands.

"It's possible."

"And even if he didn't do it himself, that doesn't mean it didn't have anything to do with him."

"Right. Which leads us back to Zuberi Youssef."

"Again, why?"

Moshe shrugged again. "That's the thing about Youssef. You never know why until it's too late."

Cam left the office just after noon, made stops at a local fish market and bakery and wound his way across the Merrimack River to the Pawtucketville neighborhood of Lowell. He found the park on a hill tucked behind a middle school.

Amanda pulled into the lot behind him. He admired her toned body as she sauntered over; he greeted her with a kiss and shook a brown paper bag at her. "Lobster rolls and a chocolate chip cookie."

She kissed him a second time. "Well played. But it *is* a bit sad."

"What?"

She smiled and widened her eyes. "We used to meet at lunch for a quickie. Now we go looking at rocks."

Cam took her hand and tugged her back toward the cars with exaggerated urgency. "The damn rocks can wait," he joked. Amanda had responded to his despondency this week with extra flirtatiousness, and it had helped lift his spirits.

Still holding hands, they walked up a path to a raised grassy area adjacent to a baseball field. The site consisted of a dozen monoliths, or standing stones, arranged on a teardrop-shaped raised mound. The stones averaged two feet in height, all of them imbedded in the ground so that they stood upright rather than in a more naturally-occurring recumbent position. The teardrop was oriented on the east-west axis, with a group of smaller stones clustered at the narrower, eastern end of the raised mound and three larger stones spaced evenly at the wide end.

They studied the site for a few seconds. Amanda broke the silence. "I'll be jiggered, Cam, this looks just like the stone circles in Britain."

"That's what Whittall said," Cam replied, "only without the jiggered part."

She pointed to the middle standing stone. "See the angle on the top here? The setting sun follows it, almost like a ball rolling down a slope."

Druid Hill Standing Stone, Lowell, MA

Cam continued, "According to Whittall, all these stones mark various astronomical events—equinoxes, solstices, cross-quarter days." He smiled. "But you guessed that already."

"What about the weathering of these stones. They look old."

"A geologist who studied them says they've been weathering in their upright position for at least a thousand years."

"Bloody hell," she said. "How many other sites are there out there that we don't know about?"

"And how many have been plowed over or destroyed?"

Amanda wandered to the narrow end of the teardrop and dropped to her knees, peering back toward the three larger stones. "Cam, I think there are some raised shapes in the ground in the middle of the circle."

He joined her. "You're right. They're not very high, but I think I see a circle and also maybe a crescent."

"That's exactly what it is, Cam—sun and moon symbols." She stood, straightened her denim skirt and wiped the dirt and grass from her knees. "Do you have a pen and paper? I want to sketch this."

He handed her his rucksack. "Okay, but while you sketch, take off your shoes."

"Nice try, cowboy." She shook her head. "But I'm not going to rut with you here in a park, even for a chocolate chip cookie."

He chuckled. "When on Druid Hill, do as the Druids do."

"Um, no."

"Trust me. Take off your shoes. They say you can feel the earth's energy here."

Amanda tilted her head. "Not a bad line, I have to admit. Okay then." She kicked off her flats. "Do I need to remove my panties also?"

He grinned back at her. "These sites," he said, "were almost always built along lines where the earth's energy was concentrated."

As he spoke, she walked slowly in a circle. "These energy lines were called ley lines," she said.

"Of course they were," he smiled. "What better place for the Druids to get laid?"

Amanda began to draw while he paced around, now barefoot himself. He thought he felt a tingling along the soles of his feet, but that could have just been him thinking about Amanda casting aside her panties.

A few minutes later Amanda handed him her drawing.

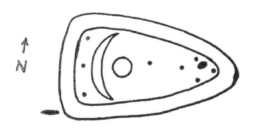

Druid Hill Stone Circle, Lowell, MA

"Nice," Cam said, folding it carefully. "Looks like we're going to be busy on the summer solstice—we need to check out both this site and our chamber, sunrise and sunset."

She took his arm. "I'm looking forward more to our chamber." She leaned into him, her breast against his bicep. "It offers much better privacy."

After their lunch at Druid Hill, Amanda returned home while Cam continued on to the office. She had an hour before Astarte got off the bus, which she planned to fill with more Baphomet research. The large manila envelope in their mailbox changed those plans.

The envelope was addressed to her, with thick, red-inked handwriting across the bottom: "PERSONAL and CONFIDENTIAL." She ripped the envelope open with some trepidation. A handful of photos tumbled out. *What the ...?*

She shuffled through the pictures. Cameron seated at a bar with a young woman with long red hair. Cam and the woman, this time with their hands touching. This time shot from behind, walking arm-in-arm down a hotel hallway. Cam inserting a key card into a door with the red-haired woman leaning against the doorframe, cleavage a few inches from Cam's face.

Blood rushed to Amanda's cheeks as she unfolded the single piece of notebook paper that had encircled the photos. Her hands shook as she read the note. *"I had my girlfriend followed last weekend because I thought she was cheating on me. These pictures were taken at a hotel near Reagan Airport last Saturday night."* Amanda's vision blurred; she blinked and refocused. *"I identified the guy based on the credit card receipt at the bar. I found his name in her college yearbook—they went to school together. Then I found you on the Internet. I thought you should know."*

She put a hand against the wall to steady herself and sank to the floor in the front hallway. At some point Venus arrived to snuggle her chin on Amanda's lap, but a cold darkness had clenched Amanda's heart and the heart, in turn, had pumped the numbing gloom through her body like deadening venom. Time passed as if in a dream. Finally reality returned, and with it the icy feeling in her chest. *This. Is. Not. Happening.* Eyes closed and fists clenched, she exhaled a long, bitter breath and forced herself to focus and analyze.

Had Cam really cheated on her? She gathered the photos, which had scattered when she dropped them, and peered at them again. No doubt the man at the bar was Cam. And he had indeed been at an airport hotel in Washington Saturday night. She had never suspected him before, but what other explanation could there be? She knew he had been a bit of a player before she met him— had old habits been hard to break? And if it happened once, had it happened before? No way could she marry a man she did not trust. Thoughts of her mother, and what her father had done to her in Marrakech, filled her mind…

And then it hit her. Could she have been such a fool? Had Cam used the Superfund mess as an excuse to delay the wedding? Maybe he wasn't ready yet, wasn't sure he really wanted to get married. Her eyes pooled. Is that what this was all about? In a world where nothing seemed to make any sense, even the outlandish became possible…

"Bloody hell," she sobbed. "I never thought I'd become *that* woman."

The sun on his face, Bartol stood on his ladder, slathering paint on the roof soffit and planning his next moves as he stared at the Norumbega stone tower in the distance. Friday was turning out to be no different than Wednesday. After killing a Mossad agent on Thursday, that was probably a good thing.

But things were different, no doubt. He had entered the battle, eliminated an enemy soldier. Which meant he was now in danger himself. He had poked a particular nasty nest of wasps—the Mossad would not rest until Raptor's death had been avenged.

They had probably found the agent by now. Wearing gloves to avoid leaving prints, Bartol had hoisted Raptor's lifeless body into the trunk of the Israeli's car, kicked dirt over the puddle of blood, driven the car to a nearby office park (being careful to stay far from any security cameras), jogged back to retrieve his landlady's vehicle, and—driving within the speed limit—returned to the North End by early afternoon with a few bags of groceries and a full tank of gas. It would be difficult to tie him to Raptor's death. In many ways, he did not even exist.

But that was not good enough. Bartol himself would now be among the hunted, which meant he needed to keep moving. The Mossad might somehow track his landlady's car; he needed to be long gone if they did. And, if he was going to fight for Thorne, he needed to be closer to him. The city of Lowell was close to Westford and might offer the needed urban anonymity, but it would take a few weeks to find the right situation. In the meantime he would need shelter. Someplace private and secluded, where he could leave his belongings during the day and return at night.

He knew the perfect place. A place where the energy of his ancestors flowed, where the memory of their greatness screamed out to the world even today. And it was only fitting that Thorne provide housing for his soldier.

Cam arrived home Friday late afternoon to a quiet house. Even Venus, who usually greeted him at the door, seemed to be absent. Only after he closed the door and yelled out did the dog slink out to greet him.

"What's wrong, girl? And where's Amanda and Astarte?" His neck tingled. Amanda's car sat in the driveway. He pushed through the house and looked out on the rear deck. Nothing. "Amanda?" he called.

Venus nosed him and began to trot away, looking back to see if he was following. The dog led him upstairs to the master bedroom, lights off and shades drawn. In the shadows he made out the shape of Amanda sitting on the floor, her back against the far wall of the room.

"Amanda," he stammered. "Are you okay?" He rushed toward her, freezing halfway at the coldness in her reddened eyes.

"No, Cameron, I most certainly am not." She tossed a few photographs at him. "And please, no lies."

"What?" Confused and alarmed, he dropped to his knees to examine the photos. Himself at a bar. Some woman with long red hair next to him. The two of them walking down a hotel corridor, another of them together by a hotel door. "Amanda, honey, I don't know what to say," he stammered.

"There's a note with it," she said, tossing it over.

He read the ugly words, his face flushing. He was under attack again. Just like with the deed to the Superfund property. But these attacks were not physical, they were psychological. Attacks on his happiness, on his psyche, on his family.

He dropped to a sitting position, took a deep breath and focused his eyes on Amanda's. "I don't know where these pictures came from. I think I recognize the woman at the bar from the Washington hotel last weekend. But no way did I bring her back to my room. I barely even talked to her—she reached over one time, tapped me on the wrist and asked me to pass her a napkin. But that was it. I had one beer, watched the hockey game on the TV and went up to bed." He sighed. "Alone, obviously."

Amanda pointed her chin at the photos. "She's with you, Cameron. Twice. And the boyfriend says you knew each other from college. Is this some old girlfriend?"

He shook his head. *This can't be happening.* "No. I have no idea who this woman even is." Cam knew trust was a big issue for Amanda, based on the stories she had told about her father's behavior in Marrakech. He studied the photos again, desperately. *There.* "Look, in both these shots in the hallway you can't even see my face."

Amanda rolled her eyes. "It's the same bloody clothes, Cam. Same shirt, blue jeans, same shoes." She again jutted her chin at the photos. "I know. I've been studying the blasted things for the past hour."

A wave of panic constrained his chest; he fought to breathe. *I can't lose her.* "Amanda, listen, that's not me." He gasped.

"Someone must have set me up. The photo's been doctored, or maybe they used a body double. But that's not me."

"I so much want to believe you, Cameron," she said, eyes closed and shoulders slumped. "More than I've ever wanted to believe anything in my life. But, well ... you know," she sobbed.

He nodded, exhaled and slid toward her, tears pooling in his eyes. She froze him, again, with a sharp glance.

"I'm not a bloody fool," she breathed. "Look. At. These. Pictures."

He lowered his voice. This shouldn't be so hard—they were both in love and they both wanted the pictures to be fakes. "I swear, Amanda, they're fakes. That's not me in the hallway. I'm not going to betray you—"

She interjected. "This has nothing to do with my parents, Cam. This has to do with you. With us."

Cam began to argue the point but caught himself.

She sniffled. "You're always talking about Occam's Razor, that the simplest solution is usually the correct one." She raised her chin. "But now you're asking me to buy into some convoluted conspiracy theory involving body doubles and unseen enemies and—"

He cut her off. "That's right. The same unseen enemies who deeded me a Superfund site."

"So what is this, some kind of blackmail?"

"Yes," he said. "I think it is."

"Then you're not thinking straight," she said, glaring at him. "How is this blackmail? They sent the pictures to *me*, not you."

He swallowed. She had a point. A blackmailer would have sent them to him, with a note threatening to share them with Amanda if he did not comply with their demands.

They sat together, a few feet apart, the only sound being Amanda's quiet sobs. His heart hurt to see her like this. He slowly reached his hand out toward her knee, but she jerked away.

"I need time," she said. "And distance."

How could this be happening? A week ago they were planning a wedding, as happy as any couple could be. Now his world was crumbling. "How much distance?" he stammered.

She shook her head three or four times, her chin on her chest. "I don't know. You should sleep in the basement. And that might not be far enough."

He had almost drowned once as a boy, the water numbing him as it filled his lungs and ears and pores. He felt the same way now, a heavy, stifling, deadening weight closing in on him from all directions. "Amanda," he whispered, in what he sensed was his last chance to reach her. "I can prove to you I'm innocent. But to do that I need to figure out who these unseen enemies are, who sent these pictures, who it is that wants to stop our research. And to do *that* I need your help—I can't do it myself. I know you feel like a victim here … and I get that … but without your help I can't do this."

She looked up at him, her green eyes narrowed in anger. "I'm supposed to help you prove to me that you didn't cheat on me." She half-laughed. "That's rich."

He didn't know what to say. He didn't know what to do. And he didn't have any idea who could have sent the goddamn pictures.

It didn't take Cam long to realize he and sleep would be strangers that night. He put Venus on her leash, grabbed a six-pack of Sam Adams from the fridge, threw on a sweatshirt, and shuffled out to the end of the dock.

Normally the lake soothed him, but tonight it seemed like just another unseen adversary. The waves lopped against the shore, eroding the foundation of his once-solid life. The spring breeze bit into him, bringing with it an odd, swampy smell. And the stars stared down at him like millions of enemy spies, each planning a sneak attack. Even Venus, normally so loyal, seemed to be eyeing him with questioning eyes, wondering if he had indeed betrayed Amanda…

He chugged a beer. But even that didn't help. Instead of numbing him it just gave him the hiccups.

Stripping to his boxers, he dove off the end of the dock, the frigid waters jolting him. He descended, forcing himself to stay underwater, allowing the lake to wash away his misery and the cold to clear his head. He surfaced twenty yards from the dock to the sound of Venus' concerned bark. *At least she still cares.*

But as he turned toward the dog, he realized she was not looking at him. Rather she sniffed at the air, her nose pointed to the wooded area next to his house. Cam peered into the darkness himself. Another unseen enemy, or just a stray cat?

He cursed. Either he was getting paranoid, or—as the cliché went—someone truly was out to get him.

Chapter 6

The better part of a week had passed, with Cam and Amanda settling into an unsettled existence. She had reluctantly agreed to help him solve the mystery of the Superfund sting which, hopefully, would reveal who sent the pictures. "I owe you the chance to prove those pictures are fake," she had said, the morning after confronting him. "And I owe it to myself, and to Astarte, to try to keep this family together if at all possible."

But it had been a tough six days, the only benefit being that he had plenty of time to organize and outline his research during his exile to the basement. Today, Thursday, he was stuck in Boston, sitting around a conference room table on the thirty-second floor of a high-rise, missing Astarte's soccer game while a team of environmental litigation attorneys ordered take-out dinner on his dime. It was a strange custom in the practice of law—lawyers charging hundreds of dollars an hour routinely also billed their clients for meals. As if they wouldn't have eaten were it not for the case they were working on. Even worse was the time they were wasting discussing the dinner order. Cam tried not to watch the clock: The partner billed at $450 per hour, the associate at $275, and the paralegal at $90. They had spent seven minutes perusing the menu which, Cam calculated in his head, had just cost him a hundred bucks. And that was without even paying for the food.

At this rate they would eat through the $20,000 retainer he had given them before the month was out. Not that Cam had any real choice. There were only a few firms in the city with the experience to battle the EPA, and none of them was cheap. In the end it probably didn't matter—he could pay the lawyers, or he could pay the government, but either way he was unlikely to walk away with anything.

They finally placed the order and refocused on his case. Cam and Nina, the partner, had worked together at a buttoned-down large firm as a first job out of law school fifteen years ago. Nina, a lesbian activist, had fit in like a giraffe grazing with a herd of cattle. Cam had been one of the few young lawyers to befriend her; they both left the firm after a few years, but had remained friends since. Nina turned to the associate, a heavy-set Asian man in his late twenties. "Jimmy, did you hear back from your sister?" His sister worked for the EPA as an analyst, and Nina was hoping to use the connection to appeal to their sense of fairness in this case.

"She called an hour ago. I didn't have much luck. For some reason they're playing hardball on this one."

Cam tossed his pen onto the table. "So much for professional courtesy."

Nina ran a hand through her long, dark, curly hair. "All right then. Hardball it is. I think our strongest defense is the one you came up with, Cam."

He had done more research into One Wing Industries. As a foreign corporation, the entity was required to register to do business in Massachusetts with the state's Corporations Division. But it had not done so. Technically, therefore, none of its actions had been legal. "You think you can set aside the land conveyance?" Cam asked.

"Honestly, no. You're the real estate expert, but my understanding of the law is that this clouds your title to the property, but does not void it."

Cam nodded. "I think you're right."

"But it does give us some leverage. If they think you might walk away completely, that might make them stop acting like a bunch of assholes."

"Okay. Let's file suit to set aside the conveyance." It felt good to have some kind of plan of action. Everything in his life was in complete turmoil; at least filing suit might eventually lead to some kind of resolution.

"It's not going to be cheap, Cam."

He shrugged. "At this point, either you guys get my money or the government gets it. In fact, feel free to make them think you're overcharging me." He smiled ruefully. "Maybe they'll start to negotiate once they see you driving a flashy new car."

Cam sat in traffic on the Zakim Bridge after finally leaving his lawyer's office. It was close to seven on Thursday evening—he had missed Astarte's soccer game so was in no rush to get home. Amanda and he had tried to keep the family routine unchanged for Astarte's sake, but their home—once ringing with laughter—had turned cold and austere. Even Venus seemed to notice.

"When rush hour traffic is preferable to dinner with the family, things really suck," he murmured. He eyed the harbor in the distance—bad as things were, at least he wasn't still in that dumpster.

Five minutes later his cell rang. The detective agency he had hired to analyze the photos. "This is Cam."

"Mr. Thorne, we have the results back on those images."

"And?"

"Inconclusive. They might have been doctored, but we can't say for sure. If they were altered, the work was done by someone fairly sophisticated."

"Can you email us your report?"

"Email to both addresses?"

In an effort to be fully transparent, he had given the agency Amanda's email as well. "Yes, both addresses." Not that it would help much. But the way things had been going for him lately, 'inconclusive' qualified as good news.

Amanda nibbled on her salad while Astarte worked on her third slice of pizza. Cam was stuck in traffic and told them to eat without him. "Hungry tonight, huh?"

The girl nodded. "It was a long game."

Amanda studied her across the kitchen table. She was growing again. And like all thoughts and feelings and realizations over the past week, this observation boomeranged right back to Cameron. Would Amanda be around to watch Astarte grow? Would the court allow the adoption if Amanda and Cam split up? And would Amanda have to fight Cam for custody of the girl if so? Amanda stabbed at a tomato, cursing as it squirted away and bounced to the floor where Venus sucked it up.

"It's just a tomato, Mum," Astarte said.

Amanda exhaled. "I'm sorry. I have a headache."

"Is that why Campadre is sleeping in the basement?"

Amanda took a bite to buy a few seconds. "Yes, honey. I've not been sleeping well because of Cameron's snoring, which is making the headaches worse."

An email chimed on her tablet, saving her from a follow-up question. The report from the detective agency. Amanda's eyes raced across it, hoping it contained the lifeline she so desperately wanted. "Blah, blah, blah," she murmured, sinking back in her chair.

"What?" Astarte asked.

"Nothing. Have your dessert and then run up to shower."

In retrospect, Amanda should have chosen the experts to examine the photos. This report was inconclusive, as useless as a chocolate teapot. If the photos were real, as she had to assume, Cam had a vested interest in using an unsophisticated agency that would reach an inconclusive verdict rather than a proficient one that might decree the photos authentic.

So they were no closer to a resolution. She had agreed to help him find his—or their—unseen enemies. She owed him that much. She owed *them* that much. If perchance he was telling the truth, however remote that possibility might be, the stakes were such that she needed to give him the opportunity to prove it.

Amanda was fairly certain he had never cheated before. But she would not be one of those women who stubbornly believed it was not happening to her. First his desire to postpone the wedding. Then his sudden decision to stay overnight in Washington. Then the incriminating pictures. She sighed. She really did have a headache.

Cam awoke Friday looking forward to his day for the first time all week. He was done with the lawyers for now, which meant he could turn back to his research and, more importantly, the question of who had decided to make him their personal pin cushion. The theory that someone would deed him the property and then send the photos as a way to stop or somehow influence his research made little sense. It was convoluted and potentially inefficient. But it was the only theory he had.

After having breakfast with Astarte and walking her to the bus stop, he headed to his Westford office. On the way he phoned Zuberi's office to ask if the Egyptian might be available for a video conference. His secretary returned to him after a slight pause. "Mr. Youssef will be available in forty-five minutes. Is that acceptable to you?"

In his office, he initiated the conference at the scheduled time.

"Hello, Cameron," the Egyptian bellowed in his familiar manner, the accent again hard on the first syllable of Cam's name.

After pleasantries Cam cleared his throat and waited until Zuberi looked straight into the camera. "I know it was you that sent the photos to Amanda."

Cam had suggested a video call because he wanted to judge Zuberi's reaction. But the man's face was inscrutable. "I am sorry, did you say photos? Like pictures?"

"Yes. But it was a sloppy job. The envelope they came in is from Great Britain. That size envelope is not sold in the U.S."

Zuberi smiled and nodded, his eyes alive. "I am not little boy selling fruit at bus stop, Cameron. I know a bluff when I see one. We have saying in Egypt; let me find English translation." He tapped at his computer with his good hand. "Here it is: *Lie to a liar, for lies are his coin; steal from a thief, for that is easy; lay a trap for a trickster and catch him at first attempt; but beware of an honest man.* I am honest man, Cameron. That is why people fear me. Not because I am liar or thief or trickster."

Cam nodded. It was not exactly a denial, but nor did Cam have a shred of evidence that Zuberi had sent the photos. In fact, Cam thought it unlikely, and the lack of even a flicker or guilt in Zuberi's eyes seemed to confirm it.

"Thank you, Zuberi. And I believe you. I hope you are not offended."

The man shrugged. "I do business all over world. Every day is new insult. But what is this about photos?"

Cam briefly explained the situation.

"I understand why you accuse me, to try to get my reaction. This is dirty business, when enemy attacks your home. I hope you find dog who did this."

"I do have another reason for this conversation. You said half of my salary would be for writing another book. My research is coming along nicely; I've already started outlining." *And I'm low on cash.* "Do you mind if I publish it early, or does it have to be at the end of the academic year?"

"Excellent! Earlier is better," he said, rubbing his bald head. "What is about this book?"

Cam summarized his research on the beehive chambers in and around New England, his belief they were built by Irish monks and Druids from the 6th century, and the ties between the Druids, the Egyptians, and the Freemasons.

"So you think Egyptians involved?"

"I actually think the Druids descended from the Egyptian priests."

"Maybe Egyptians discover America in addition to Scotland," he laughed, his dark eyes boring into Cam's from across the ocean. "Can you send outline to me?"

Cam wasn't surprised this excited Zuberi. "Sure thing. I'll send you what I have, then next week I should have the entire outline finished." He wanted to time things so royalties began to flow as soon as the Superfund litigation was resolved, but not before.

He disconnected and exhaled. Slowly he was beginning to put his financial affairs in order. He wished he could say the same for his family life.

By mid-morning he had put out a few brush fires and, still at his office, was organizing the notes for his manuscript. He had established a clear connection between the Freemasons and the

148

Druids, and between both groups and the ancient Egyptians. The common thread seemed to be sun worship. That's where he turned.

His research quickly led him to the Pharaoh Akhenaton. Prior to Akhenaton's reign in the 14th century BC, the sun god was one of many gods worshipped by the Egyptians. Akhenaton tried to change that, elevating Aton, the god of the sun, to prime and exclusive status. This attempt by Akhenaton (meaning "Worshipper of Aton," a name he adopted after taking the throne) was opposed by the many priests loyal to other gods and also by much of the populace. Eventually this attempt at monotheism, one of the first in recorded history, failed and Akhenaton was forced from power.

When Cam dove down the monotheism rabbit hole, he was surprised to find the psychologist Sigmund Freud waiting for him at the bottom. Freud, in the 1930s, theorized that the story of Moses as told in the Old Testament had been glorified. The real story, Freud believed, was that Moses—having been raised by the Egyptian royal family—had grown to become a priest in Akhenaton's temple to Aton and had been forced to flee Egypt along with Akhenaton's other followers when Akhenaton was deposed. It is this experience with monotheism, Freud argued, that made him a natural leader of the monotheistic Israelis as they fled Egypt during the Exodus.

Freud's theory, upon closer examination, had some holes in it—chiefly, why would Moses, a Jew, be an Egyptian priest? The holes closed up nicely when modern scholars began to propose that the monotheistic religion Akhenaton had been promoting—the worship of Aton—was itself actually an early form of Judaism. The Jews used the name *Adonai* for God, a name linguists concluded was identical in its roots to the name *Aton*. Somehow, the historians claimed, Akhenaton had combined sun worship with Judaism and its monotheism, most likely with the help and guidance of the priest Moses.

Cam had been at his computer for a few hours. He sat back and reflected on this revelation. Normally he would call Amanda and discuss things with her. Instead he decided to go for a quick lunchtime jog.

The Issac Question

Changing into the running clothes he left in the office, he stretched quickly and exited his office near the Town Common. Angling to a path opposite Town Hall, he found himself on the Tom Paul trail, a path lined with stone walls snaking through wooded areas in the center of town. His thoughts turned back to Moses.

A couple of things about the Exodus story as told in the Old Testament had always bothered him. First, the story of a royal princess taking in the baby Moses, the son of a slave, made no sense. It was more likely, Cam believed, that Moses was an Egyptian baby of noble birth—in fact, the name Moses was an Egyptian one, not Hebrew. Second, if the Israelites had all been slaves, how did they possess such a large stash of gold that the Pharaoh risked the renewed wrath of God to chase them across the desert for it? The Old Testament claimed the people of Egypt proffered the gold to the Israelites as back wages—but since when did slaves receive wages? Furthermore, the Israelites were the *Pharaoh's* slaves, so why would the people of Egypt be paying their back wages in any event? Cam was hardly a Biblical scholar, but he had easily been able to poke two gaping holes in the Exodus story. It stood to reason there were others.

Following the trail, Cam leapt across a small stream, his shoes splashing in the swampy ground on the far bank. He continued on, about a mile in total, before turning to retrace his steps. As he spun, he caught a glimpse of a figure ducking behind an oak tree from the direction he had just come. Someone had been following him, he guessed, and hadn't expected him to reverse course so quickly. Fingers tingling as adrenaline pumped through his body, he considered his options. He possessed the element of surprise, so why not keep it?

Averting his eyes from the oak tree, Cam ran past, hoping to lull his tail into a false sense of security. Picking up the pace a bit, he passed a pond and came to a sharp jog in the trail. Accelerating further, he cut right at the jog. But rather than follow the trail with a sharp left, he pushed through the brush into the woods. And waited.

He estimated he had probably a hundred-yard head start on his pursuit. Twenty-five seconds at a fast jog. Fighting to control his breathing, Cam counted to fifteen and peered out. Nothing. He waited another dozen seconds, scanning the trail, wondering who was following and, after another ten seconds, whether they had given up the chase…

A pair of strong hands shoved Cam's head against the tree, pinning him. "Don't move," the voice snarled. A bit of a foreign accent. French, maybe. "Wrap both arms around the tree, and don't scream." One arm slid around Cam's throat. "I could snap your neck with a single twist of my arm."

Cam fought to breathe. "Okay," he gasped. In a perverse way, he was almost relieved. Finally, his enemy had revealed himself. And if they wanted Cam dead, he'd be dead already. Or so Cam hoped. "What do you want?"

"Answers. What happened to Raptor?"

Cam blinked. The man's breath smelled of tuna fish, which Cam realized was a strange thing to notice given the circumstances. "Who?"

"The man who was following you down in Connecticut." There was anger in the man's voice; this was personal.

Cam tried to turn his head to look at his captor, but the man's grip tightened. "I didn't know anyone was following us."

"Don't lie to me." He twisted Cam's head, bending his neck awkwardly. It suddenly occurred to Cam that he might only be kept alive long enough to answer these questions. He looked around, hoping to find some kind of weapon. As if sensing his thoughts, his captor's grip tightened even further. Cam grew lightheaded and his knees began to buckle.

"I … can't … br—"

Through a fog, Cam heard a thud and felt the choke hold slacken. Cam staggered forward and, as if in slow motion, dropped to his knees. As he did so, his captor collapsed atop him, both of them tumbling into the underbrush. Cam heard footsteps scurrying deeper into the woods, but his primary focus was to get away from his captor. Rolling, he extricated himself and, using the tree for support, stood. A grapefruit-sized rock lay on the ground nearby, apparently where it had ricocheted after making contact with his enemy's head.

Cam reached down and put his hand near the man's nose. Still breathing. Which was almost more than Cam could say about himself. Cam rolled him onto his back and checked his pockets for identification. Not finding any, Cam scanned the woods and the trail. Nothing. Yet. Time to get out of here before yet a third surprise visitor appeared.

Finally able to fill his lungs with air, he sprinted the mile back to the office.

Back in his office, Cam phoned Amanda and described his encounter. He was pleasantly surprised to hear the concern in her voice.

"Are you sure you're not hurt?"

"No. I mean yes. I'm fine. But I'm not sure about the guy in the woods. I stopped at the police station and told them about it. They're checking for him now. And they're also sending a car over to watch our house." He paused. "And I called an alarm company. They're coming tomorrow morning to install an alarm system, assuming you're okay with it."

"Roger that. But Cam, who was the bloke?"

"The guy who grabbed me, or the guy who rescued me?"

"Both. Either."

"I don't know. The guy who grabbed me had an accent, heavy-set, forties. I didn't see the other guy. I'm guessing it was the guy I first saw when I did my U-turn. The guy I was hiding from."

"Someone with some training, it sounds like."

"Yeah. Whoever it was snuck up on us without being heard."

"What about that guy who sent the email? Your guardian angel?"

Cam had forgotten about him. "Could be. But that doesn't tell us who attacked me."

"Cam, I'm sorry but I need to run. Astarte will be getting off the bus soon, and this makes me even more nervous. When are you coming home?"

"Yes, go get Astarte. I have a conference call at four, so I'll be home around five." He paused. "Thanks for asking."

She exhaled. "Yes, well, I'm glad you're not hurt. Goodbye."

Cam showered, rotating his sore neck in the hot water, then took a call from the police telling him they didn't find anyone in the woods. He paced around his office, unable to focus on his law work. *Who the hell is Raptor?* It sounded like a name from a video game or something. Cam didn't know if his attacker intended to kill him or not, but there was no doubt about one thing: He could have done the job if he wanted to. He rotated his neck again. *What a shitty week.*

But it all came back to the same reality: Someone, for some reason, was trying to keep him from his research. And, for now, the only way to oppose them was to forge on. With an hour-and-a-half to kill before his conference call, he turned back to his stack of books.

Burrowing even deeper into the Egyptian rabbit hole, searching for more information about Moses and Akhenaton, Cam's eyes flew from the pages of his reference books to websites and back again while his writing hand scribbled notes. One source led to another, then to a third. Deeper he dug, making connections that never could have been made before the days of the Internet.

Patterns began to appear, and with them answers. Answers that would be controversial and disturbing. The back of his neck burned: Ideas that were controversial and disturbing were the types of things that sparked anger and aggression.

He scratched the explosive words onto his legal pad, finally able to see at least part way around the corner:

Moses and Pharaoh Akhenaton were the same person?!?

Perhaps he was getting closer to finding a motive for the attacks on him.

Working from his notes, he outlined the reasons for such a divisive and far-fetched conclusion.

First and foremost, the concept of monotheism inextricably tied Moses to Akhenaton. At no time in history prior to the mid-14th century BC had mankind conceptualized the idea of a single deity. Rather, every ancient culture subscribed to a belief set involving a pantheon of gods, each god having jurisdiction over a particular aspect of life—fertility, rain, war, crops, disease, etc. Then, almost as if by magic, after thousands of years, the radical idea of a single omnipotent God appeared out of the sands of Egypt in the mid-14th century BC. *Twice.* Cam shook his head. That was not the way the world worked. Radical ideas occurred rarely because they were, well, radical. It was far more likely that one man (Abraham) had a eureka moment which a second man (Akhenaton) later adopted. And the obvious link between Abraham and Akhenaton was Moses.

Second, the history of Akhenaton's childhood largely mirrored that of Moses. Akhenaton's older brother had been murdered by rivals to the throne, so his mother Queen Tiyee sent the baby Akhenaton—whose life as the oldest living son had now become also at risk—by boat to live with Jewish relatives (Queen Tiyee herself being of Jewish heritage). These relatives raised Akhenaton as their own in the queen's summer palace in Goshen. The similarities between this history and the Biblical story of Moses were striking: Also born in Goshen, Moses was floated down the river to the royal palace by a mother who feared that, as the oldest son, his life was in danger.

Third, both Moses and Akhenaton were trained as priests.

Fourth, both Akhenaton and Moses were exiled from Egypt as young men. Both later returned to rule their followers, only to flee a second time. Both men, in exile, lived in the same small remote village, Serabit el-Khadim, hundreds of miles away in the southern Sinai.

Fifth, and most simply, the name itself, 'Moses,' clearly derived from the name of Akhenaton's grandfather, Tuthmosis, and many other 'mosis'-named pharaohs before him.

These similarities would have been enough to convince Cam. But when he turned his attention to the story of the Biblical Joseph, he of the Coat of Many Colors, all doubt disappeared.

Joseph, in a rags-to-riches story that would make even Hollywood blush, rose from slavery to become the Pharaoh's vizier, or Prime Minister. Putting the unlikeness of the story aside, did Joseph exist in the Egyptian historical records? A scholar by the name of Ahmed Osman believed he did, in the person of an Egyptian nobleman named Yuya. Osman was especially struck by the Semitic, rather than Egyptian, features of the mummified head of Yuya. After studying the picture and remembering the admonition of his college anthropology professor that Egyptians were ethnically Africans, Cam had to agree:

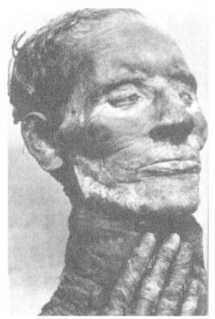

Yuya/Joseph

In addition to the Semitic facial features, Osman noted that Yuya was bearded (Egyptian nobles of that time were clean-shaven), that his hands were placed under his chin rather than across his chest in the so-called Osiris pose of other Egyptian mummies, and that the name Yuya was not an Egyptian name. So was Yuya actually the Biblical Joseph? Cam might be able to convince a jury with the evidence at hand. But his goal wasn't to win his case, his goal was to find the truth.

Yuya/Joseph, Cam learned as he continued to read, later married Thuya, a member of the royal family. Their daughter was Tiyee, whom Cam already had learned was the Jewish-descended wife of the Pharaoh Amenhotep III and mother of Akhenaton. That made Yuya/Joseph the grandfather of the Pharaoh Akhenaton, a/k/a Moses.

Cam sat back, nodding. This is where the pieces fit together. It would have been here, at the knee of his Jewish grandfather, where Akhenaton/Moses became indoctrinated into the belief of monotheism as first conceived by his ancestor Abraham.

Looking at things under the light of these revelations, the Moses Exodus story suddenly started to make sense. Moses was both Jewish and Egyptian, his identity as a child hidden to keep him safe from political rivals. As a man he returned to the palace and took the throne by marrying his half-sister, Nefertiti. When his insistence on the monotheistic worship of Aton/Adonai was met with resistance by Egyptian society, he and his followers—which included both Jews and Egyptians loyal to him, some of them presumably wealthy—were forced to flee, pursued into the desert by a new pharaoh hoping to refill the royal coffers.

Cam searched for a page in the book he had marked. Finding it, he sat back—his research had come full circle. One of the followers loyal to Akhenaton/Moses who followed him into exile was his daughter, Meritaten. After marrying a prince from Scythia, she had taken the name Princess Scythia. Her followers came to pronounce this name, and history to record it, as 'Scota.'

Cam read further, shaking his head as he read. The Scythians, though living in Persia, were renowned in ancient times for their red hair. "Just like the Scots," he murmured.

That settled it. Smiling for one of the first times this week, he scribbled the title for his new book in capital letters across the last page of his notes: "*OUT OF EGYPT.*"

☥ ✚ ⬥

Eight days had passed since Raptor disappeared. They had found his body in the trunk of his car, but the kill had been clean and professional. Tamara sat in her office sipping coffee on a Friday afternoon, waiting for Moshe to check in. Why did the shit always seem to hit the fan on Friday afternoon, just in time to ruin the Sabbath?

On cue, her cell phone rang. "Remind me I'm too old for this," Moshe blurted.

"What happened?"

He described how he confronted Thorne while on a jog. "Then someone knocked me out. I have an egg on my head the size of … an egg."

She pictured Moshe scratching at an orb on his flaky scalp. "Who was it?"

"Never saw the guy. Hit me from behind, I think with a rock."

She exhaled. This was getting messy. *They* were getting messy. "You know, we have agents for this shit. *Young* agents."

"I know. But I wanted to confront Thorne myself."

"And?"

"I don't think he knows anything about Raptor."

"But now he knows we're watching him."

Moshe grunted. "So? If he's not doing anything wrong he has nothing to worry about."

"Yes, but now the guy who conked you on the head knows also."

"Again, so what? We're the Mossad. Supposedly we're everywhere."

"The guy who hit you—if he's tracking Thorne, maybe he was in Connecticut also."

"Agreed."

She voiced the obvious. "Youssef?"

"Could be. But it doesn't really fit his M.O. He's more of a car bomb type."

"Maybe here in America he needs to be more subtle."

"Maybe we need to be more subtle." He belched. "Instead of following Thorne, we should be following the guy following Thorne."

☥ ✞ ⬡

Some days were better than others. But on the whole Amanda felt like she had spent the past week in some doctor's waiting

157

room, killing time, sloth-like, waiting for test results that would determine the rest of her life.

Today, finally, she had forced herself out of her malaise by taking the paddle boat out with Astarte after school. They circled the lake, Venus riding in the back barking at dogs on the shore. They were just pulling the boat ashore when Cam returned home. His call today had unnerved her; she met him with a hug and whispered in his ear. "You okay?"

He held her tight. "In fact, best I've felt in a week."

She disengaged gently, moved to see the moisture in his eyes. He was either really sorry, or completely innocent. The attack on him today had moved the needle in her mind—it appeared someone really was after him, based on today's attack and the Superfund sting and the lottery ticket assault. But this wasn't a more-likely-than-not situation. She needed to be one hundred percent certain Cam was innocent. There was no such thing as partial trust—either you trusted someone or you did not. Unfortunately for both of them, trust came to Amanda like bats to the sunshine.

"How about if I grill tonight?" Cam said.

Astarte returned from putting the life jackets away and jumped into a Cam bear hug. "Can we have s'mores?" she asked.

"Sure," Cam said, smiling. "But then what should we have for dessert?"

They sat on the rear deck overlooking the lake, Amanda cherishing the momentary return to normalcy. Astarte must have sensed it also, as she grabbed a deck of cards and insisted they play Crazy Eights. A half hour later she finally got bored and took Venus back to the lake to skip rocks.

"Any update from the Westford police?" Amanda asked.

"Nothing. And nothing from the Boston detective either. Nobody who fits the guy's description has cashed a half million dollar scratch ticket."

"So maybe that was some kind of setup?"

Cam shrugged. "Maybe. But to what end?"

She picked at a bowl of grapes. So much was happening to them, yet none of it seemed to be related. Where was the common thread? "The guy today said someone was following us in Connecticut?"

"Someone named Raptor. And apparently something happened to him."

They spent a few minutes trying to piece everything together. "I feel like a kid with a blindfold trying to whack a piñata," Amanda said. "Things are happening all around me that I can't see."

"Yeah, well, I feel like the piñata," Cam said, his pain not masked by his sad smile.

She covered his hand with hers. If he really were innocent, he was suffering needlessly and unfairly. They needed to figure this all out, and quickly. "You said you had some research you wanted to share?"

He brightened. "I found some really neat stuff." He explained Joseph's role in the Egyptian royal family, and how evidence strongly supported the conclusion that Moses and the Pharaoh Akhenaton were one and the same, learning monotheism at the foot of their grandfather Joseph. What he hadn't figured out was how Joseph, a lowly slave, had risen to prominence in the first place.

"That's amazing stuff," Amanda said. "Someday someone really should write a non-fiction version of the Bible."

"Well, that someone might be me. I spoke with Zuberi and he is okay with me releasing book number two as soon as possible. I'm going to send him the beginnings of my outline tonight. I'm calling it *Out of Egypt.* He's going to love this stuff—it turns out that Princess Scota is Akhenaton's—or Moses'—daughter. So all this Biblical stuff ties back to Scota and, I think, to the Druids. I'm going to start in ancient Egypt and track this history to Ireland and Scotland, then across to America with the Druids and Prince Henry Sinclair and then do a section about how it all led to modern Freemasonry."

"Wait, back up a second. Was Scota with Moses in the desert?"

"No. From what I read, the family split up to keep the blood lines apart for safety. Scota and her husband crossed the Mediterranean to Europe while Moses led a group of

159

monotheists—some Jews, some his Egyptian followers—into the desert."

Amanda furrowed her brow. "Didn't they find Akhenaton's tomb in Egypt?"

"Actually, no. They found his father, the Pharaoh Amenhotep III, and they found his son, the famous King Tut, but not him. Again, he fled. Who knows where his body is?"

She was having trouble picturing Charlton Heston as an Egyptian pharaoh. But of course that was just the Hollywood portrayal of him—Moses, being half Jewish and half Egyptian, would have looked … well, like the Egyptian actor Omar Sharif, who before his recent death had disclosed that his mother was in fact Jewish. "Are there statues of Akhenaton?"

"There is one," Cam said. "But I have to admit, it doesn't look anything like the way you'd picture Moses." He showed her an image on his phone.

The Pharaoh Akhenaton

"No, it doesn't look like the way I'd picture Moses." And nothing like the dashing Omar Sharif. "He looks … androgynous."

Cam nodded. "Some people say he wanted to be portrayed that way on purpose. Because his god, Aton, was supposed to be the mother and father of humankind, and the king was supposed to embody the creator, he wanted to be shown as having both feminine and masculine attributes."

Amanda stared out over the lake. She missed these kinds of conversations, the intellectual stimulation, the thrill of discovering fragments of truth in the dusty corners of history. How would she replace this aspect of her life if she left Cam? Not to mention everything else she adored about him...

She refocused on their conversation. "So, getting back to Princess Scota. If she was Moses' daughter, you'd expect to find some remnants of Jewish tradition and custom amongst her people, right?"

Cam smiled. "Ever wonder how the Stone of Destiny ended up in Scotland?" The famous stone upon which each of the British monarchs was coronated was, according to legend, used as a pillow by the patriarch Jacob.

"No, but are you going to tell me?"

He smiled again. "Not yet. If I give away all my secrets, you'll have no reason to keep me around."

Zuberi walked through the massive closet that separated his sleeping area from Carrington's and stuck his head through the door. "Tomorrow, my wife, I fly to Jordan." Carrington, propped against her headboard in flannel nightgown, set her book down.

"Come, husband, sit with me for a few minutes." She patted the bed.

He smiled and nodded. It hardly constituted a wild Friday night, but now that she had become resolved to the fact that their relationship would never be an intimate one, he actually enjoyed their late night chats. Sex, to the extent he desired it, he could get anywhere. But the wise and loyal counsel of his wife was a gift he cherished. As he sat she took his only hand in one of hers.

"I have been doing some reading," she said, "about Rosslyn Chapel." He had shared with her Thorne's outline of his research, which the author had emailed earlier in the evening. "And I came across some interesting information about Baphomet. I thought perhaps you would like me to forward this to Cameron and Amanda. I know she, especially, is interested in the Baphomet mystery."

"And what is this information?"

She reached for a paperback book next on her night table. "This book talks about two heads found buried in Rosslyn Chapel. Both heads had horns in them and the author thinks they may have been worshipped as a manifestation of Baphomet."

He nodded. The idea of the Baphomet head being hidden at Rosslyn Chapel made sense in light of the Chapel's strong connection to, and history with, the Templars. "Yes, I think share with Cameron and Amanda."

"I have some other information also, relating to skull worship and the Sinclair family."

"Very good. But feed to them slowly. We have old saying: Fisherman who use all his worms on first day eat no fish rest of week."

Bartol actually enjoyed the twice-daily ten mile bike ride from the stone chamber in Groton to Westford and back again. The road had a wide shoulder, and the ride kept his body tone and allowed him time to think and plan.

He didn't need to think much about what happened today. The Mossad was looking to avenge their agent, and they thought Thorne had something to do with his death. That was probably a good thing—it meant they were thrashing about, still looking for a lead. But Bartol didn't appreciate the way the fat Israeli had manhandled Thorne.

A bigger problem was Thorne's close relationship with the Freemasons. Bartol had been tracking Thorne for a week now. From the cell phone interceptor he was using outside Thorne's home and office, Bartol had intercepted a handful of calls between Thorne and the Masonic leader, Randall Sid. The conversations revolved around the Druids and Masonic ritual, but it was becoming apparent that Sid was playing Thorne. Why else would the cloistered society be sharing their secrets with a non-member? Obviously they had an ulterior motive. Now, it may be that Thorne knew he was being played and was just going along with it. But Bartol couldn't risk it.

Not when it came to the Freemasons.

The land line rang just after nine o'clock Saturday morning. Cam was tempted to let it go to voice mail—other than his parents, nobody beside telemarketers called them on that number anymore. And he wanted to continue outlining his new book. But he thought it might be the alarm company so he grabbed it on the third ring.

"Hi, is this Professor Thorne?"

Professor? "Um, yes."

A deep breath, followed by a fast-talking explanation. "My name is Rachel Levitad and I'm a student at Brandeis and I really need to talk to a professor about something and I know you're teaching a class this summer on early exploration of America and this isn't really up your alley but I thought since you were open-minded you might be willing to help me and I'm friends with Amon Youssef and he said that his father says you are a nice guy…" She ran out of gas.

"Okay, Rachel, please slow down." He wasn't thrilled with Zuberi suggesting students contact him before he even started work. But the girl seemed upset.

"It's just that I've been reaching out to a bunch of people and nobody can help me … or at least they don't want to."

Over the next ten minutes her story emerged: She and Zuberi's son were romantically involved; she was Jewish and her parents objected to her dating a Muslim, to the extent they were threatening not to let her return to Brandeis; she was hoping to prove to them that the Egyptians were different from other Arabs, both historically and in their modern-day relations with Jews; and she wanted Cam's help—that is, *Professor Thorne's* help—in building her case.

His first reaction was that no rational argument was going to change her parents' minds. But that was not for him to say. "I'm not exactly an expert on Egypt," he said.

"I know that. But Amon says you've been working on some stuff that proves the Scots descend from the Egyptians." She sniffed. "I'm sure my parents wouldn't object if I dated a guy from Glasgow."

Something about the girl's heartache touched his own aching heart. "Actually, I've got something even better for you. It may be that the early Israelites were part Egyptian." He explained the Moses/Akhenaton connection. "If so, it was none other than the Pharaoh Akhenaton who was the savior of the Jewish people."

"That's so weird," she replied. "Professor Siegel, the one I can't reach, said that the Pharaoh Tuthmosis III was the *father* of the Jewish people."

Cam's cheeks flushed. "Wait, what?"

Zuberi knew better than to leave the security of the airport. He jetted into various Middle East cities, held his meetings on the tarmac, and immediately flew away. Today his jet sat on the blistering tarmac in the late afternoon sun at Queen Alia International Airport in Aman, Jordan. Zuberi admired the architecture of the modern terminal from afar—the roof featured scores of concrete domes designed to resemble Bedouin tents. He had never stepped inside.

The jet's air conditioning purred as he waited for his guest to arrive. He needed to be especially focused today. The changing dynamic in the Middle East required that Zuberi work extra hard to develop and cultivate personal relationships. As long as the traditional currencies of trade were used—cash, power, women, favors, blackmail, revenge—Zuberi was fine. It was when the new currency of the 21st century—religious fanaticism—was employed that he found it more difficult to do business. Zuberi preferred a personal, long-lasting relationship with his customers, but he had nothing to offer these fanatics other than the weapons themselves. Even so, business had never been better. The ISIS radicals seemed intent on bombing the entire region into a smoking pile of rubble.

And when they finally decided to rebuild, he'd be there to sell them the machinery and equipment they needed.

Unless they found another supplier.

Here, again, he was back to the same problem: He needed to be able to give these radicals something beyond the traditional currencies, something they would value, something that would build loyalty and trust.

He sipped at his tea. This was the reason for today's meeting.

His guest, a bearded, angular man in his thirties wearing a black dishdasha, his head covered by a black kufi, sprang from a white Mercedes limousine, marched across the tarmac casting a long shadow, and climbed the stairs of the jet two at a time. The tails of his dishdasha flowed behind him and the billowing, white Cumulus reflected like mushroom clouds off his Ray-bans. He came alone, as did all Zuberi's guests. Only when the limousine was hundreds of yards away would Zuberi's security detail open the door to the plane. Engines running, the jet could take off on a moment's notice if someone decided to storm the aircraft. Zuberi's enemies might shoot him down as he attempted to flee, but they would never take him alive.

A few seconds passed, during which Zuberi knew the man was being frisked, and then his guest was led into the jet's cabin. Zuberi stood, smiled, and moved forward for the traditional Arab greeting. As an Egyptian, Zuberi stopped at one kiss on each cheek. His guest, being Jordanian, would continue kissing back and forth, cheek to cheek, a dozen times had Zuberi not ended it. Not that his visitor seemed to mind—his eyes were cold and distant even as his warm lips brushed Zuberi's face.

"As salam aleykum," Zuberi said, stepping back. "Welcome, Khaled. I knew your uncle," he said, speaking Arabic. "To Allah we belong and to him we return."

Khaled nodded, his eyes remaining expressionless. "All that is on earth will perish, but Allah abides forever."

The Issac Question

Zuberi motioned for the man to sit, lest an hour pass with them exchanging bereavement condolences for Khaled's uncle, a snake of a man whom nobody liked in life and surely nobody beside Zuberi missed in death. And the only reason Zuberi missed him was because Zuberi had pictures of the Jordanian with naked young boys. He had no such leverage over the nephew.

Seated in a leather chair facing Zuberi across a polished cherry table, Khaled sipped his tea, twirled his dark beard, and studied his host. He was of the next generation of Arab leaders, a generation with hatred in their hearts and disdain for the West in their souls. Life had been much easier dealing with the cocaine-snorting playboys and greedy camel-traders of the previous century. Men like Khaled were more interested in holy wars than in business. But as the saying went: *The best time to plant a tree was twenty years ago; the second best time is now.* The uncle was dead; now Zuberi needed to build a new relationship with Khaled and the other ISIS radicals.

Zuberi was content to wait, to allow his guest to control the pace of their meeting. Finally Khaled spoke, still in Arabic. "I hear your son is attending an American university, with the Jews." He spat.

Zuberi raised an eyebrow and set down his tea cup. "I commend your intelligence work. You obviously understand the importance of knowing all you can about those you are dealing with, both friend and foe."

Khaled nodded slightly.

"I enrolled my son at Brandeis for that same reason. As Sun Tzu said: *Know thy enemy.*"

"He will return to you soft and flaccid, like a cock in a cold shower. I hope you have other sons."

Zuberi let the insult pass. "It is, in fact, my son's experiences at Brandeis that I wish to discuss with you today."

A flicker of curiosity in Khaled's eyes. "I am listening."

"I am a businessman. And as a businessman I make it a habit of making gifts to my customers." Zuberi smiled and shrugged. "It has always been such, as long as there has been sand in the desert." He shifted forward, watching carefully for a reaction to the words he was about to speak. "What if I could produce for you a book,

166

written by a professor at America's leading Jewish university, offering proof from the Old Testament that the Jews have no legitimate claim to the land of Israel?" If God's covenant had been made with Abraham, and the Jews did not descend from him— because the patriarch Isaac was not Abraham's son but rather the son of the pharaoh—then their claim to the Holy Land would be null and void. "This, I think, would be more valuable to you even than the weapons I deliver."

Khaled's hand shook, tea sloshing in his cup. He set the cup down and covered his surprise by wiping his mouth with the back of his sleeve. A few seconds passed. "Yes, that would obviously be of interest to us."

Zuberi nodded. "I thought it would be." There was only one thing Muslims hated more than other Muslims. And that was Jews.

After showing the alarm technician the house layout, Cam set aside the rest of Saturday morning to research what Rachel had euphemistically referred to as the Isaac Question.

"You know," Amanda said from the kitchen as she changed a light bulb, "Rachel's parents are not going to approve of this relationship just because Isaac's father may have been an Egyptian pharaoh."

"I know. But she's desperate. It's the classic Romeo and Juliet story. I'm sure she's trying everything she can to try to change their minds, both rational and irrational. This is the rational approach."

"Okay," Amanda said, "One always feels compelled to root for love." She smiled sadly.

He held her eyes. "I know I do."

She sighed. "I'll take Astarte with me to the grocery store."

"Great. I'll be done in time for her game."

"I'm pitching today," Astarte said, "so I want to get there early to warm up."

Cam hugged her. "Your bullpen catcher will be ready, I promise."

He spread his materials on the kitchen table, opened his laptop and focused on his task. First, he needed to confirm Rachel's version of the Isaac parentage story—that Isaac had been fathered not by Abraham but rather by the pharaoh during the period when Abraham had sold his wife Sarah into the Egyptian monarch's harem. Second, if the pharaoh had indeed fathered Isaac, would this event impact the later Moses/Akhenaton story?

Cam had taken notes while Rachel spoke and compared her assertions to the actual text of the Old Testament. When necessary, he consulted secondary sources and commentaries. As he pored through the materials, he became increasingly convinced that the young student's conclusion—as revealed to her by her Brandeis professor—was, as Amanda would say, spot on. The recounting of Abraham's fathering of Isaac as told in the Old Testament looked to be an obvious coverup. And a clumsy one at that. What the writers had essentially done was push back the birth of Isaac a number of decades, creating the perception of time and distance between Isaac's birth and Sarah's time in the Pharaoh's harem.

Using graph paper, Cam made a series of timelines, one for each character in the story, and plotted the events related in the Book of Genesis for each character. If this was a retelling designed to coverup the truth, as he strongly suspected, it would be impossible to make all the dates line up. Halfway through the timeline for Ishmael, he clapped his hands. "Gotcha!"

There were two key passages involving Ishmael. First, Genesis 17:25 stated that Ishmael—Abraham's son by Sarah's handmaiden, Hagar—was thirteen years old when he was circumcised as part of God's covenant with Abraham, a covenant which produced Isaac a year later. Ishmael therefore was fourteen years older than Isaac (thirteen plus one), according to the purported timeline of the Old Testament. Second, Genesis 21:14-19 recounted the story of Hagar and Ishmael being cast out by a jealous Sarah after Isaac's weaning (which traditionally occurred at age three), making Ishmael seventeen (fourteen plus three) at the time of the casting out. But these passages described Hagar carrying Ishmael into the wilderness and setting him down under a bush to wait for him to die. Cam shook his head. What kind of woman would lift a nearly fully-grown man and carry him into the wilderness? And, even more telling, what kind of seventeen-year-old would agree to sit under a bush and wait to die? What had happened here, Cam guessed, was that the clumsy re-dating of the Isaac birth story had caused the timeline to become distorted.

Could the Koran shed any light on this story, Cam wondered? It didn't take him long to find his answer, as the Koran also recounted the story of Ishmael being cast out at the time of Isaac's weaning feast. The Koran version largely mirrored the Old Testament, with one glaring exception: In the Koran, Ishmael was a young child, an age which made the story of Hagar carrying him into the wilderness far more plausible than the Old Testament's version. Again, the writers of the Old Testament seem to have taken pains to delay the date of Isaac's birth by more than a decade, distancing it from Sarah's time in the pharaoh's harem. But Ishmael's true age revealed the coverup.

The distortion of the timeline, by itself, was fairly revealing. When combined with the circumstantial evidence outlined by Rachel—Sarah's time spent in the pharaoh's harem, the pharaoh's gift of a handmaiden/midwife to Sarah, Abraham's later willingness to sacrifice the boy Isaac—a compelling case emerged. Cam had won many court cases with less. But, again, this was about finding the truth, not swaying a jury. He kept digging.

And then he found it. A famous rabbi from the 1500s named Obadiah Sforno wrote a commentary justifying Abraham's decision to 'cast out' his son Ishmael. Relying on ancient texts and sources now lost, Rabbi Sforno asserted that Abraham did so because Ishmael had insulted Abraham at Isaac's weaning feast by alleging that Abraham was not the true father of Isaac. Instead, Ishmael claimed, Isaac had been fathered by a neighboring monarch.

Cam sat back. What a strange accusation for Ishmael to make. If the Old Testament timeline were accurate, more than a decade had passed since Sarah had left the pharaoh's harem. Even a young boy would understand that a pregnancy could not extend that long. The modern-day equivalent would be someone blaming President Obama for the Vietnam War—he would surely be miffed at the charge, but the historical timeline was so clearly at odds with the

169

claim that he would likely shrug the accusation away rather than react angrily.

But if the timeline had been altered in the Old Testament, as Cam now believed, then both the accusation itself along with Abraham's angry response made sense. A public accusation questioning Isaac's parentage—made in conjunction with a plausible timeline—might have stung Abraham sufficiently to cause him to cast his firstborn son Ishmael out, just as Rabbi Sforno opined. Cam felt certain now that Rabbi Sforno, in attempting to defend the patriarch Abraham, had unwittingly provided compelling evidence calling into question the entire Isaac birth story.

Cam walked to the refrigerator and poured a tall glass of orange juice. There was one more thing he wanted to check. When Isaac was born, God promised that Isaac and his line would rule all the land from the Euphrates River in the east to the Nile River in the west—pretty much the entire Middle East. This had always struck Cam as an odd promise, as the Israelites had never controlled such a vast territory. Why had God made such an expansive promise? Cam sensed the truth. Returning to his laptop, he found a map showing Greater Egypt as ruled by Pharaoh Tuthmosis III during his reign around the year 1500 BC. His skin tingled. The map mirrored God's promise to Isaac, comprising a swath of land stretching from the Euphrates River valley to the Nile River valley and all fertile territory in between. Cam sat back. *Of course it did.* God was merely promising to Isaac what was already his by birthright: The land of Isaac's true father, Pharaoh Tuthmosis III. The promise had nothing to do with Abraham.

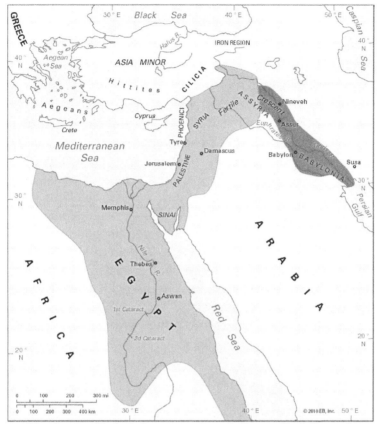

Territories Ruled (in orange) and Controlled (in red)
by Pharaoh Tuthmosis III

The Brandeis professor had been correct, Cam concluded. The evidence was overwhelming, as soon as one opened one's eyes to it.

So what did this all mean? Did the revelation of Isaac's true parentage have a domino effect on the later story of Moses and the Exodus?

Cam pulled out a legal pad and scribbled his thoughts. Primarily, and most clearly, the Isaac truth explained how the Jewish slave Joseph had made his unlikely ascension to Prime Minister—what was seemingly impossible became quite understandable with the revelation that Joseph was actually a direct descendant (the great-grandson) of Pharaoh Tuthmosis III and therefore a kinsman of the current pharaoh. But even more importantly, the revelation that Joseph descended from the pharaoh explained how he had been able to marry into the royal family and become the grandfather of—and monotheistic mentor to—Moses/Akhenaton. And it also explained the mystery of the gold: When Moses/Akhenaton and his followers fled, the group was not comprised only of slaves, but also of members of the royal family whose wealth the pharaoh coveted.

Cam stood, stretching as he walked to the picture window overlooking the lake. By focusing on timelines and maps and bloodlines and specific details of the story, he had been studying the individual trees and ignoring the fact he had wandered deep into a dark forest. He sighed and pondered the unthinkable: *What would it mean if Isaac really was not Abraham's son?*

Here things turned from being merely academic to potentially impacting world history: If God made his covenant with Abraham, and if Isaac and his line were not of Abraham's blood, then what group had the rightful claim to be called 'The Chosen People'?

This was the hidden, fundamental truth Cam had sensed was being kept from him, the corner Cam had for weeks been unable to see around. Now, deep in the forest but finally able to see, he was pretty certain he didn't like the view.

♀ ✝ ⬦

Zuberi did not completely relax until the wheels of his jet lost contact with the Jordanian tarmac. Someday, he feared, a flight to the Middle East would turn into a one-way journey. It was the nature of his business. He had diversified his dealings into high-tech and real estate, but his core operations still revolved around arms dealing. Which meant he still needed to spend time in those areas of the world where lethal weapons were part of daily life.

He checked his watch. Seven in the evening, local time. Later than he preferred, only a few minutes before dusk. He had a rule never to remain on the tarmac at night, when enemies might use darkness to approach.

He phoned Amon. "Are you awake, my son?"

"Of course, father. You know I like to rise early."

"What is that American expression of bird waking early to catch fish?"

"Not a fish, a worm. The early bird catches the worm."

"So, tell me my son, did you do as I ask? Did your little bird wake early and contact Thorne?"

The boy hesitated. "She spoke to him this morning. I think he is willing to help her. To help us."

"Excellent." He sensed there was more. "What more, Amon?"

"I am feeling guilty for not being completely honest with her, father. I did not tell her that we have a selfish motive in directing Professor Thorne's research in this direction."

The boy had told Zuberi about his romance with the American girl and asked for advice on how to deal with her parents. The solution that presented itself—in the person of Thorne—offered benefits not just to Amon but to Zuberi. And allowed Zuberi to overlook the unfortunate fact that his son had fallen for a Jewess. "The Americans have another bird expression, about killing with one rock the two birds. We have this here. It is not a bad thing if a man prays for rain to water his crops and the rainwater also fills his well."

"I suppose you are correct, father."

"Trust me on this, Amon. I know not too much about love. But I am expert on business. And this business is good for Zuberi, it is good for Amon, and it is good for Jewish girl."

"Her name is Rachel."

He laughed. "Yes, my son. So is mother of Joseph with many colors coat." Pausing, he added. "Maybe your Rachel will be important in Egypt history also."

They returned from Astarte's softball game Saturday afternoon, Amanda observing as Cam light-heartedly teased the girl on the car ride home about being so focused on cheering on her teammates that she went up to bat … without her bat.

"But I got a good hit," Astarte countered.

"Yeah, but only after you had to run back to the dugout."

She smiled. "I was just trying to distract the pitcher."

Could she in good conscience separate them, Amanda wondered?

They had accepted an invitation from Randall Sid to attend a ceremony at the Bunker Hill Monument later in the afternoon. Amanda was not sure she wanted to attend. She and Cam had not been out as a couple in the eight days since the photo bomb arrived. And she didn't particularly like Randall Sid. On the other hand, she knew the Masons were the moving force behind the monument's erection, and its design as an obelisk obviously tied back to their research on Masonic connections to ancient Egypt.

As if reading her thoughts, Cam touched her on the arm as Astarte ran into the house. "I hope you're still planning to come to the Bunker Hill thing with me."

"Honestly, I'm not sure."

He bit his lip. "It's research, not a date." And then his smile. The smile she thought would brighten the rest of her life. "I promise not to be the least bit charming."

She turned her head and blinked away a tear. "All right then."

Cam nodded toward the street. "There's the unmarked cruiser. He's was circling the neighborhood this morning also."

"Good."

An hour later Cam dropped Astarte off at a friend's house and returned to pick up Amanda. She had changed into a long skirt and blouse and slid into the SUV next to Cam for the forty-minute drive to Boston. "You look nice," Cam said.

"What happened to not the least bit charming?"

"Right. Sorry." He paused. "You're wearing *that*?"

She smiled sadly. Either he had cheated on her, in which case she could never forgive him, or he was totally innocent, in which case she might never forgive herself for doubting him. A classic lose-lose. She pushed the thought away. "So what kind of event is this?"

"It's a commemoration for the Battle of Bunker Hill, specifically General Joseph Warren. He was a doctor and also the Masonic Grand Master at the time. He died in the battle."

"I thought the battle was in June, not May."

Cam nodded. "June 17. But the Masonic calendar year starts June 24, and they have meetings and conferences that whole week. And they like to do something private. So they have a ceremony in late May every year."

"And Randall Sid invited you?"

"He said there's something he wants to show me from the top of the monument."

She turned. "He's going to climb it?"

"Apparently he does every year. He's a tough old bird."

"Then I'm glad I wore comfortable shoes."

Cam parked on a side street in Charlestown on the northern edge of Boston. They walked up a slope—Breed's Hill, not Bunker Hill, as the former was the actual site of the misnamed battle—toward the monument. Federal style row houses, both brick and clapboard, lined the street. "This whole area was burned down by the British during the battle, so most of this architecture is Federalist style, from the early 1800s." He pointed toward the large grassy area on the top of the hill, their view of the monument itself still blocked by the uninterrupted row of four-story homes. "But you can see the houses ringing the park are much fancier. They're a later style, Victorian. The committee building the monument ran out of money so they had to sell off part of the battlefield as building lots." He smiled. "I guess even the Masons run out of money sometimes."

As they crested the hill the massive granite obelisk soared above them, surrounded on all sides by lush green lawn.

Bunker Hill Monument, Charlestown, MA

They climbed a series of stone stairs toward a bronze statue of a sword-wielding soldier standing guard at the base of the obelisk. "That's Colonel William Prescott, of the famous line, 'Don't fire until you see the whites of their eyes.'"

"How high is it?" Amanda asked, glancing up. She had been to most of the historic sites in Boston but had never crossed the bridge into Charlestown.

"Just over two hundred feet. Tall, but less than half as high as the Washington Monument. But otherwise pretty much identical."

"This is in a residential neighborhood, so it seems taller," Amanda said. "Plus it's on the top of this hill."

Cam pointed. "There's Randall."

Randall and a few dozen other men—all wearing tuxedos and Masonic aprons, many of them a head taller than Randall—stood

176

in a group at the base of the monument, some of the men with wives or dates. Randall spotted Cam and walked over to greet them. The dark-skinned Mason skipped the small-talk. "I'm glad it's a clear day. You'll appreciate what I want to show you, Cameron." He turned to Amanda. "It's a long climb. Many of the wives will be waiting at the bottom."

Amanda worked a Stairmaster for forty-five minutes three times a week. "Lovely. If any of them want to lend me their cameras, I'll snap off a few shots for them."

Randall Sid eyed the crowd impatiently. He cleared his throat and waited for a couple of his lieutenants to quiet the horde gathered at the base of the monument. He refused to yell. "We'll begin the ceremony in an hour. In the meantime, those that want to climb to the top may do so now." The monument was closed to the public, but he had arranged for after-hours access. The Freemasons had, after all, built the structure. "This is the equivalent of a twenty-two-story building, and the staircase is narrow, so I urge caution."

About a dozen men, in addition to Cameron Thorne and his fiancée whose name Randall could not recall, gathered around Randall. Another woman, probably one of the wives, smiled at Randall and joined the group. Randall had never seen her before, but she wore a loose knee-length skirt over a pair of shapely legs—the climb might be less strenuous if he fell in line behind her.

She tossed her head. "My name's Samantha Handrick," she said with a Southern drawl. "I'm married to Christopher. He just joined a few months back, when we moved here from Savannah, Georgia. But my daddy was a thirty-third degree." She smiled again, wide brown eyes holding his. "Just like you."

It had been a long time since a woman smiled at him like that. Maybe it was just her Southern charm. Randall bowed slightly. "After you."

They climbed slowly, the air heavy and damp and the stone stairs narrow and winding. Samantha led, followed by Randall,

Thorne, his fiancée and a dozen of the Brothers. Randall tried to keep his breathing even. "This monument was originally built to honor General Joseph Warren."

Samantha turned and smiled. "I met my girlfriends for cocktails last week at the Warren Tavern, just down the road. The sign said it was built in 1780 and that George Washington and Paul Revere drank there. Is that true?"

Randall removed his hand from the outside railing and turned both palms upward. "I am old, my dear, but not that old." He smiled. "Yet I don't doubt the story."

She laughed gaily, the way he had always imagined well-bred, carefree women of leisure laughed. "Now, stop," she said. "I did not say any such thing about you being old. At least you are making the climb. My Christopher's idea of exercise is pushing the buttons on the channel remote."

Tiny beads of perspiration had formed above her top lip and on her nose, and a warm, floral scent wafted over him as he walked in her wake. They climbed in silence for a few minutes, Samantha and her flowing skirt setting a steady and alluring pace. Randall wished he were dressed more casually—his tuxedo constrained his movements and the dress shoes bit into his feet. He would need a long rest at the top. The ceremony could wait.

Randall turned his attention to his guest. "You seemed interested in the alignments I showed you in Washington."

"Very much so," Thorne replied.

"Well, obviously, in Washington we had the advantage of designing a city from scratch. Here in Boston, things were different. Even though ours is the third oldest Grand Lodge in the world, after England and Ireland, when the Boston Grand Lodge was chartered in 1733 the city was already a hundred years old." He paused to breathe. "The streets were already laid out and the city built up. Plus there was a time, in the early 1800s, when anti-Masonic feelings ran deep in Boston. So we needed to be more creative, and also more ... what is the word ... circumspect, with our alignments."

"I'm expecting we're going to see some of those alignments in a few minutes," Thorne said.

Samantha turned. "My daddy used to say y'all were not a secret society, but a society with secrets." She smiled again and leaned down, her breasts dangling inches above Randall's nose, her floral scent filling his nostrils. She whispered at Randall. "I just love secrets."

Randall swallowed. Secrets conveyed power. And some women, he knew, found men with power intoxicating. Especially men who reminded them of their father. It was obviously nothing more than a harmless flirtation, but it had been years, if not decades, since a woman this attractive had paid him this much attention. As the saying went, he was old, but he wasn't dead yet...

"Oh," she said, "I see the top step."

After giving his guests a few minutes to enjoy the view, and himself a few minutes to catch his wind, he gathered Thorne, his fiancée, and Samantha around the observation area's south-facing window. He pointed toward the Boston skyline and moved aside to offer Throne a clear view. "Can you find the State House dome?"

He pointed it out.

"It was built in 1795," Randall said. "At that time, there were no skyscrapers, of course. A generation later, in 1825, construction began on this monument. As you might imagine, these two structures dominated the skyline."

Thorne's fiancée spoke. "Both buildings relate to the sun. The obelisk dates back to ancient Egypt and sun worship. And the gold-covered dome resembles the sun."

Randall nodded. Thorne had picked a sharp one. "Correct. Around this time the Freemasons began to look for an appropriate location to build our Grand Lodge. It took a few decades, until 1859, but we finally found the spot we needed." He turned to Thorne. "Can you guess where?"

Thorne squinted into the distance. "Here," Randall said, pulling a pair of powerful binoculars from their carrying case. "These should help."

Thorne focused the lenses, though Randall sensed his guest already knew what he was going to find. "I think I see the Grand Lodge building right behind the State House dome."

"Yes. Yes you do."

179

Thorne handed the binoculars to his fiancée and looked at Randall. "And you're going to tell me it's not a coincidence." He smiled. "I, in turn, am going to believe you."

"You should. The Grand Lodge, the State House dome, and the Bunker Hill Monument are in perfect alignment." Randall paused while they passed the binoculars around and considered the unlikely possibility that the Grand Lodge just happened to be in line with the sun-symbolizing obelisk and golden dome. "We Freemasons love symbolism and allegory."

"And," Thorne said, "you also love sun worship. That's why you aligned the Lodge with sun symbols. Tic-tac-toe, three in a row."

Randall shrugged. "I didn't say that. You did."

Thorne shook his head and chuckled. "Well, you were right, I'm blown away."

Randall checked his watch, pleased at Thorne's reaction. Most of the rest of the group had already begun to descend. "We should be heading down."

"Can you show me again where the Lodge is?" Samantha said. "I think I spotted it but I'm not sure." She put her handbag on the window ledge, removed a tissue, and dabbed her face with it.

"Cameron, can you go ahead and tell them I'll be down soon?" Randall asked as he turned to assist Samantha. He had no idea where this might go, but there were worst places to be than alone at the top of a tower with a beautiful woman.

She leaned closer, her body brushing against his, and pointed toward the window. "Is that the dome there, to the left of the bridge stanchion?"

"That's it," he replied. He put the binoculars back to his eyes. "And just behind the dome is a gray stone building. That's the Lodge."

He lowered the binoculars just in time to see Samantha's arm arcing through the air, a black club-like object hurtling toward the side of his head. In the split-second before impact, he realized she must have waited until they were alone before removing the weapon from her handbag.

It was his last thought.

☥ ☩ ⚏

"That's pretty cool," Cam said to Amanda as they descended the Bunker Hill Monument. The connection between the Masons and the ancient Egyptian sun worshipers was becoming uncontestable. "Nobody can see the alignment today because of all the other buildings, but back in the 1800s it must have been obvious. And impressive."

"I wonder how many other old cities have similar alignments. New York, Philadelphia, London, Edinburgh, Paris—I bet they all have secrets like Boston."

Cam was about to respond when the clack-clack-clack of someone running down the stairs above them interrupted. A female voice echoed in the narrow tower. "Help! Mr. Sid has fallen!"

Cam spun and raced up the stairs, taking them two at a time, Amanda behind him. A couple of flights into his climb he nearly collided with Samantha on her way down. Breathless, she spoke. "Mr. Sid fell. He must have slipped. He was right in front of me. He hit his head and then tumbled down and down." Tears ran down her cheeks. "He's not moving. He's not breathing."

Amanda pushed by, using the railing to pull herself along. She had some first aid training from coaching gymnastics.

"You call 911," Cam said to Samantha. "Then go to the bottom and see if there's a doctor there. Or at least a first aid kit."

"Okay," she sobbed. "Okay."

Cam reached Amanda less than a minute later. She was bent over Randall's twisted body, attempting to revive him with chest compressions. She had straightened his upper body so his head rested on a stair, but his legs remained askew like an old scarecrow. She counted, compressing at each number. "Damn it, breathe," she ordered.

"Anything?" Cam asked. Blood covered Randall's ear and shirt collar. Randall's body lay sprawled only twenty steps from the top. Maybe his eyes had not had time to adjust to the dim stairwell.

"Nothing," Amanda responded. At the count of thirty she shifted, lifted his chin, pinched his nose and breathed into his

181

mouth twice, each time his chest rising slightly in response. Then she returned to the compressions.

"This is bad, Cam," she panted. "He's not breathing on his own."

In the distance a siren wailed. Amanda continued CPR, alternating between compressions and breathing, while Cam watched and wondered. He had noticed the old man looking up Samantha's skirt on the way up. On the way down he would have had a clear view down her loose-fitting blouse as the stairs spiraled.

So why would he have walked in front of her?

Twenty minutes later Cam and Amanda followed the paramedics down the monument stairs as they carried Randall Sid's lifeless body. Because of the tight stairwell they had to angle him downward as they descended, his tuxedoed body strapped to a backboard.

A policeman met them at the bottom. "You were the ones to find the body?" he asked.

"No," Cam said. "A woman was with him. Samantha. I think she said her last name was Hendricks or Handrick. She's the one who called 911." He scanned the area. "But I don't see her."

A few dozen Masons and guests remained gathered at the base of the obelisk, all eyes on their deceased Grand Master. The policeman called out. "I'm looking for Samantha." He waited a few seconds. "Samantha?"

He turned to Cam and Amanda for help. Amanda spoke. "She was at the front of the line with us. In her thirties, long brown hair. Wearing a light blue floral skirt and a beige blouse."

A middle-aged man replied. "She's the one who told us Randall fell. She asked for a doctor." He looked around. "But I don't know where she went."

"I think I saw her walking away," a woman said, pointing.

Cam's suspicions grew. Why wouldn't she stick around? "She said her husband's name was Christopher and he was a new Mason. Anyone know who he is?"

Blank faces.

Cam turned to the policeman. "I'm not so sure this was an accident," he whispered.

Tereza Bilic walked north in the fading light of dusk, toward the seamier neighborhoods of Charlestown's squat brick public housing complexes. Not that they compared to Dubrovnik during the Croatian War of Independence of her youth. More than half her city had been destroyed. From its ashes—and from ashes throughout the old Yugoslavia—rose an entire generation of citizens trained in urban warfare. Many of them, like herself, had little trouble finding work.

Careful to avoid security cameras, Tereza turned right on Bunker Hill Avenue and found the old-model sedan she had stolen from a Logan airport satellite parking lot earlier in the day. Removing her wig and skirt, she wriggled into a pair of jeans, put on a baseball cap and pair of horn-rimmed glasses and eased into traffic. She crossed the Tobin Bridge into Chelsea and followed Route 1 north for a few miles to a shopping plaza. Using a rag she found in the stolen car, she wiped clean the metal flashlight she had used as a weapon and tossed it into a dumpster.

She examined the old rag. She had opted to club the old man a second time on his temple before shoving him down the stairs, just to make sure the job was done. There might be skin tissue or blood traces on the rag, and also in her bag. No sense taking any risks. She bought a pound of ground beef in a grocery store and walked back to her car parked along the edge of the lot. After removing her passport and a few other personal items, she ripped open the hamburger and placed the beef, along with the rag, inside her handbag. She tossed it into the woods, a treat for some dog or wild animal to devour overnight.

Leaving the car in the parking lot, she jumped on the 111 bus headed into downtown Boston. As she rode she sent a quick text— *Package delivered*—before deleting the message from the phone and removing the SIM card and battery. Once in Boston she ducked into the subway, discreetly dropped the phone into a trash can and took a train to South Station, arriving forty-five minutes before her scheduled overnight train to Washington, D.C. From there she would catch a flight to Paris.

Tereza had spent almost a week in Boston, and prior to that a week in Washington, her original assignment only to follow the old man and report on his activities. Then last night the order had come in for elimination. As was her custom, she wasted no time. Nor would she waste any time disappearing.

☥ ✝ ⬦

Amanda took Cam's arm as they walked away from the Bunker Hill Monument, now illuminated by spotlights, toward their car. She wasn't a hypocrite—she hadn't much liked Randall Sid in life, so she wouldn't shed fake tears at his death. Cam seemed convinced he had been murdered, and his instincts on this kind of thing were usually spot on. "Assuming you are correct, who would want him dead?" she asked.

He exhaled through a clenched jaw. "I have to assume it's related to all the other shit going on. The lottery ticket debacle, the deed, the photographs, the guy attacking me on my run."

In a perverse sort of way, she hoped Cam was correct. If Randall really was murdered, and the crime was related to the events Cam just listed, that swung the needle even further toward the photographs being fake. It didn't prove anything for certain— Cam's enemies could have caught him in a compromising situation and used the photos to humiliate him or for some reason derail their pending marriage—but it at least made Cam's claim plausible. After all, what are a few doctored photos compared to murder? She voiced her thoughts aloud.

Cam nodded. "Your logic is sound, but you're forgetting one thing: Whoever murdered Randall could do the same to us."

"Theoretically, yes. But it seems to me that someone is trying to use you, manipulate you. Not murder you."

"For now, yes. But once they get what they want?"

They turned the corner. She felt the urge to go for an ice cream, to sit on a bench and count stars and tell each other stories about their childhood. But that's not who or where they were right now. "You know, we've been assuming there's only one person trying to pull your strings. But maybe we're wrong to look at it that way." She glanced at him. "Who wants what? Let's start with Zuberi."

"Short answer is he wanted me to take the Brandeis job."

"But why?"

"I think there are two things going on. Carrington wants to promote the story of her ancestors discovering the New World, and Zuberi wants me to find more evidence Scotland was first settled by Egyptians."

"Has he asked you to look into the Scota stuff?"

"Not directly, but it's understood. He's always sending me articles and stuff."

"Okay, who else? What did Randall want?"

"I don't know. I don't know if I'll ever know. The Masons have definitely been feeding me information about the Druids and ancient Egyptians." He shrugged. "But who knows why?"

"Well, okay, we have an intersection point here with the ancient Egyptians. Zuberi and Randall were both directing you toward them."

He nodded. "And my research on the ancient Egyptians led me to the Isaac Question revelations."

"Which is pretty toxic stuff. So maybe that's what this is all about."

He popped the lock and they climbed into the SUV. She continued the conversation. "What about the lottery ticket? Does that guy tie in at all?"

Cam shook his head. "If he does, I don't see how. That whole thing makes no sense. The fake baby, the lottery ticket, throwing me into the harbor. Just weird."

"How about the email, the guardian angel guy?"

"From what he said, he wants to help me. And I haven't heard boo from him since his first email."

"Anyone else?"

"Well, don't forget your original theory that whoever sent me the deed to the Groton property was trying to stop our research. It seems like Zuberi, Randall, even the guardian angel guy are all supporters of it."

"So maybe there's another player in all this, someone trying to stop you? Someone who might want to stop Randall from helping you? The guy who attacked you on your run mentioned someone had been following us in Connecticut? Who's that?"

Cam turned onto the highway. "Well, there's actually two mysteries here: Who was the guy in Connecticut, and who was the guy on my run trying to figure out who the guy in Connecticut was?"

"And then who was the guy following him? The guy who saved you? So there's actually three guys. I wonder if that third guy was the guardian angel?"

"Could be. Or I wandered onto a Three Stooges movie set."

She smiled. "Okay, so we have Zuberi, Randall Sid and the Freemasons, lottery ticket guy, guardian angel guy, our tail in Connecticut, and the guy who attacked you on your run."

"Plus whoever deeded me the property and sent the pictures, assuming it's not someone you already mentioned." He turned and smiled. "I'm glad you've straightened this all out for me."

"It is a bit bollixed up, I admit."

Cam stared ahead, chewing his lip. "You told me a few weeks ago the best thing to do was just keep doing our research. Someone is trying to stop us, and we can't give in." He glanced at her quickly. "But I'm worried about you and Astarte. Maybe you guys should get out of town for awhile."

Amanda shook her head. "And go where? If you're right, and someone did kill Randall, that means that Samantha woman was a paid assassin. I don't think people like that would have any trouble finding Astarte and me no matter where we hid."

"Fair point."

A ping from Cam's phone interrupted their conversation. Cam glanced down. "An email from one of the Masons who was there tonight. Randall's lieutenant. Can you read it?"

"Dear Cameron," she read. *"Randall gave me strict instructions to email the attached note to you if anything should happen to him. Obviously contact me with any questions."*

Amanda opened the attachment from Randall and continued reading. *"Not to be melodramatic, but if you are reading this it means I am dead. Perhaps from natural causes, perhaps not. It does not matter. But there are things I still have not shared with you, things that will help you better understand the connections between the Masons and the Druids. The Templars had knowledge, which they passed down to us, that the Druids came to America early in the Dark Ages to hide the head of a very important man."*

Amanda looked up at Cam, sensing the importance of the revelation. "Again with the head."

Nodding, he breathed a singled word. "Baphomet."

"Yes." In her mind, she pictured a stone chamber with a niche recessed deep inside. Inside the niche rested a treasured ancient skull, illuminated once a year—on the winter or summer solstice—by the rays of the life-giving sun. Her body reacted to the image with an involuntary shudder.

She read on. *"The Christians were taking over the British Isles at that time and the Druids did not want the Christians to have the head. The Druids believed the head possessed great power—visionary power—and that whoever possessed it would see the future and rule the land. No hiding place in Europe was safe, but the head needed to be preserved, so the Druids brought it to America. This was in the early 6th Century. Later, in the late 1100s, the Templars came back to retrieve it. This head, I'm sure you've already deduced, later became known as Baphomet. Everyone thinks the Templars came to America to hide something. And later that's what they did—they hid things from the Church. But the first time they came over, they came to retrieve the Baphomet head."*

Cam let out a whistle. "Wow. That's good stuff."

"Wisdom from the grave. I wonder why he didn't tell you before."

"He liked to feed this stuff to me in tiny morsels, like to a dog." Cam smiled. "It kept me coming back." He shifted lanes. "How far are the Catskills from the Putnam County stone chambers Shannon was telling us about?"

"I'm with you," Amanda said. They both were thinking about a twelfth-century travel log they possessed which described a Templar journey to New York's Catskill Mountains. In fact, the log—which they called a codex—along with maps and carved stones had been given to them by Astarte's uncle just before his death. If the Templars had been searching for the head in the beehive chambers of New England and New York as Randall was suggesting, that could explain why they were in the Catskills in the late 1100s.

Amanda and Cam belonged to an organization called New England Antiquities Research Association, which studied and catalogued the mysterious stone structures in and around New England. On the group's website Amanda found a list of chambers in New York's Putnam County. She pulled up a map on her phone. "It looks like the chambers are mostly located along the Hudson River, maybe fifty miles south of the Catskills. A pretty straight shot."

"Okay," Cam said, switching lanes, "so the Templars were going up and down the Hudson looking for the head. But here's the obvious question: Whose head is it?"

"It has to be John the Baptist, doesn't it?" she replied.

"You said he was beheaded by some Druid visiting Jerusalem—"

"Mug Ruith was the executioner. He left the body out to be eaten by vultures, but the head was never found."

"So maybe this Mug Ruith took the trophy home with him to Ireland, where the Druids kept it and venerated it as the grand prize in the Cult of the Head worship." He paused. "But why would the Druids venerate a Christian prophet?" Cam asked.

"At the time he was beheaded, there was no such thing as Christianity, at least not as we know it. John the Baptist was just a prophet who people believed had amazing visionary powers. And remember, that's the reason the Druids preserved these skulls— they believed the skulls could look into the future and serve as shepherds to the living. So a few centuries later, when the Christians started squeezing the Druids out, the Druids needed to hide the head, as Randall suggests."

"So off to America." Cam nodded. "It works." He paused, drumming the steering wheel with his finger. "The one thing that doesn't make sense is why would Brendan the Navigator, a Christian, hide the skull from other Christians?"

Amanda turned in her seat. "Don't forget, the legends say there were three Druids on the voyage with Brendan. Maybe Brendan had no idea."

Cam nodded. "The pieces fit together. Later the Templars learned of the head across the Atlantic. And they had long venerated John the Baptist."

"Would the Templars have risked crossing the pond to get his skull? At the time, it would have been considered incredibly dangerous." Amanda had a strong opinion on this question, but she wanted to hear Cam's thoughts first.

"Would they?" Cam sniffed. "They would have swum across if they had to."

☥ ✝ ⚒

During the rest of the car ride home from Charlestown they discussed whether it made sense for Amanda and Astarte to go into hiding. In the end Amanda carried the argument. "Honestly, Cam, I don't think Astarte and I have anything to do with this. If they want to stop your research, they'll come after you, not us. But even so, I think we're safest here. We have the alarm system now, the police are watching the house, and we know all the neighbors so any strangers lurking around would stick out like an Adam's apple on a beauty queen."

Cam smiled. "I've never heard that one before."

"I thought about using turd in a punch bowl, but it seemed vulgar even for me."

He smiled again. He actually liked her vulgarity.

"Anyhow," she continued, "like I said earlier, if some professional assassin is after us, I doubt we'd be able to hide for long anyway."

He nodded. "Okay. But no more school bus. And no more babysitters—one of us always needs to be with her."

Ten minutes later they pulled into Astarte's friend's driveway. "Let's go for an ice cream," Cam said as they left the house with Astarte. It was important to keep up some sense of normalcy, even as the world swirled around them.

"I thought you liked mayonnaise for dessert," Astarte teased.

He hoisted her over his shoulder in a fireman's carry. "You better watch out or you'll find mayo in your toothpaste."

At the ice cream stand Astarte joined some friends on a swing set. "Sorry to talk shop again," Amanda said, "but I've been thinking about something you told me when you got back from Washington, about how Rosslyn Chapel was meant to tell the history of Scotland with its carvings and symbolism."

Cam kept one eye on Astarte. "You don't agree?"

"No, I think you're spot on." She spooned some black raspberry frozen yogurt into her mouth. "But I don't think you took it far enough. In addition to the Green Men and the sun worship and the ties to the Druids and the Egyptians and Freemasons there's one other thing—carvings that depict North American plants."

Cam knew about these. The theory was that Prince Henry Sinclair brought back drawings or even samples from his 1398 journey and the Earl of Rosslyn, Prince Henry's grandson, carved them into the chapel as a nod to the journey.

Amanda continued. "Everything else carved into the chapel describes early Scottish history, things that tell the story of early Scotland. These plants are out of place. They tell the story of America, and even of the Sinclair family, but not of Scotland." She paused. "Unless there was something in America that relates back to the early days of Scotland."

"Ah," Cam smiled. "You're talking about the head."

"Yes. The Sinclairs were prominent members of both the Knights Templar and the Freemasons. If anyone knew about the head, it would be them." She lifted her chin. "And I'll take it one step further: I bet the head is now hidden someplace at Rosslyn Chapel. There have long been rumors of a skull hidden in or under the Apprentice Pillar," she said, referring to the ornately-carved pillar in the center of the Chapel. "In fact...," Amanda said, pausing as she tapped at her phone. "Yes, here it is."

"What?"

"A letter from Mary of Guise in 1546 to William Sinclair. Mary of Guise was Queen of Scotland and later served as regent for her daughter, Mary Queen of Scots. During the gap between these two reigns she visited Rosslyn Chapel. Apparently William Sinclair showed her some important secret, because afterward she wrote to Sinclair and said to him: '*We shall be loyal and a true Mistress to Sinclair, his Council and the Secret shown to us, which we shall keep secret.*'"

"That's fairly ... subservient language for a queen to use toward a lord, isn't it?"

"Very much so. Rather than Sinclair pledging his loyalty to the queen, it is the queen promising to be loyal to the Sinclairs and not betray their secret."

"So that must have been some secret Sinclair showed her."

Amanda smiled. "That's why I read it to you."

As Cam scooped up the remains of his ice cream, he considered the possibility of the venerated head originally hidden in America being later secreted within Rosslyn Chapel, and eventually shown to the queen under an oath of secrecy. "So how would the head make it to Rosslyn? We know that when the Templars fled France in 1307, lots of them ended up in Scotland."

Amanda nodded. The Templars, commanded by another William Sinclair, fought on the side of Robert the Bruce in 1314 at the Battle of Bannockburn. The famous battle for Scottish independence took place—perhaps not coincidentally—on June 24, John the Baptist's birthday. "The Templars turned the battle for the Scots after all was thought lost at Bannockburn," she said. "After that, Robert the Bruce welcomed the Templars with open arms."

"Along with their treasures," Cam said. Including, quite possibly, the priceless head they retrieved from America more than a hundred years earlier. Cam smiled. "Think about it: What better place to hide a Druidic skull than inside a chapel filled with dozens of little pagan Green Men to stand guard?"

Cam tossed and turned on the pull-out couch. It was Saturday night and he was sleeping alone. Or not sleeping. What had happened to his idyllic world?

Venus, hearing his movements, trotted down the basement stairs to keep him company. She rolled onto her back and he rubbed her stomach. "Your only worry in life is who's going to give you your next belly rub." She cocked her head in an apparent effort to remind him she also chased squirrels from the yard. "Well, if I'm not going to sleep, I might as well do some research." He opened his laptop and sat on an old recliner in the darkened basement

One of the loose ends he needed to chase down was the Scottish Stone of Destiny. The stone, also known as the Stone of Scone, was an oblong block of red-gray sandstone used for centuries in the coronation of Scottish and English monarchs. Cam found a picture of the stone, with a couple of metal rings at either end to aid in transportation, in its location at Edinburgh Castle.

Stone of Destiny, Edinburgh, Scotland

The stone was believed to have originated in the Middle-East and was also called Jacob's Pillow—it was upon this stone that the Biblical Jacob supposedly rested his head while he dreamt of God promising him the land of Canaan. Was this dream inserted into the Old Testament by early writers, Cam wondered, as another attempt to buttress Jacob's claim to the Holy Land in light of his father Isaac's questionable parentage?

In any event, tonight Cam's research focused on how the stone found its way to Scotland. But what he uncovered as he dug made him want to shake Amanda awake and share the revelation.

Using as his source a 14th century book called the *Scotchichronicon,* or *Chronicle of the Scots,* Cam learned that the original Stone of Destiny—rather than being a block of red-gray sandstone—was actually an ornately carved marble throne of Egyptian origin. In a spine-tingling case of dots connecting perfectly, this marble throne had been brought out of Egypt by none other than Princess Scota at the behest of her father, the Pharaoh Akhenaton. Akhenaton had abdicated his throne, but apparently only in the figurative sense—he took steps to make sure the actual seat of power remained in his family.

Cam stared blankly at the wall. The moon had broken through the clouds, bathing the room in a soft yellow glow. Here was another tie-in to the Scota legend, another piece of tangible evidence tying the Scots to the ancient Egyptians. Akhenaton surely kept for himself other symbols of his kingly authority—his scepter, for example. But his daughter Scota would need authentication of her claim to the royal throne as well. What better validation could there be than the throne itself?

So what happened to this throne? How had it morphed from an ornately carved seat of marble to a hunk of sandstone? The answer, as was often the case, was convoluted.

Best Cam could tell, in 1296 the Scots—knowing that Edward I of England intended to invade Scotland and take the Stone of Destiny as plunder and as validation of his rule over Scotland—substituted the throne with another famous stone known as the Bethel Stone. It was the Bethel Stone, not the Stone of Destiny, which the Biblical Jacob had used as his pillow and which now was on display in Edinburgh Castle. The Scots allowed Edward to plunder this ancient Biblical relic, saving for themselves the even more valuable marble throne of Akhenaton.

Which begged the question: Where was the marble throne? Not surprisingly, Cam's old friends the Sinclairs now entered the picture. The family, like the Druids, seemed to pop up in almost every chapter of this saga. Relying on a Scottish history book, Cam learned that in the year 1069 Scottish Queen Margaret appointed Sir William Sinclair as Keeper of the Holy Relics. This position, which the Sinclair family held for centuries thereafter, made the Sinclairs custodians of both the Stone of Destiny and the Bethel Stone, along with the Holy Rood, a piece of the Christ crucifixion cross. The implication was obvious: If anyone knew the location of Akhenaton's throne, it would be the Sinclairs. And the obvious hiding place, of course, would be the family's Rosslyn Chapel. All roads seemed to lead back there.

Cam shook his head. From somewhere across the Atlantic he could hear Zuberi chuckling.

Chapter 7

Amon stood at the gate at La Guardia Airport, straining his neck as a swarm of disembarking passengers rolled toward him after their late morning Tuesday arrival. He breathed into his hand, checking his breath. Stale. But what did he expect? His mouth was as dry as camel dung in the desert. He chugged some water and popped an Altoid.

He didn't remember ever being so nervous. What if she no longer liked him? He had heard numerous stories of love affairs that flamed up in hours and then turned to ash just as quickly. They had spoken every day, usually multiple times, but two weeks had passed since they had seen other, held each other, caressed each other. Would it be the same?

Somehow Rachel spotted him before he saw her, a bright smile and a wave announcing her arrival. He felt his mouth contort itself into a wide grin, like one of those clowns at the circus. What a dork he was. But getting his mouth to close was like trying to put your hand into a flame, his brain powerless to override his body's reflexive reaction.

And then she was in his arms, her face against his, her eyelashes fluttering against and moistening his cheek. He pulled back and smiled. "Are you crying, Rachel?"

She grinned, her hazel eyes watery. "Sorry. I'm just so happy to see you."

He kissed her gently on the mouth, lingering, tasting her. He had never wanted to be one of those people who publicly displayed their affection. But he couldn't help himself. "Come," he said. "Let's get out of here."

He took her overnight bag as she looped her arm through his and leaned into him, matching his stride. She sighed. "I'm sort of, like, nervous to see you."

He stopped. "Really?" he asked, facing her. "Me too. I was worried that what we had was like … magic … or something."

She flashed a wet, white smile. "It was. It is."

Five minutes later they were in the back of a cab on their way to a Manhattan hotel. "So," she said, turning to face him. "I figured we should talk now." She smiled. "So we don't have talk when we get to our room."

He had arrived the night before, splurging for a room at the classic Carlyle Hotel on Madison Avenue near Central Park. "That is a good plan," he grinned.

She handed him a green file folder. "This is what I found so far. We need to check out this obelisk behind the Metropolitan Museum of Art."

"And you think this obelisk will help convince your parents to give approval to our … relationship."

She kissed him on the mouth, apparently happy with his choice of words. "I don't know. But we have to try. And we'll need Professor Thorne's help also."

He thumbed through the file as she continued. "Just so you know, I told them I was going to my friend Shannon's beach house. My mother has an app that lets her track my phone, but she doesn't know that I know she has it. Shannon's really going to her beach house, so I gave her my cell phone to take with her." She held up a cheap disposable phone. "I forwarded all my calls to this. But if my mom tracks me—and I'm sure she will—she'll think I'm on Lake Michigan."

Amon chewed his lip. "I don't like you lying to your parents."

"I don't either. But they're the ones being assholes about this, not us."

Amon nibbled at her ear, waking Rachel from a dream about him. He smelled fresh—toothpaste and hotel soap and aftershave. "How long have you been awake?" she mumbled.

"I never slept." He grinned. "I watched you."

"What time is it?"

"Four."

They had spent the afternoon in bed. She sat up and stretched. "Give me ten minutes. Then we have work to do." She smiled. "The sooner we get it done, the sooner we can come back to our room."

A short walk later, hand in hand in the late afternoon sun, they approached the Metropolitan Museum of Art. Rachel turned left onto a path into Central Park. "We need to go around back behind the Met."

"Tell me again why this obelisk is important." He smiled that shy smile of his. "I was a little distracted earlier."

She took a deep breath. The key was proving a historic connection between the ancient Jews and ancient Egyptians. A familial relationship. Even her parents would be hard-pressed to object to Amon if it turned out the Jews and Egyptians were of the same stock. Actually, that was not true. They still would probably object. But at least she had some ammunition against them. "I was researching the pharaoh, the one Sarah married after Abraham passed her off as his sister. Tuthmosis III. And I figured if Professor Siegel was right, if this pharaoh was Isaacs' father—the true father of the Jewish people—then he must be important. It made no sense that history just forgot him."

"Okay."

The path angled right behind the museum. "So I came across this obelisk. Want to guess who built it?"

"The Freemasons?"

"Good guess, but no. It was built by this pharaoh, Tuthmosis III. The one who married Sarah."

Amon stopped mid-stride. "But how could that be? You're talking, like, thirty-five hundred years ago."

She increased her pace. "That why I was so excited to find it. Somehow the Freemasons got hold of it and brought it to America."

"When?"

"Around 1880."

He shook his head. "All the Western countries were stealing our artifacts back then."

She stopped and looked at him, suddenly realizing the obelisk had special meaning to Amon—it would be like an American seeing the Washington Monument sitting in Gorky Park. She squeezed his hand. "That sucks. And there were two others just like it," she explained. "One went to Paris and the other to London."

They walked in silence, rounding a clump of trees. She pointed. "There it is."

Cleopatra's Needle, Central Park, NY

They stared up at the seventy-foot-high stone obelisk. "It's called Cleopatra's Needle," she said.

"But Cleopatra lived more than a thousand years after Tuthmosis III." Amon shook his head. "If they're going to steal our history, they could at least get the dates right."

She studied the structure, trying to wrap her head around the fact that it dated back to the time of Abraham and Sarah and the pharaohs, back to the earliest days of the Old Testament. It was likely the oldest extant structure in the entire hemisphere—older than anything from the Incan, Mayan or Aztec civilizations. And here it stood in Central Park, largely ignored.

Amon angled his head. "I still don't understand why the Freemasons brought it here."

"I don't either." She pulled out her phone. "But they must have had a reason. And I know who might have some answers."

After his all-night research marathon Saturday night, Cam had slept in on Sunday and spent the afternoon boating with Amanda, Astarte, and some friends, enjoying the lake before the government got around to seizing his 18-foot bowrider. On Monday, Memorial Day, again trying to keep things normal for Astarte, they had gone to see the Red Sox play at Fenway Park. In between family time Cam had fleshed out the outline for *Out of Egypt*. His lawyers were burning through his money and the government continued to play hardball. It seemed like the only path back to solvency was to plant a seed now—in the form of a new book—that might bear fruit a few months down the line once the Superfund litigation was behind him.

He had spent Tuesday with his lawyers. Late in the afternoon on his drive home he got a call from Rachel Levitad.

"Professor Thorne," she said after exchanging pleasantries, "do you think the Freemasons know anything about this Isaac Question?"

"Good question. They seem to know a lot about the ancient Egyptians, so it wouldn't surprise me. Why do you ask?"

She explained she was in Central Park looking at an obelisk built by Tuthmosis III 3500 years ago.

He pulled into the breakdown lane and put on his hazards. "Wait, what?" Another obelisk?

"It's called Cleopatra's Needle. It's behind the Met. I'm texting you a picture now. In 1880, nine thousand Freemasons marched up Fifth Avenue for the cornerstone ceremony. I didn't realize Masonry came from Egypt."

Cam angled his head. "Most people don't. How did you learn that?"

"I read the speech they gave when they laid the cornerstone. The head guy, the Grand Master, talked all about it."

Cam shook his head. Randall Sid had made it sound like such a big secret. And Cam himself had to dig around for days to prove the Egyptian connection. But Rachel found it after surfing the Internet for a few minutes. He glanced quickly at the image she sent.

"Rachel, do you know why they picked that location?"

"Actually, nobody does. It was chosen in secret. The guy who was in charge of dragging it across Manhattan said it was the worst possible location."

Cam smiled. "Not if you're interested in alignments."

"Alignments?"

He asked Rachel to pull up Google Earth while he waited. "See if you can find the Masonic Grand Lodge."

"Got it. On West 23rd Street."

"Now, if you draw a line from the Lodge to the obelisk, what do you see?" Obviously, any two points would connect, but Cam was looking for something more significant.

"Well, for one thing, the line runs parallel to all the north-south avenues of Manhattan."

"Good, that makes sense." He was beginning to learn how to think like the Masons. "They would want the alignment to be in balance with the layout of the city. One more question: When was the Grand Lodge built?"

"1873."

Cam laughed. "So as soon as the Lodge was built, that's when they started making plans to get the obelisk."

"Yes. The planning for Cleopatra's Needle began in 1877."

"Please do me a favor and see if there are any other obelisks in Manhattan that are on this line."

He waited while she navigated around the Google Earth site. "I can see one obelisk already," she said, "the one in front of Saint Paul's Chapel near the World Trade Center." She chuckled. "You're right, it's on the same line."

"I'll bet you can find others also. That's why they put the obelisk in the so-called 'worst possible location'—they had to keep the alignment going."

"This is cool stuff, Professor. I can't wait to take your class this fall." Her voice dropped. "Assuming my parents let me come back."

"Well, hopefully this will help convince them. Tell me, in your research, did it say anything about why they picked this particular obelisk, from Tuthmosis III?"

"No. Do you think it's because of the Isaac Question?"

"I wouldn't doubt it. With the Freemasons, nothing is ever random. They have lots of secrets, and they love to hide them in plain sight. They talk about having 'eyes that see'—in other words, being educated enough to understand what you're looking at."

Cam thanked Rachel and hung up, mulling over what he had just learned as he merged back into rush hour traffic. He had established that the Masons based much of their ritual on the ancient Egyptians, and he had assumed it was because of sun worship. But perhaps it was more complicated than that. Perhaps the Freemasons, like Rachel and her Brandeis professor, had stumbled upon the inconsistencies of the Old Testament and deduced that Isaac was not the son of Abraham but rather the son of Pharaoh Tuthmosis III. If that were the case, erecting an obelisk honoring Tuthmosis III would be perfectly appropriate for a group that, being largely Judeo-Christian, descended from this forgotten patriarch.

Rachel had said that nine thousand Masons marched to commemorate the laying of the obelisk's cornerstone. Of that group, probably only a handful—the 33rd Degree Brothers—understood the true significance of the monument. The more Cam thought about it the more convinced he became that this was

201

another case of the Freemasons taking their most cherished secrets and, as he explained to Rachel, hiding them in plain sight.

Amanda watched Astarte run into school, a bright smile on her face. Unfortunately the girl's exuberance was not contagious.

Amanda had mixed feelings about spending the day in the car with Cam. On the one hand, the time they spent researching constituted pretty much the full extent of their quality time together. But it was also a sad reminder of how far they had fallen—a car ride was now as good as it got. No passion, no intimacy, no planning their future together...

Cam stepped away from the passenger side door after cleaning some debris off the floor. He did so almost apologetically, as if he sensed he might be invading her space. "Ready to hit the road?"

She nodded. "As long as we're back by three."

The highest concentration of stone chambers in America existed in the Hudson River Valley north of New York City. Dozens of chambers dotted the landscape, themselves only a small percentage of what once stood in the area. So it made sense for Amanda and Cam to make the drive. They had time to visit only a few chambers, but having examined their own Groton chamber, along with the Gungywamp chamber and a few others in Massachusetts Cam had visited, they had a good sense of the things that differentiated the Colonial root cellars from the earlier Druid structures.

Ten minutes later Cam turned onto the highway onramp heading southwest, Venus chewing on a rawhide bone in the backseat. Amanda had not seen Cam much the previous day, and they did not like to discuss Randall Sid's murder in front of Astarte, so Amanda was a bit in the dark. "Did you hear anything from the Boston police?" she asked.

"Nothing. They probably think I'm a kook. First my dip in the harbor, then this."

"You don't think they agree it was a murder?"

Cam shrugged. "All they really have is me saying he was a dirty old man who liked looking up Samantha's skirt."

"And the curious fact she disappeared."

He shrugged again. "You could see where they might assume she was upset and went home."

"But they would have been remiss not to at least question her."

"Maybe they did. I'll follow up with Randall's Masonic Brothers to see if they've heard anything."

"Speaking of the Masons, can you explain to me this obsession of theirs with the Egyptians? Is it a historical connection, or a religious one?"

"I think it's more historical, maybe even cultural. I don't think the Masons really worship the sun. But I do think they admire and trace their history back to people who did. And don't forget, if they know about this Isaac Question stuff—and based on Cleopatra's Needle, I think they do—then Pharaoh Tuthmosis III would in their mind be the patriarch of the Judeo-Christian people. The Masons would think of him the same way most people think of the Biblical Abraham."

She chewed her lip. The Isaac Question revelations could be toxic. "You say it's not religious. But in some ways it's very religious—the Isaac Question changes the entire dynamic in the Middle East."

He nodded. "I agree. But the Masons are coming at it from a historical viewpoint, not a religious one. If anything, the Masons are anti-religious. I read once that Masons believe man is naturally good and does not need religion. Obviously most religions feel the opposite."

Somehow this ancient Egyptian history had led them thousands of miles west and thousands of years into the future to examine stone chambers in the Hudson Valley…

Amanda stared out the window, letting her mind drift, watching as an endless sea of trees whipped past. American forests, she knew, had been key to attracting European explorers across the Atlantic. Few Americans realized that the Vikings, who needed massive tree trunks to build their ships, had cleared the forests of Scandinavia. When they stumbled upon the soaring woodlands of the New World—an area they named Markland, meaning 'Forest Land'—they must have been ecstatic at the possibility of an unlimited source of timber.

These kinds of things—the need for timber, land, resources—were what motivated exploration of the New World. These, of course, and religion. It always seemed to come back to religion. Cam's comment about the Mason's believing religion not to be necessary dovetailed with her own beliefs. "The thing about religion," she said, breaking the silence, "is that it puts people on a one-way, dead end street."

"How so?"

"Just think about it. Religions ask you to believe some truly outlandish things—immaculate conceptions, seas parting, virgins in paradise, reincarnations as a mosquito. Most people, being rational, would normally think it all rubbish. Who would believe such fairy tales?"

"Apparently, lots of people."

"Exactly. And they believe this bunk because they've convinced themselves it must be true. Here's the thought process: *I know I'm not an idiot. I believe in virgin birth. Only an idiot would believe such a thing ... unless it were true. Therefore it must be true.*"

"Well, what about other people who believe in other religions?"

"Exactly, what about them? Let's continue the exercise. *Since I know my religious beliefs are true, any contrary religious beliefs must be false. And what kind of fools would believe such obvious rubbish?*"

She paused. "See what's happening here? It is almost impossible for me to have strong religious beliefs while at the same time respecting members of other religions. They are, after all, misguided at best and idiots at worst." She exhaled. "And don't forget, they feel the same way about me. From there, it seems, conflict is almost inevitable."

Cam weighed her argument as he drove. "Don't you think you're overstating things a bit?"

She chewed her lip. "Yes, I suppose I am. I agree, not everyone who is religious is so intolerant. But those that are the most intolerant often seem to be able to lead the herd. History has taught us that."

"That doesn't paint a very rosy picture for our future. Most people are religious in some way. Are we destined to always be at war with one another?"

"No. Perhaps your Masonic friends have the right idea. They essentially teach that all religions go back to the same place, to one deity, and as long as you believe in that, the other details don't matter. That gives them a pretty large tent. And I don't recall them starting many wars."

"No," Cam smiled. "But they do want to take over the world, according to the Church."

"The Church fears anything it can't control. As do all religions. Again, the rest of us are just idiots."

Cam turned and smiled. "Well, this idiot feels a bit more educated than he did ten minutes ago."

After stopping for a quick break in Connecticut, Amanda and Cam drove in silence, listening to music, while Amanda researched the Putnam County chambers on her phone.

"Listen to this," she said, "from a *New York Times* article in 2001. Some geologist used something called a proton procession magnetometer to measure the magnetic fields at four stone chambers in Putnam County in the 1990s. He said he got, quote, 'The strangest readings I ever got in this area. It was strong enough to reverse a compass. Each stone chamber had a significant magnetic pull right in front of the door.'"

"Wow."

"Wait, it gets better. This is the geologist again: 'This magnetic anomaly is a true clue that they are much older than the early colonists. Builders put metallic material below the chamber's doorstep plate either to aid in finding the chambers with early compasses or to help early religious leaders perform magnetic tricks during ritual ceremonies to convince people of their special powers.'" She smiled. "Just like you said."

"All us pagans think alike."

As they approached the Connecticut-New York border, Amanda pulled up a map on her phone. "Let's head to the town of Kent. You can stay on 84; it's just over the border. There's a cluster of chambers there, over fifty by one count. And some bloke was kind enough to map them all out for us."

A half hour later Cam pulled onto the shoulder of a winding country road fifty miles north of New York City. The rural setting only an hour away from the country's largest metropolis surprised Amanda. "There," Amanda said, "about fifty feet into the woods."

"Wow," Cam replied as they approached. "Look at the size of some of those stones. A farmer *could* have moved those stones, but why bother? There are plenty of smaller stones that would have done the trick."

"What's the old expression? Most great architecture is meant to impress the gods."

"Speaking of the gods, it's fun to imagine which of these chambers might have housed John the Baptist's head."

"I'm guessing it was at Gungywamp, since that seems to be the main complex. But who knows? Apparently the Templars were looking around here."

They ducked in, Cam pausing to test his compass. He smiled. "Unless the morning sun is in the north, we have ourselves a magnetic anomaly."

They passed through a six-foot high entryway into a rectangular space the width of a single-car garage running over twenty-five feet deep into the hillside. Amanda did some quick math in her head. "It's over two hundred square feet. Would a single farm need a root cellar so large?"

"Only if they were feeding an army. But if you were holding a religious ceremony, or building a shelter, this would be the perfect size." He examined the way the stones fit together so tightly. "I'm getting a bit tired of the root cellar theory."

"I don't doubt some of these chambers were built as root cellars—the records are clear on that. But larger ones like this, with magnetic anomalies and dressed stones and massive lintels, seem older."

She had found something in her research which she hadn't shared yet with Cam. "Did you notice the orientation?"

He stepped outside and found the sun. "Looks like it opens to the southeast."

"And?"

He grinned. "Winter solstice orientation."

"Gold star for you." A couple of weeks ago she would have kissed him on his forehead; today she tapped him lightly with her forefinger. "I found a picture someone took of the solstice illumination." She showed him a picture of the same chamber they were standing in front of, taken at the winter solstice.

Kent Chamber, Winter Solstice

"That light box runs almost right down the middle of the entryway opening," Cam said. "And with a chamber this deep, the sun probably only penetrates all the way to the back wall for a day or two on either side of the solstice."

They hustled back to the car. Continuing their tour, they inspect four other chambers, at least two of which seemed not to be root cellars, before calling it a day.

"That was well worth it," Cam said as they found their way back to the highway.

"We have time for one more quick stop," Amanda said, checking her watch. "Something I think conclusively proves the ancient Celts were here."

She directed him southwest, about ten miles as the crow flies, along a country highway to North Salem, New York. They parked next to an old barn and walked down a short path. An enormous gray boulder sat perched atop five smaller stones like a circus elephant balancing on a unicycle.

Balanced Rock, North Salem NY

Cam grinned. "That's amazing." He peered under. "It's resting on all five stones."

"Some people say a retreating glacier left it perched there."

"No way," he responded. "The weight is too evenly distributed. That doesn't happen randomly. And it's just a coincidence that it's so close to all the chambers?"

She nodded. "That's why other folks say it's a dolmen, a ceremonial site erected by the Celts. It's similar to other dolmens in the British Isles."

He stared at the balance boulder and shook his head. "Unbelievable."

They examined the marvel for a few more minutes before she led him back to the car. He looked back over his shoulder.

"Between the chambers and the dolmen, there's a pretty compelling case the ancient Celts were here." He began to navigate back to the highway. "I don't know how anyone could subscribe to the root cellar theory with this dolmen so close by."

Cam's root cellar comment reminded Amanda of something else she wanted to share with him. She tapped at her phone as he started the engine. "I think we can put the root cellar theory to rest," she said. "Take a look at this." She showed him a picture of a squat, narrow stone chamber.

America's Stonehenge Chamber

"What is it?" he asked.

"It's one of the chambers up at America's Stonehenge." Many experts believed the America's Stonehenge site in New Hampshire dated back 3,500-4,000 years ago, probably built by the ancient Phoenicians. Ironically, this dated the complex to around the time of Abraham—it was possible, therefore, that the complex's chambers were as old as Cleopatra's Needle. "This goes back before the Celts and the Druids," she continued, "but to me it proves ancient explorers built chambers for ceremonial purposes. Look how small this chamber is—the only possible purpose is for a priest to crawl in there to observe an astronomical alignment. It has no other functional use—it's too small for shelter and too open

209

to the elements to store food." She put the phone away. "It simply must be ceremonial."

"Just playing devil's advocate, but who's to say the Native Americans didn't build it?"

She shook her head. "Again, for what reason? It's clearly not a sweat lodge." She had visited the site with a Native American chief a few years earlier, just before meeting Cam. "I think I told you what that tribal elder told me. He said, 'This is an amazing place, but my people didn't build it.' He was certain of it."

Cam nodded. "Okay then."

Amanda unwrapped their sandwiches as Cam turned onto the interstate. "Whenever we visit sites like these, I'm left wondering why others don't reach the same conclusions we do. Why is it so hard to imagine the Atlantic Ocean as a highway rather than some impenetrable barrier?"

Cam took a bite. "Other people have reached the same conclusions. Just not enough of them." He told her about a book written in the 1970s by a Harvard professor named Barry Fell, called *America B.C.* "That book had a lot of people out in the woods looking for Ogham."

She had seen examples of Celtic writing, called Ogham, in museums. It was comprised of a series of horizontal and vertical lines. Something connected in her head. "Wait one second." She tapped at her phone again. "Here it is. I knew I had read this before. It says here that the Ogham script was invented by a Scythian king."

"Scythia again? Really? That can't be a coincidence."

She continued. "And get this: It says here the Scythian king's son married the daughter of an Egyptian pharaoh." She lowered the phone into her lap and smiled. "Apparently her name was Scota."

They rode in silence for a few seconds, each contemplating the meaning of yet another remarkably odd connection tying both the Druids and their American research back to the Scota legend.

Amanda broke the silence. "So what happened with Fell's book?"

"Unfortunately he overreached—he got to the point where he believed every scratch on a stone was a message from the past. Eventually people stopped taking him seriously."

"But that doesn't mean the whole of his work should be discarded."

"You're right. I haven't looked at his research in a while, but he was convinced the Druids were here. Can you find his book online?"

She did, and found her way to a section on the Druids. "Give me a few minutes to skim through this."

Fifteen minutes later she leaned back in her seat and smiled. "Mr. Fell was not shy with his opinions. Like us, he was convinced the stone chambers were Celtic, probably Druidic. But he also found massive phallic stones—seven feet tall—near some chambers in Vermont that he believed were used during Beltane celebrations. Folks would dance around them as part of a fertility celebration."

"Sort of like the maypoles today."

"Not sort of, exactly. That's what the maypole is, a giant phallus to dance around every May."

"So where are these giant stones?"

"Most of them have fallen over, but he found a good number in Vermont, like I said. And they all had Ogham script on them."

"What did the Ogham say?"

She found the passage. "One stone said, 'Beltane Stone,' another said, 'Let it swell,' and a third said, 'To inseminate the birth passage.'"

"Not much room for doubt there."

"And from the pictures in the book, the Ogham marks were clear." She pulled an image up on her phone and showed Cam.

Vermont Beltane Stone

"I agree. These are much clearer than the faint scratches that he became famous—or infamous—for later."

"So here's the thing," Amanda said. "If you're going to have a Beltane celebration, dancing around the maypole and such, you need to have ... dancers. Brendan brought three Druids with him. Not exactly a party."

"I've been thinking about that. My guess is that some of them stayed, became part of the community, took wives, had children. Or maybe there was more than one voyage back and forth. Either way, eventually the custom took hold and was passed down. All cultures have fertility celebrations in the spring. To the Native Americans, this probably looked pretty normal." Cam smiled. "The terminology may be unique, but I think the 'Let it swell' concept is fairly universal."

She moved the conversation onto safer ground; the talk of fertility only served to remind both of them of the deep freeze in their sex lives. "So what's the bottom line on all this?"

Cam chewed his lip. "I think there's a lot of evidence the Druids came here sometime during the Dark Ages and built these chambers. And according to Randall Sid, they came to hide a skull—probably John the Baptist—which the Templars later came back to retrieve."

She nodded. "Not to mention this all ties back to Scotland and the ancient Egyptians."

212

Cam stared straight ahead at the highway. "It's even bigger than that." He paused. "I can't put my finger on it, but I have a gut feeling that this also somehow ties back to the Isaac Question."

Cam and Amanda made it back from New York in time to pick up Astarte from her after-school activity. Cam checked his emails in the parking lot while Amanda went into the school.

A message from Carrington Sinclair-Youssef caught his eye:

"Dear Cameron," it began. *"I hope you don't think me impertinent for writing to you directly. I assure you that Zuberi has given his permission for me to do so."*

Shaking his head, Cam smiled. When they had first met and had dinner, Zuberi relayed Carrington's food order to the waitress for her. And Amanda had noted how she seemed to wait for some kind of nonverbal permission from him before speaking. He read on:

"Zuberi tells me you and Amanda have been researching the Cult of the Head and how it might relate to the Sinclair family and Rosslyn Chapel. Did you know that the first Sinclair/St. Clair to take that name—a man by the name of Clare, in the late 9th century—met with an unfortunate death? Apparently he had chosen to live the life of a hermit, rejecting the overtures of a wealthy heiress. Eventually he became famous as a holy man and healer. The heiress, seeking revenge, sent agents out to kill him. They beheaded him, and the figure of a headless man carrying a skull in his arms became the symbol for the Sinclair family thenceforth. His bones are interred in a nearby church, but the head is missing."

Cam smiled wryly. Another missing head. And more symbolism connecting the Sinclairs with holy skulls.

Rosslyn Chapel's Apprentice Pillar was massive, he knew. Perhaps it needed to be in order to house all the missing heads.

"What the fuck is going on, Moshe?" Tamara had insisted on meeting outside. Nothing made sense, and everything was on the table. Including the possibility that their Brandeis offices were bugged.

Moshe huffed along beside her, his gray slacks and blue sweater vest standing out on the school's outdoor track in the mid-afternoon sun. Tamara had changed into sneakers and sweats, looking forward to the opportunity to perspire away some of her frustration. They kept to the outer lanes to allow the runners to race by, and also to keep out of earshot. "You want the bad news, or the really bad news?"

She didn't need him to make a list for her. First, Zuberi Youssef had met with the Jordanian militant, Khaled, which meant ISIS was that much closer to obtaining another shipment of weapons. Including, perhaps, a small nuclear device. Small, of course, being a relative term—a small nuke would only destroy a city, not an entire country. Second, the Freemason, Sid, had been murdered. The Masons had been working behind the scenes to neutralize ISIS, and his death could only be seen as an attack on these efforts. So another ally lost. Third, Thorne and the young girlfriend of Youssef's son were continuing their inquiries into the Isaac Question, a line of research that Thorne either had shared with Youssef or likely soon would. And, fourth, they were no closer to figuring out who killed Raptor.

They walked in silence for a few seconds. "Moshe, what do you do when you're playing chess and you are losing badly."

He shrugged. "Maybe play for a draw. Or hope my opponent makes a mistake."

"That's bullshit, a loser's mentality." She slapped her palm against the side of an equipment shed, making a loud thwack sound. "If you're losing that bad, you knock the fucking pieces off the board and start over."

He scratched as his skull. "I'm not following you."

"Look, we're getting our asses kicked right now. We need to change the game."

It was hard to rattle Moshe. "You're speaking euphemistically," he said calmly. "Please give specifics."

"Okay. We need to stop watching and start acting. We need information, and since nobody seems to want to give it to us, we need to take it from them." She resumed her walk, increasing the pace. "And it starts with Cameron Thorne."

Amanda had plans to meet an old university friend for dinner in Boston, so Cam threw a few hot dogs on the grill while Astarte pulled the stems off a bowl of fresh pea pods. The meal had become a tradition for them when Amanda was out—Astarte called it their 'peas-in-a-pod-with-a-dog' dinner.

"Campadre, there's no room on the kitchen table." Cam had adopted the practice of printing out pictures of items he was researching in the hope that the visual montage would help him infer connections—dozens of photos of sites, artifacts and other images lay scattered across the table.

"I know. I need to hang them. We can eat in front of the TV if you want. Just don't let Venus steal your food."

Astarte mumbled an "okay," her attention obviously elsewhere, as Cam went to check on the grill. When he returned a few minutes later, the girl was leaning over the table studying a group of photos.

"What're you doing?"

She held up a photo of a skull and crossbones. "What's this?" she asked.

Skull and Crossbones

"It's one of the symbols for the Knights Templar. When they were in battle, if one of the Knights died and they couldn't carry the entire body home, they would take just his head and thigh bones back for burial. Later, pirates started using it because they wanted their enemies to think they were good fighters like the Templars. It's called the Jolly Roger when pirates use it."

She nodded and reached for another photo. "What about this one?"

Chi-Rho Symbol

"That's called a Chi-Rho symbol. The early Irish monks used it." Standing over her, he explained that the Greek letters were the first two letters in the Greek word for Christ.

"I think it looks sort of like the other one."

She reached for a third photo as Cam nodded. The round part of the 'P' was off-center, but otherwise the symbols were nearly identical. "I never noticed that, but you're right."

"What about this one?" she asked.

Crook and Flail

Cam's neck tingled, his body intuiting the importance of her observation even as his mind processed it. "That's an Egyptian pharaoh," he whispered. "He's holding a crook and a flail, which are symbols of power."

"They all sort of look the same to me," Astarte said.

Of course they do, he thought, focusing on the head above the crossed X.

Three symbols, all similar, tying three groups together as sun worshipers, just as he had theorized while in Washington. First, the Templars, and with them the Freemasons; second, the early Druids as they were becoming Christianized; and third, the ancient Egyptians. All three using a variant of the skull and crossbones in their symbolism.

But there was another connection he had not made, one that he saw only now because of Astarte's astute observation. The

217

symbolism did not merely tie the three groups back to ancient Egyptian sun worship. It tied the groups to a specific pharaoh, a pharaoh who championed the sun god over all others, a pharaoh who named this god *Aton* after the Hebrew word for the Lord, *Adonai*. The Templar/Masonic and Druidic fixation on ancient Egypt was far more specific than Cam had realized: Through their symbolism they were all paying homage to the exiled, monotheistic Pharaoh Akhenaton, a/k/a Moses.

Cam awoke early on Thursday morning. Or, more accurately, Venus woke him by jumping on his head. He wondered if she was insulted by the installation of the house alarm, as if she somehow wasn't up to the job. He checked his watch: not even six o'clock.

Ascending the basement stairs, he disabled the alarm—including the motion detectors on the main floor set to detect any movement above Venus' thirty-inch height—and put the dog out on her leash. A faint glow illuminated the eastern horizon; the sky was clear and he was tempted to wake Amanda with a fresh cup of coffee and invite her to sit on the deck with him and watch the sun rise. But he was afraid she'd decline the offer.

He wanted to go for a run, but he and Amanda had agreed to avoid putting themselves into risky situations. Instead he let Venus in, threw his workout clothes into a duffel bag, and wolfed down a breakfast bar. After leaving Amanda a short note and resetting the house alarm, he headed for the gym.

He turned right out of his driveway; the neighborhood was quiet, including any sign of police surveillance. A retired CIA operative had once complained to Cam that modern agents were soft and lazy. "God forbid they have to do something early in the morning, before they've had a shower and cup of coffee. You know," he had said, winking, "sometimes the bad guys set their alarms early."

Windows open, Cam drove slowly along the long side of the lake, into the rising sun. The cool morning air invigorated him even as his gloveless fingers tingled in the cold.

A garbage truck pulled out just ahead of him from an intersecting street, blocking his way, a loud and malodorous intrusion on his morning. He nodded to the man perched on the rear of the truck, then again at the burly driver walking toward him. What a horrible job, he thought—not just because of the work itself, but because of the way most people looked down upon them. Who wanted to roll out of bed every day and spend eight hours with their nose in other people's trash while those same people stuck their noses up at the sight of them?

And then it hit him. *It's not garbage day.* The men raced toward him and had guns pointed at Cam through both front windows even before the thought had fully formed. "Get out," the burly man on the driver's side grunted, his demeanor controlled and matter-of-fact. He had done this sort of thing before. "Now."

Cam's mind raced. Could he throw it in reverse and make a run for it? As if reading his thoughts, his assailant reached in, turned off the ignition, snatched the keys, and tossed them over a fence into a neighbor's shrubbery. He aimed the gun at Cam's knee. "We can do this hard, or we can do this easy."

Cam cursed and unbuckled his seatbelt. A flash in his side-view mirror caught his eye—a bicyclist cruising down the street toward them. "What do you want from me?" he said, hoping to buy some time.

The burly man saw the bicyclist also. "Say a word," he whispered, leaning in, the smell of cigarettes on his breath, "and we kill the guy on the bike." He shielded the gun with his body from the bicyclist's view.

Cam bit his lip. "Okay."

"Just sit there, until he passes."

The bicyclist pedaled past without slowing. Cam exhaled. Didn't the guy think it odd to see a pair of garbage man leaning into opposite windows of a passenger vehicle?

"Okay, get out," the burly man ordered. "Now."

Cam didn't know what else to do. Something about the man's icy calmness convinced Cam that he could, indeed, do this the hard way if Cam didn't cooperate. Cam unlatched the door and slowly stepped out of the SUV.

His captor edged up against him, the hard barrel of the gun pressed into Cam's side. "Walk. Toward the truck." They were going to toss him in the back. This was becoming eerily similar to being locked into the dumpster. "Now get in."

Through his fear an odd thought rose into his consciousness. *Today the bad guys set their alarm early.* He lifted his leg, took a deep breath and, almost retching at the smell, hoisted himself into the back of the garbage truck.

The burly man motioned to his shorter cohort. "Stay back here and watch him. Now let's get out of here."

Cam eyed the man left to guard him. Cam probably outweighed him, and could probably outrun him as well. But the gun offset any size advantage, and Cam could not outrun a bullet. He'd have to use his brains…

The truck suddenly rolled forward. "What the—?" the short man exclaimed, still a few feet away from the truck.

Who was driving? Cam wondered. The burly man could not yet have reached the driver's door.

The truck lurched ahead. The short man reacted and, sprinting, lunged for the metal platform on the rear of the vehicle. Thinking quickly, Cam rolled to his knees and, as the man leapt, shoved both arms into the man's chest, knocking him sideways and away from the platform. The man tumbled to the pavement. The truck swerved to the left, and a second later the body of the burly driver bounced along the side of the road opposite his cohort—apparently the loser in some kind of confrontation with the truck's driver.

Cam leaned back, the truck continuing to accelerate, the bodies of the two henchmen in its wake. The burly man stood, stared angrily at the disappearing truck, and delivered a vicious side-kick to a bicycle leaning against a nearby tree.

Bartol pulled the garbage truck into the lot of a small office park a mile from Thorne's house and exhaled. That was close. He had arrived for his daily surveillance of Thorne's home just as the

SUV was leaving the driveway. A minute or so later and the Mossad would have had Thorne.

Which, Bartol was beginning to believe, might not be such a bad thing. Based on the cell phone calls Bartol had intercepted, Thorne's research seemed to have taken a turn into some dangerous territory. It was one thing to glorify the accomplishments of early European explorers. But what benefit would it be if doing so undermined Judeo-Christian culture and all its accomplishments? This idea that Thorne was exploring, that the covenant God made with Abraham extended to the descendants of Ishmael rather than Isaac, was a toxic one.

It would be one of many things he and Thorne would be discussing this morning.

Bartol stepped from the cab and, giving wide berth in case Thorne tried to jump him, walked toward the back of the truck.

Thorne stood at the edge of the nearby woods, a thick branch in his hand. He had not run, just as Bartol expected. His curiosity would win out—who had rescued him? Plus he probably figured the one-on-one odds were the best he would ever get if he wanted some answers.

Bartol smiled, enjoying the look of recognition and then shock on the author's face. "You," Thorne stammered. "With the scratch ticket."

"Yes, me. You can call me Bartol. I was testing you." Bartol stopped ten feet away, giving Thorne plenty of space. "I imagine you have some questions. We can start at the beginning, or we can start at the end and work our way back."

Thorne held up his cell phone with his left hand. "First of all, all I need to do is push one button to call 911. The police know my number, they know I've been attacked, and they will respond quickly. So don't get any closer."

Bartol nodded and took a step back in response.

Thorne lowered the tree branch. "Now who were those guys with the guns?"

"Mossad. At least I think so."

"Wait, what? Israeli intelligence?"

"You can't get into bed with Arab arms dealers and expect the Israelis aren't going to notice."

221

"Wait again. Hold on." Thorne's jaw tightened. "Zuberi Youssef is an arms dealer?" Bartol nodded. "What did you think he did?"

"Import-export."

Bartol arched an eyebrow. "Okay, you can call it that."

"How do you know?"

Bartol turned his palms to the sky. "I know a lot of things. Like I said, we can work backward, or I can start from the beginning."

"Either way, I'm not in bed with anyone," Thorne said defensively. "I'm doing research. That's all."

"Research that could destabilize the Middle East."

Thorne lifted his chin. "People have a right to know the truth. If it changes things, so be it. Who am I to decide which truths to tell and which to hide?"

Bartol nodded slowly. Thorne's argument carried weight— Bartol had always hated the idea of Big Brother deciding what the populace should know and not know. That was what had first attracted him to Thorne's writing, the fact that he was exposing the true history of early American exploration. But there was still the question of the arms dealer. "And you don't think this arms dealer is using you?"

Before Thorne could answer his eyes widened in fear.

Bartol dove instantly, his training kicking in. Rolling toward the shelter of the truck, he pulled a Glock .45 from a shoulder holster. Slowly he peered out from behind the rear tire of the truck. Two men had positioned themselves at either corner of the office building. Somehow the Mossad agents had followed. In Thorne's SUV, he guessed, after retrieving the keys they tossed. They had probably used some kind of tracking device in the garbage truck. Bartol's entire body tensed. He needed to protect himself, and more importantly his charge.

The adrenaline surged. This is what soldiers did.

222

Cam pushed the "call" button on his cell phone just as the shot rang out. Lunging for the shelter of the woods, he listened for the ping of the bullet ricocheting off the truck or pavement. Instead he heard a dull thud, followed by a low moan.

"Got him. Should I go after Thorne?" A man's voice, across the parking lot.

The burly garbage truck driver responded. "No. We gotta get out of here before the cops come."

Cam's 911 call connected as he watched the two gunmen run toward the main road, where presumably they had parked Cam's SUV. He quickly explained the situation, his hand sweaty and shaking. "A guy's been shot. He needs an ambulance." He described the culprits and his SUV. "They're going east on Route 40."

"Thorne," a raspy voice called.

Cam crouched next to the truck. "An ambulance is coming."

"They got me good," Bartol panted. "Lucky shot, right in the gut."

Cam ripped his sweatshirt off and pressed it to the wound; within seconds his hands were drenched in warm blood. "What else can I do?"

"Just listen." He gulped air. "The property ... in Groton ... it's not contaminated."

"What?" How did he know about Groton?

"Trust me," Bartol said, his voice barely more than a whisper. "They set you up." He coughed, blood dripping down his chin, his face otherwise an unnatural shade of white. "I dug ... there's some kind ... of retention tank ... buried."

A siren approached. "Are you saying the chemical is in the tank, but not in the ground itself?" Who was this guy?

He grinned, his teeth red with blood. "Yes."

The ambulance sped into the lot. Bartol reached a shaking hand out to Cam. "Keep writing ... the truth."

A pair of paramedics rushed over. Cam had dozens of questions for Bartol, but they would have to wait. Perhaps, he sensed, forever.

Cam arrived home just as Amanda and Astarte were sitting down for breakfast. Hard to believe less than an hour had passed; the police had agreed to drive him home and let him clean up before taking a full statement. "How was your workout?" Amanda asked.

"Um, okay," he said, his bloody hands hidden in his pockets. "But I think I got a splinter in my foot." He caught her eye. "Can you come try to get it out for me?"

In the bathroom he showed her his hands and quickly summarized his morning.

"Is Bartol dead?" Amanda asked.

Cam nodded. Later he would explain to her that Bartol was the lottery ticket guy, though Cam never did get an explanation for why other than that Bartol had been testing him. "He bled out before they could even get him out from under the truck."

"How horrible."

"There's a squad car in the driveway now. He's going to wait while we pack." He turned the water on and began to scrub the blood off. "We need to disappear. Now."

She nodded. "Where shall we go?"

"The police have done this a few times before in domestic violence cases. They have a protocol to make sure we won't be followed. We'll get a bunch of American Express gift cards to pay for things. And the police know of hotels and car rental places that won't ask questions."

"What will we tell Astarte?"

He appreciated Amanda trying to be rational, but the blood had drained from her face and her pupils had dilated with alarm. "Good question," he answered. "If she weren't so damn sharp, we could lie to her. But I think we have to tell her the truth, or at least a version of it. Bad guys are trying to stop my research, and until the police catch them we think it's safer to stay in a hotel."

Amanda nodded. "That should work. And we'll need to bring Venus."

"You'll need to take some time off from work, and obviously Astarte will be missing school."

"What about you?"

"Same. I'll have someone cover my closings and cases. And at some point I'll need to make a decision about teaching the summer course at Brandeis. But I am going to continue my research."

"Good. Once you've discovered whatever it is someone doesn't want you to discover, presumably then the cat will be out of the bag and there'll be no reason to intimidate you into silence." She smiled nervously and shrugged. "Or something like that. It made sense in my head."

He turned off the water. "There's just one thing I need to do before we go." He related what Bartol said about the contaminant. "Like I said, I need to give a statement about today's shooting. But the detective agreed we can do it while he drives me out to Groton." Cam's cousin owned a landscaping company. "I've arranged for a Bobcat to meet me out there. It's going to take the police a few hours to arrange our escape anyway. You'll be safe with a detail parked out front."

"Do you think Bartol is correct?"

He shrugged. "Bartol's claim is no more ridiculous than anything else about that property."

She touched his arm. "That would be amazing if the property wasn't contaminated."

He tilted his head. "Yeah, I guess." With their lives in danger and his future with Amanda unsettled, somehow it didn't seem so important anymore.

Tamara and Moshe sat in her office at Brandeis, listening to the report from their field agent on a speaker phone. "I think I got the son of a bitch that killed Raptor, so it wasn't a totally wasted morning." She dipped a spoon into some yogurt while Moshe ate the parts of a blueberry muffin that didn't end up in his lap.

Moshe asked a few operational questions then issued his orders. "Get to New York. Next flight to Tel Aviv." He didn't need to be more specific than that.

They hung up; Tamara tried to control her anger. "Shit, Moshe, was that really necessary?" It was a good thing she had a solid relationship with her boss.

"What do you mean?"

"Going all Rambo like that?"

"How else we going to get Thorne in here?"

Boys. Everything was about guns and trucks and fast cars. "Here, watch." If Moshe had consulted her first, they could have avoided this whole mess. She found a phone number in a manila folder and dialed it. "Hello, Professor Thorne, this is Dean Maxson from Brandeis University."

"Um, hello."

He sounded distracted, but she plowed ahead. "I was wondering if you might be available to come in for a quick meeting? We want to go over some administrative matters, and also get you set up in an office here. And I'll need a syllabus from you so we can order the books your students will need. As you know, summer classes start in two weeks already."

"Hold on one second, it's loud here." She heard heavy machinery. "Okay, that's better. As for coming in, this week will be tough. Can I just email you the syllabus?"

"I'm sorry for the short notice, but we really do need to meet in person. Can you come in tomorrow at all?"

"It's really not a great week."

She pushed harder. "The thing is, we need to get you into the payroll system, and we can't do that until we complete a background check, and we can't do that until we get some paperwork done, and, well, you know how this goes. Plus Mr. Youssef said you have some requests as to how we structure payments to you, which we're happy to cooperate on if possible. But we really need to get started."

He exhaled. "Okay. I can come in tomorrow, say eleven o'clock."

"Great." She winked at Moshe. "See you then."

Tamara hung up. "Now, was that so hard? No guns, no cops."

"And no information yet." Moshe licked blueberries from his fingers. "You still need to figure out a way to get him to talk."

Cam hung up from the call with the Brandeis dean. He wanted to keep as low a profile as possible, but at some point he needed to make the trip to Brandeis if he ever expected to get paid. So might as well get it over with. And if he felt like he was being followed, he'd just cancel. He had no idea if it would be safe to begin teaching in two weeks.

He turned back to watch his cousin's workman push a wheeled box in a grid-like pattern in the area next to the old foundation of the Groton property, where the soil contamination had been found. The box, a ground penetrating radar device, sent radar pulses into the ground in order to detect subsurface voids and disturbances.

"It's weird," the workman said. "There's nothing buried here, and there's no void or anything like you'd find if there was a septic tank or something. But there's a rectangle area where the soil seems … looser. Like it was dug up and then thrown back in, but wasn't tamped down. Outside the rectangle, it's more compacted."

"Bartol mentioned a retention tank," Cam said to himself. He gestured to the Bobcat. "Can we dig?"

"Sure. There's no utilities or anything under there."

They marked a rectangular area the size of a single-car garage with landscaping flags, drove the Bobcat over and began to dig in the center, removing dirt from one side of the rectangle and piling it on the other.

"Careful to keep all the dirt within the rectangle," Cam said.

A half-hour later, the man jumped from the machine and dropped into the four-foot hole he had dug. He kicked at a solid gray object. "I think it's the bottom of that retention tank you mentioned. Fiberglass."

So Bartol had been correct. Cam watched as the man, using a shovel now, cleared away a portion of the bottom of the retention tank, then dug sideways until he found a wall. "It's sort of like an in-ground swimming pool," the man said.

"Okay." Cam had seen enough. Someone had buried the retention tank and then, apparently, injected trichloroethene into the soil inside the tank's perimeter. Anyone testing the soil would find the contaminant. But the surrounding environment was totally protected, the chemical solvent unable to flow beyond the barrier. The whole thing was a set-up, designed so that a test of the soil would reveal contamination, but also designed so that—unbeknownst to the testers—the contamination would be contained within the four walls of retention tank.

"Whatever you do," Cam said, "don't puncture the walls of the tank."

The man nodded. "Roger that. How much more you want me to dig?"

"You know what, that's enough." The Westford cop was waiting patiently for them to finish. "If you can put the soil back and flatten it out, that'd be great. Just make sure the dirt you dug up stays within the perimeter of the tank."

Cam walked around, taking one final look at the hole in the ground that had put such a hole in his life. As always, the question of why pounded at him. Who had come up with such an elaborate ruse, and to what end?

Whatever the reason, this was the first good news in weeks—without the threat of groundwater contamination, the potential liability had been drastically reduced. The site still needed to be cleaned and monitored, but the costs now would total in the tens of thousands rather than the millions. But, again, someone had not only gone to the trouble of deeding him a contaminated property, but also had first taken steps to ensure the contamination had been secretly contained. Did they plan to reacquire the property at a later date? Were they concerned about their own liability for cleanup costs? Perhaps someone who was more than happy to screw Cam but morally opposed to doing actual damage to the environment?

He thanked the workman and began walking back to the street. He phoned his lawyer, Nina, and gave her a quick update as he approached the cruiser. At least he could stop incurring legal bills. "But please don't say anything to the EPA yet," he said to her. "Someone's trying to fuck with me. Let them think they're getting away with it for a while longer."

Amanda pinballed around the master bedroom, trying to decide what items to pack. Would they be gone for a week, a month, longer? In the end she opted to go light on clothes—she could always buy more if she needed—and heavy on things like important papers and photos and keepsakes that were irreplaceable.

Just after nine her cell phone rang, her body involuntarily clenching in response as she recognized the number. She had never lied to Cam. And this technically was not a lie. She just hadn't told him that she had taken the photos to another lab for a second opinion. What if, on the verge of fleeing, the lab confirmed the validity of the photos? Would she then just take Astarte herself and disappear?

The last thirteen days—yes, she had been counting—had been hellish. She felt like an old married couple just staying together to make it easier on the kids. The uncertainty was paralyzing, stifling. Were they building a life together or not?

On ring number three she swallowed and answered.

A man's voice, professional and respectful. "We have the results back on those photos."

"Yes?" She leaned against the bed's footboard.

"Whoever did this did a good job. But I'm pretty sure one of the photos—the one with the gentleman inserting the key card—has been altered. The light isn't quite right, and one of the shadows is at the wrong angle. I think the woman was added later."

Her knees buckled even as the weight of an uncertain future lifted from her shoulders. She tried to speak but nothing came out.

"Ma'am? Are you there?"

"Sorry, yes," she mumbled. "Are you certain?"

"No, not certain. It's possible there was light reflecting off a mirror not in the shot, which could explain the discrepancies, but that seems unlikely. I'd say we have probably eighty percent certainty on this. Maybe even ninety."

Was that enough? "What about the shot of them walking down the hallway."

"I didn't see anything on that one. But, as I'm sure you know, we don't see the gentleman's face. If one shot was altered, this one could have been done with a body double."

"And the shot at the bar?"

"Nothing questionable about that one." He paused, apparently uncomfortable saying anything more.

"Please continue. Speak freely."

"Well, she could have just been reaching over to ask him to pass the pretzels, you know? If someone wanted to set him up, they would have had the camera ready to catch the second or two her hand was on his. But I'm just guessing, in light of the other picture likely being altered."

Astarte appeared at the bedroom door, her packed suitcase next to her. Venus bound over, nuzzling Amanda's thigh. "Okay, thanks, thanks very much," Amanda said, hanging up. And to Astarte, "Come give me a hug, honey."

The girl's cobalt eyes widened as she strode over. "What's wrong, Mum?"

"Nothing," she sobbed. "Nothing at all."

"Husband," Carrington said, knocking on his home office door, "please pardon my interruption."

He glanced at his watch. Three o'clock. He rarely worked during business hours from their home; he much preferred his office in a strip mall on the outskirts of Edinburgh. Most of his employees were Egyptian expatriates like himself, many of whom he had known his entire life, but there was no sense in tempting fate by being an absentee boss. As the saying went, *Opportunity makes a thief.*

When he did work at home, Carrington knew not to interrupt him unless it was important. "Yes, my wife. Sit down."

Zuberi turned to Bennu, doing her homework on a small desk adjacent to his. On the rare times he worked at home, he liked it when she joined him. Over the past couple of years he had to bribe her to do so, today (at Carrington's suggestion) with tickets and a limo to some rock concert all the kids were going to. She had actually given him a hug in response. He had been dismayed to smell cigarette smoke in her hair, but said nothing.

"Would you excuse us, little bird?" he said.

She sighed and stood. "Whatever."

Carrington carried a tray with a cup of tea and a bowl of dried figs, which she set in front of him. "I just received a phone call that I wanted to share with you," she said. "It was from an elderly chap by the name of Duncan Sinclair. He and my grandfather Malcolm were second cousins, best I can ascertain. He just returned from a conference in Washington, D.C. Your name came up, Zuberi."

Zuberi sipped his tea using his good arm. He recognized the Duncan Sinclair name; now retired, the man at one point had chaired the Bank of Scotland. "What kind of conference?"

"The Freemasons. Apparently Duncan is a high-ranking member."

"And what does cousin Duncan want?" Something about this didn't feel right.

"He wants to meet with you. He claims the Masons are concerned about ISIS. They are hoping you will curtail your arms sales to them."

Zuberi sniffed dismissively. "You can tell him only way Zuberi not sell to ISIS is if Masons pay higher price." He chuckled as he pictured a bunch of middle-aged men in funny hats and aprons running around with rocket-propelled grenade launchers.

She nodded and stood. "Of course, husband." Halfway out the door she stopped. "One thing to think about, Zuberi, is that Duncan is one of the trustees of Rosslyn Chapel. Do you foresee any reason we might want to have access to the chapel? Perhaps even dig?"

He smiled. Carrington had been holding this nugget back; this was what he sensed earlier. But the question was a valid one: If Cameron's research was correct, there could be hard evidence of Egyptian settlement of Scotland hidden in the chapel. "Very well," he said. "I am businessman. I will meet with him. Everything is for sale, and anything can be bought."

Cam, Amanda, and Astarte drove in Amanda's car to the police station with a police escort. Once there, they eased into the station garage, the doors closing behind them. Two windowless police vans and three SUVs with tinted windows sat in a row.

"Five choices, pick any one you want," Lieutenant Poulos said. A balding, paunchy, bear of a man, he had been Cam's baseball coach in high school. "All five vehicles will leave the station at once, all going in different directions. Whoever's after you won't be able to follow all of them. And even if they happen to get lucky, the guy driving you is an expert at spotting tails."

"Where we going?" Cam asked.

"Two choices. One of our guys has a brother who owns a motel up in Salisbury Beach. Straight shot up Route 495. There's a two-bedroom cottage they rent out. It's preseason, so it won't cost you much." He smiled at Astarte. "Heated pool, plus a big game room. And Wi-Fi, which I'm guessing you'll want. Second choice is closer, a furnished apartment near Lowell General that they use for visiting nurses. It's empty now." He again smiled at Astarte. "But no pool."

It was an easy choice; they wanted to make this as stress-free as they could for Astarte. "Did you bring a bathing suit?" Cam asked.

"No," she frowned.

"Well, I guess that will be our first purchase when we get there."

Two hours and one unremarkable trip in a police van later they arrived in Salisbury. They had unpacked and were now sitting by the pool watching Astarte swim in a pair of shorts and t-shirt. Their cottage overlooked the beach and was disconnected from the main hotel, offering just enough privacy. Amanda picked at a slice of pizza. "So, now what?" she asked.

"You mean we can't just sit here and enjoy ourselves?" he smiled.

She took his hand. "I'd like that. I really would. But I think we have some work to do first."

He wondered about her sudden affection, but now was not the time to bring it up. He told her about his conversation with his lawyer regarding the Groton property. "Someone thinks they have leverage over us that they don't really have. I'm willing to let them keep thinking that."

"Good idea."

"And tomorrow I need to go into Brandeis." He related the phone call from the dean.

"Is that wise?"

"They're dropping off the rental car here this afternoon. I'm pretty sure we haven't been followed, and if we have it doesn't matter if I go to Brandeis or not. And I don't think anyone will be looking for me there."

"Okay. Please be careful. Perhaps wear a disguise."

He nodded, his eyes on Astarte diving to the bottom of the pool to retrieve a coin. "Bartol said something today that has me wondering. He says Zuberi is an arms dealer. And he thinks he's using me in some way to help his business."

"Odd. How would your research affect his arms sales?"

"The Scottish history stuff not so much. But the Isaac Question—that could be like lighting a bonfire in a munitions dump."

She nodded. "I could see that." She weighed it in her mind. "Although, when Zuberi first approached you, this Isaac Question stuff hadn't even come up yet. So maybe not."

Cam took a deep breath. "Which leads to the other thing Bartol said: He thinks it's the Mossad that's after me."

Amanda's green eyes widened. "Bloody hell, the Mossad? Why?"

"Again, because of the Isaac Question."

"But you just stumbled upon that last week. And nobody knows about it, right?"

"True." He thought about it. "Maybe they're just concerned about Zuberi in general. And when I entered the picture, they took an interest in me also."

"Well, either way, the Mossad being involved explains a lot." She looked out over the ocean. "So did they off Randall Sid?"

Cam shrugged. "I don't know why they would. The Masons are trying to get Zuberi to stop selling to ISIS. You would think the Israelis would want the same."

"So perhaps it wasn't the Mossad. Then who?"

"Maybe ISIS? If they want to buy from Zuberi, and the Masons were trying to stop the deal, then that's their motive."

"We're just guessing now. That woman Samantha who bashed Randall's head was many things, but based on the cleavage she was showing I'd wager a Muslim fundamentalist was not one of them."

☥ ☦ ⊛

They found an arcade near the hotel and spent Thursday evening in good-natured video game and air hockey competitions while munching on fried dough washed down with flat soda. "Tomorrow morning I'm taking the car and doing a food shop," Amanda announced. "If we keep eating like this we'll need to find a larger cottage."

"Speaking of which," Cam said, "we left Venus there alone. Let's go rescue her."

As they walked home, the main strip starting to come to life for the summer with a few t-shirt shops open and a gaggle of teenagers gathered by the beach, Amanda took Cam's arm. He wondered, had she done so unconsciously, out of habit? Two weeks had passed since the photos arrived in the mail, two weeks of uncertainty and doubt. Cam had taken a philosophy class in college and the professor had written a quote on the board that popped into his head now: *To believe with certainty, we must begin with doubting.* Maybe Amanda had examined her doubt, wrestled with it, studied it and plumbed its depths, and concluded it was unsubstantiated. He relished the feel of her fingers on his skin, the smell of her hair in the evening breeze.

Back at the cottage, Amanda helped Astarte unpack and settle in while Cam walked Venus and checked in with Lieutenant Poulos using a disposable cell phone.

"Our guy's pretty sure nobody followed you up to Salisbury," the officer said.

"And I haven't seen anything suspicious up here."

"Good. We'll keep an eye on your house. And Cameron?"

"Yeah."

"If you see the Mossad, run like hell."

Cam kissed Astarte goodnight and slid into an Adirondack chair on the cottage porch, listening to the ocean crash ashore. A half-moon lit the nighttime sky and a warm breeze kept the bugs away. He closed his eyes and sipped on a light beer, Venus curled at his feet. But for the fact that he was on the verge of bankruptcy, his fiancée refused to share his bed, and someone was perhaps trying to kill him, life was pretty good.

Amanda joined him on the porch, surprising him by dropping onto his lap and draping an arm around his neck. "I need to tell you something." She took a deep breath. "I sent the photos out to another lab. I simply couldn't live with the uncertainty."

He swallowed. She was sitting on his lap, which should mean good news. Or maybe she was really pissed and was just leading him on to punish him.

"They're pretty certain the picture of you putting the keycard in the door has been altered," she said.

Cam's entire body unclenched as relief washed over him. "Like I said, that was me, but there was no woman with me."

"That's what the agency said. It looked like she was added in later."

He exhaled. "And?"

She held his eyes. "And, in my mind this matter is as close to being settled as it can be. Based on all the other craziness going on, it hardly seems a stretch that someone doctored the photos to manipulate you somehow."

He smiled, even as his eyes misted. She gently took his beer bottle from him, brought her face close to his and peered into his eyes. "I just need you to tell me one more time, Cameron. Did anything happen in Washington?"

He spoke softly and slowly, his response like a prayer. "I swear to you that nothing happened. I have no idea who that woman in the picture is."

The Issac Question

She brushed his cheek with her hand, sighed, and touched her lips softly against his. "I believe you," she breathed. "And I want you back."

She didn't need to ask twice.

Chapter 8

Venus nosed at Cam, her warm breath on his face. He rolled out of bed, in as good a mood as he could ever remember. "Okay, girl."

He kissed Amanda on the cheek, breathing in the scent of her hair, before throwing on some sweats and sandals, finding the leash, and leading Venus out to walk the pre-dawn beach. The tide was low and Venus dragged him away from the cottage, curious at the strange smells of the sea. A few seagulls circled and cawed, but otherwise they were alone on the edge of the continent, the Friday morning horizon aglow in oranges and pinks.

Remembering his experience at yesterday's dawn—an encounter that in some ways seemed weeks ago—he kept the cottage in site and stayed alert for other activity along this stretch of beach. He kicked off his sandals and waded up to his knees, the warm, sweet memory of Amanda's return to him fresh in his mind even as the May Atlantic waters numbed his toes. The sun on his face, he closed his eyes and exhaled. The Superfund thing would, with luck, soon be behind them. His research for *Out of Egypt* was almost complete—with it, presumably, would come an end to the efforts of whoever was trying to manipulate him. And, most importantly, Amanda was back. His life—the same one that last night had seemed like such a train wreck—might finally be getting back on its rails.

But he knew that would not be the end of it. Someone had come after him, and come after him hard. They said that one sign of maturity was the ability to bear an injustice without wanting to get even. Well, if so, he had some growing up to do. He was pissed at whoever did this to them, whoever was putting them through this hell...

Amanda and Astarte surprised him by emerging from the cottage, interrupting his thoughts of revenge. They joined him, Astarte throwing a stick into the surf for Venus to retrieve while Amanda, in a pair of cut-off shorts and t-shirt, nestled up against Cam as they watched the sun's rays play off the waves. "This is nice," she whispered, her breasts pushing against him. "I'm sorry I doubted you."

He smiled, his thoughts of revenge evaporating in the sea mist. "Last night almost made up for it." They had abandoned the Adirondack chair for a chaise lounge, and then again later for their bed. *Their bed.* After two weeks on the couch, the words sounded like poetry. "Maybe we can just stay here for the summer. Call in sick for three months."

"Tempting," she answered. "It would be nice to come back once we put all this behind us."

"Speaking of which," he said, wishing he didn't have to ruin the moment, "I'm supposed to be at Brandeis at eleven. And I know you want to do a food shop."

"Have you given any thought to a disguise?"

"Actually, yes. I'm going to stop in Cambridge on my way to Waltham. There's a great costume place there."

"Let me guess, you're going dressed as Underdog."

"No," he smiled. Last Halloween he had dressed as Underdog and then, halfway through the night, changed into the cartoon character's alter-ego, Shoeshine Boy.

"What then?"

"A priest," he deadpanned. "What are the chances a Mossad agent would be able to see through the disguise?"

Cam didn't think the folks at Brandeis would appreciate him arriving in a priest's costume, so he entered the administration building, found a restroom, and removed his black shirt with clerical collar, replacing it with a light blue button-down. And he stashed the Bible in his briefcase. As far as he could tell, he had not been followed. But with the Mossad, who knew?

Dean Tamara Maxson occupied a large, neat office overlooking a pond on the edge of campus. A professional-looking woman in her late thirties, she greeted him with a smile and a firm handshake. "Please call me Tamara. Have a seat." She smiled again. She was a bit horsey-looking, but her face exuded both confidence and warmth. Not pretty, but not unattractive either. "And welcome aboard."

"Thanks." He pointed his chin toward the pond; a mother duck and a parade of ducklings paddled along near the shore. "Nice view."

"It's called Chapel Pond. We have three chapels surrounding it—one Catholic, one Protestant and, of course, one Jewish. They are built in such a way that none ever casts a shadow on the other two."

He opted not to remark that none of the three was a Muslim chapel. "I think this is the first time I've been here since I was an undergrad at Boston College."

She angled her head. "I can't imagine you came *here* for a road trip. We're not exactly known for our hopping social life."

He laughed. "No. I was doing research on something called the Rat Line—after World War II the Catholic Church helped a bunch of Nazis escape to Latin America. As you might imagine, Boston College didn't have a ton of books on that subject."

"I see," she said slowly, her face asking the question her mouth had not uttered.

"I'm half-Jewish, on my mom's side. My grandmother lost most of her family in the Holocaust."

"I've read about the Rat Line. Nothing to be proud of. But a fascinating little dusty corner of history." She tilted her head. "One of many you've explored, it seems."

He nodded. "I appreciate Brandeis being open-minded about my pre-Columbian research. Some people think it's bunk."

"Well," she smiled, "to be honest, Zuberi Youssef can be very persuasive."

He nodded, swallowing a comment to the effect that it was his money that was, in fact, so persuasive.

She seemed to read his thoughts. "He has been very generous in endowing this chair. And I'd be lying if I said we aren't hoping his generosity continues." She shifted forward. "But even more important than the money is the relationship. He is a very powerful man in the Middle East."

"Honestly, I only recently learned he was an arms dealer."

"I did not know either." She smiled. "You can imagine my surprise when Israeli intelligence contacted me a couple of weeks ago."

He sat up. "They contacted you?"

She eyed him for a few seconds. "You know what? I'd like to be perfectly candid with you, but I need to check with my boss first. We are in very sensitive territory with this stuff. Can you give me a few minutes?"

"Sure." The more he could learn about the Mossad and its interest in him, the better.

She handed him a stack of paperwork. "In the meantime, you can get started on this."

Five minutes later she returned, making a point of closing the door behind her. "Okay, I got permission." She took a deep breath. "The Israeli government, and apparently all the Western governments as well, are extraordinarily concerned about the rise of ISIS. The Middle East has always been a volatile place, but ISIS is a whole different kind of threat. I'm an academic dean, but my background is in history—I read a fascinating article recently, comparing ISIS to something you are an expert on: the Knights Templar."

He waited for her to continue.

"Like the Templars, ISIS is not a nation or a political party or an ethnic group. It is an army, with sworn allegiance to a religion. As such, its fighters are fanatical and single-minded. And from a strategic point of view, they are hard to attack. They have no capital, no homeland to defend, no populace to protect and serve. They move across borders, answerable to nobody. The last time the world saw an army like that was almost a thousand years ago, when the Templars and the Crusaders tried to take back Jerusalem."

Cam nodded. "It's an interesting comparison."

"And a scary one. As you know, the Templars became the most powerful force in Europe for almost two hundred years."

Cam thought about it further. "The Templars grew powerful because of their wealth. Without money, you can't fight a war."

She put her hands on the desk in front of her. "Think about all that oil money. Just as the wealthy families of medieval Europe contributed to the Templars to assure their path to heaven, so also do the oil sheiks of the Middle East. ISIS has money to burn."

Cam saw where this was going. "And Zuberi has arms to sell."

She nodded. "Yes. But there are other arms dealers as well—it is the nature of things. What makes Zuberi different, what makes him, frankly, a unique threat, is the research he and his son are conducting on something we call the Isaac Question."

Cam swallowed. "I'm familiar with that."

"The entire foundation for the existence of Israel, the reason almost the entire Judeo-Christian world recognizes its right to exist, stems from the covenants God made with Abraham in the Old Testament. Covenants that promised the land of Israel to Abraham's descendants."

She paused and held his eyes. "What if it turns out that the promise applies not to the Jews, but to the descendants of Ishmael, the Arabs?"

A Biblical claim for the Arabs to retake Jerusalem. All of it. "I can see how that would be a problem."

"Historically, Israel's greatest protection has always been that the Arabs were so busy fighting each other that they never banded together to take on Israel. But a revelation like this might be the catalyst to bring them all together. For one glorious holy war."

"Just like the Crusades brought the warring nations of Europe together a thousand years ago," Cam said.

"Exactly. And in a holy war, there can be only one acceptable result: total annihilation."

Cam now understood the Mossad's keen interest in Zuberi, and in anything and anyone within his circle.

Tamara continued. "To make matters worse, Israel's popularity around the world has never been lower. The revelation that the Jewish people were not, in fact, the true Biblical claimants to the Holy Land would only erode that popularity further." She looked out over the pond. "One wonders how many nations would rise up to defend her against a wave of ISIS-backed attackers."

"You paint a pretty bleak picture."

She smiled sadly. "I've been given a palette which only contains browns, blacks and grays."

She hadn't told him all this just to kill twenty minutes. He asked, "So what can I do to help?" Obviously he didn't want to do anything to contribute to the destabilization of the Middle East, much less Israel's destruction.

"For now, nothing. For now, it is enough that you know of the threat." She looked him in the eye. "But there may come a time when you and I both need to stand up to Zuberi Youssef."

☥ ✝ ⬙

The text came in into Tamara's phone even as the door was still swinging shut behind Cameron Thorne. "Should we follow him?" it read.

"Yes," she quickly replied.

A few minutes later Moshe waddled into her office. "We have a guy tailing him."

"Okay. But be careful. We don't want to spook him. No more garbage trucks." She peered out her window. "Did you listen?"

He nodded.

"And?" she asked.

"We'll run the audio through our lie detection software, but the guy sounded sincere to me."

"Agreed."

"You didn't offer to help make his Superfund problem go away."

"As it was, I thought I came across a bit too hard. I'm supposed to be a college dean, not an international powerbroker. Or a Mossad agent. How would a dean make a problem like that go away?"

"Fair point."

"Besides, it's good to have a card still in our hand."

Moshe clicked his tongue against his teeth. "Speaking of unplayed cards, when do we take the boy?"

"Zuberi's son?"

"Of course. It's the ultimate leverage."

"Or it's a declaration of war against one of the most powerful men in the Middle East. In case you haven't noticed, we don't exactly have a lot of friends right now."

"It's not about friends. Like I said, it's about leverage." He gestured with his chin. "The boy is, literally, in our back yard."

She shook her head. "Please, Moshe, I think that is a big mistake. At least wait and see how the Thorne thing plays out."

Moshe picked at his cuticles. "All right. For now." He exhaled. "Do you think Thorne will really stand up to Youssef if it comes to that?"

That was the crux of it all. They needed to get close to Zuberi in order to defang him, but to do so they needed to let another potential snake, Thorne, into their house. With so many snakes slithering about, it would be a wonder if nobody got bit. Looking back, perhaps it would have been the better choice to keep the snakes away altogether. But it was too late for that. She recalled an old saying her first Mossad handler, who had grown up in Eastern Europe, often spouted: *In times of great danger, you are permitted to walk with the devil until you have crossed the bridge.*

She finally answered the question. "I don't know. Thorne seems like a good man. And I think he wants to do the right thing. But his idea of the right thing and our idea of the right thing might not be the same."

Moshe nodded, his small, dark pupils peering out from deep within his fleshy cheeks. "Which is why it's good we are following him again."

☥ ✞ ⬡

Cam had a lot to think about, and an hour drive back to Salisbury Beach to do so. He didn't like making rash decisions, but the idea that he was in bed with an arms dealer—first suggested by Bartol, and now confirmed by Tamara Maxson—gnawed at him.

He dialed Zuberi's number, not expecting the business titan to answer on the second ring.

"Cameron," he bellowed. "How are you?"

"I'm actually a bit bothered by something, Zuberi." He decided to be blunt. "I just learned that you are an international arms dealer."

"So?"

Not exactly a denial. "But you told me you were in the import-export business."

"And so I am. I import weapons from one country and export to other."

"I'm not sure I'm comfortable with that."

"You are big boy, Cameron. I hope you do not think my business is oriental rugs and big-screen televisions. I diversity some into high tech and real estate, but mostly my business is weapons. And also heavy equipment and machinery like helicopters and cranes to rebuild the things the weapons destroy. When the world makes war, Youssef makes money. When the world rebuilds after war, Youssef also makes money. When no war, Youssef makes not so much money. Is simple equation."

"It may be simple, but it is still blood money. I'm not sure I'm comfortable accepting it."

"Blood money!" Zuberi laughed. "All money is blood money, Cameron. Your nation was built with blood of slaves. Today, clothes you wear and cars you drive and food you eat are made with blood of child workers." He lowered his voice. "What do you think happens if I don't sell weapons? I tell you: Other dealers take my place. As long as there is war, there is men to sell guns."

Cam didn't have a response, so Zuberi continued. "And these other men, these other dealers? They take profits and give to Al-Qaeda. Or to Hezbollah. Or to ISIS. I give profit to you, to write book about true history. So am I such really bad man?" Zuberi lowered his voice. "Don't forget, Cameron. We have deal. Zuberi Youssef always keeps his word. And I expect same from you."

The line went dead before Cam could reply.

Amanda and Astarte spent the morning at the cottage's simple square kitchen table working on schoolwork Astarte's teachers had emailed them. Cam texted just after eleven, saying he'd be home by noon.

"Let's take a break until after lunch," Amanda said to Astarte. She wanted to focus on an email Carrington Sinclair-Youssef had sent earlier in the week. Amanda sensed Carrington was sharper than she first appeared. The message directed Amanda to a passage discussing Rosslyn Chapel in a 2004 book entitled *Guardians of the Holy Grail*, by Mark Amaru Pinkham.

She found the passage: "*Two human heads were recently discovered under the Rosslyn Chapel's floor, examined, and then sealed back up in the crypt. Both skulls had holes in locations that correspond to the horns emanating out of some Green Man heads. Could these skulls have been worshiped as manifestations of Baphomet?*"

Amanda sat back. Horned manifestations of Baphomet at Rosslyn Chapel. Hmm.

The message from Carrington continued, explaining how her maternal grandfather, from whom she got her Sinclair blood, used to work as a carpenter at Rosslyn Chapel. Because he was a Sinclair, the other hired hands often shared stories and legends with him. One such legend was that there was a skull hidden inside or under the Apprentice Pillar.

More skulls, more heads. Due to the Templar's close association with Rosslyn Chapel, Amanda had long suspected a connection between the iconic structure and Baphomet. This information from Carrington only strengthened her suspicions.

Something that Cam had observed last week, about Akhenaton looking androgynous, had nagged at her. Tapping at her laptop, she went back to review her Baphomet research. She pulled up an image of Baphomet.

Baphomet

And then it hit her. How had she missed it? *Breasts*. The horned figure was so fearsome looking, and so full of symbolism, that she had never focused on the feminine breasts. Baphomet, like Akhenaton, was depicted androgynously.

Baphomet's androgyny made a lot of sense, based on what they knew of the Templars. She and Cam believed that one of the main causes of the conflict between the Templars and the Church had been that the Templars, drawing on early Gnostic Christian teachings they discovered in the Holy Land, believed in the duality of the godhead—that God possessed both feminine and masculine qualities. Because of this the Templars worshiped and venerated the Virgin Mary and, to a lesser extent, Mary Magdalene. The Templars had tried to push the Church to become more balanced, more feminine, less patriarchal. The Vatican had resisted, eventually driving a schism between the army of the Church and the Church itself...

Cam's car pulled into the cottage driveway, interrupting her research. They made sandwiches and had a picnic on the beach, Venus barking at the encroaching seagulls, then played Frisbee for a half hour. But Amanda's mind was on her research.

When Astarte tired of the game and began to build a sand castle, she and Cam sat on the sand nearby, hands linked. "How was your meeting at Brandeis?"

He glanced at Astarte. "Interesting. I'll tell you about it later."

"Okay, well I'll tell you what I did." She summarized her morning's work.

"So do you think there's something to the fact that both Akhenaton and Baphomet are portrayed androgynously?"

She shrugged. "Let me turn the question around to you: Is there a chance that Scota and her gang would have preserved Akhenaton's head and brought it with them to Scotland?"

"Sure," he said. "They were Egyptian. They preserved all their royalty. And Akhenaton's tomb in Egypt is empty—nobody knows where the body is."

"So..." she said, letting her mind wander. "Is it crazy to think that the Baphomet skull the Templars worshiped could actually be the head of Akhenaton-Moses?" That would explain the Templar's obsessive veneration of the head, and also the Church's violent putdown of the Templar order. If the Templars had learned that Akhenaton and Moses were the same person, they also had surely followed the trail back and discovered the truth about Isaac's parentage. That was not a secret the medieval Church—in the middle of a series of Crusades to win back the Holy Land—could afford to have revealed...

"Not crazy," Cam responded, interrupting her musings. "In the hierarchy of Christian relics, Moses would be pretty high up there. Even above John the Baptist." He shrugged. "But we don't really have any evidence."

She stood up and brushed the sand off her shorts. "Not yet we don't. You stay here and watch Astarte. I'm going back to work."

Amanda spent the next couple of hours back at the kitchen table of the cottage with her laptop, scrolling through thousands of images of Rosslyn Chapel. The chapel boasted hundreds of thousands of visitors per year, and it seemed like most of them had posted pictures of their visit. But how many images of the ornate Apprentice Pillar could one look at before—like the jealous master mason of Chapel legend—wanting to bash in the head of the apprentice who carved it?

Amanda needed something that would tie Moses to the chapel, something that would give some traction to their musings. Ready to give up, she clicked on one more set of images. Her breath caught in the throat. What was this?

Moses Carving at Rosslyn Chapel

She stared, blinked, rubbed her eyes, and stared again. A bearded man carrying a stone tablet in his right hand, the caption reading, 'Moses carved onto a pillar along the south wall.' *With horns.*

Horns. Just like Baphomet. Could it be? Could this be the proof that the Templars worshiped the head of Moses as the horned Baphomet?

But a voice in her head whispered to her, reminding her that wisdom is knowledge tempered with judgment. Something about this conclusion seemed premature. She had plunged deep into the

Baphomet mystery, and until today had never bumped her head against Moses. The voice spoke to her again: *Extraordinary claims require extraordinary proof.* A single carving of a horned Moses was not enough to assert he was Baphomet.

Was there another possible explanation for the horns on Moses' head?

Five minutes later she had her answer: Due to an error in translating the Bible from Hebrew to Latin around the year 400 AD, Moses' "radiant face" had become his "horned face" throughout Europe for over a thousand years, as evidenced by Michelangelo's horned sculpture of Moses in Rome. And, apparently, in Rosslyn Chapel as well.

So did this settle the matter? Was the horned carving of Moses a meaningless clue? She wasn't willing to go that far. If the Scots indeed did descend from the Egyptians—and more specifically from Akhenaton/Moses through Scota—they would surely know Moses was not horned. So why depict him that way? It was possible, she concluded, that the Chapel builders had used the translation error to hide the clue in plain sight. To a casual observer Moses' horns would be attributed to the translation error. But to those aware of the true history, perhaps the horns conveyed a far different message: *I am the horned one you revere; I am Baphomet.*

She stood, closed her laptop, and jogged toward the beach. She needed a second opinion. "Cam," she called, "you have to see this."

Amanda ran toward them across the sand. Cam stood, alert, his eyes arcing the horizon for signs of danger. "Are you okay?" he called.

"Yes, fine. But you have to see this."

"What?"

Carrying her laptop, she dropped to her knees on their blanket, nudging Venus out of the way. "Look at this picture. It's a carving from Rosslyn Chapel."

He did a double take at the horned representation of Moses. "That can't be."

"Well, it is."

Astarte put down her book and leaned in. "Why does Moses have horns?"

"It's a clue," Amanda said.

Amanda had clearly made the same Baphomet association that he had. "How come nobody's ever made a big deal about it?" Cam asked.

"Probably because there's, like, a thousand strange carvings at Rosslyn Chapel. What's one more?"

He looked at the image again. "You're the Baphomet expert. So could Moses be Baphomet?"

"Possibly. But there's another explanation." She took a deep breath and explained how the Bible had been mistranslated, 'radiant' turning into 'horned.' "It turns out there are many representations of Moses with horns."

He made a face. "Yeah, but not among the Jews, right?"

"Right. The Hebrew clearly says 'radiant.'"

"So anyone who knew Hebrew, or anyone who had access to Bible experts or Hebrew speakers, would know better, right?"

She smiled at him knowingly, as if he was going down the same path she had just traveled. "Right again."

"Look, the Sinclairs were smart people. Very smart. And they brought in religious experts, including rabbis, from all over Europe to help them design Rosslyn Chapel. I can't believe they would allow a mistake like this."

She nodded. "That's what I thought also." She explained her theory that the horns had a hidden, secondary meaning, meant for those who had 'eyes that see'—a term they had coined for those trained to see hidden meanings and messages among Templar and Masonic symbolism. "What do you think?"

"Well, it's either one or the other. Either the Sinclairs didn't know their Bible history, which I have trouble believing, or they were using these carvings in the Chapel to convey secret, coded messages."

She grinned. They both believed that's exactly what the Sinclairs were doing.

"So does this change things?" Cam asked.

"I think it does."

They had been working under the assumption that Baphomet was the head of John the Baptist, and they had tracked his skull back and forth across the Atlantic. First, his executioner Mug Ruith brought the head home with him as a keepsake to Ireland; second, the Celts venerated the prophet's skull and its visionary powers as part of their Cult of the Head; third, Druids voyaging with Brendan the Navigator brought the skull to America to keep it out of the hands of the invading Christians; fourth, the Templars (having heard legends of the head's existence) traveled to America to retrieve the skull of their patriarch; and fifth, after the downfall of the Templars, the Sinclair family built Rosslyn Chapel as a repository for this and other Templar treasures. It had been such a neat, tidy theory. But maybe they had the wrong skull.

He looked out over the Atlantic, toward Scotland, wondering.

Amanda broke the silence. "Let's walk through it, step by step."

"Okay," he sighed. "Akhenaton, now known as Moses, leads his group of mixed Israelites and Egyptians into the desert. Eventually he dies. Does anyone know where his body is?"

She shook her head. "No. Like you said, the tomb in Egypt is empty." She tapped at her phone for a few seconds, doing some quick research. "The Jewish belief is that God buried Moses' body and nobody knows the exact location."

Cam smiled. "How convenient. Okay, so his daughter Scota somehow ends up with his remains, or at least his head, in the Egyptian tradition. Scota and her people carry the head with them—along with his throne, the Stone of Destiny—on their journey westward across Europe."

"But if Scota settled in Scotland, how did the skull end up with Brendan the Navigator in Ireland?"

He smiled again. "I don't think I told you this part of the Scota story. Scota and her followers actually settled in Ireland before moving on to Scotland. Scota's son, Hiber, led the attack that defeated the Irish natives. That's where the name Hibernia comes from." Ireland was often referred to as Hibernia. "They stayed in

Ireland for many generations before some moved on to Scotland. Maybe they left the skull in Ireland for safe-keeping."

She shifted on the blanket, her movements conveying her excitement. "Well, clearly, the skull of Moses would have been quite a prize in Cult of the Head worship, even more so than John the Baptist. And I suppose the same logic works for Moses as for John the Baptist: The bloody Christians were coming, and the Druids would want to protect their valuable skull."

After that, the story would mirror that of John the Baptist's head, bouncing back and forth across the Atlantic before finally ending up at Rosslyn Chapel. And the Templars would have learned all about it during their time in the Holy Land. The Knights were there purportedly to fight the Muslims, but they also made numerous alliances and friendships in their two centuries in and around Jerusalem. If anyone could have ferreted out a secret like this, it would have been the Templars.

Cam pondered the possibility. If the Templars did end up with the skull of Moses, it would be a powerful symbol of their ties back to the Holy Land and to the Old Testament. Cam had been convinced the Baphomet skull was that of John the Baptist, but in the pantheon of great Biblical figures, Moses clearly stood above the Baptist. Not only that, but the skull would have been a veiled threat to the Church, an indication that the Templars knew the version of the Exodus story the Church was telling was simply not true...

"You know," Amanda interrupted, "there's another possibility. It's possible the head of Moses is buried in Rosslyn Chapel, even if Moses was not Baphomet. The carving of Moses with horns could be a clue saying, 'Hey, *I'm just like* Baphomet,' rather than, 'Hey, *I am* Baphomet.'"

"The 'just like' part meaning his skull was being worshiped as part of the Cult of the Head, in the old Druidic ways."

"Right."

Cam nodded. "That makes sense also." In the end it didn't really matter whether Moses was Baphomet. What mattered was that the head of Moses might be hidden inside Rosslyn Chapel.

Cam had another thought. "And you know what, if the head is Moses, that would explain something that's always bothered me.

252

People always talk about these important skulls and relics and treasures hidden at Rosslyn Chapel—well, why didn't they display them out in the open like all the other churches and cathedrals did?"

"You're right," Amanda replied. "It's one thing to have the tooth or little finger of some saint. The head of John the Baptist or Moses is something else entirely. The Church would likely insist on taking it."

They sat on the blanket, staring at the surf.

"Odd how our research has converged," Amanda said. "Again."

He nodded. It seemed to happen often. Who would have thought that the beehive stone chambers of New England that Cam had been studying would somehow link back to Amanda's Baphomet research, and that both of these paths would lead back to Zuberi's Scota legend. "Usually when it happens like that, it's because we're on the right track," he said.

"Yes. We follow different paths, both leading back to the same truth."

"You know who's really going to love this?"

"Zuberi. Not only did the bloody Egyptians settle in Scotland, but it may be that they brought the head of Moses with them as well."

Cam smiled. "And his wife's family has been keeping it safe for the world for all these years. What a story."

"Not to mention the whole thing begins with the revelation that Isaac was not Abraham's son. Without that, it's impossible to make the Moses/Akhenaton connection."

They sat in silence for a few seconds. "So is that it?" Amanda asked. "Is your research done? Are you ready to write it all up?"

"I think so." He had not yet told Amanda about his conversation with Zuberi and his arms dealings, or about Dean Maxson's request that he keep secret his Isaac Question research. "I'm ready to write. I'm just not sure this is a story the world is ready to hear."

253

Zuberi had agreed to meet Duncan Sinclair for an early Friday evening dinner. Sinclair had invited Zuberi first to his country club, and then to a fancy restaurant along Edinburgh's Royal Mile, but Zuberi had suggested the White Hart pub in the gritty Grassmarket section of the city. Men like Duncan Sinclair felt comfortable around linen tablecloths and crystal decanters. Men like Zuberi preferred paper napkins and a foamy pint.

Zuberi waited outside for his guest, admiring the massive Edinburgh Castle looming over the strip of Victorian architecture built along the base of its hill. The Castle purportedly housed the Stone of Destiny—but if Thorne were correct in his research, the stone on display was actually the Bethel Stone, not the true Stone of Destiny which had served as the throne of Akhenaton. That throne, Zuberi now believed, was hidden at Rosslyn Chapel. His goal tonight was to convince Duncan Sinclair to let him go find it.

A tall, white-haired man in a dark suit eased his way out of the back of a black sedan and began loping past the skateboarders and sidewalk musicians toward Zuberi, a look of bemused curiosity on his face as if he were strolling through an exhibit of exotic animals. Zuberi guessed it had been years since the soles of the banker's wingtips had trod upon working class detritus. He'd probably need to throw them away.

Zuberi offered his left arm to the banker and they shook, a greeting far preferable to the silly Arab exchange of kisses. Sinclair seamlessly accepted Zuberi's left hand, which Zuberi took as an indication he had conducted a background check on Zuberi beforehand. Which, in turn, meant the meeting was important to him. Zuberi would adjust his price accordingly.

"Mr. Sinclair," he said, speaking slowly, "it is a pleasure to meet you."

"Aye." The elderly man's blue eyes sparkled as he showed a row of even gray teeth. "Apparently we are cousins, Mr. Youssef," he said. He spoke with a thick Scottish accent that Zuberi always had trouble understanding.

"Some of my least favorite people are my cousins," Zuberi sniffed, not untruthfully.

"Well, then, that should make it easier for me not to disappoint you."

They found a table in the front corner of the pub; a harried waitress dropped a couple of menus and some silverware onto the middle of the table. "Place your orders at the bar," she said.

Sinclair smiled. "I used to come to Grassmarket as a student at the University of Edinburgh, after the war. They still don't have table service, eh?"

Zuberi nodded. He had been surprised at the practice when he first came to Scotland, but many pubs followed the same procedure. "When you know what you want, I will order for us," he said.

Five minutes later Zuberi returned with a couple of pints, one tucked into the crook of his elbow. He got right to the point. "I assume you are trying to convince me to not sell arms to ISIS."

"I am indeed." The elderly man leaned forward. "I do not need to explain to you the geopolitical danger ISIS presents. You know this as well as anyone, yet you still choose to arm them." He sat back. "So I will not attempt to appeal to your sense of decency."

Zuberi did not take offense. "Good. Many people believe I do not have one."

"But I do have something to offer. It is my understanding that you believe ancient relics may be buried at Rosslyn Chapel."

Zuberi nodded. This was a dangerous game he was playing, potentially reneging on a deal with ISIS. But he wouldn't have many chances in life to ferret around at Rosslyn Chapel. And he could placate ISIS with the Isaac Question bombshell. "And you are prepared to let me dig?"

"Within reason. We, too, have long been curious as to what relics may be buried there. This arrangement you and I come to, assuming we do, would be the kick in the arse we need to find out what is hidden. The crypt, as well as the Apprentice Pillar, seem like obvious places to look."

Zuberi sipped at his pint. "How long would be moratorium?"

Sinclair peered at him. "A year. No arms sales for a full year. That should give our allies enough time to destroy ISIS."

"Three months," he countered. "After that it will not matter—they will find another supplier."

"Perhaps another supplier, but not one nearly so well-stocked."

In the end, as they picked at their steak and ale pie, they settled on a six-month embargo, provided the Rosslyn Chapel excavations began in the next sixty days. Zuberi knew how these things worked—without a firm deadline, it would be years before the excavations began. If the dig were delayed beyond the sixty days, Zuberi would not be bound by the embargo.

They finished their pints and shook on the deal. Zuberi stood to leave.

"Where are you going?" Sinclair asked.

Zuberi cocked his head. "Home. Our business is done."

"Very well. Good night, cousin." He grinned. "I think I'll stay and have another pint."

Perhaps Zuberi had underestimated the old Scot.

Chapter 9

Tamara hated working on Saturdays. It wasn't that she ascribed literally to the Ten Commandments, including observing the Sabbath. It was more that she appreciated the tranquility and peacefulness and rejuvenative powers of a weekly day of rest spent with her family. Her body, and her soul, had grown accustomed to it, in the way others grew addicted to exercise or meditation. But Israel was at war, and her job was to fight to protect it.

Moshe had phoned, waking her, and asked her to meet him in their Brandeis offices. He shuffled in and dropped into the chair opposite her desk. "I just heard from Tel Aviv," he said, scratching at some dry skin on his forearm. "They want us to take Thorne's fiancée and daughter."

Tamara's body clenched. "Why?"

He gave her a funny look. "As leverage, of course."

"But he said he'd cooperate."

"That's what he says now." Moshe shrugged. "People change their minds. Or they get cold feet. We can't take any chances with the stakes this high."

"But how do we gain leverage over a man by kidnapping his family? That's how we make enemies."

"One can have leverage over one's enemies. And also over one's friends. Leverage is leverage."

She stared out the window. Just yesterday Thorne had sat in this office with her, offering to help if he could. And this is how they repaid him. She sighed. "You know, Moshe, in many ways we're no better than the terrorists we are fighting."

257

"Not true. They would abduct the fiancée and the girl and abuse them, rape them, probably behead them. We are not animals. We will do only what is necessary.'

Cam woke early on Saturday, walked Venus, and went for a long run along the beach. His body relished the release of endorphins, and his mind appreciated the quiet solitude to think and analyze.

He had spent yesterday afternoon and evening writing, turning his thirty-page outline into what would eventually become a three-hundred-page manuscript. In truth, the hard work was already complete—the outline contained all the information, all the arguments and conclusions, needed to tell the fascinating story of Scota and Moses and the Cult of the Head and the Druids and the North American stone chambers and the Templars and Prince Henry Sinclair. He just needed to add the connective tissue.

The big question, of course, was whether to include the Isaac Question research. Dean Maxson made a compelling case: In Zuberi's hands, the material could, quite literally, alter the history of the Middle East. Who was Cam to play God with the fate of millions of lives?

On the other hand, he and Amanda both held strong beliefs that the truth was paramount in these types of situations. He had once heard the Holocaust survivor Elie Wiesel speak, and his words resonated even these many years later: 'May I never use my reason against truth.' There were many reasons for suppressing this particular truth, but who was Cam to decide which truths were fit for the world to hear and which were not? Suppression of this information sounded distressingly similar to the medieval Church burning books it didn't agree with—and murdering those who read from them.

Whatever Cam decided, he was relatively free from the financial pressures of the Superfund case. He still had no idea who had set up the ruse—Zuberi, the Freemasons, and the Mossad all seemingly had both the capability and motivation to do so.

Eventually someone might offer to make the problem go away as some kind of incentive, which would reveal the culprit. But, again, in the meantime he could make decisions on the content of his book without fear of imminent bankruptcy.

Like the Superfund problem, he also had no good sense who had sent the fake photos to Amanda. The same three suspects were in play, all again having both motivation and capability. At some point someone might offer to make the photos, like the Superfund problem, go away.

For the murder of Randall Sid, he assumed the Masons were not involved, though he suspected both Zuberi and the Mossad. And Bartol as well—he could have been working with an accomplice, and he had expressed anti-Masonic opinions.

He picked up the pace, his bare feet slapping against the wet sand. He was in a strange place, on an imaginary island surrounded by sharks. While on this island he had been tasked with writing a book. The contents of the final chapter of that book would determine which of the sharks would attack him when he attempted to flee.

☥ ✝ ⚒

Amanda and Astarte ate bowls of cereal on the porch, huddled in sweatshirts against the early morning chill. "So, do you like it here?"

Astarte was nothing if not introspective. She swirled her bran flakes around in the bowl before responding. "I would like it if it were a vacation. But it feels like … we're hiding." She looked up sadly. "When do we get to go home?"

The short answer, of course, was when it was safe. But that didn't seem like a fair response. "I think that once Cameron finishes the book he's working on, it will be time to go home."

"A whole book? How many pages?"

"Perhaps three hundred."

"Won't that take, like, a year?"

"Not nearly so long as that. He has outlined it already, and he writes very fast."

"So how long?"

Working from an outline, she had once pushed out a ten-thousand-word university term paper in a day-and-a-half. Cam was equally motivated to put this behind them. Amanda did the math in her head for an eighty-thousand-word manuscript, some of which Cam had already written. "I reckon ten days."

Astarte bit her lip, then brightened. "Why don't you help? You're a good writer. Then it would only take five days, right?"

Not a bloody bad idea. Amanda knew the material as well as Cam did. "It would mean you would have to keep yourself entertained."

Astarte nodded. "I have homework. And books to read. And Venus to play with." She smiled. "And maybe you can let me watch a little extra TV?"

When Cam returned from his run, Amanda bounced the idea off him.

"Sounds great. We could alternate chapters," he said, stretching his legs.

"We keep saying that someone is trying to stop you from finishing your research. The sooner this book is done, the sooner that someone will leave us alone."

"Okay," he said, "but first I need to talk to you about something." He quickly explained that Dean Maxson had told him Zuberi was an arms dealer, and that Zuberi himself had confirmed it.

She pondered the revelation, not really surprised by it. "I suppose it doesn't really change anything. The plan is the same: Finish the manuscript so we can put this chapter of our lives—no pun intended—behind us and get back to normalcy."

He nodded. "I'm glad you said that, because I'm not sure Zuberi is the type we want to back out of a deal with."

Putting the plan of two authors into action, they spent the rest of Saturday on dueling laptops, tapping away in a friendly competition. "How many words," Amanda asked, stretching as the late afternoon sun cast long shadows across the beach.

Cam checked his word count. "Just over six thousand." He smiled. "A few dozen of them actually make complete sentences. But it's rough. Definitely a first draft."

She nodded. There was no way to write that fast and maintain quality. "Well, you beat me. I'm under five thousand."

"Given that you're working from someone else's outline, that's pretty impressive."

She smiled back at him. "You'd be even more impressed if you knew what a dingbat the person who made the outline is."

"Let's break for some dinner, then we can get back to it tonight. I hear that dingbat makes a mean grilled chicken."

She nodded. If they kept up this pace they could be finished before the week was out, as she had promised Astarte. Then, finally, they might be able to get their lives back to normal.

Tamara took an early Sunday morning flight out of Logan Airport to Chicago and immediately checked into a hotel at the airport. By nine o'clock she had put on a wig, changed her eye color with contacts and added ten years to her face with some simple makeup tricks. As far as she could recall she had never met Rachel Levitad, but she couldn't take the chance of being recognized.

She hailed a taxi for the twenty minute ride to the modest cul-de-sac north of the city. She would be arriving unannounced, relying on the odds that on a Sunday morning most people would be home at half past nine. And that their college-aged daughter, just back from a three-day tryst with her boyfriend, would still be asleep.

In her younger days Tamara would have prepared a speech, or at least made a list of key talking points. But there was no right way to ask what she was about to ask. She decided instead just to follow her instincts. She tapped gently on the door of a neatly maintained split-level, hoping not to wake Rachel. A thin, unshaven man in a bathrobe answered the door. She recognized Martin Levitad from their surveillance photos.

"May I help you?" he asked not unkindly. This was his second marriage, Rachel a product of his late forties, which made him in his late sixties.

"I hope so, Mr. Levitad. I am here to speak to you and your wife." She held his eyes. "I work for Israeli intelligence. The Mossad."

He nodded slowly, his eyes alert. "I'm guessing you don't carry any identification."

She pursed her lips. "No. For obvious reasons. You can call me Leah, though of course that is not my real name."

A smile crept onto this face. "I don't suppose the boys from the swim club put you up to this?"

"No. I'm afraid not."

He looked past her toward the street, ascertained she was alone, and stepped aside to allow her to enter. "I imagine this has to do with Rachel's new boyfriend?"

"Yes."

"Let me get my wife," he exhaled. "Would you like some coffee?"

Five minutes later they gathered in a sun room off the rear of the house, Martin's dark-eyed wife Audrey wearing a damp t-shirt from a workout Tamara had obviously cut short. She dabbed at her face with a towel and sipped water from a bottle. Martin took her hand and smiled. "My wife is training for a triathlon." He picked up a half-eaten bagel smeared with cream cheese. "I am training to watch her."

Audrey didn't share her husband's casual attitude. "I'm sorry to be rude, but why are you here?"

The words tumbled from Tamara's mouth. "I'm here because the Jewish people are under attack. In Israel, in Europe, in America." Sometimes she felt like crying when she talked about this, or stomping her feet, or ripping at her hair. Why did no one else see the dangers? Had the nightmarish memories of the Holocaust already faded? "I'm here because we need your daughter's help."

"She's just a girl," the mother said.

"She's a young woman," Tamara corrected. "Were she living in Israel, she'd be serving in the armed forces."

"Well, she's not living in Israel," came the retort.

Tamara nodded. "Thankfully for us, you are correct. I say 'thankfully,' because she is in a rare position here, at Brandeis, to be of invaluable service to her people."

Martin leaned forward. "Can you be more specific?"

"My understanding is that you are not happy about her new boyfriend."

"He is Muslim," the father said. "We are not racists, but we did not send our daughter halfway across the country to date a man whose religious leaders criticize Hitler for being not efficient enough."

"So you do see the danger," Tamara said. "You understand what we are fighting against."

The mother jumped in. "We see the danger to our daughter. Which is why we want to end this little romance now, before it gets going too far."

Martin spoke. "You still haven't told us what you want from us. From Rachel."

Tamara took a deep breath. "Amon's father is an arms dealer by the name of Zuberi Youssef." She outlined Youssef's role in the Middle East arms supply game and the danger ISIS posed to Israel. And she explained how Israel was trying to neutralize him. "As you might imagine, it has been very difficult for us to penetrate his inner circle. Now, with your daughter, we have a chance."

Rachel's mother's face flushed. "So you want us not only to allow our daughter to date this ... son of a terrorist, but to spy on him as well? Are you crazy?"

"No. I'm not crazy." Tamara looked back and forth, trying to hold both their eyes at once. "In fact, I have a thirteen-year-old daughter myself. So I can imagine how terrifying this must be for you—"

Rachel strode into the room, interrupting their conversation. In a t-shirt and sweatpants, her hair wild about her face, she spoke with a calm dignity. "You can all stop trying to make decisions for me. I'm not a little girl." She looked at her mother and father. "I am going to continue dating Amon, with or without your approval. We might stay together the rest of our lives, we might not last the summer. But it will be *my* decision, not yours. And for the record, he has nothing to do with his father's business." And then at

Tamara. "And you're crazy if you think I'm going to betray him like some modern-day Delilah." She straightened herself. "You know, maybe if all you so-called grown-ups just stayed out of things, my generation would figure out a way to get along just fine." She folded her arms across her chest and glared at her parents.

Tamara's shoulders slumped as Rachel's parents retreated to a corner of the room, their voices low but heated. Tamara remembered having thoughts similar to Rachel's as a young woman herself. That was before the piles of dead bodies suffocated her idealism. But how could she convince a nineteen-year-old to give up her ideals? What was that expression? *To be young and have no ideals is to have no heart.* If the girl would not help, there was nothing Tamara could do...

Tamara turned to smile at Rachel, but the young woman's eyes remained focused on her arguing parents. After what seemed like a half hour, but was probably only six or seven minutes, Rachel's mother nodded abruptly and the two parents, hands linked, returned to the center of the room. The father spoke, his voice soft but firm. "We have always supported you, Rachel, in whatever you do. And we are very proud of you. But in this matter we are going to exercise our rights as parents. You *will* help the Mossad in this, or you *will not* be returning to Brandeis. If, as you claim, Amon is not involved in his father's business, then you will not be betraying him in any way. In fact, there will be nothing at all to report. But to the extent you have an opportunity to prevent war in the Middle East, we must insist you do so. It is your duty as a Jew, as an American." He held his daughter's eyes. "It is your duty as a human being. Sometimes the needs of the many outweigh the needs of the few."

Rachel stood motionless in the sun room while her father walked the Mossad agent to the door and said goodbye. She and her mother held each other's eyes, neither so much as breathing until the door closed and her father snapped the deadbolt into place.

Rachel exhaled. "Wow, that was intense. What a way to wake up."

Her mother pushed back her chair and gave Rachel a hug. "You did great."

"Do you think she bought it?" Rachel asked.

Her father called in from the kitchen. "I think so. You were very convincing." He smiled.

Rachel returned his smile. "All those years of theater training. And you and mom were pretty good yourselves."

Her father opened the pantry door. Out stepped a man in his sixties wearing a wrinkled blue suit over a white shirt and yellow tie. "I agree. You were very good," the man said. From what Rachel knew, the man and her father had served in Vietnam together; he was now a senior CIA official. He and her father joined them in the sun room.

Her dad turned to his war buddy. "How were you so certain she'd come here?"

The man, paunchy but with kind blue eyes, reminded Rachel of a math teacher in her high school who used to play Santa Claus in the mall at Christmas. "Once she got on the plane to Chicago, it was pretty obvious where she was going."

"So now what?" Rachel asked.

"Now we wait." The man exhaled. "As I explained, the Freemasons are close to brokering a deal with Zuberi Youssef. Very close. The last thing we want is the Mossad poking around and ruining things." He smiled. "The Mossad is very good at what it does. Unfortunately sometimes it does the wrong thing."

"So can I tell Amon?"

The agent shook his head. "No, sorry."

She frowned. "I guess the story would sound a little crazy: The Mossad asked me to spy on you, but the CIA got to me first so I agreed to be a double-agent and feed them misinformation."

Her mother said, "Are you sure you're comfortable with this?"

Shrugging, Rachel replied. "I'm not really spying on him, so why not? And as Dad said, I'll be doing the right thing." She held their eyes as she spoke, confident they had no idea she way lying to them just as she had lied to the Mossad agent...

She didn't like lying to her parents, but they had brought this on themselves. They were being racist and bigoted and hypocritical in not wanting her to date Amon, and now they were asking her to spy on him and his family. In essence, they had forced her into lying to them. They had nobody to blame but themselves.

A Nor'easter had moved in overnight, buffeting their cottage and roiling the ocean. Amanda and Cam sat at the kitchen table, each writing on their laptop, while Astarte bounced a tennis ball off the bathroom door and watched Venus leap to catch it. Amanda exhaled. It was difficult to write using someone else's outline. But it also afforded her the opportunity to look at Cam's research with a fresh set of eyes.

"Hey Cam," she said. "I think I found another connection between the Egyptians and the Scots."

"What?"

They had found over the years that, when they were on the right track with their research, later evidence tended to corroborate earlier conclusions. "If you're right that the Scots descended from the Egyptians, then there should be cultural similarities between the groups, right?" She didn't wait for a response. "The Egyptians were matrilineal—the pharaohs all married their sisters, because it was *her* sons that were ordained to rule. Well, so were the ancient Scots. Which was pretty rare back then—most of Europe was patrilineal."

"And still is." Cam smiled. "Good find." He stared out the window at the storm. "And you know what else, that helps explain the whole conversation God had with Sarah after the Pharaoh kicked her and Abraham out of Egypt. The Old Testament says that God told Sarah that 'the kings of people shall be of *her*.' Not of Abraham. But of her, in the Egyptian tradition of matrilineal descent. If the son she was about to have had been fathered by Abraham, then the rules of Judaic inheritance—through the father—would have applied and nothing would have been needed to be said. But with the pharaoh being the father, the Egyptian hereditary customs came into play."

Amanda nodded. "That's a subtle point, but a good one. And if you follow Sarah's bloodline, you do indeed get to all the Biblical kings: David, Solomon, Asa—"

Cam interrupted. "And Jesus."

She angled her head at the strange interruption. "Yes. Jesus also I suppose."

Cam grinned. "Don't you get it?"

"Get what?"

He got out of his chair and began to pace around the table. "All along I've been thinking this whole Isaac Question is bad for the Jews, bad for Israel. But it's also bad for the Christians."

"I'm sorry, I'm not tracking you."

A flash of lightning, followed a few seconds later by a thunder rumble, highlighted Cam's point. "The Book of Matthew makes a big deal about Jesus being descended from the House of David, that he was the true king because he was part of the Davidic bloodline. Well, if so, that also makes him part of the pharaoh's bloodline, not Abraham's."

Now she understood. "Aha. So the Christians are in the same boat as the Jews."

"Yes. And that boat does *not* sail to Jerusalem. Whatever claims the Christians have to the Holy Land stem from Jesus being of the Davidic line. If that line is tainted, so is the Christian claim."

Smiling, she reached out and squeezed Cam's hand as he stood next to her. "First the Jews, now the Christians. You sure do have a rare talent for making enemies."

Amanda took a break to play a board game with Astarte while Cam continued to write, the Sunday storm darkening the cottage even though the clock read mid-afternoon. Now reclined on the couch, he still hadn't decided whether to include the information about the Isaac Question in the book: On the one hand, the material was highly inflammatory, calling into question Judeo-Christian claims to the Holy Land. On the other hand, the information appeared to be factual. And facts, as the saying went, were stubborn things. They were like weeds—nobody liked them, but they couldn't be ignored.

He figured he had a few more days to decide. He was actually ahead of pace, his level of focus reminding him of the week he spent cramming for the bar exam. Other than meals with Amanda and Astarte, five hours of nightly sleep, and a morning run on the beach with Venus, his entire existence revolved around turning his outline into a full-fledged, and fully fleshed-out, manuscript. The project had become his life because, until he was finished, he could not get his life back.

And even that was a leap of faith. He and Amanda had been working from the presumption that everything that had happened over the past month had been designed either to get him to finish, or to keep him from finishing, his research. The Bartol lottery ticket and abduction in the North End, as best he could figure, was some kind of test to see if Cam was worthy in Bartol's mind of championing the revisionist history brigade. The Groton property conveyance was designed to get him to focus on the ancient stone chambers leading back to the Druids, and also to put him under behavior-altering financial pressure. Zuberi's offer of employment was a way to focus Cam's research on Zuberi's pet research projects— proving the Scots descended from the ancient Egyptians and enhancing the Sinclair name. And, perhaps, also, shining a light on the Isaac Question. Randall Sid's assistance was a way for the Freemasons to cultivate close ties with Cam, presumably with an eye toward using Cam to gain access to and influence over Zuberi. And the fake photos were someone's attempt—he did not know whose—to create turmoil in Cam's domestic life, presumably in an attempt to alter the direction or pace of Cam's research. Would all of their enemies, and all of their enemies' dirty tricks, suddenly disappear once Cam's research was complete? The answer, Cam sensed, depended largely on his conclusions. And since it was unlikely all the puppet masters in this little game had an identical agenda, Cam feared the answer was no.

But he was otherwise out of options. So he kept typing.

An hour later his email pinged and the ground underneath them shifted again. "Shit," he whispered, reading the message. "Amanda, I need to show you something."

Amanda and Astarte were on the living room floor huddled over the Monopoly board. Amanda rolled over to him. "Just in time. The girl's a tyrant. What?"

He turned his screen toward her, showing her an image. "Speaking of tyrants, recognize this?"

She angled her head. "It looks like a drill of some kind."

"Yes. A hand-held, industrial drill. Based on the description included with it, it can drill down ten meters."

"I don't get it."

"Maybe I should have read you the message that came along with it: *Retention tanks can leak.*"

"Oh." She leaned against the couch. "A threat."

"And not a very subtle one."

"Who sent it?"

Cam sighed. "I don't know. It's not an email address I recognize. But someone was obviously watching us and saw me digging around the property."

"Well, as threats go, it's not much of one. It doesn't tell you to do anything."

"Does it have to? Basically it's saying that the Groton property is still a sword hanging over my head. Someone could easily scale the fence with one of these drills and poke a bunch of holes in the tank. Within a few weeks the whole area would be contaminated and we're back to millions in liability." He closed his eyes. This was one problem, at least, he thought was behind him.

"But like I said, what kind of threat is it if there's nothing they're trying to get from you?"

He exhaled. "Just because they haven't asked yet, doesn't mean they won't."

"I think, my wife, that I would like to invite Cameron Thorne to visit Rosslyn Chapel with me later in week." Zuberi and

The Issac Question

Carrington sat in his office for late Sunday afternoon tea and figs, as was their custom on days when he worked from home.

"Will he have completed his manuscript?" she asked, pouring him another cup of Earl Grey. For breakfast he still preferred a strong cup of sugared Turkish coffee, in which the grounds were allowed to settle at the bottom of the cup. But he had grown accustomed to the British tradition of late afternoon tea.

"I think yes."

She nodded. "And will he bring it with him?"

Zuberi chewed on a dried fig. "Of course."

"And you have worked out the details with Duncan Sinclair regarding excavations at Rosslyn Chapel?"

He was not used to her questioning him like this. "Yes, of course," he replied in a dismissive tone.

She bowed her head. "I am sorry to pry, husband. It is just that I know how hard you have worked for this moment."

He reached over and patted her hand. "My thanks are to you, my wife. You have been valuable partner in this project."

They sat in silence for a few seconds. "May I ask one more question, Zuberi?"

He inclined his chin.

"Do you really think the head of the Pharaoh Akhenaton, of Moses, is hidden at the Chapel?"

This was, after all, the key question. He took a deep breath. "We have saying in Egypt: *Words are like dry sand, actions are like strong wind.* I think you have similar saying in English, that actions make more noise than words."

"Actions speak louder than words."

He nodded. "So my actions are loud, like strong wind. I lose much business with ISIS to make deal with Duncan Sinclair. I would not do this if I do not think Moses head is in Chapel."

"Would it not be wiser to not risk your relationship with ISIS and wait for others to look for the skull?"

He ignored the fact that one more question had turned into two. "We have second saying in Egypt: *Do not buy either the moon or the news, for in the end they will both come out.* But this Rosslyn Chapel, she keeps her secrets forever. How do we know what is hidden? I do not think Duncan Sinclair and others want to know truth. I think they never dig unless I push them." He popped another fig into his mouth.

Carrington nodded and stirred her tea. "You know, husband, I think you are correct. I have known people like Duncan my entire life. They only really take action when strong men like you come along and force them into it." She sipped at her cup, smiling at him.

Zuberi smiled back, pleased at his wife comparing him favorably to her highborn cousins. But for some reason Carrington was swaying side-to-side in her seat, like a person staggering through the desert. In fact, the entire room rocked. He swallowed. Perhaps, rather, it was he that swayed. Blinking, he set his cup down, the liquid splashing onto his desk as a wave of nausea washed over him. "Wife, I feel sick."

She nodded, her legs crossed, and took another sip of her tea. "How so?"

"Dizzy," he gasped. "Hard to see." The sound of his own heartbeat filled his ears.

"Yes," she replied. "That is to be expected."

Blinking more, he tried to focus on her. "What say you?"

"Zuberi, the correct English is, 'What are you saying?' You really need to work on your grammar."

What? The room darkened as panic rose in his chest. *Of course, the figs.* Carrington was a smart woman, and her mother—who had never liked him—was a chemist with access to any number of poisons. With a shaky hand he reached for his cell phone, only to have Carrington snatch it away.

"We only have a few seconds, Zuberi. Or, more accurately, you only have a few seconds. So listen carefully. You are going to die. That much is unavoidable. What is in question is the fate of your children. If you cooperate with me, I will make sure they are cared for and protected—"

He tried to interrupt her but she spoke over him.

"But if you do not, I will make sure ISIS knows it was Amon and Nasser who, after your death, reneged on the deal you made. I do not need to tell you how that will end. As for Bennu, I will do nothing. Without her brothers, she will find misery on her own, I am certain."

What was going on? He fought to stay focused even as his head spun and his throat constricted. "What … you … want?" he gasped.

She nodded, her eyes cold. "A baby would have been nice." She shrugged. "Now, not much, really. Not compared to what I deserve for this nightmare of a marriage." She set her cup down. "The password. To your computer."

His eyes widened even as bile rose in his throat. She had played him. Everything she needed to control his empire—his bank accounts, his list of client contacts, his files on both friends and enemies—was on that computer. He shook his head. "No."

She leered at him, an expression he had never seen from her. "You know, Zuberi," she said, her voice a loud imitation of his accent, "there is old saying we have in Egypt: *The house of a tyrant is in ruin.* You are a tyrant, Zuberi." She cackled. "And if you don't give me that password, your house will be in ruin." She stood. "Last chance. They are your children. I care not what happens to them."

"Wait," he gasped. He turned his head and focused on the photo of Bennu, Amon, and Nasser propped on the corner of his desk. They would be the last thing he saw. So be it. "Password is this," he whispered. *"One arm man rules world."*

She lifted her chin and laughed, turning toward the door. "Apparently not."

Carrington Sinclair-Youssef returned to her husband's study an hour later. She had no desire to watch him die. That he was dead was enough.

She edged the door open enough to peer in and see his body crumpled on the floor near his desk. Using a disposable cell phone, she texted Duncan Sinclair. *"A bird with one wing may think it can fly, but does so at its own peril."*

Now the hard work began. For the next few days she would need to hide the death. After that it would not matter. She closed the door.

It being a Sunday, the household staff had the day off. And Bennu was at a concert with tickets Zuberi had given her, at Carrington's suggestion. In Edinburgh, as in all large cities, anything could be arranged for a price. Carrington descended the stairs, opened the front door, and motioned to a man sitting in an unmarked dark blue van that had just pulled into the gravel driveway.

He opened the van door. A clean-cut chap wearing a gray jumpsuit and cap. Younger than she expected.

"We alone?" he asked.

"Yes."

"To confirm: Fifty thousand, in cash. The body stays here."

"Yes."

"Half now, half when I finish."

She handed him a small duffel bag filled with rolled bills. "This is half." She held his eyes. "Just so we are clear: If you try to blackmail me for more, I'll have you killed."

He nodded, spent a few seconds counting the cash, and stuffed the bag under the driver's seat. "And there's a bathroom I can use?"

"The body is upstairs in an office; there is a private loo next to it."

"With tub?"

"Yes."

He nodded, exited the van, and retrieved a couple of suitcase-sized containers from the rear of the van. "Bring me to the body."

Three trips up and down the stairs later, the man had set up a portable embalming lab in Zuberi's office bathroom. She helped lift the body onto a wheeled, metal table, reflecting for a moment on the irony of her husband being embalmed in the manner of his Egyptian ancestors. "Remember, I want the eyes open and his face to look alive. He'll need to be propped up in bed. I'll show you where the bedroom is."

The embalmer nodded. "Where are his clothes?"

"I'll bring you a suit and tie." She reconsidered. A sick man in bed would not wear a suit. "Actually, I'll bring you a shirt, trousers, and sweater."

The man shrugged. "Whatever."

273

"How long will it take?"

"About three hours."

"And there will be no evidence you were here? No residue or waste?"

"It'll smell like formaldehyde for a few hours." He smiled wryly. "Other than that, they'll be nothing left besides the body." He turned to her. "And it'll be another fifty grand if you want me to come back for it."

"No. There will be no need for that."

Chapter 10

Tamara Maxson put the phone down and stared out her rain-soaked office window. What a way to begin a Monday morning.

She called Moshe on his cell. "You close by?"

"Be there in ten."

"Come see me right away." She shook her head. "We have some work to do."

Tamara made a couple of quick calls to clear her morning and hung up just as a jacketless Moshe sloshed into her office. "No raincoat?"

He shrugged. "Couldn't find it."

"Umbrella?"

He dried his eyeglasses with her curtain. "It's just water. What's going on?"

She took a deep breath. "I just got a call from Tel Aviv. Our man in Edinburgh received a proposal from a high-ranking Freemason."

"What kind of proposal?"

She rolled her eyes. "You know how this works. They wouldn't tell me, other than it involves Zuberi Youssef."

"What *did* they tell you?"

"Not much. But they gave me an assignment. They want me to contact Rachel Levitad and ask her to find out the name of Zuberi Youssef's dog when he was a child."

Moshe chewed on his thumbnail for a few seconds. "Sounds like a test of some kind. This Freemason in Edinburgh wants to see if we really do have access to Youssef. The only way to get this kind of trivial information is by asking him."

"Easier said than done."

"Why?"

"Well, picture my conversation with Rachel: We need you to find out your boyfriend's father's dog's name. How do I justify that?"

Moshe's beady eyes darted around the room, as if looking for an answer to her question in the patterns of the wallpaper. "How about this: Tell her we are trying to access his computer files and one of the security questions asks for his dog's name."

She thought about it. "Not bad. But what does she tell Amon? In the end, only the boy is going to be able to get this information from his father."

"So maybe she lies to the boy, tells him she is getting a puppy and is trying to come up with a unique name."

Tamara shook her head. "Sorry, not going to work." She smiled. "But I do realize you at least are throwing out ideas. I'm just sitting here being negative."

Moshe stood. "I'll give it more thought. When do they want this information, this dog's name that is going to save Israel?"

"By tomorrow, Wednesday at the latest."

Moshe left, leaving Tamara to try to figure out what to tell Rachel. Twenty minutes of pacing and staring at the rain brought her no closer to a solution, so she picked up her phone and dialed the girl's number.

"Hello," Rachel said sleepily, answering on the fourth ring.

"Sorry, I realize it's still early." Tamara explained her assignment. "We need the dog's name to access Youssef's credit card information, which we think will help us to track his travels," Tamara lied. "Can you think of any way to get it?"

"It's just to track him?"

"I promise not to buy myself a big-screen TV," Tamara chuckled.

Rachel paused. "Okay, I guess. Amon is teaching me Egyptian words. I can just ask him to teach me some pet names. He's very trusting—he'll never suspect I have an ulterior motive."

"And you're okay with this?" This was a risky game they were playing, making things personal with Youssef.

"There's no way Amon could get blamed for it, is there?"

"No."

She sighed. "Then okay, I'll get the dog's name."

☥ ✠ ⬦

Her hair still wet from her shower, Rachel walked into the kitchen of her parents' home. Her mother sipped from a cup of coffee and watched a Monday morning news show on the television while her father read the sports page. The cat lounged in the sun next to a window. The idyllic American family. Except their daughter was a spy.

"Good morning," she said. "I need to talk to you guys about something."

Her father looked up from the newspaper. "Yes, honey?"

"If I'm going to do this spying thing, you need to let me go visit Amon. Or let him come here. I just got a call from the Mossad woman. She wants me to get some information for her."

"What information?" her mother asked.

"It's nothing important. But the point is, if I'm going to do this you guys need to let us see each other."

"Where would you stay if you go to Boston?" her mother asked.

Rachel exhaled. "With Amon, of course."

"Perhaps, then, he should come here," her dad said.

"What, so we have to sneak around behind your backs?" She had not told them about her trip to New York last week—they still think she had spent a few days at the beach with a friend. She crossed her arms in front of her chest. "Funny how I'm old enough to spy for my country but not old enough to have sex with my boyfriend."

"Don't be crude, Rachel," her mother scolded.

"Well then don't ask stupid questions about where I'll be sleeping in Boston."

Her father stepped in to diffuse the conflict. "What would you prefer, going to Boston or him coming here?"

She exhaled. "Boston. Nothing personal, but I'm worried you guys won't be too welcoming."

Her parents exchanged a look, each of them nodding slightly. "Very well," her mother said. "When will you be going?"

Rachel turned. "This afternoon. My flight leaves at one. I've already packed."

☥ ☩ ⬥

The weather had cleared and turned warm, and his fingers were numb from typing, so before lunch Cam decided to take a half-hour break from his writing to build a sand castle with Astarte. Venus helped out also—whenever Astarte needed sand she buried a milk bone and waited for the dog to dig it out. It probably wasn't the best choice for activities—every time they dug down, Cam thought about the industrial drill penetrating the Groton property retention tank.

Wiping the sand from his hands, Cam checked his email. A message popped up from Zuberi: *"Hello Cameron. How close are you to finishing your book? We may have a chance to excavate at Rosslyn Chapel and your conclusions in book might help with this. Carrington and I would like you to be at dig if it happens."*

Cam's eyes widened. *A dig at Rosslyn Chapel*. He could think of no place else he'd rather excavate. Of all the structures in the world, the Chapel held more secrets than any except perhaps the Egyptian pyramids. But there was something about the email that sounded ... funny to him.

"Hey, Astarte, let's go back to the cottage and grab some lunch."

They found Amanda hard at work, writing on her laptop. Cam showed her the email. "What do you think?"

"Think? I think I'm jealous."

He smiled. "Don't worry. I'm not going without you. But does the email seem ... odd ... to you?"

She studied it. "Yes, in fact. When he writes that 'Carrington and I' want you to come dig. I don't remember him ever referring to her as anything other than his wife. And he never seems to give her equal status—in his mind, the invitation would be coming from him and him alone."

278

Cam nodded. "That's exactly what I thought."

☥ ☩ ⌖

Amon stood at the arrival gate at Logan Airport on Monday afternoon, just as he had a week earlier in New York. Again he was nervous, though not quite so much. Again he popped an Altoid. Sighing, he wondered if the butterflies in his stomach would ever leave. "I hope not," he whispered to himself.

In the cab she smiled at him, repeating the words from their New York taxi ride. "We should talk now so we don't have to talk later."

He remembered his line. "That is a good plan."

She took a deep breath and whispered, "I had an interesting weekend. The Mossad and the CIA both want me to spy for them." She explained yesterday's encounters with both agencies, along with her parents' insistence she help the CIA and her apparent agreement to do so. "But," she continued, her jaw raised, "I'm not going to help any of them. What we have, for as long as we have it, is ours. It's private. I'm not going to poison it by spying on your father for them, no matter what my parents say."

Amon sat back in his seat. Until now his father's business had been just that—business. Now, suddenly, it had intruded into Amon's most intimate affairs. And he found himself embarrassed that Rachel had learned the nature of his father's affairs. He spoke slowly, also in a hushed tone. "Did they say why they want you to spy on my father?"

She nodded. "The Mossad says he is selling arms to ISIS. The CIA says the Freemasons and your father are close to making a deal where he would agree to stop selling arms to ISIS, but they are worried the Mossad will mess things up."

Amon pursed his lips. All of this was news to him. "And they think you can get information through me?"

"Yes."

He mulled it over for a few seconds. He recalled his father's directive to befriend members of the Jewish community, and to win their trust. Presumably that included Rachel's parents. "Okay, I'll do it."

"Do what?"

"Help you give them information."

She shifted in the seat. "But I just told you I'm not going to do it."

"Yes, but I want to win your parents' trust. I want them to approve of me. And if you give them nothing, your parents will learn of it, yes?"

She squeezed his hand. "I suppose so."

"Then it is settled." He smiled. "So what is it they want you to learn about my father?"

She smiled. "Well, the Mossad wants to know the name of his dog when he was a child."

"His dog? I did not know he had a dog."

"Well, apparently he did."

Amon pulled out his phone. "I did not expect this spying to be so easy."

"Wait," she said, stopping him from dialing. "You can't just come out and ask. Won't he be suspicious?"

Amon smiled. "He is always suspicious. But you are correct. I need a reason." He looked out the window as the tunnel walls flew by, marking their passage under Boston Harbor and into the city. "I know. I will tell him it is for a writing assignment. I am taking a writing class this summer to improve my English skills. I will tell him the teacher told us to write a story about our parent's pet." Amon smiled and pushed the speed dial for his father's number. "My father will think it is just ridiculous enough to be true."

☥ ☥ ⬦

Venus in tow on a warm, windy Monday afternoon, Amanda walked barefoot along the mostly-deserted beach in the wet sand, wondering about the meaning of Zuberi's odd email. Perhaps it was nothing more complicated than him telling his secretary to compose a message and send it under his name.

A young woman approached from the opposite direction, her path parallel to Amanda's but higher on the beach, in the dry sand. Amanda probably wouldn't have given her a second look, but the woman hesitated as she spotted Amanda, her hands reflexively rising in front of her in a defensive posture. Spinning instantly, the woman marched away from the ocean, her long red hair swinging behind her. Amanda gasped. In that split second, Amanda had seen her face. It was a face she would never forget, a face she had studied for hours. The face of the woman in the photos with Cam.

A wave of nausea swept over her, forcing her to one knee. Venus whimpered, nuzzling her ear, while a rogue wave broke and soaked her legs. *What was this woman doing here?* There were, Amanda quickly deduced, only two real possibilities: Either the woman was following them, part of the same team that had doctored the photos for some unknown reason, or she was here clandestinely to continue her affair with Cam.

Would Cam be so bold, and so careless, as to bring his mistress along while they were in hiding? Amanda doubted it, but then again she never considered him capable of an affair in the first place. And he did disappear for an hour every morning, usually without Venus, purportedly for a run on the beach. Was it possible he was using the time for a tryst?

The frustration and turmoil of the past few weeks boiled over. Without thinking, Amanda stood and raced after the woman, covering the twenty yards soundlessly in the soft sand. Leaping, she grabbed the woman around the neck and threw her to the sand, landing atop her back.

The woman reacted quickly, wriggling herself free and kicking at Amanda with sandaled feet. She caught Amanda in the ribs, dazing her, and rolled away. Hunched low, she leered at Amanda. "Stupid bitch," she spat. She lunged, swiping at Amanda's ankle with her hand. But Amanda's gymnastics training kicked in and she somersaulted away, landing on her feet. Before the woman could recover, Amanda charged, burying her shoulder in the woman's gut and taking her down with a football tackle.

They hit the sand with a thump, the weight of Amanda's body knocking the wind from her adversary. Amanda pushed in, her shoulder on the woman's neck, pinning her. But the woman was bigger than Amanda, and apparently had some training. Pivoting on her hip, she threw Amanda off and rolled onto her stomach. Before Amanda could react, the woman threw a handful of sand into Amanda's face, temporarily blinding her. Panicking, Amanda rubbed at her eyes, for the first time realizing this attack may not end well. Barely able to discern the woman's form, she backed away slowly, her fists up in a defensive position.

The woman might have pushed her advantage had Venus not stepped in. Growling, she snapped at the woman's legs, distracting her and causing her to spin away. Blinking the sand away, Amanda charged again, knocking into the woman's back and sending her face-first into the sand for the second time.

This time she would not give up her advantage. She grabbed a handful of carroty-red hair and shoved the woman's face into the sand. "I know you've been following us. Why?" she demanded.

The woman wriggled in an attempt again to free herself, but a low growl from Venus froze her. She spat out some sand. "I don't know what you're talking about."

Amanda pushed a knee into the small of the woman's back. "Bullshit. Who are you working for?"

The woman lifted her chin slightly. She was pretty, Amanda hated to admit. Something made the woman smile. "You want to know who I work for?" she said, her tone more defiant. "They're coming now." Amanda glanced up. Two men in street clothes, large and fit, ran toward them from the road. "I'm sure they'll be happy to answer any questions you have," the woman sneered.

"Bloody hell," Amanda murmured. There was no way she could fight off all three of them. Shoving the woman deeper into the sand, Amanda spun off and leapt to her feet. "Venus, come!" Sprinting, she raced away, her eyes burning, slowing to a jog once it became clear nobody was following.

Amanda cursed. So close to some answers, only to have the opportunity slip away. One thing, though, had become apparent: The woman did work for *somebody*. She had said so herself.

But that left Amanda no closer to any real information. If someone had doctored the photos, there must have been a reason for doing so. She had half-expected that reason to become apparent over the past couple of weeks. For example, a demand upon Cam to alter his research at the threat of more incriminating photos being produced. But, as far as she knew, nothing. Someone had gone to a lot of trouble and expense to gain leverage over Cam. At some point it only made sense that the leverage would be applied.

Carrington had not slept well overnight. She wasn't a superstitious person, but her husband's embalmed corpse lying in the bed in the room next to hers came alive in her dreams, swooping down at her like a rabid bat whenever she drifted off to sleep.

But there was no time for fatigue. The household staff had returned after their weekend off. She gave strict instructions to stay out of the master suite that contained their adjoining bedrooms and private baths, explaining that Zuberi had contracted some highly contagious disease during his travels. That should keep the staff away for a few days, at least. And that was all she needed.

Mid-afternoon she had prepared tea and a bowl of dried figs, as the staff knew was her custom when her husband was home, and carried a tray to the master suite. Now, nearing nine o'clock, she did the same with his dinner—some soup and pita bread. Locking the door behind her, she entered his room and sniffed. A faint smell of formaldehyde, but not nearly as bad as the night before. And, more importantly, no smell of decay. She set the tray down and went to Zuberi's desk to check his phone messages and email.

She focused on his business affairs first, referring to his meticulously-kept files and notes before replying to the various inquiries. She moved some money around as was required, careful not to move too much or in such a way as to create suspicion. In the game of murder, she knew, the spouse was always the primary suspect and money the main motivation. The allowances made in their pre-nuptial agreement and Zuberi's life insurance policy, plus the money he had recently gifted her as a reward for her assistance in the Scota research, would allow her to live comfortably, though she would be unable to afford to keep the castle. But she hadn't done it for the money. If greed had been her motivating factor, she could have just left the scoundrel alive.

Carrington turned to his personal communications. Two phone messages, along with a text and a voicemail, from Amon. The name of Zuberi's dog? She had no idea. No doubt the poor animal had been kicked and otherwise neglected.

But what was she to do? The boy would grow suspicious if his father did not reply—and with four separate communications, he clearly wanted an answer. With access to Zuberi's computer, she was in position to deal with whatever business matters might come up over the next week. But this stumped her. She could give the boy a fake name, but if he heard the name before and was just looking for a reminder, he would know she was lying.

She opened Zuberi's computer and typed: *"Hello my son. In Egypt we have saying: The barking of a dog does not disturb the man on a camel."*

She had no idea what this meant, and Amon likely would not either, but perhaps it would discourage further questioning. She hit send.

♀ ✝ ⚏

Leading Venus and blinking the sand out of her eyes, Amanda trudged the final few yards back to the cottage, her mind racing. They had been followed. Presumably by the same people who had already killed Randall Sid and/or Bartol. Which meant they were also in danger. She was tired of waiting around for danger to find them.

She opened the cottage door. There was no time for delay—the red-haired woman and her team, knowing Amanda had spotted them, might feel the need to act now.

She barged in on Cam and Astarte eating a mid-afternoon snack at the kitchen table. Cam immediately recognized the change in her body language. "What's wrong?"

She exhaled. "We've been followed. I'll explain later, but we need to leave. Now."

He eyed her for a second, no doubt noticing her flushed cheeks, disheveled hair, and sand covering her body. He nodded and pushed his chair back. "Okay."

"Just grab the essentials," she ordered, marching to the bathroom to wash the sand from her eyes. "I want to be gone in five minutes."

They grabbed their computers, tossed some clothes and toiletries into suitcases, and threw a few incidentals directly into the trunk of the car. Cam raced the engine of the rented Camry. "Where to?"

"I confronted them, so we have to assume they're expecting we might make a run for it," Amanda said. It was Monday afternoon, the early part of rush hour. They approached the onramps to Route 95. "If you go south, we'll just get stuck in Boston traffic. So head north. We need to see if we have a tail." She turned to face Astarte, huddled in the back seat with Venus. "Please don't be frightened. I think we left before they could follow."

"I'm thinking I should call Lieutenant Poulos," Cam said.

Amanda vetoed the idea. "If they're watching us they may have figured out a way to listen to our phone calls also." Which made her consider something else. She tapped at her phone, searching the Internet for a carwash. "Take the next exit."

"To see if anyone's following us?"

"Yes. And for another reason also."

He glanced sideways at her. Keeping his voice low, he said, "You going to tell me what happened?"

"Later." Being on top of the red-haired woman, touching her, smelling her perfume—it was like rubbing salt on a sunburn. Had Cam done the same? Amanda shook the vision away and pointed. "Go into that carwash. Make sure to get the treatment that washes the undercarriage. If there's a tracking device on our car, that should knock it off or short it out."

Fifteen minutes later they were back on the highway. "I didn't see anyone following," Cam said.

"If they're pros, you probably wouldn't," she replied.

They drove in silence.

Within minutes of the taxi dropping them off at his apartment on Monday afternoon, Amon and Rachel were naked in his bed. He felt like the gentlemanly thing to do was to talk a bit, maybe cuddle. "I have missed you," he said, nibbling on her shoulder.

"Mmm," she purred. "Me too."

"Have you thought about what you'd like to do for dinner?"

"Amon," she said, smiling, her eyes closed. "I didn't fly all this way for the food. Now please shut up and make love to me."

A half hour later she rolled off him, kissed him on the nose, threw on his tee-shirt, and strolled to the bathroom. From behind the door she shouted out to him. "Did you hear back from your father?"

He checked his phone. "Not since the camel response." It was unlike his father to be so … cryptic. He was nothing if not direct and literal, though he did love his Egyptian proverbs. Amon had replied, asking the name of the barking dog that did not disturb the man on the camel.

"Do you think maybe he doesn't remember?"

"No. He remembers everything."

Rachel returned, Amon's eyes involuntarily drifting toward her naked thighs. She sat next to him on the bed and ran her hand through his hair. "Maybe he's embarrassed by the name."

Amon shrugged, Rachel's warm breath on his neck sweeping away any interest he had in the dog. "My father does not get embarrassed."

She reached between his legs. "I bet he'd be embarrassed if he saw what I'm about to do to you next."

Tamara had gathered her things and was walking across the abandoned, late-afternoon Brandeis campus to her car when her cell rang. The campus looked beautiful this time of year, full of colors and birds and deep green lawns. But without the students it didn't feel right. There was something about having a few thousand curious intellects around that kept her young.

She took a moment to appreciate her surroundings before answering the call. "Yes."

"We have a situation up at Salisbury Beach."

They had decided not to abduct Thorne's fiancée and daughter for the time being, choosing instead to watch them. "Tell me."

"For some reason they bolted. They're driving up to Maine. Looks like they left in a hurry."

"Are you with them?"

"Yes."

"Any idea why they left?"

"A theory, nothing more."

"Go ahead."

"Looks like someone else is following them. Maybe Thorne spotted them and decided to make a run for it."

"Any idea who it is?"

"No. But I can give you a plate number. Maybe you can track it down."

Tamara sighed. So much for getting home for dinner. She reversed course. "Give it to me. I'll call you when I have something."

☥ ✝ ⬦

Cam drove north into New Hampshire and exited the highway when they reached Portsmouth, turning west on Route 16 into the setting sun.

"Where are you going?" Amanda asked.

She had refused to tell him what was going on, and was definitely giving off an angry vibe. He let it go for now—the important thing was to find safety. "This will take us up to the Lakes Region. We used to vacation up there when I was a kid. I know the back roads; if anyone is following us, I can lose them."

She turned to study his face. "One could argue that on back roads the danger is greater."

He nodded. "One could argue that. But I think the first thing we need to do is figure out if anyone is following us, and if they are, lose them. I don't know how else to do that."

She tapped at her phone for a few seconds. "I do. Get back on the highway, going north."

"To where?"

"Portland," came the one-word answer.

Cam had no idea what he had done to deserve the attitude. That is, other than putting their family in danger with his research.

Amanda turned and faced Astarte in the back seat. "I have a job for you, okay?" The sedan had a split backseat, allowing part of it to fold down and create an opening to the trunk for things like skis to be transported. Per Amanda's instructions, Astarte folded down part of the seat. "Now I want you to reach back and start to pull things out of the trunk."

Over the next half hour Astarte grabbed the items from the trunk that they had thrown there in their rush to leave Salisbury Beach. Amanda either took them from the girl and stashed them at her feet, or instructed Astarte to throw them on the floor of the back seat. When they had finished, Amanda stuffed the front seat items in an overnight bag she had emptied. "Now give me the suitcases, one at a time." From them Amanda pulled passports, a few toiletries, Cam's diabetes medication, a few milk bones for Venus, phone chargers, and one change of clothes for each of them and stuffed the items into the overnight bag. "Okay, this is the stuff we need. Everything else we can live without."

Cam still had no idea what was going on. Amanda rarely got in a bossy mood, but he knew enough to give her space when she did.

Ten minutes later she pointed at a highway sign on the Maine Turnpike. "That's your exit. Follow the signs to the ferry."

Cam turned. "Ferry?"

"Trust me, Cameron."

Amanda checked her watch. "Ferry for Nova Scotia leaves at eight o'clock. Final boarding is in five minutes."

"Should I rush?"

"No. It's off-season. They'll not turn us away."

"What's your plan?"

She answered his question with a question. "Let's suppose you were assigned to follow us. We pull into a ferry station, buy a ticket, and drive our car onto the ferry. Do you follow, or do you just call it in and expect someone to meet the ferry at the destination point?"

Cam thought about it. "Probably both. My job is to follow you, so I'd buy a ticket and get on the ferry. But I'd also call ahead so someone was waiting at the far side in case I get stuck on the ferry or something."

"Good. I see it the same way."

Cam pulled into the ferry lot. "Be right back," Amanda said, carrying the overnight bag with her. "You might want to walk Venus while I'm gone."

She returned five minutes later without her bag. Cam spent the time trying to identify any possible tails, but had no luck. Other than someone traveling with young children, anyone could be the tail. "Okay," she said, "drive onto the ferry."

Cam did so, pulling the Camry onto the boat and parking it among the other vehicles. A half dozen cars remained lined up behind them—one of them could be the tail.

"Okay," Amanda declared. "Everyone grab a sweatshirt. Cam, you and I should carry our laptops. Astarte, you have Venus. The luggage stays here. Make sure you have your phones."

It must have been high tide, because the pedestrian gangway rose at a steep angle up to the ship's main portal on the second deck. Once they had boarded, Amanda led them on a lap around the ship. "Stay close to me," she said, lingering near the pedestrian gangway at the stern. "When you see the crew begin to pull the gangway in, we run for it, okay?"

Cam smiled. It was a good plan. "I'll go last."

Ten minutes later the ship's horn sounded and a pair of crewmembers moved into place to wheel the metal pedestrian walkway away from the ferry. Amanda bolted. "Now."

Cam held back as Amanda, Astarte, and Venus scurried down the angled gangway and past the startled dock workers, their shoes echoing off the metal surface. Just as Cam moved to join them, a tall man in a long leather jacket slipped through a portal only a few feet away, near the entrance to the gangway. He moved to block

289

Cam's path, his eyes narrow and his jaw tense. "Don't make a scene," he commanded, reaching for Cam's arm.

Cam exhaled. If there was one guy, there was likely to be another, probably on his way. The odds would never be better than now.

Cam ripped his arm free, spun, and sprinted away from the gangway. He assumed the man, tasked with following him, would do just that and run after him. If nothing else, it would give Amanda and Astarte time to escape. And if Cam's plan worked, he might still be able to join them.

Racing along the side of the ship, Cam charged up a set of stairs to the third deck. Cutting left, he entered a large lounge area that looked out the back of the ship through a wall of windows. He crossed to the far side of the boat and leapt into a stairwell opposite the one he had just ascended—he had essentially run up, across and now was headed back down, making a full circuit. Behind him a heavy set of feet pounded after him, like a rhythmic war drum. Halfway down Cam jumped, landing on the second deck and racing back toward the wheeled gangway.

He approached the portal. The crew had begun to roll the gangway away from the stern. Not hesitating, Cam leapt, past a startled crewmember assigned to monitor the area, his hands reaching for the retreating metal platform. Halfway into his jump, with the concrete pier twenty feet below him, he realized he would not make it. The gangway was too far and his leap too short. *Shit.* For some reason he remembered himself as a four-year-old, jumping off the front porch in his Superman cape. He had crashed to the ground then, and he would do the same now. He braced for impact,

"Cam!" Amanda shouted. Somehow anticipating his jump, she had raced back and shouldered the gangway back toward him. It was just enough. Stretching and contorting his body, he managed to claw at the metal structure, his hip barely finding the edge of the platform atop the ramp. Rolling, he banged against a metal rail post and skidded down the incline a few feet before he finally came to a rest.

He looked up to see his pursuer readying himself for a similar leap.

"Pull it away!" he yelled to Amanda.

She had already begun yanking the gangway away from the ferry, the sloped pier and the momentum created by Cam's landing assisting her. Cam met his pursuer's eyes. "You'll never make it."

The man nodded, stepping back from the edge. "No." His dark eyes held Cam's. "But what makes you so sure we're the bad guys?"

Cam jogged down the gangway, his hip throbbing, wondering at the man's words. Had he made a wrong move? A few crewmembers stared at him, curious at the sudden disembarkation. One asked if he was okay, but none moved to follow in the few seconds it took him to reach Amanda and Astarte.

Amanda didn't give him time to think further. She turned. "Come on. They're probably calling in backups right now."

Jogging ahead, she reentered the ticket office and grabbed their overnight bag from a locker. "I already called a cab," she said. "It's waiting out front." Without a smile, she led them away. "Now let's get out of here."

Amanda sat in the back of the taxi, her head turned, staring at the departing ferry. The ferry steamed slowly into the twilight, their pursuers hopefully with it.

"Where to?" the cabbie asked.

She had dropped nearly four hundred bucks on the ferry ticket, not to mention the loss of their car and most of their supplies. They would need to be careful with their money. "The bus terminal, please."

Cam leaned in. "Where are we going?"

"Assuming we're still being followed," she whispered, "at some point they'll question the cabbie. So we need to throw them off our path. Once we get to the bus terminal, we'll need another feint." Amanda pulled up the bus schedule on her phone. "There's one more bus leaving tonight at 9:15, for Augusta. I'll buy tickets for us. But we're not getting on."

"So what are we doing?"

"I'm not sure yet." But she could help the cabbie deceive their followers. She raised her voice. "By chance do you know of any interesting things to do in Augusta? We plan to spend a few days there."

"No, sorry," he replied.

The taxi dropped them off a few minutes later at the Portland Transportation Center. "Any late trains?" Cam asked.

"No. Last thing out tonight is that bus to Augusta."

Cam pointed his chin at a plane landing at the airport across the river. "Maybe a flight?"

"Too much paperwork. I'm afraid whoever is following us will pick up our trail."

Astarte tugged at Amanda's arm. "Why don't we camp out? It's warm enough."

Amanda weighed the idea. "You know, I saw a Wal-Mart up the road." She tapped at her phone. "And there's a campground not far away. We could catch another cab from the Wal-Mart. We still have money on our gift cards—let's buy a tent and some sleeping bags."

"And some s'mores," Astarte said.

☥ ✝ ⬥

Rachel woke up in a dark room, her head on Amon's chest. She had no idea what time Monday night it was, but her throat was dry and scratchy. Careful not to wake him, she grabbed her phone and tiptoed out of room. The display told her it was only nine o'clock and that her Mossad contact, who called herself Leah, had phoned.

After chugging orange juice from the carton, she retuned Leah's call.

"Hello, Rachel. I was wondering about the dog's name."

"You know, it's weird. Amon can't reach his father. His father did send an email, but it was … unresponsive."

"Okay, please keep trying."

"Hold on one second." Amon had shuffled into the kitchen, his hair askew. "Amon, did you hear back from your father?" Rachel asked, muting the phone.

"Yes, actually, another email. But I find it quite odd. He said I should name it anything I wanted, since it does not matter anyway because the dog is dead."

"Why is that odd?"

"Because he wrote it twice. First, he wrote it as I just said. Then he wrote it again, this time in capital letters: *THE DOG IS DEAD.*"

Four hours after Tamara had thought she was leaving her Brandeis office for the evening, she placed a call to the field agent. "Are you still with them?"

"Yes. At a campground in Maine. They pulled a neat trick on a ferry and nearly lost us. And I think they did lose their other tail."

"That's why I'm calling. We traced that license plate. It took some digging, but the car belongs to Randall Sid. He's the Freemason who died ten days ago, the one we think may have been murdered. He was helping Thorne with his research. And the Masons are also trying to broker a deal with ISIS. Anyway, this Randall Sid owned a driving school, and the plate is registered in the school's name."

"So the Freemasons are tracking Thorne also?"

It made sense; he was an obvious conduit to Zuberi Youssef. "Looks that way," Tamara replied.

"How did they find him? We followed him from Brandeis that day, but nobody was with us."

"We think through the dog."

"The dog?"

"Turns out another of the high-ranking Masons up in Boston is a vet." She paused. "Thorne's vet." Once they had traced the car back to Sid, Tamara started looking for other Masons with connections to Cam and Amanda. "We're guessing he planted some kind of GPS device on the dog that allows for tracking.

Probably tucked it inside the dog's collar." Tamara didn't doubt the technology; the Mossad possessed GPS devices the size of her fingernail.

"Well," the agent said, "in that case the Masons can easily pick up the trail again."

"Exactly. So keep your head on a swivel."

"I might be able to do better than that. I can try to jam the signal."

It was still preseason so Cam was able to secure a campsite even at the late hour Monday night. They pitched their tent and toasted some marshmallows, but Astarte and even Venus seemed to sense Amanda's irritability. Astarte yawned. Cam felt tired also, but he knew a late night lay in front of him.

Twenty minutes later, as Astarte snored softly in her sleeping bag, Amanda motioned for Cam to join her by the fire, Venus by her side. "You must be wondering what's going on," she said in a low voice.

"You think?" he smiled.

She remained serious. "I saw the woman with the red hair on the beach this morning."

Cam sighed. So that explained it. "The one from the pictures?"

"Yes."

"Are you sure it was her?"

"I spent two weeks staring at her face. And when I saw her, she panicked. It was her. She admitted as much when I shoved her head into the sand."

He turned. "You did what?"

"You heard me. But before I could question her a couple of guys came running over."

"And you think she was there ... what, to see me?" He smiled wryly. That explained Amanda's anger. "What an asshole I must be. Not only do I have an affair, but I bring her on vacation with us."

Amanda resisted the bait. "I thought that might be a possibility. But based on the guy at the ferry it seems apparent that she's part of a team following us."

"Okay. Makes sense."

"So let's talk that out for a second." She obviously had been thinking about it. "If the pictures were doctored, then why?"

They'd gone over this a dozen times. "Maybe to influence my research in some way."

"And in what way would that be?"

Cam shrugged. "I don't know."

"So why go through all that trouble then?"

"Well, Randall Sid is dead. Maybe he was the one behind it. Or maybe even Bartol. Maybe they never had the chance to try to influence the research before they died."

Amanda nodded. "That's logical. But if Randall or Bartol are to blame, why is someone still following us?"

Cam had no response to that. He stared at the fire for a few seconds. "I don't know, Amanda. Honestly I don't." He took a deep breath. Obviously the sight of the red-haired woman had re-stoked Amanda's suspicions. And anger. "This month has been a nightmare. And most of what is happening I don't understand. But like we keep saying, once the book is done, all the dust should settle." If he thought abandoning the manuscript would keep them safe, he'd happily do it. But it was just as likely that their enemies—people like Zuberi—wanted him to finish. This had all started, after all, with someone leading him to the stone chamber on the Groton property. He stood. "I'm close to finishing. I'm just going to keep writing until it's done. It may not be very good, but we need to put this behind us." He squatted down in front of her, his eyes even with hers. "Can you just give me one or two more days?"

She studied his face, looking for answers he couldn't provide. After a few seconds she sighed. "Okay then. But this is really hard for me, Cam. Images of that ... woman ... with you ... keep popping into my head. One or two more days. But I can't promise more than that."

Amanda curled up with Astarte and Venus in the tent, leaving Cam tapping away on his laptop at a picnic table in the dark. She had no idea what to believe anymore. Only one thing was clear: Cam was either one hundred percent guilty, or one hundred percent innocent. So why was she fifty-fifty on which it was?

In the middle of the night she awoke with a start, a heavy feeling pushing down on her chest. She had always assumed there were only two choices: Either Cam was romantically involved with the red-haired woman, or she was part of a surveillance team following them. It now suddenly occurred to her, in the dark cool air of the campground, that there was a third choice: It could be both. The woman could be an operative and have seduced Cam at the hotel bar as part of some plan to influence his research. Cam had confidently maintained that he did not know her—that she was not a college girlfriend as the letter claimed—because he had just met her that night at the hotel bar.

The realization should have made her feel better. At worst, her fiancé had succumbed to a one-night temptation while alone in a strange city. But it did not. The reality, she now feared, was that her fiancé had cheated on her *and* they were being followed by a group that appeared to have both lethal intentions and lethal capability. She didn't *believe* Cam had done so, but she couldn't get it out of her head that he *might* have. And that doubt, she knew, was poisoning her love for him.

The sounds of the woods around them suddenly seemed ominous, foreboding, menacing. She would not sleep more tonight. And perhaps never again with the man she loved.

Chapter 11

Duncan Sinclair's secretary stuck her head in the door of his corner office overlooking the majestic Edinburgh Castle, glowing gold in the morning sun. The castle, along with the soaring gothic tower honoring Sir Walter Scott rising up in the foreground, reminded Duncan of the great Scots who had come before him. Men like Robert Louis Stevenson and Sir Arthur Conan Doyle, true literary giants. And economists like Adam Smith and inventors like Alexander Graham Bell. And, of course, his own Sinclair ancestors. "Yes, Dolores."

"You have a call from a gentleman named Dov." They were the only two people in the bank at this early hour; he was technically retired, as was Dolores, but he had continued his lifelong habit of being at the office by six every morning. "I believe he is calling from Israel."

"Yes. Put him through."

The man did not waste time on niceties. "I am afraid I have bad news. This dog's name you asked for—we are unable to obtain it."

Duncan smiled. It was as he expected. "I thought you had access to the son?"

"We do. And this should have been a relatively simple assignment. But sometimes things are not as they seem."

Indeed. "And you are certain the son pushed for this?"

"We believe so, yes. Pushing further would jeopardize our source."

"Sir, are you in a position of authority?"

"I am."

"In that case I think you would find it worth your while to visit Edinburgh. It is beautiful this time of year. And I have a proposal that I believe you will find enticing."

"I have a plane at my disposal. I can be there in six hours."

Duncan hung up and stared out over the city, just beginning its morning bustle. This call provided the confirmation he was looking for. The son could not discover the name of his father's dog because Zuberi Youssef was dead. The tyrant's wife had done it, just as she claimed.

Duncan smiled. One must never underestimate a member of the Sinclair Clan.

☥   ✟   ⟐

At four in the morning Cam had grabbed a couple of hours sleep wrapped in a blanket in the corner of their tent, but he woke with the sun, stiff and sore. He made some instant coffee, resisted the urge to go for a run, and clicked on his laptop to continue working.

"Last day of May," he whispered to himself. "What a freaking month." It would be nice to put *Out of Egypt* behind him before the calendar turned to June.

An hour later Amanda and Astarte awoke, and Cam joined them for a quick breakfast of granola bars and juice. "There's a convenience store down the road," Amanda said. "Astarte and I will take a walk with Venus."

"I'm closing in. With any luck, I'll finish the manuscript today."

She nodded. "I have a few things to add to that chapter I was working on. I'll be done by lunch." She studied him for a second. "Do you really think all this goes away once you send the manuscript to Zuberi?"

He exhaled. "I'm hoping none of this—the Groton property, the photos, the guys tailing us—is personal. They want to stop my research, yes, but they don't really care about me personally. So once the research is out, hopefully they just move on. Maybe they'll try to discredit me in some way," he said, shrugging, "but after this past month, they can say whatever they want as long as they leave us alone."

"So are you going to include the Isaac Question stuff?"

Cam swallowed. He had been thinking about it most of the night. "I don't think I have any choice—Zuberi is going to insist on it. And even if he didn't, I'd want to include it. Think of all the horrible things done over the centuries by the Church just to whitewash religious history. I can't be part of that." He sighed. "But I do have an idea on how to mitigate its impact."

Duncan's mid-afternoon meeting with the Israeli intelligence official who called himself Dov had gone as smoothly as could be expected. Like Zuberi Youssef, the man had refused his invitation to dine at one of the many fine restaurants in Edinburgh's New Town district. Men today simply didn't appreciate the importance of sealing a deal with prime rib and a fine brandy. Doing business over a cup of coffee and a pastry did not carry with it the same level of ceremonial formality.

But the Israeli, again like Zuberi, had been reasonable in his demands. Two hours after they first sat Dov phoned Tel Aviv, and a half hour after that received approval to proceed. "It is good that you work quickly," Duncan had said. "The widow no doubt has her hands full keeping her ruse going."

That was five hours ago. In the interim Dov, presumably with help from the local bureau chief, had put together a team of three men and two women. The five of them, along with Duncan and Dov, rode in silence in a van west along A90. A few miles from the city they turned onto a local road and ascended Corstorphine Hill. At the end of a winding gravel drive a stone castle rose in front of them, the top of its single turret lit by the last rays of the setting sun. Duncan nodded; it was a home worthy of the four-million-pound price Youssef famously had paid for it.

Hopefully for him it had been a good place to die.

Carrington met them in the driveway. Duncan stepped from the van while the others waited. This was his first face-to-face meeting with his cousin. He eyed her as he approached—he had expected someone darker and more menacing. This woman looked like a book store manager, not a killer. Duncan reminded himself that Zuberi Youssef had made the fatal mistake of underestimating her; he would not do the same. He extended a hand and bowed to her. "It is a pleasure to finally meet you, cousin Carrington."

"Likewise." She smiled, a bit of perspiration on her upper lip. Unfortunately for her, she did not possess the high cheekbones and thin face of most Sinclairs.

"I assume you have sent the staff home," he said.

"Yes. The gardener and his family are in the caretaker's house, but the home itself is empty." She eyed the van. "Who is with you?"

"Trusted associates. That is all you need to know."

She nodded. "Very well. I will bring you to the body." She edged closer. "And if you betray me, I'll have you killed."

The words, coming so matter-of-factly from this dowdy woman, disconcerted him. He forced a smile. "I'm eighty-four. What difference would it make?"

"You may be old, but you are full of life. You love life, every second of it." She motioned to the van. "Otherwise you'd be in some home with the other codgers."

He nodded. "Guilty as charged." What else was he to say?

"I'm not bluffing, you know. I offed the other Freemason, Randall Sid."

This time Duncan could not hide his surprise. "*You* did that?" The Sovereign Commanders had assumed it had been ISIS, or perhaps an accident as the police maintained. "Pray tell, why?"

"Put your team to work, then I'll tell you," she responded.

Ten minutes later, now inside the master suite, she continued her explanation. "I killed Sid because of the photographs. There was no reason for that. You almost spooked Thorne. I couldn't have that."

Duncan nodded. He guessed Zuberi—or perhaps Carrington, as things now appeared—had decided to monitor Randall Sid once Sid began to take a special interest in Thorne and his research. "That was a poor piece of work, I must admit," Duncan said. "But Randall insisted upon it. Randall believed at some point Thorne

300

might need an incentive to continue his work, a reason to help us broker a deal with Youssef. Perhaps a problem could be made to go away." He shrugged. "A gentle push, if you will."

"Yes, well, it was Mr. Sid who got the push. And not so gentle a one." She pursed her lips, her eyes narrow. "Because of those doctored photos, and the implicit threat behind them, there was a risk Thorne would walk away from his research. He even accused Zuberi of being behind the photos, which is how I learned of them. Fortunately Zuberi was able to assure him otherwise and Thorne continued his research for us."

Duncan merely shrugged. Perhaps she had been right to eliminate Sid before he could advance his ham-fisted attempt to influence Thorne's research.

Carrington continued. "At a time when we needed Thorne to be focused, your clumsy play only served to distract him." She held his eyes. "And Amanda as well. Did it ever occur to you that her contributions to this research were almost as important as his? You Masons think you're so smart, but how intelligent could you be when you still do not understand the importance of a woman like Amanda in her partner's research?" She snorted. "You still do not even admit women to your little club. Sid and his clumsy ploy left me no choice. I assume you will not be so imprudent, *cousin*."

Duncan smiled and put a hand up defensively. "Neither imprudent nor *impudent*. We have a deal. I have nothing to gain by betraying you. And you are correct, I do cherish my remaining time in this fascinating world, however short it may be." He moved the conversation to safer ground. "You expect Thorne's manuscript shortly?"

"Today or tomorrow. Thursday at the latest."

"But this will be only a first draft."

"Yes. But once it is submitted, there is nothing Thorne can do to prevent it from being published. He signed a contract to produce a book, for which he will be entitled to remuneration. The publisher is authorized to make reasonable edits and revisions, so long as the substance is not changed."

Duncan nodded. "I see. So first draft or not, once Thorne sends the manuscript to you he loses the right to alter its content."

"Yes. Zuberi was concerned he might get cold feet, so he inserted the appropriate language in the contract."

Duncan paused. "And do you think Thorne will broach this Isaac Question, as everyone seems to be calling it?"

Carrington exhaled. "Zuberi seemed to think he would. And Zuberi was an astute judge of character."

Two team members wheeled Zuberi's embalmed, fully-dressed corpse down the hallway in a wheelchair. Duncan smiled at Carrington, his respect for her having grown many-fold over the past hour. "Apparently not as astute as he might have been."

Tamara's phone rang, the ringtone like a metal fork scraping across a porcelain plate. She fumbled for a night light and jabbed at the infuriating device. Of all the things about her job, the one thing she would never get used to was being awoken in the middle of the night.

"What?" she mumbled, seeing Moshe's number on her screen.

"The plane left Scotland five hours ago, at two o'clock their time. It will land in Jordan in an hour, where it is already morning."

She checked her clock. One in the morning. "I assume Zuberi Youssef is on board." It was an obvious observation, but she needed a few seconds for her brain to engage.

"Yes. Our agents are serving as pilot and crew."

"Were you able to arrange a meeting with that swine Khaled?" The thought of that butcher swept away her drowsiness.

"Through Youssef's email account, yes."

She knew the plan. Khaled would be let aboard the plane and searched, per Youssef's normal protocol. The crew of Mossad agents would then quickly disembark to another waiting plane, which would be ready to depart immediately. "Have the Jordanians agreed to cooperate?"

"Cooperate, no? But they are willing to not interfere. They have no love for ISIS either. They will allow our plane to depart."

"And Khaled? Is the plan unchanged?"

"Unchanged. He will enter the cabin and find a dead Youssef waiting for him. It is a subtle, but unmistakable message: Fuck with us, and we'll get you."

They had made the decision not to kill him. "I still think we should take him out," Tamara argued.

"No. It is better this way. Plus the Jordanians might then not allow our crew to depart. Khaled will leave the plane like a dog whose nose was pushed into his urine after peeing in the house. He will know who his master is. This is more valuable to us than making him a martyr."

She sighed. "Very well. But why are you so sure Khaled will assume it was Mossad who killed Youssef?"

"The large Star of David hanging around Youssef's neck will be a good clue. Even a donkey like Khaled should be able to figure it out."

Tamara couldn't help but smile at the imagery. Khaled would try to keep it quiet, not wanting other arms dealers to know what happened to those who sold arms to ISIS. But the story would run on the morning news. Worldwide.

This, Tamara knew, was the real beauty of the plan. Mossad would get credit for assassinating a feared arms dealer, but without fear of retaliation. And the message to other arms dealers was both clear and stark: Sell arms to ISIS, and you'll likely end up dead like Zuberi Youssef.

With a Jewish star around your neck.

Chapter 12

Cam sat at the campground picnic table, staring at the clock on his laptop screen as the sun rose along the Maine coast. After an all-nighter he had, twenty minutes ago, finally finished the manuscript. It was attached to an email, ready to be transmitted across the Atlantic.

Flash. The clock changed, now reading 6:01 A.M. He hit the send button. 6:01 on June 1, or 6/1. For some odd reason it seemed important to him. Not as important as, say, waiting for the summer solstice. But his research was so filled with symbolism that he felt compelled to wait the extra few minutes and indulge in a little symbolism of his own.

The message transmitted almost immediately. Eighty thousand words and dozens of photographs, across the ocean with the tap of a key. He yawned and rubbed the back of his neck. He wanted a long, hot shower and some pancakes. Then a nap with the sun on his face and Venus curled at his feet. Then he'd figure out how to get their lives back.

Twenty minutes later he stepped from the communal shower and, yawning, threw on his t-shirt and a pair of sweatpants. Trudging across the campground, he was surprised to see Amanda jogging toward him. "Is everything okay?" he called.

"Yes." She stopped a car's length away from him. "Or maybe not. There's something you have to see."

Carrying a bottle of shampoo and wet towel, Cam followed her past a line of recreational vehicles back to their tent, Astarte and Venus greeting him as he entered. Amanda's laptop was open atop her closed suitcase. "This is a news feed from the BBC, from about an hour ago. Watch."

Cam clicked the play button. A news anchor teased the story: "A prominent Middle-Eastern businessman has been found dead in Aman, Jordan. Authorities believe the man, identified as Zuberi Youssef, was assassinated. Our sources indicate Youssef may have been an arms dealer and this could have been the work of Israeli intelligence operatives in retaliation for Youssef selling arms to the militant group, ISIS. More on this story as it develops."

Cam dropped to the ground. "Wow," was all he could muster.

Amanda sat next to him. She leaned her head against his shoulder, her blond hair blanketing his arm. "The witch is dead."

Cam shifted to look at her. "That seems harsh. Was he really that bad?"

She shrugged. "He was an arms dealer. And as soon as he entered our lives, horrible things began happening. It will be interesting to see if those horrible things continue now that he is dead."

As if in response to her musing, Cam's phone rang. He pulled it from his sweatpants pocket and looked at the caller ID. "It says Zuberi," he whispered to Amanda, as if afraid to wake the dead.

"It must be Carrington. Or maybe the authorities. Answer it."

"Hello, this is Cameron."

"Cameron, this is Carrington Sinclair-Youssef." The voice was flat and distant. "Have you heard the news?"

"Yes," he said, angling the phone so Amanda could hear. "We just heard. We are shocked. Is there anything we can do for you?" He didn't really know what else to say. It wasn't like they were close friends, though their lives had become intimately intertwined.

"I happened to see your email come in a few minutes ago. I wanted to thank you for that. Zuberi would have been pleased to know you completed the manuscript. I will, of course, make sure it is published." She swallowed. "In his honor."

"Of course." Cam searched for the right thing to say. "I only wish I had sent it a day earlier."

"He knew you were close to finishing, that is the important thing." She paused, and he sensed what she was about to say was the real reason for her call. "Zuberi was not particularly religious, but he was a Muslim, which requires the body be buried as soon as

305

is practical. The funeral therefore will be Friday, here in Edinburgh."

Cam was pretty sure today was Wednesday. "I see." It made no sense that she was going to pressure them to attend, but it seemed to be angling that way.

"Zuberi's son is a student at Brandeis University, and we will be sending a private jet to bring him home tomorrow. I plan to be on that plane. I was hoping to meet with you when it lands."

"Um, we're out of town right now."

Carrington's voice dropped an octave. "Cameron, please make every effort to make yourselves available. I'm going to email you the meeting particulars. As I think you know, there are things we need to discuss." She paused. "Including a certain excavation. I see no reason to delay that excavation merely because of Zuberi's death."

Rachel rummaged around Amon's apartment, dressed only in his t-shirt and a pair of socks, searching for a coffee filter. The sound of the shower muffled the morning news on the television, but somehow her subconscious homed in on the name as if it had been a siren—*Zuberi Youssef.*

She dropped into an easy chair, forgetting the coffee, and turned up the volume. Her shoulders slumped as she processed the news, imagining the devastating effect it would have on Amon. With a loud, long sigh she clicked off the TV and padded toward the bathroom. Standing at the door, she waited. There was no reason to rush the news—Amon could hear it just as well with his hair rinsed as with a head full of shampoo.

Waiting, she considered the ramifications. Would Amon need to return to Scotland to run the family business? Would it change his upbeat personality? One thing seemed certain: Her brief career as a spy was over, since the person she was supposed to be spying on was now dead.

The water stopped. She took a deep breath and knocked.

His laugh answered her. "You are too late, I am out. Why did you not join me?"

She grimaced. They had spent the past day enveloped in a flowery cocoon of young love. Now the ugly world had sliced through their little paradise like an angry chainsaw. "Um, I have some bad news, Amon. Some really bad news."

Carrington puttered around in her garden, yanking tiny weeds and breathing in the rich smell of the dark soil—the soil of her ancestors, going back dozens of generations. She loved to grow things, to tease life out of nothingness. As a teenager she had looked on with fascination as a Roslin Institute team of scientists (which included her mother, albeit in a minor role) produced Dolly the sheep out of nothing but an adult cell. Talk about teasing life out of nothingness. And, from what her mother told her, huge advances in the science of cloning had been made over the past twenty years…

Last night she had shared with her mother the news of Zuberi's death.

"Everything went as expected?" came the simple response.

"Yes. Just as you said it would." In fact, the poison had worked even more efficiently than Carrington anticipated.

"Well, thank God it's over then," her mother said. "A man can buy a castle, but that doesn't make him a prince. Good riddance."

Carrington repeated the utterance in a whisper. "Yes, good riddance." She was more than happy to delegate the funeral details to a local funeral director. The tyrant was dead, that was all that mattered. And she had more important things to focus on.

The game was nearing its end. Some of the players had served their purposes and had been eliminated or neutralized—Randall Sid, Khaled, Zuberi of course. Others she still needed, some to be sacrificed like pawns and others to champion her cause. It was this latter group she planned to meet with in Boston. Amon, as Zuberi's son and heir, still was useful. Thorne and Amanda had continuing roles to play. As did Duncan Sinclair. And, of course, the Mossad would insist on a seat at the table.

She thought back to October, to when they had first visited Westford, Massachusetts. The encounter had set into motion a series of events that even she could not have foreseen. Her original plan had simply been to enhance the reputation and standing of her clan, of the Sinclair name. Zuberi's obsession with proving the Egyptian origins of the Scots had not concerned her—his fixation had been merely a way to convince him to fund Thorne's research. But, ironically, Thorne's research into the Egyptian history had become a key part of her grand plan.

Zuberi's dream of proving the Egyptian origin of Scotland would come true. But, by a matter of a few days, she had denied him the satisfaction of seeing those dreams become reality. She yanked a weed and tossed it aside. In many ways, that had been her ultimate revenge.

Cam and Amanda sat on opposite sides of an aging picnic table a few feet from their tent while Astarte threw sticks for Venus to fetch. Many campers had not arisen yet for breakfast, but Cam felt lifeless from the morning's events. The tension from fleeing trained and presumably dangerous operatives, the exhaustion of writing all night, the euphoria at having finally completed the manuscript—all combined with the shock of Zuberi's murder to numb him. Each event, by itself, provoked a rich, emotional reaction. But collectively they pooled into a nondescript brown bog of … nothingness.

"I feel like someone shot up my whole body with Novocain," he said.

Amanda studied him. "I can't imagine why. There's been nothing on your plate this month."

He smiled weakly in return. Zuberi was not a close friend, but the two of them shared a passion for history and Cam had a certain fondness for the gruff businessman. Beneath his numbness, he felt a dull sense of despair at the man's death.

"You know, Cam, they say things come in threes."

"What are you referring to?"

She held up three fingers. "There've been three deaths: Randall Sid, then Bartol, now Zuberi." She shrugged. "Under the rule of threes, that means we're safe."

"I'm not sure it works that way. Besides, you forgot the Mossad agent, Raptor. That makes four."

"He doesn't count; we didn't know him."

A few seconds passed. Amanda broke the silence. "Three deaths or four, my point is still the same: This game is coming to an end, if for no other reason than it is running out of players. Someone deeded you the property. Someone killed Randall Sid. Someone killed the Mossad agent. Someone killed Zuberi. Someone has been following us. Someone sent those photos. Those 'someones' are either dead or, if I'm right, will be sitting around a conference room table at the airport tomorrow."

"Yes, just waiting to make us dead body number five and six."

She shook her head. "I don't think so. It's too public a setting—these people may be killers, but they're not reckless."

"So you think we should attend?" Attending the meeting would, of course, mean coming out of hiding.

She nodded. "Like I said, the gang will all be there. And you can tell Lieutenant Poulos where we'll be. It might be our only chance to get some answers."

"Okay. But how do we get to the airport without being seen? We don't have a car, and there's a hundred miles between us and Boston. We might be safe once we get to the meeting, but getting there's a different story."

She smiled. "Go take a nap. I'll handle the logistics."

Cam had slept most of the day after hearing of Zuberi's death, woke to share a meal of take-out Chinese with Amanda and Astarte and slogged his way through a late evening jog before showering and finally feeling human again. He and Amanda then stayed up late to plan for the next day's meeting in Boston. Now, on the morning of that meeting, they woke early, packed, settled their bill at the Portland campground using an American Express gift card, and grabbed a taxi.

"Airport, please," Cam said.

"What airline?"

Amanda replied. "Private jet." She gave him directions.

Cam smiled. It was a good plan. By the time their name showed up on a flight manifest, the plane would be landing in Bedford's Hanscom Field, the small airport not far from Brandeis that Carrington had chosen for their meeting. Instead of arriving at their destination via car or bus, they would be dropping in from the sky, presumably beyond anyone's reach. And Cam's parents had agreed to meet them at the Portland airport and take Astarte and Venus with them to their vacation house in New Hampshire for a few days.

At the airport, Astarte seemed nervous to leave Cam and Amanda, and Amanda had almost made the decision to leave Cam and stay instead with Astarte at his parents' home. But the girl took a deep breath and announced that she thought it best Amanda stayed with Cam. "You guys are a good team," she said. "And every time Campadre goes off on his own, he gets in trouble."

They said their goodbyes and entered the charter terminal. Amanda completed some paperwork and handed over the last of their American Express gift cards. "How much is this costing us?" Cam whispered.

"Just over two thousand." She smiled. "But your second bag is free."

Carrying the bags they had brought off the ferry, they strolled across the tarmac to a turbo-prop twin-engine Cessna 310. Amanda pointed at the propellers. "You and I will need to take turns pedaling. The good news is that the flight is less than an hour to Bedford."

He rolled his eyes. But at least Amanda's playful nature had returned. "Did you specify that we need the plane to pull right up to the terminal?"

She nodded. "In fact, I found a map of the airport and told them which door I wanted them to use. I'm fairly certain we'll march into this meeting room without incident."

He smiled warily. "It's marching out that I'm worried about."

Amanda took Cam's arm as they disembarked, crossed the tarmac, and approached the meeting room tucked into the corner of the office-park-like airport terminal. "Ready?" she asked. Zuberi's death had convinced her that she and Cam were mere pawns in some international game of intrigue—a game that included murder. And if it included murder, it was highly likely it included doctoring some photos as well.

He smiled in response to her taking his arm, his eyes on hers. "Not quite." Leaning in, he kissed her full on the mouth, lingering for a few seconds. She melted into him, her eyes closing. "Now I'm ready," he breathed.

She had been worried about him yesterday, about his lethargy and lack of vitality. But he was his old self today. She touched his cheek with her fingertips. "Me too."

Amanda pushed the door open without knocking. Someone in the room—probably multiple someones—was a killer. They'd get over her lack of decorum. They entered a square, white-walled room with a rectangular table in the middle, a couple of cheap prints on the walls, and a drooping houseplant in one corner. Other than the view of the tarmac below, they could have been in any of a hundred strip-malls in suburban Boston.

Amanda's eyes swept across the table. A horsey-looking woman who nodded at Cam, her presence at the table a clear indication that her Brandeis job was merely a cover. Carrington, of course. An older gentleman, tall and erect, wearing a plaid kilt. A lithe, handsome young man, his eyes pink and swollen. Hardly an intimidating lot. The two alpha males, if you could call them that, could not have been less menacing, one in a skirt and the other red-eyed from sobbing.

Carrington did the introductions. Amanda and Cam nodded at the others, all eyes in the room alert and wary, before taking a seat side-by-side next to the horse-faced woman Amanda assumed worked for the Mossad. The kilted Duncan Sinclair and Zuberi's son Amon sat opposite them, the young man glaring at the Mossad agent. Carrington sat at the head.

"Before we begin," Carrington said, "I want Cameron and Amanda to know that this room has been swept, by two separate security firms, for any recording devices." She spoke with confidence, an air of aristocratic gravitas in her bearing and a custom-cut olive suit hanging gracefully from her shoulders. Amanda had trouble believing this was the same woman who had worn an outdated pantsuit and let her husband order her dinner last fall. "Cameron and Amanda, I will need you to place your phones on the table and power them off. In this way we can all be certain that none of what will be said here can be transmitted or recorded."

"Why two different security firms?" Cam asked as he and Amanda relinquished their phones. Amanda guessed he knew the answer but was testing his opponents.

Duncan Sinclair spoke. "Because, frankly, nobody in this room trusts each other." He smiled at Amanda, a smile conveying both old-world charm and modern-day savvy. "And you two have more reason to be distrustful than anyone."

"This distrust is why," Carrington said, "I have invited you all to this meeting. We all want different things, and for the past month many of us have been wrestling each other for them. But I believe there is a way for all of us to walk away today having secured for themselves a victory." She scanned the room. "To do that, I feel we need to put that distrust aside." She straightened her back. "I believe there is no better way to earn someone's trust than to tell them a damning secret about oneself. I will begin." She paused dramatically. "I ordered the murder of Randall Sid. There is not a shred of evidence to prove it, and I will deny it outside this room, but I hired a professional assassin and had him killed."

"Wait, what?" Cam blurted. "Why?"

"That, I will explain later," Carrington said.

Duncan lifted his chin. "I suppose this is a good time for me to show my cards as well. I am a thirty-third degree Freemason, part of a group working to prevent ISIS from taking over the Middle East. As part of these efforts, Randall Sid befriended Cameron, hoping to gain access to Mr. Youssef. Randall, unfortunately, became a bit too zealous." He looked at Cam. "At some point he was planning to blackmail you. He possessed evidence proving the photos Amanda received had been doctored."

A wave of relief flooded over Amanda. *Doctored.* What a wonderful word. Here, finally, the evidence she needed. The evidence *they* needed. Under the table, she squeezed Cam's hand.

"Let me guess," Cam said, keeping her hand in his. "To get this evidence, all I had to do was change my research conclusions."

Duncan nodded. "Or perhaps feed us information about Mr. Youssef. I don't believe Randall knew exactly how he was going to use this particular hammer ... only that he had it if needed."

Cam exhaled. "So it was blackmail after all, but sort of reverse. Instead of threatening to reveal something, he would make the revelation *go away* if I did what he wanted."

The Scotsman sat back, his liver-spotted hands on the table in front of him. "That was his plan."

"So it was Randall who sent the photos," Amanda said. She never had liked the man.

"Yes," Duncan responded. "And they were, I can assure you, altered."

In her head, she had already reached that conclusion. But her heart still hurt when the photos flashed in her mind's eye. The Scotsman's assurances swept those images away, allowed her finally to relegate those memories to some deep dark part of her subconscious.

Carrington addressed Cam. "At a time when Zuberi and I needed Amanda by your side, assisting you with your research, Randall Sid was trying to drive a wedge between you. In short, he was pushing while we were pulling." She shrugged. "When he refused to stop ... we gave him a push of our own."

Cam flinched. "That seems a little excessive."

"Perhaps," she responded. "But the stakes were high. Are high."

Amanda studied Carrington. The stakes were high because she had invested so much in her plan—marrying a man she hadn't loved, kowtowing to him for years, obsessing over her ascent up the social ladder. And she had played her part well.

Cam exhaled and turned to the Mossad agent. "Are you next in this little game of Truth or Dare?"

313

She smiled, not unkindly. "I don't suppose I can pass?"

"No," Cam replied. "And I don't suppose when you told me you were helping the Mossad that you were understating things a bit?"

"More than a bit," she said matter-of-factly. "My position at Brandeis is a cover, obviously." She took a deep breath. "Our interest in this originally was merely to monitor things. We obviously are concerned about arms sales to ISIS. But then we lost a field agent, Raptor." She gritted her teeth. "That tends to get our attention."

"That was the work of Bartol, my supposed guardian angel," Cam responded. He looked around the room. "Anyone want to take responsibility for him?" He waited a few seconds, blank faces looking back at him. "So he really was just an idealistic soldier without an army," Cam said, shaking his head. "He saw the Mossad agent following me and took him out."

"And we returned the favor," the Brandeis woman said. "But other than that, and following you, our hands are clean." She smiled. "That doesn't happen very often."

"That is a lie," Amon snarled. "You killed my father."

The Mossad agent shook her head. "That is what we want the world to believe but, no, we are innocent of that particular crime."

Carrington turned to her stepson. "I wanted to tell you alone, Amon. What she says is true. Your father died of natural causes, a sudden stroke." She smiled. "I think he would have been proud of our ploy to turn his death into a profitable venture. One last piece of good business on his way out of this world."

Amon's face turned pale. Amanda eyed him—what a horrible few days for such a young man.

"You claim your hands are clean," Cam challenged, "but what about the Superfund site?"

The Mossad agent looked back at him blankly. "I don't know what you're referring to."

Carrington cleared her throat. "That was Zuberi's work, I am sorry to say. I found notes in his office after his death. He acquired the property soon after meeting you in October, on the off chance he might need to pressure you to work for him."

Another mystery solved. Amanda glared at her, wondering whether the grieving widow was as innocent as she claimed. Cam must have shared her suspicions. His upper jaw pulsated—this 'on the off chance' contingency plan of Zuberi's had nearly bankrupted him.

Carrington continued. "Zuberi believed that the financial predicament caused by this property would make you more willing to accept the teaching position at Brandeis."

"Which it did," Cam said.

"Why bother with the retention tank?" Amanda asked.

Carrington eyed Cam, her face expressionless. "You know, Zuberi had a true affection for you, Cameron. That is—that was—a rare thing. He had no desire to bankrupt you."

"Unless he needed to pressure me," Cam replied, an edge in his voice.

"Yes," she nodded, "business always came first with him."

After a few seconds of silence, all eyes turned to Amon, the only person at the table who had not told his story. He cleared his throat. "First of all, I had no idea my father was selling arms to ISIS." He lifted his chin. "That will end now." His eyes settled on Cam. "Second, I have no interest in holding Mr. Thorne to the terms of his contract with my father as it seems to me that my father acted ... perhaps a bit dishonorably ... in their dealings."

Cam nodded, noncommittal.

Amon continued. "Third, I wish to be part of this excavation at Roslyn Chapel. It meant a lot to my father, so it means a lot to me."

Duncan pursed his lips and rocked forward in his chair. "I do not object to that. Access to the results of the dig is, in fact, the price your stepmother insisted on for the use of your father's corpse in this little ruse we all just participated in to damage ISIS." He smiled. "The proceeds from his last business deal, if you will." He looked at Amanda and Cam and took a deep breath. "I believe Mr. Youssef had extended the same invitation to you, as well. Unfortunately, I regret to inform you that this invitation expired along with Mr. Youssef. I will do my best to convince the other Trust members to allow you to join us, but I am not hopeful."

315

Cam sat back and eyed the elderly Freemason. Amanda knew he had been looking forward to the dig, to being there when centuries-old secrets were revealed. Cam spoke softly and calmly, which he tended to do when he was at his most angry. "That's fine, sir. But with some extra time on my hands, I will be going to the press with the details of Mr. Sid's attempt to blackmail me." He smiled coldly. "The Freemasons do, after all, make for juicy fodder for all the conspiracy theorists out there."

The kilted man eyed Cam across the table; Amanda imagined he had been involved in hundreds of high-stakes negotiations in his lifetime. "You have no evidence of wrongdoing, Mr. Thorne. And I do not appreciate being threatened. As I said, I'll do what I can."

Cam shifted in his seat, his eyes and the elderly Freemason's locked.

The Mossad agent cleared her throat, breaking the standoff. "Actually, there is some evidence. Mr. Thorne's veterinarian, a Masonic brother of Mr. Sid's, put a tracking device in his dog's collar." She turned to Amanda. "That is how they've been following you. It should be easy to track the device back to your vet's office."

So that was it. Amanda shook her head. Another mystery solved. And another mystery born—why would the Mossad, presumably working with the Freemasons on the Zuberi murder ruse, now risk alienating the men's group by disclosing their secrets? She could only conclude that they were trying to curry favor with Cam.

Cam turned on Duncan, smiling. "Perhaps the gentleman from Scotland would like to reconsider his position on the matter?"

Duncan's blue eyes narrowed as he eyed the Mossad agent. He ran a shaky hand through thinning white hair. Amanda guessed he was not used to not getting his way, but he recovered quickly and offered a slight bow. "Very well, provided the appropriate non-disclosures are signed."

"Fine," Cam said, conceding the small point to allow his opponent a bit of honor in defeat. He sat back. "I'm glad we are all satisfied."

"Not exactly," the Mossad agent said. She addressed Cam. "When we met at Brandeis, I asked for your help in keeping the Isaac Question quiet."

"And I said I would consider it."

"And?"

Amanda now understood why the agent had told them about the tracking device in Venus' collar. She was hoping to trade favors with Cam.

Cam shook his head. "I'm sorry, but I'm going to include it. I'm a researcher. I don't believe in censorship."

The agent exhaled, her face visibly pained. She had obviously misread Cam. "That is a very idealistic way to view the world, Mr. Thorne. But in Israel we can't afford to indulge in lofty ideals. If we do, we will likely find ourselves annihilated, our people and culture and religion erased forever." She raised herself in her seat. "The Mossad wishes to make its position perfectly clear: We will not allow this book to be published with the Isaac Question materials in it."

Amon surprised Amanda by replying. "Are you threatening us?"

"Yes. Yes I am. And I believe you all know that the Mossad does not make idle threats."

Amon did not hesitate. "And I believe you know that my family does not do the Israeli government's bidding—"

A knock on the door interrupted the angry exchange. "Sorry to intrude." A frumpy man in a blue blazer addressed the Mossad agent. "There's something on Al Jazeera you need to see." He entered and plugged in a flat-screen TV mounted on the conference room wall. "Something you all need to see."

Cam had been fascinated by the interplay of the group around the table in the airport meeting room. The grieving Amon seemed to be playing it straight, but Carrington, Duncan Sinclair, and the Mossad agent clearly were playing a high-stakes game full of feints and threats, bluffs and coercion. Cam didn't really care how it all turned out. All he wanted was to get these people out of his life.

The frumpy man found the channel and stepped away. A bearded, angular figure wearing a black dishdasha, his head covered by a black kufi, stood in front of a podium, the black flag of ISIS hanging behind him.

"That is Khaled," the Mossad agent Cam knew as Dean Maxson said. Khaled spoke in Arabic, with Al Jazeera translating his words in a running scroll across the bottom of the screen. She turned to the frumpy man. "What have we missed?"

"He has been speaking for almost fifteen minutes. It started off with the usual bullshit, but then he started talking about Zuberi Youssef and some great secret. That's when I thought I should interrupt."

In Arabic, his voice rising, the terrorist pointed his finger at the camera. "Zuberi Youssef was not murdered because he was selling arms to the army of Muhammad in its holy war against the infidels and the dirty Jews." He shook his head. "No. Our Egyptian brother was murdered because he had uncovered the truth about Palestine, the truth about The Most High's covenant with Abraham, the truth about which people can rightfully call themselves The Chosen Ones. And this truth got him killed."

An image of the dead Zuberi Youssef appeared on the screen, the words 'Assassinated by the Mossad' scrolled beneath it. "But Zuberi Youssef is not the only victim," Khaled said. "The Jews will attack even one of their own. This is Professor Siegel of Brandeis University, a Jewish university in America." A second image appeared, of a man in a wheelchair with his head and arm bandaged. Siegel was the professor who first told Rachel about the Isaac Question "He, too, had learned the truth about Palestine. When he began to discuss this with his students, he, too, was silenced."

Khaled leaned into the camera. "This truth is too much for the Zionist devils to bear. They have no choice but to try to keep their secret hidden." Khaled smiled. "But it is too late. Allah has seen fit to open my eyes so that I may see the truth, so that I may expose the lies."

Khaled, his voice now modulated, proceeded over the next five minutes to summarize the evidence calling into question Abraham's parentage of Isaac. Cam and Amanda shared a grimace—the summary was almost a word-for-word recounting of Cam's research. Zuberi, obviously, had shared Cam's outline with the terrorist.

"Now," Khaled continued, "here is the important thing. The Most High promised to Abraham that his descendants would inhabit the land between the Euphrates and the Nile. All religions agree on this—Islam, Christianity and Judaism. This land is to belong to the descendants of Abraham. The lying Zionists refer to this as the Promised Land. Here, you can see a map."

An image showing the Middle East, with the Nile and Euphrates Rivers hash-marked in, appeared on screen.

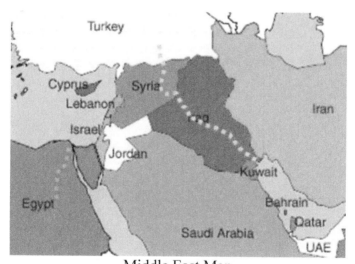

Middle East Map
Nile (left) and Euphrates (right) Rivers Marked by Dotted Lines

"Now," the Islamic extremist continued, "you can clearly see that this land encompasses much more land than what we now know as Palestine. And, in fact, the greedy Jews refer to this wider area as Greater Israel and, I am certain, have plans to wipe away the area's historical residents and claim the land for themselves.

319

Here is a drawing depicting this area which the Zionists claim as Greater Israel."

Another map appeared on screen, this one with a circular blob-like area delineated over much of the Middle East.

Map Showing "Greater Israel"

"The Western apologists, of course, claim Israel has no such intentions," Khaled continued. "But let us examine a modern Israeli coin, the 10 agorot coin."

Another image appeared, a coin with a menorah superimposed over what looked like a roundish plot of land.

Israeli 10 Agorot Coin

320

The corners of Khaled's mouth lifted. "Compare the shape of the land on the coin to a map of Greater Israel. I will let you decide what the image on this coin depicts." He paused and sipped some water.

Cam leaned into Amanda. "I've never heard of this claim, have you?"

"No."

He glanced at the Mossad agent, who was clearly uncomfortable at the revelation.

Khaled continued, leaning forward. "So, what does the image on this coin depict? It is obvious, yes? But," he paused, before speaking staccato-like, "it ... does ... not ... matter. It does not matter. Why? Because the land was promised to the descendants of Abraham. The Promised Land. And the Jews do not descend from the great patriarch. They do not descend from Abraham. No. As I explained to you earlier, and as Zuberi Youssef discovered and was killed for, the Jews descend from the pharaoh Tuthmosis III, husband of Sarah, through their son Isaac."

He stared into the camera, his dark eyes afire. "There is no doubt. The truth is out. The truth that Zuberi Youssef died for at the hands of the Mossad. The Promised Land does not belong to the lying Jews. It belongs to the descendants of Ishmael, the first son and true heir of Abraham. The Promised Land—including Palestine—rightfully belongs to the Arab people, the descendants of Ishmael." He held his arms up to the sky. "Allah is great! He has revealed to us this great truth. It is now up to us to take the words of The Most High, as accepted in all three religions, and turn them into reality."

Turning on a heel, Khaled marched off camera.

Cam broke the silence, the weeks of tension perhaps eroding his filter. "Well, I guess no one will care if I include the Isaac Question stuff in my book now."

The Issac Question

Cam and Amanda strolled out the front door of the airport terminal into the late morning sun of a warm summer day. An American flag whipped in the wind atop the glass-faced terminal building. The meeting had broken up after the Khaled news conference. Carrington had denied sending the Isaac Question research outline to Khaled, instead blaming Zuberi. Cam wasn't sure whether to believe her or not. And he didn't really care anymore. He just wanted to put this all behind him.

"So where to?" Amanda asked. She called for a taxi on her phone.

They had no car, no destination. "Home sweet home," Cam replied.

"You think it's safe?"

He shrugged. "The game is over. Other than finding the skull, there's nothing left to be done."

"You mean other than war in the Middle East?"

It was the last thing he wanted. But the idea that this Isaac Question could be bottled up indefinitely was ridiculous. In the age of the Internet, and with Professor Siegel already discussing it with his students, it was only a question of time before the information went viral. But Khaled had misplayed his hand. "You know, this revelation would have had a lot more impact if it had come from a Brandeis professor rather than an ISIS terrorist."

"That was Zuberi's original plan."

"Right. And I think ISIS saw the value in it also. But they needed to get out in front of the Zuberi assassination, needed to convince the other arms dealers it was safe to do business with ISIS. The price for doing that was disclosing the Isaac Question information now, rather than waiting for *Out of Egypt* to come out."

They sat on a Jersey barrier positioned to block a path to the terminal building, waiting for the taxi. "So are you going to include it in the book?"

He shook his head. "No. I don't believe in censorship, but now that the information is out there there's no reason for me to add fuel to the fire by adding Brandeis' stamp of approval to it. Khaled has all my research—I'm sure they'll package it up nicely and make it available to anyone who wants to see it."

322

"And you're okay with not getting credit for it?"

"Credit for inspiring another generation of terrorists and Jihadists?" He took her hand and looked up at the American flag atop the terminal. "I can live without that, yes."

Chapter 13

A week had passed since the meeting in the Hanscom Field airport terminal. The Khaled news conference had been picked up by all the major networks, the Isaac Question revelation fanning the hatred in the Middle East even beyond its normal feverish level. With so much loathing, and so many weapons, the next spark could turn the region into a wasteland.

May had turned to June, and Cam and Amanda now waited in another airport terminal, this time Boston's Logan Airport, for a flight to Edinburgh via Dublin. They had returned to their Westford home, Astarte and Venus in tow, and—in stark contrast to the turmoil in the Middle East—spent a blissfully uneventful early summer week swimming and boating and watching Astarte play softball. Lieutenant Poulos still had a squad car circle their block every couple of hours, but it seemed as if the Mossad and the Freemasons and the guardian angels and the Middle East arms dealers had all moved out of their lives.

All that was left was to break through a pillar in Rosslyn Chapel and perhaps rewrite history again. "The fun stuff," as Amanda called it.

Their flight was a red-eye, leaving in the evening and arriving the next morning. They had a couple of hours to kill in the airport and grabbed a pair of vinyl-covered seats along the outer wall near their departure gate.

"Let's play a game," Amanda said. "Write down what you think we'll find inside the pillar. I'll do the same. Then on our flight home we can see who got closest to getting it right. Winner gets backrubs for a week."

"What if we have the same answers?"

"That's a draw," she said. "House wins all ties. Since I'm the house, I get the backrubs."

"Why are you the house?"

"Because it's my game." She handed him a small spiral notebook. "Don't write too much. I don't want those back-rubbing hands of yours to get sore."

It seemed like every visitor to Rosslyn Chapel had a theory as to what holy relic or secret was buried or hidden there. Popular theories included the Holy Grail, the bones of Jesus, the Templar treasure, records of the Jesus and Mary Magdalene family bloodline, and the Ark of the Covenant. But Cam was convinced, based on his Cult of the Head research, that the pillar safeguarded an ancient skull. The Moses possibility was the most intriguing, but John the Baptist seemed possible also—the skull having been taken from Jerusalem after his beheading and carried back to Ireland, where it was worshiped by the Druids for its visionary powers, hidden in America in a stone chamber by the Druids accompanying Brendan the Navigator, retrieved and returned to Europe by the Templars where it was worshiped as Baphomet, and finally ensconced within Rosslyn Chapel by the cabalistic Sinclair clan. He sensed that Amanda would choose Moses, and it struck him that there were worst bets to lose than having to give his beautiful fiancée backrubs for a week. Smiling to himself, Cam scribbled his answer in the notebook: *A skull in a limestone box. Baphomet. Probably the head of John the Baptist. And maybe other relics such as the Stone of Destiny and a piece of the Jesus crucifixion cross.* He handed the notebook back to Amanda.

She read his answer and handed her his. "I'm with you on the skull, and I agree the skull was worshiped by the Templars as Baphomet. That's why the Sinclairs and the Freemasons preserved it. But I went for Moses rather than John the Baptist." She shrugged, smiling. "In for a dime, in for a dollar. Zuberi was obsessed with the Egyptians settling Scotland. I think he knew more than he let on."

"And that 'more' was the Moses stuff?"

She nodded. "It would explain a lot. Including why the Church put the Templars down—in the end, the secret was just too big, too explosive. In order for Moses to have made it to Scotland, it would

325

require acknowledging that he was actually Akhenaton, actually an Egyptian pharaoh—how else would his head have gotten to Scotland if not with Scota and his other descendants? The skull being Moses would inevitably lead back to the Isaac Question. The Church couldn't have that."

He nodded. "You make a strong case."

"And as your research shows, the story holds together. Scota and her family brought Moses' head to Ireland with them on their way to Scotland." She shrugged again. "You know the rest."

"Too well. I'm a little nervous about the fallout once my book comes out."

"Speaking of fallout, I have another reason I think the skull is Moses and not John the Baptist." She shifted to face him. "If the head was John the Baptist, why wouldn't they just display it like all the other holy relics and saintly body parts? I know we talked about the Church coming in and taking it, but the Sinclairs were powerful enough to prevent that. I mean, if you have the head of John the Baptist, tell the world and let them come make pilgrimages." She smiled. "And, of course, leave your donation at the door."

"I get you," Cam replied, pausing as a flight was called. "That's what all the other churches did. And, to continue your point, if the head was Moses, they'd have to keep it hidden because it would be too controversial."

"Yes, precisely. Again, it would lead inevitably back to the revelation of Isaac's parentage. Even the powerful Sinclairs couldn't open that can of worms."

Cam nodded. Perhaps the skull was indeed Moses.

Amanda stared out the terminal window, the jets on the tarmac casting long, bird-like shadows in the late afternoon sun. "I almost hope I'm wrong. The Moses skull at Rosslyn, along with the Isaac Question stuff, could be really destabilizing. It's too much."

"Good," Cam said, lightening the moment. "So we both want me to win the bet." He smiled as he rotated his shoulders and neck. "You know, these long flights really do a number on my back."

Amanda and Cam had landed in Dublin, boarded a connecting flight, and arrived in Edinburgh without incident. From the airport they took a taxi to the Apex International Hotel in the Grassmarket section of the city. While waiting for an early check-in, Amanda snapped a shot of Edinburgh Castle looming over the city in the morning sunlight like something out of a fairy tale.

Edinburgh Castle

She sighed as she stared at the massive structure. She enjoyed Boston because it possessed a richer history than any other American city. But it still paled in comparison to Great Britain. As a history buff, Amanda sometimes felt like living in America was akin to being limited to reading short stories rather than novels.

Cam interrupted her thoughts. "So do you think that's the real Stone of Destiny on display in the Castle?"

According to their research, the actual Stone of Destiny—the marble throne of Akhenaton—might be hidden away in Rosslyn Chapel. She smiled. "I can give you a better answer tomorrow."

They checked in, breakfasted, napped, and showered before spending the afternoon wandering the city. Carrington sent a car for them at three o'clock, which should get them to Rosslyn Chapel in plenty of time to explore the chapel before the excavation began at six, after the tourists cleared out.

"I used to visit the Chapel often," Amanda said, their car following the signs toward Rosslyn Chapel, bypassing the nearby

Roslin Institute where the sheep Dolly had been famously cloned. "But that was before all the *Da Vinci Code* madness."

"Well, you've got me beat. I must be the only Templar researcher in the world who's never been there."

She sighed and leaned her head against his shoulder, still fatigued from the flight. "You'll want to stay forever. Every inch of the walls and ceiling is carved, and every carving hints at another mystery or secret. I may never get you back."

Ten minutes later they hopped out of the car and entered a modern visitor center, built to accommodate the more than one hundred thousand people who visited the Chapel every year. Amanda gave their names at the ticket counter and a tall, middle-aged man immediately appeared. Politely, he addressed Cam. "Mr. Sinclair said you'd have some paperwork for me?" Cam nodded. The non-disclosure agreement. Cam handed it over and the man escorted them through the visitor center and into the courtyard outside the Chapel structure.

As they stepped through the door Cam froze, his eyes sweeping the Gothic edifice. Amanda grinned, her eyes on him, enjoying watching him experience the Chapel's magic for the first time.

Rosslyn Chapel, Scotland

"It has almost … an energy flowing from it," Cam finally said.

"Many people believe it was built along ancient ley lines to capture the energy from the earth. You'll often see dousers here, tracking and measuring the energy fields."

Cam stared. "But it's smaller than I expected."

"It's unfinished. It was supposed to be much larger." She pointed to her right. "That's why that western wall is so rough—it was erected just as a temporary barrier to keep the weather out."

Amon emerged from the Chapel's front entrance and strode out to meet them, dressed smartly in a blue blazer and crisp pair of khakis. He greeted them warmly, his melancholy from their meeting at the airport terminal replaced with a quiet confidence. He smiled kindly. "I am glad you are here. My father would have wanted it this way." He bowed slightly. "None of this would be possible without your research."

He escorted them inside and introduced them to Rachel, his affection for her obvious in the way he spoke her name and grinned in her presence. Amanda smiled, glad that the young man had someone to help him through this rough time.

Amon spoke. "The final tour of the day is set to begin. I suggest you join them. The guides know far more than I."

Amanda had taken the tour before so she left Cam and wandered off alone. The most prominent features of the Chapel were on its east side, near the altar. But they would be spending the evening excavating there, with plenty of time to examine and explore, and Amanda wanted to check out the veracity of something she had recently read. She strolled to the foot of the Chapel, at its west end. One of the pieces of evidence often cited in support of the Prince Henry Sinclair journey to North America in 1398 was the existence of North American maize and aloe carved onto the walls and ceiling of the Chapel. The Chapel was built in 1456 by Henry Sinclair's grandson, William Sinclair, and the thought was that William possessed drawings or even samples of these plants from his grandfather's journey and that the carvings were commissioned as a nod to this exploration. The problem was that different varieties of maize and aloe existed outside North America, and some argued that the carvings depicted these varieties rather than the North American.

The trillium cernuum flower, on the other hand, was uniquely and indisputably North American, native to eastern Canada and New England. Amanda walked slowly along the perimeter of the Chapel, scanning the walls and ceiling. *There.* On a pillar near the back wall. Ignoring the prohibition on photography, Amanda snapped a quick picture with her phone, then pulled up an image from the Internet and compared the two.

The Trillium Flower on Rosslyn Chapel Pillar and Growing in North America

She was no expert, but the report she had read alerting her to the trillium was written by a botanist. Now she had seen it with her own eyes, and the evidence seemed compelling. To state the obvious, someone from Scotland must have traveled to North America and seen trillium—and/or North American aloe and maize—prior to 1456 in order for it to have been carved on the Chapel walls.

Amanda checked her watch and made her way back toward the front of the Chapel. The trillium was an important piece of evidence proving the Prince Henry journey to America. But it was nothing compared to what they might find hidden within the Chapel's Apprentice Pillar.

Amanda was correct—Cam could have spent a week inside the Chapel, just sitting and letting his eyes wander. If the Chapel kept secrets out in the open on its walls and ceiling, imagine what kind of mysteries might be concealed within its crypts and other hiding places...

A voice called for attention. A team of Chapel Trust officials that included a kilted Duncan Sinclair, along with a handful of workmen, had gathered near the Apprentice Pillar with Carrington and Amon. Cam had been staring at the pillar for ten minutes, wondering at its workmanship. And wondering if the legend of it being a repository for the Chapel's secrets was true.

Apprentice Pillar, Rosslyn Chapel

Amanda sidled up next to him. "What did you learn?"

"So, according to Amon, over the past couple nights they've been using metal detectors and radar and anything they can think of to figure out if there's a void inside the pillar. Best guess right now is that there's a cavity the size of mailbox in the base of the pillar. Last night they drilled a hole and pushed a camera in there; nobody will say what they saw, but it was enough so that they're going to cut away a bigger portion of the base tonight."

Amanda studied the pillar. At least the base hadn't been ornately decorated, so any damage they did could be easily repaired.

Amon approached. "As expected, everyone is arguing," he reported. "Some people don't want to cut away the base. Even the stonemason is reluctant. This is sacred space, and the pillar is over five hundred years old."

"If you don't cut, how would you retrieve whatever is inside?" Amanda asked.

"Exactly," Amon smiled. "I think not cutting is the true agenda of some of the trustees. But I believe Duncan is handling things."

Apparently Duncan did so quickly, as he and Carrington walked over to greet Cam and Amanda. Despite the Freemason's original reluctance to allow them to participate, he greeted them with a warm handshake. "On the one hand," he said, adjusting the knot on his plaid bowtie, "I am excited to get to the bottom of this mystery. But I also know that Rosslyn does not give up her secrets easily. Often one mystery solved leads to the birth of two others in its place."

Carrington was less circumspect, her stylish blood-red business suit over a black blouse matching her aggressive bearing. Cam guessed there was no tissue tucked inside her sleeve this night. "There's only one mystery I care about," she said. "The images from the camera were blurry, but I'm pretty sure there's a box under that pillar." She leaned in to whisper to Cam and Amanda. "A box the perfect size for a skull. An ossuary. Cameron and Amanda, I believe your research was correct—inside that box is the skull of Baphomet. In fact, I'm certain of it. These old coots think they're going to keep me from taking it." She lifted her chin. "Not a bloody chance. Duncan made me a deal, and I'm going to make sure he honors it."

Cam and Amanda exchanged a quick glance. This was not the same demure housewife they had dinner with in Westford.

Cam edged Amanda away from Carrington and out of earshot. He whispered to her, "If it is Baphomet, that would be an amazing find." He smiled. "Sorry to state the obvious."

"That's okay. In this case the obvious is also astounding. Like you said, whoever Baphomet is—Moses or John the Baptist or someone we haven't even thought of—it would be an incredible discovery."

Cam rotated his shoulders and smiled. "What's this *whoever* stuff. I told you, it's John the Baptist."

The workmen had spread drop cloths and protective plastic around the pillar, and with surprisingly little ceremony a goggled stonemason dropped to his knees, leaned to his side and began to drill into the pillar base with a pneumatic chisel. Ten minutes later, amidst a cloud of stone dust, he set down his tool. In a thick Scottish accent, he announced, "I've hit a void. Don't want to drill any further, lest I damage whatever is tucked inside."

Duncan stepped forward. "Can you make the opening larger?"

"Aye. But I reckoned you might want to have a peek before I do so."

The Sinclair elder shook his head. "We've had enough peeks, I believe. It's time to reach in and grab whatever is in there."

The workman shrugged. "So be it then."

Moving his chisel along a rectangular path, the mason sawed into the pillar base over the next twenty minutes. When he completed his rectangle, he inserted a long iron lever into the cracks and worked the newly-loosened block of stone free from the base. With little ceremony he shoved the stone aside and motioned toward the opening. "I'll not be the one to reach in there."

"I will," Carrington said, striding forward.

As she did so, two of the workmen reached into their duffel bags, pulled out handguns, and turned them on the group.

"And I suggest nobody tries to stop me," Carrington sneered as she approached the pillar.

Cam could not help but think there was something farcical about the red-suited socialite, splayed on her belly, arms reaching into the base of the ornate pillar like a farmer reaching in to deliver a calf. But there was nothing lighthearted about the look on the two henchmen's faces. They were professionals, and they were paid for results.

Cam took Amanda's elbow and pulled her slowly toward the back of the group. They had no dog—or skull—in this fight. Assuming Carrington pulled a head out from the pillar, he was dying to learn what could be learned from it after DNA testing. But those answers would not come tonight no matter who made off with the skull.

"Got it!" Carrington announced. Slowly she extracted her arms from beneath the pillar, dragging something along. All eyes, except for the henchmen's, remained fixed on her arms—first elbows, then wrists, then hands, then fingers, and finally, slowly, a beige stone box emerged from the cavity. Carrington rolled to her side, her red suit blotched with stone dust and dirt. Silence echoed off the Chapel walls. On her knees, with shaking, grimy hands, she reached for the box's square lid.

"Carrington, don't," Duncan commanded. "Being sealed in the pillar, and within the ossuary, may be all that has kept the bones from decaying all these years. They'll turn to dust in your hands."

She didn't even take her eyes off the box. "You're bluffing, Duncan. And not particularly well."

Amanda whispered to Cam, "She's right. A few minutes in the air won't matter much."

Still on her knees, and using two hands, Carrington lifted the lid and set it gently aside. Leaning forward, she peered in, her hands clasped in front of her chest as if in prayer. A sharp intake of breath, followed by a wide grin, announced her find. "A skull," she breathed. "Baphomet. Just as we thought."

Her eyes moist, she replaced the lid, pushed herself to her feet, and motioned to the two henchmen. Carrying the ossuary herself, Carrington led them to a side exit, their guns still trained on the Chapel visitors. "Don't dream of trying to follow," she said, her eyes on Duncan. "I think we all know just how serious I am. Some would say obsessed." She coughed out a sharp laugh. "My men are carrying hydrofluoric acid." Her words sunk in. "I'll destroy the skull before I let you take it from me."

Edging sideways, Cam caught Duncan's eye as Carrington ranted. Cam blinked, not certain his eyes weren't playing tricks on him. Rather than anger, the elderly Freemason wore a bemused look on his face.

♀ ✝ ⟁

Duncan's Sinclair's voice rose above the mayhem within Rosslyn Chapel as Carrington and her two henchmen slipped out a side door with the stone ossuary containing the ancient skull. "Everyone remain calm. Do not, I repeat do not, pursue them."

"Shall I call the police?" a woman asked, her cell phone in hand.

"No. I believe Ms. Sinclair-Youssef when she threatens to destroy the skull. We will handle this without the authorities." He scanned the room. "I suggest you all wait a few minutes and then proceed in an orderly fashion to your vehicles. Tonight's festivities have now concluded."

"Shouldn't we at least look to see if there's anything else in the cavity?" Cam asked. He found it odd that the Freemason had not thought of this already.

Duncan arched his eyebrows. "Quite so." He nodded to one of the Chapel employees, who dropped to his knees on the drop cloth and felt around inside the void.

"It's empty," the man reported, his dark suit soiled with stone dust.

Cam approached Duncan. "So you're just going to let her go?"

He shrugged. "If you had the skull, what would you do with it?"

"Have it tested," Cam replied. "The molar contains a treasure trove of DNA. You could determine age and region of origin, maybe even derive physical characteristics."

"And that is precisely what Carrington will be doing. Having it tested. And since her mother works at The Roslin Institute, my guess is that is where the skull is headed. No doubt such a sophisticated lab can complete the testing rather quickly."

"So you're going to grab it there?"

Duncan looked at Cam disdainfully. "I'll do no such thing. You Americans are such cowboys, always ready to go storming in. Why should I interrupt the testing process? It is, after all, the results that we all are awaiting. The skull itself is secondary." He gave Cam a long stare. "Now, I suggest you go back to your hotel and get some sleep."

The text message alert woke Cam from a sound sleep. Fumbling in the dark Edinburgh hotel room, he found his phone and reoriented himself.

"What time is it?" Amanda mumbled. Then she bolted up to a sitting position, obviously concerned about Astarte. "It's not your parents, is it?"

"No," he replied. "It's Carrington. And it's just after four in the morning."

Amanda sank back into her pillow. "What does she want? I'm surprised she bothered to reach out to us."

Cam skimmed the message, now fully awake. "She wanted to share the DNA results with us."

"That was quick," she mumbled.

"Like Duncan said, her mother works at the Roslin Institute." He swallowed. "It's still preliminary, but the tests show a male skull, Middle-Eastern or northern African in origin, approximately thirty-five hundred years old."

"Bloody amazing,"

"More than amazing. It might actually be the skull of Moses. Wow. Just wow."

"I guess we're awake now," Amanda said. She propped herself up on one elbow, facing Cam, her flaxen hair willowing over her face. "One thing I don't understand is why Carrington felt the need to steal the skull."

"I don't think she trusted Duncan to be honest with the results, whatever they were. This stuff is pretty controversial. We're rewriting the whole Book of Exodus, and that doesn't even include all the Isaac Question stuff. I'm not sure the Rosslyn Chapel Trust officials are going to be too excited about all this."

"Why? It'll just add to the tsunami of tourists passing through there. The Jesus Bloodline *and* the skull of Moses in one place. And it turns out Baphomet was Moses—no wonder the Templars worshipped the head. And that means the Templars must have known about the Isaac stuff."

He nodded. "It makes sense. If the Freemasons know, the Templars must have known also." Shifting, his mind alert, he continued. "You know what else? This all pretty much conclusively proves the case for early cross-Atlantic exploration. Brendan and the Druids, then the Templars, then Prince Henry."

She yawned and stretched her arms. "So what next?"

"I guess we catch our flight."

"So that's it? End of adventure."

"I guess so, yeah."

"Incorrect, sailor." She jumped from the bed. "I'm going to go wash up. We have all morning to kill, and I believe you owe me a backrub."

Chapter 14

Just over eight weeks had passed since Carrington liberated the ancient skull from its stone prison within Rosslyn Chapel. She nibbled on a late breakfast of yogurt and granola, enjoying one of her last days in the castle. Bennu had returned to Cairo to live with her mother's sister, and Carrington no longer needed or could afford the sprawling home. Her limited funds were best spent on other necessities, and if things panned out she'd soon have more status than a dozen castles could give her.

The final test results on the skull had come back after four days, confirming the preliminary findings she had texted to Cameron—the skull was indeed a male of Middle-Eastern or northern African origin dating from approximately thirty-five hundred years ago. There was no doubt in her mind that the skull was that of Moses. She smiled as she licked her spoon. Zuberi had been correct after all. How sweet it was that he had died not knowing.

Today, August 7, one of the four ancient cross-quarter days, marked the pagan holiday of Lunasa, a day celebrating the beginning of the harvest season, a time when Mother Earth finally began to yield her fruit. Carrington rested one hand on her abdomen as she ate. Would she, too, reap what she had worked so hard to sow?

The grandfather clock in the living room rang for the eleven o'clock hour and Carrington, dressed in a khaki skirt and pink blouse, ambled to the front door. Her mother, driving a navy blue compact car, pulled into the circular driveway, punctual as always. A worker bee, driving a perfectly middle-class vehicle. Carrington wanted more, deserved more.

"Hello Mother," she said, getting in and offering a quick peck on the cheek. Her mother, as always, tasted like cold cream.

"Did you wire the money?" her mother replied, hunched over the wheel as she navigated the long drive.

"I can't wire anything. It's Sunday. I'll wire it in the morning."

"The agreement was the funds were to be wired at seven weeks."

Carrington sighed. "I can't change the banking laws, Mother." She had already wired a half-million pounds, with two more installments of a quarter-million still due. The expenditures would wipe her out—representing the entirety of her savings, the proceeds of Zuberi's life insurance, and what he had left her in his will. But it was worth it. It would all be worth it.

"If things don't work out, you can come back home until you get back on your feet." Her mother's mouth contorted as she spoke the words, in the way it would had a bug flown in.

"That won't be necessary, Mother. But thank you."

"You can't be certain."

"The Americans have a wonderful expression, about putting one's money where one's mouth is. Were I not certain, I would not have wired the funds."

"But you *can't* be certain."

Carrington rolled her eyes. "Honestly, Mother, you can be infuriatingly small-minded sometimes."

They drove in silence. Sometimes the best way to shut her mother up was to sass her and let her sulk a bit.

Ten minutes later they turned off a main road and into the University of Edinburgh's veterinary school campus. A hulking linear structure comprised of two parallel buildings, one resembling an elongated glass and mosaic jewelry box and the second an elongated mahogany toy chest, dominated one corner of the campus. "The two buildings are meant to represent two separate strands of DNA," her mother said, breaking the silence.

"How appropriate," Carrington said.

A sign identifying the company housed in the building dominated a wall near the main entrance. Had it been Carrington's choice, instead of signage she would have commissioned a sculpture of a giant sheep. The sheep, along with the DNA-like buildings, would tell visitors all they needed to know.

This was, after all, The Roslin Institute.

☥ ☩ ⬡

Carrington and her mother stepped from the car and into the haze of an inordinately muggy August day.

"Looks like it might rain," her mother said, sniffing the air like a beagle.

"It's Scotland, Mother. It always rains."

They had purposely chosen a Sunday, a day when the building would be mostly empty. Her mother swiped her ID card into the elevator and they ascended to the fourth floor. Dr Wilcox waited for them in his corner office. A heavy-set, humorless man with fleshy jowls and darting eyes, he remained seated behind his desk as they entered. "Did you wire the funds?" he asked by way of greeting.

"They will be wired in the morning," Carrington said. "Assuming the test results are acceptable."

He sighed. "They were due today." He pointed across the hallway. "The technician is waiting for you."

"Are you joining us?" Carrington asked.

He made a face. "I am a geneticist, not a medical doctor."

And not a particularly ethical one. Though very well paid.

"Why don't you wait with Dr. Wilcox, Mother," Carrington said, making her exit.

She made a point of not making eye contact with the young female technician in a light blue lab coat. The less said the better. Carrington disrobed, climbed atop the examination table, and spread her legs. The woman lubricated a beige wand resembling an electric toothbrush and inserted it into Carrington's vaginal canal. As far as the tech knew, Carrington was Dr. Wilcox's mistress, here on a Sunday to avoid undue publicity.

The technician spoke matter-of-factly as she maneuvered the wand. "There's the sac. And the fetus."

Carrington lifted her head and peered at the monitor. It just looked like a blob to her. "How large?"

"About a centimeter in length, the size of a dried lima bean. Looks healthy. I can see some facial features. I can detect a heartbeat. A strong one." She smiled for the first time as she removed the wand. "Everything looks fine. It's a boy."

"Yes, I know," Carrington replied. Half-naked and spread-eagled, Carrington had never felt more confident. She lifted her chin. "His name is Moses."

♀ ✝ ⬡

Only fifteen minutes had passed since Carrington had left her mother and Dr. Wilcox alone in the doctor's office. But the world had changed.

"The fetus is healthy," she announced. "Moses is healthy."

The geneticist nodded smugly. "I will expect the funds first thing tomorrow morning."

"So what are the odds of a healthy birth?" Carrington knew that a healthy heartbeat at the seven-week mark for traditional human pregnancies put the odds of a healthy birth at over ninety percent. But this pregnancy was anything but traditional.

"In other primates," Dr. Wilcox replied, "the seven-week mark has been a tipping point. After seven weeks, viability jumps from twenty percent to almost sixty percent. I have no reason to believe it will be any different with humans."

Carrington's face flushed. He had said sixty percent, but in her heart she knew it to be a certainty.

Her mother, however, remained skeptical. "Yes, but with primates you were working with fresh DNA. This DNA is over three thousand years old."

"That's why this seven-week mark is so important. It seems we have overcome any shortcomings with the DNA we extracted from the molar."

As Carrington understood it, the cloning process generally required undamaged cell nuclei that could be inserted into a surrogate parent, and even then the odds for success were low.

341

Over the past decade researchers at Roslin had advanced the science, increasing the odds and making even damaged or old cell nuclei viable. Of course, nobody had ever tried to clone a human. Until now.

Carrington stood. She had no desire to spend more time with the geneticist. In fact, spending time together only increased their chances of getting caught. It had not been difficult, using her mother as an intermediary, to convince the rogue scientist to accept the million-pound bribe. For him it was a chance to both get rich and change the world. But that didn't mean Carrington had to like him. Or trust him. In the end it might be safer to eliminate him the way she had eliminated other obstacles in her path. After all, his idea of changing the world might not run in lockstep with hers.

They walked in silence to the car. Once inside, her mother exhaled. "This is dangerous for me, you know."

Carrington laughed. The woman's daughter was about to give birth to the Bible's most famous prophet, and all she could think about was losing her job. "I appreciate your sacrifice, Mother."

They began to drive. "Does the American know?" her mother asked. "His research is crucial to all this."

"Nobody knows. Just you and Wilcox." But her mother was right about Thorne's research. It would be possible to prove to the world that her baby had been cloned from DNA extracted from the skull. But to prove that the baby was a clone of the Biblical Moses would require a plausible explanation for how Carrington came to be in possession of Moses' skull in the first place. For that she needed the research in Thorne's new book. "As for his research, his book will be released a couple of months before Moses' birth." Just enough time to let people get used to the idea.

Her mother peered ahead, hunched low over the steering wheel. She took a deep breath. "Even sixty percent is no guarantee. You realize that, don't you?"

"Yes, mother. I'm not an idiot. One hundred minus sixty equals forty. That means there is a forty percent chance of … non-viability." They had been over the science a dozen times.

"Forty percent is significant."

Carrington fought to control her tone. "Mother, do you believe in God?"

"That's a ridiculous question. You know I do."

Carrington had never been particularly observant, but she had never doubted the presence of some omnipotent power that first created and now controlled the world. "Well, then, let me ask you this: Why would God go through the trouble of allowing me—whose mother just happens to work at the world's foremost genetic cloning laboratory—to recover the skull of Moses, clone him, and use my womb to carry the fetus, if the entire procedure was fated to fail?"

"One cannot hope to know what God intends for us."

"No. But when God walks me to the front door and hands me the key, what am I to do but walk on in?"

The doorbell rang early one August morning, on one of the hottest, most humid days of the summer. The house was cool from the air conditioning having been on overnight and the thick, heavy air almost took Cam's breath away as he opened the door. The sight of the white-haired Duncan Sinclair standing on his front porch served as a second blow to the gut.

Cam fought to find his voice. "Duncan," was all he could muster.

"Mr. Thorne," the elderly Freemason replied, his cream-colored dress shirt sticking to his body. "Good morning." A dark sedan idled on the street in front of Cam's home.

Cam had just stepped from the shower, his hair still wet. Amanda was doing yoga in the basement while Astarte, in her pajamas, sat on the living room couch watching cartoons. White index cards littered the kitchen table, remnants of last night's effort to finalize the seating arrangements for their upcoming Labor Day wedding only a month away. They were hardly ready to receive company. But Cam couldn't turn the man away. "Please come in. I apologize for the mess."

Venus trotted over to sniff their kilted guest, surprising Cam by licking gently at the back of his hand. Normally she was a better judge of character. Or maybe Cam himself had judged the Sinclair clansman too harshly. Duncan bowed. "I apologize for coming unannounced, and at such an early hour. But today is Lunasa, and I thought it an appropriate day to pay a visit."

Cam nodded. Lunasa marked the traditional beginning of the harvest season. It also was a traditional time to gather and trade. No doubt the Freemason was here to barter, but for what? Cam pushed the index cards aside and pulled out a chair for his guest. "Can I get you a cup of coffee, or maybe tea?"

"Just some water, if it would not be too much trouble."

Cam served his guest and sent Astarte to tell Amanda they had company. Duncan sighed. "I am, frankly, exhausted. It is all we can do to keep the Middle East from erupting."

"I've never understood why the Freemasons are so involved in this."

Duncan fixed his watery blue eyes on Cam. "Governments, and their diplomats, come and go. But we have relationships in the region that go back centuries. A certain level of trust has developed." He shrugged. "But we can only do so much. This Isaac Question revelation has been most unfortunate." He brightened. "But it could have been much worse, had the information come from your book as Zuberi had originally planned." He paused. "You understand, don't you, that this is a secret we Freemasons have kept for millennia? It is at the core of our beliefs—that we Westerners *all* are children of the ancient sun-worshiping Egyptians. Jew and Gentile. All of us. The Judeo-Christian religions, at their most basic, are merely differing versions of pagan sun worship."

Cam nodded. "The clues are everywhere—why else would you have so much Egyptian symbolism in your Masonic rituals? But what I don't understand is, with the clues so obvious, why has it remained a secret for so long?"

Smiling knowingly, Duncan leaned forward in his chair. "Sometimes the truth is so incomprehensible, so inconceivable, that we simply can not fathom it. Even after all you have learned, do you think religious Jews or Christians will ever believe themselves to be descended from the pharaoh Tuthmosis III rather than from Abraham?" He waved a hand. "Of course not. The truth has remained a secret not because it is hidden, but because there is no desire to see it. Very few people have eyes that truly see. You are rare in that respect."

Duncan broke the few seconds of silence that had settled over their conversation.

"Moving from the sublime to the mundane, I trust your problems with the polluted real estate are behind you?"

The retention tank had, in fact, done its job, and the contaminated soil been trucked away. In the end, even after the cleanup costs and attorneys fees, they would net a profit if they ever sold the land. "Yes," Cam replied. "But I'm guessing you didn't come all this way to discuss my legal problems, or even Judeo-Christian philosophy."

"No. I felt the obligation to bring you some news personally, rather than by telephone or email."

Cam leaned forward. "What news?"

Amanda entered the room in a t-shirt and shorts, her face flushed and her hair in a ponytail. Duncan greeted her, spread his arms, and responded, "Carrington is pregnant. Or, to be more accurate, she is carrying a baby in her womb."

Cam and Amanda exchanged quizzical glances as she dropped into a chair. "I don't understand," Cam said. But his fingers tingled in a way that told him danger loomed.

"She has extracted DNA from the Rosslyn Chapel skull, from what she believes is Moses, and had it cloned. In seven months she believes she will give birth to a baby that is genetically identical to Moses."

Amanda rose in her chair, as if standing to object. "How is that possible?" she asked. "Human cloning is still only theoretical."

Duncan shook his head. "Publicly, yes. But The Roslin Institute has been quietly pushing the envelope on this. Others also. Carrington was able to find a rogue geneticist to assist her. I just received a phone call: She underwent an ultrasound examination mere hours ago. The fetus is healthy and viable." He paused. "A boy, of course."

Cam picked up on an extraneous word Duncan had used. "You said she *believes* the skull is that of Moses. Do you have reason to doubt it?"

The Sinclair elder smiled. "I have every reason to doubt it. In fact, I know the skull is a fake because I placed it there myself."

"A fake?" Cam asked. These guys were unbelievable. Everything was a house of mirrors, a parlor trick, a ruse. He recalled Duncan's bemused smile the night Carrington stole the skull…

"Yes. The night before we all gathered at the Chapel, a trusted associate and I dug up into the pillar from the crypt beneath. We removed the skull that was hidden there and replaced it with the skull Carrington now possesses."

"But testing showed the head to be Middle-Eastern and thirty-five hundred years old," Amanda challenged.

Duncan shrugged. "It is not difficult to purchase ancient skulls in the antiquities markets in Beirut. We procured a dozen and tested them until we found a male that dated back to the time of Moses."

"So Carrington is carrying the clone of some random Middle-Easterner?" Cam asked.

The Freemason smiled. "One of the tenets of Freemasonry is that any man can lift himself to greatness. Perhaps this baby she is carrying will, indeed, become a great prophet. But I assure you, he is not a clone of Moses."

"Why are you telling us this?"

"Your book will be released next month I believe? As I understand it, Carrington will be making a public announcement soon thereafter. You will no doubt be questioned, since it is your research that makes it plausible that the head of Moses found its way to Scotland in the first place." He bowed slightly. "We have not always been completely honest with you, Mr. Thorne. We feel as if we owe you this courtesy. I would not want you to go on record validating Carrington's claim, only to later be repudiated. What is that expression you Americans use, egg on your face?"

Cam wasn't sure this was purely an altruistic gesture. With Duncan and the Freemasons, there was always a reason for something, and then the *real* reason for something. He probed. "So if Carrington has a fake skull, where is the real skull?"

"Safe."

Amanda replied before Cam could. "I think you owe us more than that. Has it been tested?"

He shook his head. "No, it has not. The Knights Templar worshiped the skull as Baphomet. As such it was sacred, and therefore remains sacred to our brotherhood today. Subjecting it to testing would desecrate it."

"With all due respect, that's bullshit," Cam replied. "The testing is non-invasive. If you wanted to test it, you could."

The Freemason placed his liver-spotted hands on the table, one finger brushing against the stack of index cards listing their wedding guests. He exhaled. "I concede the point." He stood. "I am old, and I am tired. These past few months have sucked the very marrow from my bones. I will not lie to you: I have indeed had the skull tested. And the other artifacts found beneath the pillar as well. I alone am privy to the results."

"And?" Cam pushed.

"And nothing. As you know, we Freemasons like to say we are not a secret society, but a society with secrets. And this is one of our biggest secrets of all." He offered Cam a wry smile. "The fact that you have, through the force of your intellect, pulled away the veil covering this secret does not make it any less of one. A secret it is, and I trust a secret it shall remain."

Cam knew that was about as close to a confirmation that the skull was Moses as they were going to get. So be it.

Without preamble, Duncan offered a hand to Cam to shake. When Cam reciprocated, the elderly Scot, with surprising strength, pulled Cam closer. He focused his blue eyes on Cam's. "I have one last favor to ask, though I realize you owe me nothing. This silliness of Carrington's has the potential to do serious damage in the Middle East. I ask that you do what you can to cast doubts on the merits of her claim. As I have just told you, the DNA she has used is not that of Moses. Her claim relies on your research, so you are in a unique position to refute her."

The Freemason disengaged, turned, and began to walk toward the door, talking over his shoulder. "We disagree on many things, Mr. Thorne. But on this I think we are in accord: It is up to your generation—the two of you and others like-minded—to deal once and for all with the volatility in the Middle East. Your research

347

will, I think, help in that regard. This Isaac Question revelation may force people to stop looking at these ancient texts, if you'll excuse the word play, as the gospel. The Old Testament, the Koran, the New Testament—they are the words of men, written by men. There is nothing the least bit divine about them."

Duncan stopped and turned again to face them, the light from the front door window bathing his pale face in an ethereal glow. "Your quest for knowledge, your thirst for the truth, your ideals— these are all admirable traits. But sometimes action is needed. There is such a thing as good and evil, as right and wrong. Do not let your ideals cloud that reality. What ISIS is doing is wrong. It is wrong. It is evil. Again, sometimes action is needed in support of one's ideals."

Cam watched the man, uncertain how to respond.

Duncan sighed, the fatigue of his eighty-plus years apparent in his sloped shoulders and watery eyes. Finally he straightened himself for one final missive. "Fighting to stop ISIS is the right thing, the moral thing, the good thing." His voice rang with conviction. "Sometimes in this complex, befuddling world, things really are that simple."

Cam shook his head as he watched the elderly Freemason walk slowly back to his car.

"What?" Amanda asked, standing next to him at the front window.

"It just hit me, as I watched him walk away."

"What did?"

"He's bluffing. It was a great speech, all that stuff about ideals and doing the right thing. And I agree with him. But underneath it all, he was bluffing."

"About what?"

"About the skull." He shook his head again. "He didn't go into the Chapel the night before. The skull's legit. Which means Carrington really did clone Moses."

"How can you be so bloody certain?"

348

"Logic." He took her hand and led her back to the kitchen table. "Okay, do you agree that Duncan and the Freemasons don't want Carrington to clone Moses?"

"Yes, totally."

"Why?"

She sighed. "For the same reason they didn't want the Isaac Question stuff to come out. It's totally destabilizing. What if this new Moses decides the Jews should abandon Israel? Or if he decides Israel should bomb Iran? You're talking Moses here—people will do what he says. The Isaac Question revelation was bad enough. But adding a cloned Moses to the equation could lead to, well, Armageddon."

"I agree. So here's another question: Why did Duncan fly out here?"

"That's obvious. He needs you. Carrington's whole story is based on your research, so you're in a unique position to put the kibosh on everything."

Cam nodded. "Agreed."

"Okay," she said. "So where's this logic of yours come in?"

Smiling, Cam slapped the table lightly with his palm. "Here. If you were Duncan, and you really did plant a fake skull in the Chapel for Carrington to find, how old would it be?"

"How old?" she repeated… "Aha!" She grinned, leaning forward. "I'd choose any age *except* thirty-five hundred. Probably something easily explainable, from the 1400s when the Chapel was built."

"Exactly. But he chose thirty-five hundred. He had no choice. Once Carrington's testing came back at thirty-five hundred, and Duncan really had *not* gone in the night before, he had no choice but to use the actual age for his fictional fake skull. He had to base his lie on a foundation of truth. He had to use a thirty-five hundred year old skull. But he was smart about it, he set it up well—he made sure that I saw his bemused smile that night in the Chapel when Carrington stole the skull, as if he was fine with it. He was already planning his next move."

She shook her head. "Remind me never to play poker with you guys. But now what? If Carrington really is cloning Moses, what do we do?"

"Well … I suppose we ought to send a gift."

"A gift." She laughed. "What exactly does one give to a baby prophet? A staff?" Amanda stared out over the lake for a few seconds. "Actually, I do have an idea: Let's give him the gift of anonymity."

Cam angled his head. "What do you mean?"

Her green eyes sparkled with intensity. "No kid should have to grow up with that kind of pressure." Before Astarte came to live with them, her uncle had declared her to be some kind of savior, the expectations of which had nearly crushed her. "Let's contact Carrington and offer her a deal. We'll vouch for her story—the skull, the research, all of it—if she agrees to keep everything quiet until the boy turns eighteen. But if she doesn't agree, you'll come out and publicly state that you have knowledge that the skull is a fake."

Cam leaned over and kissed his soon-to-be wife. "That's brilliant. Absolutely brilliant." If Duncan Sinclair insisted he planted the skull, and Cam—upon whose research Carrington was relying—backed him up, Carrington's claims would be widely panned. But if he vouched for her and refuted Duncan's assertion, it would add crucial credibility to her claim. And then he thought of something. "But why would she trust us? What if eighteen years pass and we renege on the deal?"

"I suppose that's a risk she has no choice but to take. After all, *we* have never lied to *her*. And why would we renege? You've made it clear that you want this history to come out. We just want the lad to have a normal childhood first."

Cam nodded, swayed by Amanda's arguments. Carrington might just go for it. "And maybe by the time the boy turns eighteen people won't be so caught up in all these so-called holy texts. Maybe by then people will laugh at the idea that he's some sort of prophet."

Even as he spoke the words, he doubted them. More likely was that young Moses would never escape the shadow of his name.

"You know," Amanda said, "this adventure all began on Beltane and now it's ending on Lunasa, one full cross-quarter day later."

He nodded. The past few months had been difficult, harrowing, tumultuous. But now, here, it felt like he was finally gaining control again, finally taking his life back. *Their* life back.

"You know what else?" Amanda said, smiling. "In addition to harvesting and bartering, there was another traditional Lunasa activity."

"What's that?"

"Handfasting."

"I don't know what that is."

"It's a pagan wedding ceremony." She called to Astarte to join them as she walked to the pantry, retrieved a broom, and pulled Cam to his feet. His chest tightened, sensing Amanda's fervor. "We take hands, like this." She smiled and handed the broom to Astarte. "And we pledge to love each other for either a year and a day, or for life—"

"Wait, there's a rental option? You can just rent for a year?"

"Careful."

"I choose life," Cam said quickly, grinning.

"Smart boy." She paused and turned serious, squeezing his hands. "And I also. I choose to spend my life with you." She instructed Astarte to hold the broom parallel to the floor, a foot in the air. "Then, together, we step over the broom." She lifted one leg and waited for Cam to do the same.

"And that's it?" He leaned closer to her. "We step over and we're married?"

She nodded. "Yes. In the old traditions of Lunasa." Her eyes held his. "With Astarte as our witness. And me wearing a sweaty t-shirt."

He nodded and pulled her closer. "Sounds perfect to me," he whispered.

Together they took a deep breath. Together they smiled. And together stepped over the broom.

The End

If you enjoyed *The Isaac Question,* you may want to read the other books featuring Cameron and Amanda in David S. Brody's **"Templars in America"** series:

Cabal of the Westford Knight
Templars at the Newport Tower (2009)

Set in Boston and Newport, RI, inspired by artifacts evidencing that Scottish explorers and Templar Knights traveled to New England in 1398.

Thief on the Cross
Templar Secrets in America (2011)

Set in the Catskill Mountains of New York, sparked by an ancient Templar codex calling into question fundamental teachings of the Catholic Church.

Powdered Gold
Templars and the American Ark of the Covenant (2013)

Set in Arizona, exploring the secrets and mysteries of both the Ark of the Covenant and a manna-like powdered substance.

The Oath of Nimrod
Giants, MK-Ultra and the Smithsonian Coverup (2014)

Set in Massachusetts and Washington, DC, triggered by the mystery of hundreds of giant human skeletons found buried across North America.

Author's Note

Inevitably, I receive this question from readers: "Are the artifacts and historical sites in your stories real, or did you make them up?" The answer is: If they are in the story, they are real. I sometimes do, however, take creative license: For example, the so-called Groton chamber in this story is actually located in Upton, Massachusetts—I relocated it to Groton to facilitate the story.

Likewise, the historical and literary references are accurate. When, for example, I quote from the Old Testament or the Scottish Declaration of Arbroath, or refer to the writings of Sigmund Freud or a medieval rabbi, those quotes and references are accurate. How I use these artifacts and references to weave a story is, of course, where the fiction takes root.

For inquisitive readers, perhaps curious about some of the specific historical assertions made and evidence presented in this story, more information is available here (in order of appearance in the story):

- There are many versions of the legend of Brendan the Navigator, but most of them have the Irish monk and his crew sailing westward across the Atlantic, accompanied by two or three "pagans," to a new land during a seven-year voyage in the early 6th Century. As stated in this story, in 1976 British explorer Timothy Severin recreated this voyage using a historically-accurate replica of Brendan's vessel.
- The so-called Groton chamber described and pictured in this story is, as I stated earlier, in reality the Upton (Massachusetts) Chamber. The Upton Chamber, which is indeed aligned to mark the summer solstice sunset, is open to the public: http://www.upton.ma.us/pages/uptonma_bcomm/historical/UptonHeritagePark2012.pdf . Although many chambers do

exhibit magnetic disturbances at their entryway as I write in the story, the Upton Chamber does not.

- The Norumbega Tower is open to the public and can be found on Norumbega Road, Weston, MA.
- The Westford Knight carving, including the newly-discovered Hooked X, is located along Depot Street in Westford, MA. Park at the Abbot School, 25 Depot Street, and walk up the hill fifty yards to carving on your left.
- A virtual tour of the Gungywamp site, along with information on how to visit the actual site, can be found here: http://www.dpnc.org/gungywamp
- The Druid Hill stone circle site is open to the public and can be found in Leblanc Park, at the corner of West Meadow and Gumpas Roads, Lowell, MA.
- For a book discussing the possibility that Moses and the Pharaoh Akhenaton were the same person, see Ahmed Osman, *Moses and Akhenaten*[sic]*: The Secret History of Egypt at the Time of the Exodus* (2002)
- The obelisk called Cleopatra's Needle is located in Central Park, behind the Metropolitan Museum of Art, in New York City.
- For a discussion of Druid/Celtic sites in New England, see Barry Fell, *America B.C.* (1976).
- For a discussion of the Stone of Destiny and the missing throne of Akhenaton, see Keith Laidler, *The Head of God* (1998).

Lastly, the possibility that Isaac may be the son of an Egyptian pharaoh rather than Abraham is largely a result of my own research and contemplations. One website I found helpful was this, though I do not necessarily agree with all its conclusions: http://theancientsacredmysteries.com/who_was_father_isaac.htm

So, did the writers of the Old Testament take some liberties with both the timeline and the story of Sarah's time in the pharaoh's harem? And if so, does this help explain Joseph's seemingly remarkable ascension to power in Egyptian. In turn, does Joseph's prominent role in the Egyptian ruling elite explain the monotheistic religious beliefs of Pharaoh Akhenaton? And does all of this give us a different understanding not only of the Book of Exodus but of the history of Scotland and Ireland as well? Most fundamentally, do these revelations change the way the world views the conflict in the Middle East?

These are the questions that fascinate me, that keep me up at night. Hopefully this novel has caused you to focus on them as well, and also provided you with some entertainment and intellectual stimulation. Thanks for reading.

Photo/Drawing Credits

Images used in this book are the property of the author, in the public domain, and/or provided courtesy of the following individuals (images listed in order of appearance in the story):

Drawing of Groton chamber:
Courtesy of Kimberly Scott

Image of Masonic House of the Temple decoration:
Credit: http://scottishrite.org/headquarters/virtual-tour

Image of Newport Tower Winter Solstice:
Courtesy of Richard Lynch

Images of Gungywamp chamber and Chi-Rho symbol:
Courtesy of Vance Tiede

Images of Gungywamp stone circle:
Courtesy of Brad Olsen

Drawing of Druid Hill stone circle:
Courtesy of Kimberly Scott

Map of land ruled by Pharaoh Tuthmosis III
Credit: http://www.crystalinks.com/Thutmose_III.html

Image of Kent County stone chamber winter solstice illumination:
Credit: Thomas Maxson

Image of America's Stonehenge stone chamber:
Courtesy of James and Mary Gage

Image of Edinburgh Castle:
Courtesy of Kimberly Scott

Acknowledgements

Diving down an unexplored rabbit hole and (to mix my animal metaphors) ferreting around there for a few months doing research for a new novel is my idea of a great time. Honestly. Thankfully for me, I have managed to surround myself with fellow researchers who share this passion. Heartfelt thanks for assisting me in my research go out to (in alphabetical order): Michael Carr, Matthew Cilento, Mark Eddy, David Goudsward, Richard Lynch, Jeff Nisbet, Jim Pecora, Matthew "Doc" Perry, Vance Tiede, Scott Wolter, Michael Yannetti, and Zena Halpern. I am grateful to you all. (Please note that inclusion in the above list does not in any way constitute an endorsement of this work or the themes contained herein.)

I also again want to thank my team of readers, those who trudged their way through early versions of this story and offered helpful, insightful comments (listed alphabetically): Allie Brody, Jeff Brody, Spencer Brody, Michael Carr, Jeanne Scott, Richard Scott, and Eric Stearns.

For other authors out there looking to navigate their way through the publishing process, I can't speak highly enough about Amy Collins and her team at New Shelves Distribution—real pros who know the business and are a pleasure to work with.

Lastly, to my wife, Kim: Thanks once more for your unending patience and support. You slog through the early drafts, you help me wrestle with the plot, you offer gentle but firm support, and you even do the cover art. But most of all you offer invaluably wise and astute counsel. I am lucky to you have as a life partner.

Printed in Great Britain
by Amazon

47227529R00214